Windhaven Plantation

A torrid, tempestuous novel of men and women driven by ambition and greed, and damned by their desires.

Rich and authentic in historical detail, earthy and true to life in its characterization, exciting and sensual in the swift storytelling, this giant saga became a national bestseller within weeks of publication.

Now, a lusty sequel to once again bring Marie de Jourlet's special brand of writing to the continuation of the adventures of the Bouchard Family.

★　　　★　　　★

It is 1834 and the first tremors of the Civil War are reverberating across the land. And the unrest of the nation is reflected in the turmoil of Windhaven Plantation, very much a living portrait of the American South. Fathers and sons, mothers and daughters—and lovers—will soon see their lusts and loyalties put to the test of fire. Will Windhaven survive the private battles of a proud family, the terrors of a vicious war?

Dark clouds are gathering, tempers are high, and blood is running hot in the veins of the men and women who have inherited Windhaven.

STORM OVER WINDHAVEN

Pinnacle Books by Marie de Jourlet:

WINDHAVEN PLANTATION
STORM OVER WINDHAVEN
LEGACY OF WINDHAVEN
RETURN TO WINDHAVEN
WINDHAVEN'S PERIL

Storm Over Windhaven

by Marie de Jourlet

PINNACLE BOOKS   LOS ANGELES

STORM OVER WINDHAVEN

Copyright © 1977 by AMP Publications, a Division of American Medical Products Corporation

An original Pinnacle Books edition, published for the first time anywhere.

Produced by Lyle Kenyon Engel, Canaan, New York

ISBN: 0-523-40643-6

First printing, October 1977
Second printing, October 1977
Third printing, November 1977
Fourth printing, August 1978
Fifth printing, November 1978
Sixth printing, February 1979
Seventh printing, April 1979
Eighth printing, June 1979
Ninth printing, October 1979

Cover illustration by Bruce Minney

Printed in the United States of America

PINNACLE BOOKS, INC.
2029 Century Park East
Los Angeles, California 90067

Gratefully dedicated to the memory of Helen M. Little, whose high artistic standards I shall constantly strive to follow.

ACKNOWLEDGMENTS

No writer of historical fiction can consider his or her work authentic unless every effort has been made to achieve complete accuracy of detail, whether it be in describing the clothing of the period, the prices of everyday staples, or the actual topography of the locale. The author wishes to acknowledge her indebtedness to Milo B. Howard, Jr., Director of State Archives at Montgomery, Alabama; Rose Lambert, Librarian, Louisiana State Museum, New Orleans; Brad Rush of Kroch's & Brentano's, Chicago, whose diligent ferreting out of valuable reference books facilitated the author's task; Rich Padnos, good friend and history minor at the University of Illinois, who helped locate data on the notorious breeding-training farms of the South; and to Mrs. Doris Samuels, not only the finest transcriber any author who dictates her material to could hope for, but herself an eminent teacher and historian who contributed several vital facets to the overall concept of this book. To these, all heartfelt thanks!

Marie de Jourlet

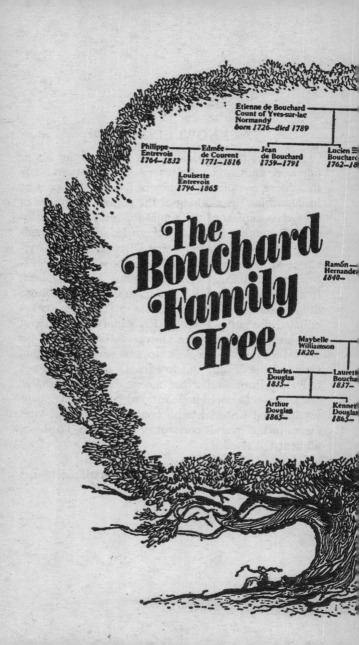

Etienne de Bouchard
Count of Yves-sur-lac
Normandy
born 1726—died 1789

Philippe
Entrevois
1764–1832

Edmée
de Courent
1771–1816

Jean
de Bouchard
1759–1791

Lucien
Bouchard
1762–18

Louisette
Entrevois
1796–1865

The Bouchard Family Tree

Ramón
Hernandez
1840–

Maybelle
Williamson
1820–

Charles
Douglas
1835–

Lauret
Bouchard
1837–

Arthur
Douglas
1865–

Kenneth
Douglas
1865–

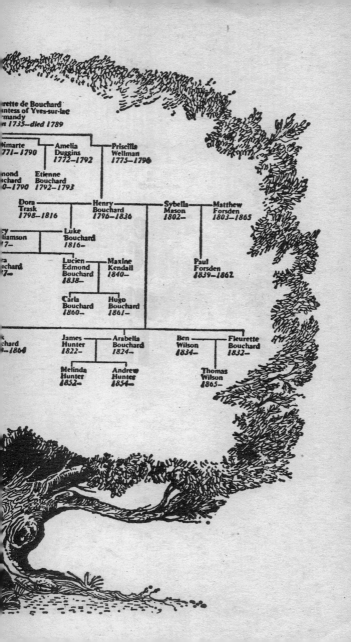

...rette de Bouchard
...ountess of Yves-sur-lac
...rmandy
...n 1735—died 1789

...imarte
...771—1790

Amelia Duggins 1772—1792

Priscilla Wellman 1775—1796

...mond ...chard ...0—1790

Etienne Bouchard 1792—1793

Dora Trask 1798—1816

Henry Bouchard 1796—1836

Sybella Mason 1802—

Matthew Forsden 1803—1865

...cy ...liamson ...7—

Luke Bouchard 1816—

...ra ...chard ...7—

Lucien Edmond Bouchard 1838—

Maxine Kendall 1840—

Paul Forsden 1839—1862

Carla Bouchard 1860—

Hugo Bouchard 1861—

...hard ...9—186?

James Hunter 1822—

Arabella Bouchard 1824—

Ben Wilson 1834—

Fleurette Bouchard 1832—

Melinda Hunter 1852—

Andrew Hunter 1854—

Thomas Wilson 1865—

STORM OVER WINDHAVEN

CHAPTER ONE

Although this 18th day of December in the year 1834 marked his seventy-second birthday, Lucien Bouchard sat erect, his white-haired head held high, in the great hand-carved chair at the head of the long cherrywood table in the dining room of Windhaven Plantation. High above the table, the tiny tongues of flame from twenty-one red wax candles set into the ornate silver chandelier cast a fascinating interplay of lights and shadows upon the tapestry-covered walls as upon the white-plastered ceiling. Three silver candelabra decorated the long table, each with three tall white tapers which rose imposingly, their even brighter and unwavering glow illuminating the elegant chinaware from Delft, the silver service and the lace-edged tablecloth. Their three tongues of flame seemed to bend toward him who was truly the *seigneur* of Windhaven, as if in tribute to this special natal day.

He wore, as he had for many years and as was his preference, buckskin jacket and breeches, leggings and moccasins, with a necklace of bear claws. His angular face was weatherbeaten and so darkened by the Alabama sun that he might have been taken for his own Ashanti overseer, Thomas. Yet the characteristic features of his youth seemed to have remained with him: a firm, deeply cleft chin, the frank mouth with its humorous curve, and above all, the large, dark-brown eyes in which there always seemed to lurk a twinkle of

1

amusement at the changing world they surveyed. He was still wiry and lean, with his hands calloused from working on the land. And he could still walk without a cane up the stairway to the tower which faced the red bluff where his beloved Dimarte and their infant son lay buried.

At the opposite end of the table, his improvised tree-branch crutches on the floor nearby, a cushion under his left foot and the left leg of his breeches split to accommodate the thong-strapped splints to his broken leg, sat his thirty-eight-year-old black-haired son Henry, his fawn-colored waistcoat unbuttoned and the lingerie cravat loosened at the neck of his ruffled silk shirt for greater ease. At his right, his lovely auburn-haired wife, Sybella, sat, her glossy hair piled in a regal pompadour with curled puffs at the temples. She wore a long blue silk gown with bell-shaped skirt which just revealed her dainty heelless slippers, the edge of the skirt stiffened with buckram and ornamented with rows of trimming. She leaned toward him now and whispered something which made his glum, drawn face brighten, and he sent her a quick intense smile and whispered something back to her which made her cheeks suddenly flush and her eyes demurely lower.

At Henry's left, coquettish black-haired little Arabella looked proudly around the table, not quite eleven years old and reveling in the thought of being allowed to stay up so late and be accepted by her elders. With pardonable femininity, she glanced down from time to time at her pretty pink cashmere dress with its white frills and the short puffed sleeves and her new soft cloth slippers and neat gray lisle stockings.

But more often her eyes sought out her half brother, Luke, across the table, for she idolized the tall, slender, blond eighteen-year-old youth who never teased her and who often brought her flowers or whittled a toy for her. He caught her gaze now and smiled and nodded, as he bent toward little auburn-haired Fleurette, her nearly three-year-old sister, who was perched in a special high chair which had been made by Thomas especially for this occasion and the holidays ahead.

2

Luke was dipping a spoon into a dish of sago pudding and dutifully feeding his little half sister, who clapped her hands and gurgled with delight at all this attention from the serious-faced, gentle young man beside her.

At Lucien Bouchard's left, Mark glanced uneasily down the table at his father, then speared a morsel of roast chicken with his fork and downed it. He wore a dark-blue suit with vest and trousers, a wide-knotted blue silk tie and stiff shirt collar, which made him look much older than he was. Lucien looked at him searchingly then murmured, "It will be all right—this time, Mark. I'm sure your father can forgive you. But learn from this—about violence—and its consequences."

"Yes, I understand, Grandfather. I—I'm sorry I fought with him over that woman—I didn't mean to push him down the stairs, but he was so angry with me I had to defend myself." The boy seemed genuinely repentant.

"Well, well. Once your father can walk without crutches again, he'll be busy with his crops and you'll be back at school. The incident will be forgotten. We'll say no more about it, Mark. Ah, here comes Mammy Clorinda's famous spice cake, and just one candle on it. Now do you suppose she's being tactful about my age, boy?"

Clara, a pretty, slender Kru kitchen girl, had just borne in a huge cake on a silver platter and, her eyes apprehensively rolling, very gingerly set it down before the white-haired old man.

"It looks wonderful, Clara. You be sure to tell Mammy Clorinda how pleased I am that she'd bake this for my birthday. And tell her, too, I've never tasted better roast chicken nor a more appetizing dressing."

"Yassuh, Ah will, jist lak you said, suh." Clara smilingly bobbed her head. Matthew, a stout, good-natured Fulani in his late forties, resplendent in the red waistcoat and black breeches of a house servant, now entered with a decanter of Madeira and carefully filled old Lucien's glass.

"I think Arabella may have a sip, just this once, Sybella my dear?" Lucien raised his glass and smiled down at his daughter-in-law.

"Well, perhaps just this once, but only the tiniest sip. I can't refuse you anything on your birthday, Father."

Matthew ceremoniously filled all the glasses, and then discreetly withdrew to the immense sideboard, where he set the decanter on its silver tray.

"Blow out the candle, Grandfather!" Arabella irrepressibly giggled.

"I will, my darling. But first, a toast. A toast to all of us here at Windhaven, that we may enjoy this beautiful home which my son Henry so generously arranged to build for his doddering old father."

"Come now, Father," Henry Bouchard chuckled as he lifted his glass, "no one would ever call you that. I'll wager you can still outride me whenever you've a mind to do so."

"I doubt that very much, my son. And besides, winning a race wouldn't prove anything at all." He stood a moment in reflective silence, then lifted his glass again: "I think the best birthday present of all is to be with every one of you, including little Fleurette. We're a family now, with a home that I hope will stand not so much for the good fortune that made it possible, but rather as a testament to family loyalty and love."

"I'll drink to that, Father," Henry Bouchard staunchly declared, and reached his other hand out to Sybella, who brought it to her lips and kissed it.

"Now that's what I like to see, my son," Lucien said, winking broadly. "There's the true Gallic touch of *l'amour*. You're fortunate to have a wife like Sybella, as I am to have her as my daughter-in-law." He paused again, and this time his voice took on a more serious note: "We've had our differences through the years, and yet tonight as I look back on the years I've spent on the land which the Creeks gave me so long ago, I've learned that all the adversities are part of the debt each of us owes through life. To be able to cope with them, to resolve them, and always with integrity and honor, that's the crux of life itself. And when one has love and

4

devotion to strengthen one against these adversities, then the true meaning of home and family is revealed. Always remember that a family divided against itself cannot endure. But now, I didn't mean to make a speech. To all of you, long life, good health, and every happiness."

He turned to look at his grandson Luke, who raised his glass and looked back at the tall white-haired old man, his blue eyes shining with so fervent an admiration that old Lucien quickly put his glass to his lips and drained it to hide the sudden well of tears.

Young Mark had been first to rise from the table, with a last uneasy glance at his father, and then turned to the man at the head of the table. "Happy birthday, Grandfather. I hope you have many more. I'll say good night now."

"Thank you, Mark. Try to make peace with your father, for my sake. And when you go back to school, take my advice and give some attention to your studies. A little book learning never hurt anyone, you know. One day, when you take charge of your own land, you'll be grateful for the knowledge."

"I'll try, Grandfather. Just the same, I could learn a lot more staying here and finding out how to take charge of things the way Father does. Let Luke do all the studying he wants, he's bound to be a fancy gentleman anyway. Well, good night." With an abrupt nod, his face sullen again, the boy left the dining room.

Henry Bouchard watched his younger son leave, an angry frown creasing his forehead. Sybella squeezed his hand again and shook her head: "Don't spoil Grandfather's birthday, darling, please. He's proud and stubborn, just the way you are. You know he's sorry about your leg." She leaned over to brush his cheek with her lips, then added, "In a way, I'm not, if you want to know something. It's given us a chance to be together again, Henry. All you ever think of is your land and your slaves, and I'm still reasonably young enough to be jealous of your lack of interest. As soon as I've put Fleurette and Arabella to bed, I'll come to see you.

5

And I want to talk to you about Luke, too, darling. Can you manage by yourself all right?"

"Of course I can." Henry Bouchard glowered as he reached down to retrieve his crutches, then slowly got to his feet and adjusted them.

Sybella moved to the high chair and bent down to kiss her younger daughter, who put her arms around Sybella's neck with a happy little cry of "Mama!" Sybella smiled at her stepson: "Fleurette adores you, Luke. She didn't leave a scrap of food on her plate, thanks to you. It's so good to have you home again. And before you go back to school Monday, I want to talk to you about something that's been on my mind for quite a while. Come along, Fleurette darling, time for bed now." She lifted the little girl in her arms, cradling her against her bosom and playfully brushing Fleurette's nose and eyelids with her lips. Then she turned to Arabella: "It's time you were saying good night to everyone, sweetheart."

"All right, Mother. But can't I please walk Grandpa up to the tower?"

"Why, if he wants you to, of course you can, Arabella. But then, you make sure that he gets to bed himself and then you go straight to your room, do you understand?"

"Oh yes, Mother!" Arabella scrambled out of her chair and ran to the head of the table as old Lucien rose. "Can I go with you, Grandpa, can I?" she eagerly demanded.

"I'd like that very much, dear Arabella." The old man took her hand and bent down to kiss her forehead. "Come along."

Sybella watched her husband carefully make his way out of the dining room, and as she cradled the already drowsy Fleurette in her arms she drew a quick, deep breath as a shiver of anticipation surged through her. As she turned to leave, the red-liveried Matthew entered with the candle snuffer and respectfully inclined his head.

"Thank you, Matthew. Tell Mammy Clorinda and

6

Clara that everything was just perfect tonight. Good night."

"Good night to you, Miz Bouchard."

She saw Arabella lead smiling old Lucien out of the dining room and her dark-blue eyes softened with an affectionate glow.

"Am I walking too fast for you, Grandpa?" Arabella anxiously looked up at Lucien Bouchard as they reached the second-floor landing of the stone stairway that led to the tower.

"No, Arabella, not at all, my dear child." Lucien smiled down at the pretty black-haired little girl. She smiled back. "Grandpa, did you wear those clothes when you lived with the Injuns, did you?"

"Why, yes, Arabella. You see, the Creeks hunted deer and then they skinned and tanned the hides to make jackets and breeches and skirts. They're very comfortable. They were the first people who lived where we are now, Arabella. They lived on and from the land, and they gave back what they took from it. That's what made it so rich and good, you see."

She frowned, not quite understanding, but nodded solemnly as if to reaffirm her complete trust in whatever he told her. "Uh huh. And those claws around your neck are from the bear you had to fight when you first came here. Did you really kill the bear all by yourself? I'd be so scared if I just saw one, Grandpa!"

They had come now to the top of the tower and Lucien stood looking out through the clear glass of the casement window toward the bluff beyond. The moon was full, but with a hazy ring around it, and it seemed to send a ghostly light down upon the dark trees and bushes which flanked the bluff. He drew open the window, put his right arm around Arabella's shoulders and pointed toward the moon. "That's a sign of rain, when you see that ring around the moon, Arabella. Well, to tell you the truth, I was scared too. You see, I was on my pack pony riding up all the way from Mobile, and there was a little bear cub playing with a comb of honey the bees had left in a dead log, and the next

7

thing I knew, the mother bear was coming at us because she thought I was going to hurt her cub."

"But you weren't going to, were you, Grandpa? You wouldn't hurt anybody, I know that. Mama says how good and kind you always are to everybody. That's why I love you so much, Grandpa."

Lucien blinked his eyes to clear them of the sudden tears, smiled tenderly down at the anxious little girl who stood on tiptoe to stare out toward the bluff. "Your mother is good and kind herself, Arabella, and so are you. No, of course I didn't mean to hurt the cub. But she wanted to protect it, and perhaps she'd never seen a man before and was afraid for her cub. She sprang at my pony, and my gun wouldn't go off, so I had only my knife. I was very lucky I wasn't killed. But you see, Arabella, it was God's will that I live long enough to see you, your mother and your little sister Fleurette and your daddy and Mark and Luke at my birthday party."

"Uh-huh, Grandpa. I'm awful glad that bear didn't hurt you too much, either, Grandpa. And Mama says you come up here all the time because someone you love is buried at the top of that bluff over there."

"That's true, my darling. Her name was Dimarte, and she had lovely black hair like you, and she was sweet and kind and very wise and understanding. We had very little time together, and yet all my life I've remembered her and how wonderful it was to be with her. I hope, Arabella, that one day you'll find someone whom you love just as much and who will love you all the rest of his life. You see, darling, loving someone and sharing all the good things with someone is what makes life so very beautiful. I didn't really know that until I came here, and I was a young man by then."

Again Arabella nodded solemnly, looking up at him and then tugged at his hand and pressed herself against him. "I hope it's someone nice like you, Grandpa."

He stroked her black curls, his eyes fixing on the distant bluff. *My beloved Dimarte, you are still alive in my heart and you will be even as I draw my last breath. And I pray to your God as to mine that all of my descendants and their families will be blessed with the gift of love which you brought me so many years ago, a gift that restores my soul when I am saddened by the greed and selfishness of those who have come to this land, not in gratitude but in avarice and distrust of their neighbors. Oh beloved woman, let your sweet spirit seek out the hearts of Arabella and Fleurette, and of Luke, my older grandson, and even the troubled heart of my son Henry and his second son Mark who shows already the fierce worldly ambitions of his father. I cannot blame Henry and Mark because they differ in their alikeness from me, for it may well be that in my blood I passed on to them the traits of my older brother Jean, who placed possessions and conquest above love and honor. Oh beloved one, I know there are only a few years left to me upon this earth before I come to join you there—from your resting place, watch over Windhaven with love and compassion so that all who dwell here may be imbued as I was to rejoice in the gift and wonder of lasting love and faith and honesty.*

Very slowly he closed the window and then, lifting Arabella in his arms, kissed her gently and said, "And now, it's time for bed, my darling. I'll walk you down to your room and then I'll go to mine."

Sybella, her tawny cheeks flushed, quickly slipped into the first-floor bedroom adjoining Lucien's and whispered, "The girls are safely in bed, and I've come to look after you, Henry darling."

Henry Bouchard had doffed his waistcoat and cravat, laid his crutches down beside the bed and lay on it now, propped up by two thick pillows filled with goose feathers. He stared glumly at his left leg, the splints and thick, buckled thongs exposed by the long slit along the left leg of his breeches. Experimentally, he wiggled his stockinged toes and frowned. "It's a bit better. In a few weeks I'll be able to throw these damned crutches away. Well, I'll be glad enough when Mark goes back to school, and I shouldn't mind if I didn't see him again till the end of the spring term."

9

"Now you hush, Henry Bouchard!" Sybella chided as she came toward the bed, bent down and, slipping her hands under his shoulders, pressed her mouth to his in an ardent kiss. "You know perfectly well you can't be too angry with him. After all, he was just trying to prove he was as grown-up as his own father—and you know perfectly well what would have happened that night if he hadn't noticed your trying to hide Cellia."

He scowled and turned his face away from her, self-consciously embarrassed at her frank allusion to his lubricity. "Just the same, to dare to fight me over a bed wench," he grumbled.

Sybella very matter-of-factly began to remove her blue gown, standing in her stays, made in two layers of white cotton sateen, with a light linen interlining and narrow shoulder straps. They were beautifully quilted around the waist and lightly boned, with worked eyelet holes. They gracefully accentuated the swell of her still superbly firm bosom, and delineated the shapely waist and the flare of robust, voluptuous hips. Beneath them, she wore a pair of lace-trimmed pink nainsook drawers. Hearing the rustle of her gown, he turned and sat up erect, his eyes widening. "What the devil—"

"Well, since your accident, you've moved down to this bedroom, Henry darling, and a wife's place is with her husband, isn't it?" she blithely commented as she began to unfasten the stays. "Grandfather was looking awfully fit this evening, don't you think so?"

"Yes—yes, of course. Whatever possessed Mammy Clorinda to put only one candle on his birthday cake, though?"

"You know perfectly well that Moses, our chandler, has been down with river fever the past few weeks, so he couldn't make the tiny little birthday candles. And you just couldn't put seventy-two large ones even on that big cake. Now, have you anything else to complain about before we go to bed?"

"Damn it, Sybella—" he began, and then tilted back his head and burst into hearty laughter. "What a woman you are!"

10

"I was hoping you'd come around to that notion, Henry. I rather think I still am too, woman enough to take care of you so you don't have to go hiding bed wenches in the wing of the second floor. And that reminds me—if you've no objection, I'd like Celia as my personal maid. With these fashionable new stays they're bringing in from France, a woman needs help in her boudoir, and of course you'll be out in the fields once the planting season starts."

"Well, I don't see any objection to that. Take the wench and good riddance to her. Just make sure you keep her away from Mark while you're at it."

"Certainly. I intend to keep her away from both of you," Sybella retorted as she let the stays slither to the floor and stood there naked to the waist. Reaching up to undo the ornate pompadour, she let her glossy auburn tresses cascade down over her lush round breasts. Now, Lilith-like, with a coquettish smile at her surprised husband, she brushed away the silken strands and cupped her breasts, as if offering them to his inspection. "Do you think I'd make a salable bed wench, Henry? How much do you think you could get for me at New Orleans?" she teased.

His face darkened with his sudden desire, and he made a motion to lean over toward the little nightstand on which a single candle flickered in its candelabrum.

"No, don't blow it out. I want you to see exactly what you're getting. Just the way you must have seen Celia on the auction block, Henry. The difference is, I'm your wife and you don't have to pay for my services, and I still happen to be in love with you. If you'll give me a chance, I think I can keep you sufficiently occupied so that you won't be going to New Orleans to buy any more Celias."

"My God, you're—you're absolutely brazen!" he gasped, his voice becoming hoarse as he watched her stoop and tug down her drawers.

"You just won't understand, Henry Bouchard, that a perfectly respectable married woman could be in love with her own husband and have desires just as he does.

11

I thought you learned that on our wedding night, but apparently not. Oh, there's just one other thing."

"And what's that? Hurry, come to bed, Sybella, I do need you, I want you!"

"That's not quite good enough. I didn't hear you say you loved me, Henry."

"Damn it, woman. I don't know any other man who'd put up with your tantalizing ways. Now what's this other thing?"

"Two, really. First off, since you've told Grandfather you'd rather have a white overseer than Thomas, though he's been wonderful for Windhaven, why not let Luke stay home from school and be overseer? Then Thomas can be his assistant, you see, and he can help Luke learn what he doesn't know already. He's so much like your father, Henry. And I know he loves the land and he gets along so well with the slaves."

"That's not such a bad idea, come to think of it." Henry Bouchard meditatively pursed his lips and rubbed his stubbly chin with his hand. "But you'd best speak to Luke about it. He's doing so well at the Lowndesboro Academy that he may not want to give up his studies."

"I plan to discuss it with him, Henry. Now the other thing. It's time Windhaven had a proper housewarming. It was a lovely party we had this evening for Grandfather, and think how nice it would be if, perhaps sometime about the middle of next month, we could invite our neighbors and let them see what a beautiful château you built for your father. You would certainly rise in their esteem, once they found out how devoted you are to him, Henry."

Henry Bouchard chuckled and shook his head. "I can see that the best day of my life was when I stopped over to meet old Grover Mason," he said, his voice husky with furious yearning. "Yes, a housewarming would be a capital idea. And now, will you take pity on an invalid who's half out of his mind and give me a proper bedwarming before the housewarming, if you please?"

"Why, that's what I had in mind all along, Henry

12

darling," Sybella laughed softly, triumphantly, as she bent down over him and deftly began to remove his breeches. "Besides, didn't I promise to look after you the way a good wife should? Don't scowl at me like that, sir, or I'll go off to my own bed and leave you just as you are now—really, I don't think there's much danger of your going prowling among the cabins tonight."

"Damn you, Sybella"—his eyes glittered at the rich jut of her naked breasts as she slowly straightened, then at the snug drawers which shaped out her voluptuously ripe hips, clung to the plump mound of her love-core—"you're driving me crazy parading around like a New Orleans bordello hussy—"

Hands on hips, cocking her head at him, her red lips deepening their mocking curve, Sybella laughed softly again. "I take that as a fair compliment, sir, considering that you must surely speak as a man of considerable experience. *Tsk, tsk,* didn't I tell you not to scowl like that? La, sir, I always thought when a man wanted pleasuring, he was all smiles and flattery—"

"Oh my God, Sybella, you beautiful, heartless, scheming hussy you, don't stand there talking—you know I want you, I love you, I—"

"Ah, that's better. Want me? Oh, I can plainly see that, sir. But when you said that magic word 'love,' then there's still hope for the two of us, isn't there? Now you be a very good boy and don't move about too much or you'll hurt your leg—arch up a bit so I can slip your drawers off—my gracious, yes, you want me very much. Does it hurt—there?" Her soft hand roguishly touched his straining manhood, and Henry ground his teeth and groaned aloud, shuddering in his fierce tumescence.

"Now, sir, you'd best shift that splinted leg of yours as far away as is comfortable for you, and not try to be overly energetic." She straightened, her pink tongue wetting the corners of her mouth, as her fingers slid inside the waistband of her drawers, then slowly inched them down. Henry groaned again, lifting his head to stare at the lascivious unveiling of her satiny na-

13

kedness, his fingernails digging into his sweating palms as he watched, spellbound, his throat too choked to speak. Then, scuffing off her slippers, she knelt down beside him, her glossy auburn hair tumbling over her round swelling breasts. "If I keep on my stockings, Henry, you can pretend I'm your bordello hussy, can't you?" she teasingly whispered.

"I don't want to pretend—Sybella, my God, please—my darling, you're killing me—" he gasped, knowing the pleasures to come.

"Then you'll admit you can do as well at home as on your little jaunts to those sinful places in New Orleans, do you?" Again her soft hand stroked him . . .

"Yes, yes, better than any of them—all I want is you, Sybella!" And he meant it. He always meant it—until the beauty of another woman sent the familiar fire through his loins. . . .

She tossed her head so that her auburn tresses danced against her neck and shoulders as she lowered herself on her palms, making a saucy moué at him as her lips approached his. Tantalizingly, she brushed herself against his ferociously rampant manhood till, with a hoarse cry, he could bear no more. His hands seized her succulent hips and drew her down upon him, his fingers clenching possessively into her ripe, warm flesh as their mouths fused, and he groaned again to feel her hungering response.

As she drove him to the peak of ecstasy, she thought to herself, *Maybe I can make him love me just a little . . . the way it was . . . the way it could be . . .*

CHAPTER TWO

Arabella Bouchard coquettishly pirouetted before the cheval glass in the bedroom she shared with her little sister Fleurette and made an impish face at it. It had been a Christmas present from her mother, and by now the latter was almost regretting her impulsive gift. Arabella, having seen the elegantly framed, tiltable mirror in her mother's room, had almost daily begged Sybella to let her have one for her very own, ever since the afternoon of her grandfather's birthday when she had gone into her mother's room and found Sybella trying on her exquisite blue gown.

"Look, Fleurette," she called to the little, auburn-haired girl who stood near the window, watching as the rays of the early afternoon January sun brightened the luster of the casement panes. "See how pretty I look in my pink dress, Fleurette! I'm going to the party this evening, 'cause I'm grown up, I am!"

She had very nearly added that she would be allowed with the grownups tonight but that Fleurette wouldn't because she was much too young for all that excitement. But she couldn't help thinking it with ecstatic pride as she turned back to the mirror and studied her reflection from head to toe. Her face was oval-shaped, with large dark-brown eyes, a dainty, upturned little nose, and high-set cheekbones. Her mouth was willful, with the lower lip riper and mercurial in its ability to change from sulky pout to delighted smile. She had painstakingly combed out her black curls, which tumbled below her slim neck, and then made little twisted curls all along the top of her high-arching forehead. She examined these now as Fleurette continued to stare out the window.

"If only I were twelve or thirteen," she said half aloud to herself as she turned sideways to examine her profile. "There's sure to be some nice boys at the party tonight and they'd pay lots more attention to me if I were just a little older, I know they would! Even Mama says I'm bound to be a heartbreaker some day—what fun it'll be to have boys make a fuss over me and think I'm awfully pretty. But then, I guess I am." Turning, she raised her voice and called, "Fleurette, come see how pretty I look, and tell me if you like my dress for the party."

But the little girl standing before the window was impervious to her sister's words. A yellowhammer had just perched on the window ledge, ruffling its feathers, bending its graceful head to peck at its claws and then to look in on the two girls.

"Pretty birdie!" Fleurette exclaimed, gleefully clapping her hands. Her sweet round face shone with pleasure, and her green eyes were wide and glowing. "Come see pretty birdie, Bella, before he flies away!" she called.

Arabella frowned, momentarily disgruntled by her sister's failure to acknowledge her own self-evident attractiveness. Then again she decided to be generous. After all, Fleurette was just a baby and Mammy Clorinda would bring her her supper here in her room, while she, Arabella, in her prettiest dress, would be sitting at the table with all the people Mama and Daddy had invited to see Windhaven. And besides, it didn't matter whether Fleurette thought she was pretty or not; tonight, if someone like that nice Bobby Jordan would say that, it would mean a great deal more.

"Yes, it's a very pretty birdie, Fleurette," she agreed as she walked over to window and reached down to stroke Fleurette's auburn curls.

"Oh, you scared him away, Bella!" Fleurette reproachfully exclaimed as the yellowhammer, cocking its head at the sudden appearance of Arabella, took instant flight and disappeared from view.

"I wanted to see the birdie. Maybe he would have come in to play with us, Bella!" Fleurette's eyes were misty with sudden tears.

"Silly, he couldn't because the window's closed, Fleurette. But I'll tell you what. I'll ask Mama if maybe you can have a bird in a cage for your very own. Would you like that, Fleurette?"

"Oh yes, Bella!" Fleurette nodded, clapping her hands again. "And you're pretty too, Bella!"

Arabella quite forgave her little sister for the latter's earlier neglect. She hugged Fleurette and kissed her, then whispered, "Just for that I'll bring you up a piece of Mammy's angel food cake when I come back from the party."

"Well, now, Father," Henry Bouchard said, sitting on the edge of Lucien's bed, "have a good nap before the party this evening. I want you to have energy enough to lead the dancing after dinner. We'll have Jeb with his fiddle and Moses with his harmonica to play us some waltzes and quadrilles in the drawing room, and I expect you to start things off by taking Sybella first on the floor."

Lucien Bouchard chuckled softly. "You'd better tell Jeb and Moses not to make the first time too lively, then, Henry. My old legs aren't as spry as they once were, certainly not the way they were when I used to dance at the green corn festival so long ago." His smile faded and he uttered a long sigh. "This housewarming is a fine thing, boy. Now that we're getting neighbors around us, it's a good thing to have them over and be close to them."

"Not quite all of them, Father." Henry's eyes narrowed speculatively. "Just the ones who really matter. There'll be Edward Williamson, of course, because he's

17

got four hundred acres of prime land a few miles down-river from my own holdings. Besides which, he's a widower with two nice, marriageable daughters. And with Luke being eighteen and overseer now, Father, it wouldn't be a bad idea if he thought about taking himself a wife."

"He's too young yet, Henry. Besides, what with school and working on the land, he's had no time at all to learn the social graces."

"True enough, and all the better reason for having him take an interest in Williamson's older girl, Lucy. She's his own age, and from what I hear, shy and sweet."

"Well, young as he is, Luke has a good mind of his own and I think he'll know whom to pick when the right time comes. Who else will enjoy our hospitality tonight, Henry?"

"Well then, there's Frank Ellerby and his wife, Wilma, from upriver. Frank's got two hundred productive acres and twenty slaves. He's done right well in the two years he's had his land. Then there's Silas and Helen Jordan and their two boys, Bobby and Ashton. They're not far from the Ellerbys, you know."

"That's fine." Lucien Bouchard chuckled again. "I'm sure, if Sybella is allowing Arabella to attend the party, my older granddaughter will be quite happy that the Jordans are bringing their boys over. She's a saucy little minx, that one is, and you and Sybella had best be keeping a tight rein on her. I shouldn't wonder if she'll be married by the time she's sixteen or so."

"Advantageously, Father, that's how she'll be married."

"Of course, it's expected that when she falls in love it'll be with a fine upstanding young man who has the means to support her."

"And, hopefully, Father, so far as I have anything to say about it, with a man whose land is close enough to mine and whose ideas about working it dovetail with my own."

Lucien propped himself up on the pillows, stared

18

earnestly at his son. "I hope you won't try to manipulate your children like pawns in a game of chess to give you material profits, Henry. You know that I never tried to manipulate you."

"Of course I know that, Father," Henry impatiently countered. "I learned a great deal from you and I'm the first to admit it. Only, as I've told you so many times, things have changed. When you got your land from the Creeks, there weren't any other whites around for miles and miles. No competition. If you produced a hundred bales of cotton or so a year, that was fine. But now we've got steamboats on the river and we've got slaves to work the cotton and the gin to ready it for market. And the more cotton we can produce and the more slaves we have to work the land, the better off we'll all be. I want to make Windhaven the biggest plantation in all of Alabama before I'm done."

Lucien Bouchard grasped his son's hands in his and leaned forward, his eyes bright and searching. "Can't you learn the difference between possession and stewardship, Henry? Yes, I can understand your passion for the land. When I came to Econchate, when I saw the hill on one side and the bluff on the other and the sloping, rich valley-like land between them, I remembered my father's land at Yves-sur-lac. It was a kind of miracle, that after wandering across the ocean I found Windhaven. It's so like my own birthplace. But when old Tunkamara gave me the land as a gift for my labors, I pledged myself not to own it for my own selfish ends, but to keep it in a kind of trust, to produce for the good of those who had taken me in as a stranger, wounded and impoverished, a foreigner who could not even speak their own tongue and who knew nothing of their customs."

"Yes, yes, Father, that was all very well before Alabama became a state. But now the land belongs to the whites. And the deeds to the lands that you own and which I've acquired are registered, and they'll hold up in any court in the years ahead, and you don't owe the Indians a thing. It's time to think of the present and the future, Father, and that's what I'm going to do."

19

Lucien stared silently at his son for a moment, then leaned back on the pillows and closed his eyes. "You are my only son and heir, and what I've worked for has been for you and for your children, Henry. You've always scolded me for lecturing you. Well, I shan't try. But remember, in your own best interests, that you can wear out even the richest land by not diversifying crops or by letting it lie fallow for a year or two. Haven't you seen what happened in the Carolinas and Virginia, how all their good land was ruined by the incessant cultivation of tobacco? Any good farmer knows that he needs more than one steady crop to balance his books at the year's end, especially if some disaster strikes that single crop."

"And that's precisely why I intend to get more land, Father." Henry Bouchard rose from the bed and smoothed his waistcoat. "There'll be a few others here tonight, Father, who are beholden to me. They've had to mortgage their crops pretty heavily for this year, and last year they ginned their cotton in my shed. I'm keeping it there to be taken to Mobile, and if they can't pay what they owe me and what I've already advanced for their seed and their equipment, Sybella's father will just take up their mortgages."

"You'd do that to your own neighbors, Henry?" Lucien Bouchard gasped.

"It's only business, Father."

"If you're so greedy for land that you must acquire it at the expense of decent, hard-working neighbors, then I venture to say you'll pay a dearer price for it than you can guess, a price far in excess of the worth of that land you're so eager to add to your already quite adequate acreage."

"Oh Father, there you go lecturing me again! Take your nap, and let's not talk business. Let's enjoy the housewarming. I've something to celebrate, you see. I don't need my crutches anymore, I'm strong and fit as I ever was, and this is 1835 and a new year and one I want to see as the best Windhaven has ever known."

"Amen to that, my son," Lucien Bouchard said with

a sad smile as he closed his eyes and lay back on the pillows.

The large, well-planned kitchen of Windhaven was at the very back of the red-brick château, a separate unit which looked like an additional wing to the original building, with its wide chimney and its roof rising slightly above the first floor of the château itself. As Sybella entered, the delicious odors of cooking made her nostrils dilate, and fat Mammy Clorinda turned with an alacrity which her portly weight belied to hurry toward her mistress.

"You needn't worry none, Miz Bouchard," she beamingly asserted. "Everythin's gwine be jist lak you wants it foah tonight, you'll see. Amy gal, see dat de spit keeps turnin' slow and easy, so's de pig'll baste right proper and be cooked to a turn. You lemme find it's jist a mite raw anywheres, gal, I'se gwine baste youah backside with my ladle, and dat's a promise!" She turned with a great show of authority to harangue the timid young Hausa girl who, with a taller, slightly older Gullah girl named Ruby, was engaged in turning the handles of the long spit on which a suckling pig hung over a steep fire in the great stone hearth. From the stone oven there came the mouth-watering aroma of a side of venison, along with baking yams and pumpkin and winter-apple pies liberally doused with cloves and cinnamon and sugar. Clara was inspecting the oven and, catching sight of her mistress, made a hasty curtsy.

"Are you sure you'll have enough help, Mammy Clorinda?" Sybella asked.

"Don't you worry none 'bout dat, Miz Bouchard. So long as dese yeah gals do jist lak Ah tells dem, it'll be all ready when you is, m'am. Anyways, Ah'll have three new gals at least to serve tonight, and you'll want Matthew too, won't you, Miz Bouchard?"

"Yes, Mammy Clorinda, he'll be a kind of butler, you see. And the girls can follow his example. It might be a good idea to have him tell the ones you've picked for tonight just what to expect."

"Ah'll see to dat, count on me, m'am! Now den, whyn't you go take youahself a little nap so's you kin be fresh and purty foah tonight?"

"Well, I must confess there doesn't seem to be anything for me to do at all. Mammy, you're such a wonderful cook and I just know our guests are going to pay you lots of compliments."

"Thank'ee, m'am. Now, is dat new gal Celia pleasin' you? Is she bein' a proper maid, Miz Bouchard?"

"Why, yes, she's fine, Mammy. Why do you ask?"

The plump black woman surreptitiously glanced toward her helpers, then approached the auburn-haired matron and whispered in a confidential tone, "She ain't had the vapors none yit, has she, m'am?"

"The vapors—no—what do you mean, Mammy?" Sybella's dark-blue eyes widened questioningly.

" 'Cause she's gwine drop a suckah mebbe befoah next fall, dat's what. Ah knows. She done tol' me she missed her last two times, beggin' youah pardon, Miz Bouchard."

Sybella paled, bit her lips, then odded. "Thank you for telling me. I didn't know, Mammy. But you needn't worry, she's going to stay my maid and nobody's going to bother her."

"Yassum. She a mighty sweet l'il gal, she try hard to please."

"I know. But I'd just as soon you wouldn't let any of the girls gossip about her having a baby, Mammy. I know I can count on you. You mean so much to Windhaven already, I find it hard to remember what it was like before we had you as our cook and housekeeper."

Before Mammy Clorinda could begin her thanks at such lofty praise, Sybella added, "Just to make sure you know how many to prepare for, we'll have Mr. Williamson and his two daughters, the Ellerbys, the Jordans with their two boys—and they're twelve and fourteen and I warn you, they eat like horses—and two bachelor gentlemen. That makes eleven guests in all. Oh yes, and I'd appreciate it if you'd have Clara take a special tray up to Fleurette so she doesn't feel slighted at not being at the party."

"You kin rely on me foah ebbrythin', Miz Bouchard. Ah's much obliged foah what you jist said to me. It's real nice to wohk foah a lady lak you, m'am."

"Thank you, Mammy. And your girls are doing very nicely too. Be sure they get a good share of the food they're cooking for us once our guests have had their fill. And I'll see that Matthew brings out a little wine for you and them as well."

"Thank'ee, m'am, thank'ee!" the black woman acknowledged this unusual generosity of her mistress with a wide grin.

Sybella went back into the house, silent and troubled. So Celia was pregnant—it could only mean that young Mark had got her with child on that terrible night when he and Henry had fought over the poor girl. Well, when Celia's pregnancy became more evident, she'd see if she couldn't get Henry to give Celia her freedom so that the child could be born free, too. It was the least he could do. And in another year or two, she thought, it might be well for Mark to marry. Perhaps that would curb his lustful appetites, in which he so resembled his father. And ardently, she wished that her husband would satisfy his desires with her alone, his proper wife and bedmate.

CHAPTER THREE

"Oh, this is truly a treat for me, Mr. Bouchard!" Wilma Ellerby exclaimed in her high-pitched voice as she entered the elegant drawing room on the arm of her husband, with Henry Bouchard following at her side. "Land's sakes, I declare, I haven't been dancing since dear Frank brought me here from Boston! And just look at those beautiful settees—why, I declare, they must be by Duncan Phyfe."

"As a matter of fact, they are, my dear Mrs. Ellerby. You see, Father believes that, as an American citizen, despite his French birth, it's patriotic to pay tribute to our own native skills. And the furniture made back East is certainly as good as anything one can find anywhere these days."

"Oh, to be sure it is!" the attractive, light-haired young woman agreed. "I do hope I haven't forgotten how to dance in all this time." She sent her husband a quick, contemptuous glance.

The floor of the drawing room had been oiled and then waxed two days before the housewarming. There were five beautiful mahogany settees, with fluting on the back and rails, fluted legs with brass ball feet, reeded arms, posts and lower back rail. Thick red-velvet curtains had been drawn over the two large windows, and at the far left, on a little stand, the two middle-aged Jamaican slaves Jeb and Moses stood, awaiting their master's signal to begin.

"And those lovely upholstered wing chairs, too—my gracious, it must have cost a fortune to build and furnish this wonderful house," Wilma Ellerby rhapsodically went on. Henry Bouchard's lips curled in a cynical smile, for he read the attractive matron's envy and frustrations all too well in her praise of Windhaven's accommodations and decor. Throughout the eight-course dinner which had just been served and at which she had been seated at his right, Wilma Ellerby had intimated to him more details of her disappointing marriage than he had known or could have guessed from Frank Ellerby's meek, almost withdrawn behavior. He knew that Frank Ellerby was thirty years old and eight years older than Wilma; that he had been the son of a wealthy auctioneer in Charleston, visited Boston four years ago where he had met and married Wilma, then brought her back to Charleston. Two years after that, upon his father's death, Frank Ellerby had come to Alabama and purchased two hundred acres of prime land as well as twenty slaves for the house and the fields. Yet, if only from Wilma's rapturous reaction to the tour which he had conducted for all his guests through the château, Henry had been made aware that Wilma was unhappy in her marriage and bored to tears with plantation life.

Sybella, who as hostess had been seated at the opposite end of the dinner table from her father-in-law, was standing beside Lucien now over at the little stand where the two Jamaicans were softly testing their instruments. She had already observed how much attention her husband had paid to Wilma Ellerby, whom she considered vapid and affected. Besides, Wilma Ellerby's red marcelline frock with its low-cut bodice—even granting that she wore a lace fichu round her neck—was in her opinion somewhat brazen for an occasion of this sort. It was plain to see that Henry constantly stared at that bodice which revealed just the beginning of the valley between the young woman's high-perched, full round breasts and the generous expanse of pale white skin afforded to even the most casual gaze. Lucien, observing her turn now in the

26

direction of the door to the drawing room, leaned over to whisper comfortingly, "Never mind, Sybella my dear. He is simply reacting like a predatory rooster that's been kept out of the hen yard for a very long spell."

"I suppose that's his right as a male, Father. But I dare say that if he were to catch me looking in the direction of some other man, I'd hear about it soon enough. Why is it that men always have a double standard, two for themselves and none for their wives?"

"Perhaps because society has imposed monogamy on men and it's a condition they really weren't suited for," Lucien wryly responded.

She turned back to face him, put her hands on his shoulders and kissed his weatherbeaten, wrinkled cheek. "But you're the exception to the rule, dear Father."

"In one sense, yes, because I've been faithful to Dimarte all my life. If God had granted us long life together, I don't think I should have been tempted by any other woman. If only you'd known her, Sybella! How gentle she was, yet how wise, mature beyond her years—and she was much younger when I first saw her than Mrs. Ellerby is now. Yet there was a joyous, happy, sometimes almost prankish side to her nature, which balanced so wonderfully with her gracious compassion and her understanding of people." He lifted his head, as if again he were in the tower staring out at the red bluff beyond, and a tender smile curved his lips. "But it wasn't to be, and then there were Amelia and Priscilla. And each of them was destined, each in her own way, to give a man all the happiness he could ask for in a single lifetime, and I was privileged to know such women. Perhaps that's why I've known the value of continence, because each of them had such ideal qualities that I intuitively knew that any other women would fail in the comparison."

"And yet Henry's so different from you, Father. When he had that—that—well, accident—we were brought together again, and it was good. In fact, if you can keep a secret, I'm really hoping that I'll give him another child. Another son, someone just like you, Father. That's what I'd really like."

"You mustn't flatter an old man like that, Sybella dear. Besides, there's your stepson Luke, and he's all that any father could ask for. He has something of Dimarte's wisdom too, that grave, gentle, secretly contained wisdom which will never let him be swayed by passion or greed or intolerance. Yet how strange it is, Sybella, that Luke, in whom I sometimes see myself when I was his age, was born not to you but to an unhappy girl who was the daughter of a crooked land speculator. How strange our destiny is upon this earth, Sybella—my only surviving son who is your husband cost the death of his innocent, orphaned mother Priscilla, whose only living kin had been murdered by the Choctaws. No, it's not possible for man to chart his own destiny, not as he would plan it. But that's enough of somber thoughts. Let's get my part of the ceremony over with quickly, for I feel myself getting tired after all this excitement. Have Jeb and Moses play an old tune, not too fast, so that I shan't make a disgraceful spectacle of myself with you."

"You could never do that, Father." Sybella squeezed his hand as she turned to the two Jamaicans and whispered, "Do you know 'Greensleeves'? Please play it for us."

As the two slaves began to play the old English folk song, Henry Bouchard excused himself to the Ellerbys and went to one of the settees on which his two bachelor guests were sitting. One of them was tall and lean, in his mid-thirties, James Cavendish, the only son of a Georgia plantation owner, who had compromised the honor of neighboring plantation owner's seventeen-year-old daughter. When he had refused to marry the girl, his widowed father disowned him, gave him $2000 in gold and told him to make his own way henceforth. He had come to Lowndesboro not quite two years ago, purchased fifty acres of land and five slaves, and was producing about forty bales of prime cotton for the Mobile market. He had come to Henry Bouchard to have his cotton ginned but had been unable to pay for the service; Lucien's wily son intended to take over that acreage before the year was done, as he did that of the other bachelor guest, Benjamin Harnesty, a stout, reddish-haired former surveyor from Huntsville, who, according to rumor, had been discharged from his post for taking bribes and who owned forty-five acres of land near Cavendish's holdings. Henry knew him to be a confirmed womanizer, and a frequent patron of brothels in Natchez, New Orleans, and Mobile.

"Don't look so glum, you two," he blithely admonished them. "We'll have a quadrille, and you'll get the chance to dance with Wilma Ellerby as well as with Helen Jordan. And of course, with my own dear wife Sybella and Edward Williamson's two delightful daughters. Besides," he glanced back across the room at Sybella and Lucien, "I'll see to it that each of you is provided with a pleasant bed wench when it's time to retire."

"That's damned decent of you, Bouchard," Benjamin Harnesty muttered, his watery pale-blue eyes glinting with anticipation.

"You boys won't mind sharing the same bedroom, in that case," Henry added with a worldly wink. "The other guests are staying the night, and the guest rooms are close to the children's bedrooms. So keep it quiet, there's no need to let them know about bed wenches this early in life." His face momentarily soured as he remembered how his precocious younger son had not only found out about Celia, but actually enjoyed her body while to this very moment he had been deprived of it.

"We can keep our mouths shut, Mr. Bouchard, sir," the younger man muttered. "I'm mighty obliged for such hospitality."

"It's part of the Windhaven tradition, Jim, Benjamin," Henry Bouchard affably explained. "And of course, no need to rush away in the morning. Stay for lunch, even supper if you've a mind to. Besides, we've a little business to talk over. Seems to me I'm holding your cotton in my shed, the both of you. But I'm sure it will fetch a good price in Mobile, and the better the

29

price, the sooner our little accounting can be happily settled. Enjoy yourselves, my friends." He clapped each man on the back, nodded cordially, and then moved over to one of the wing chairs in which pretty Arabella had ensconced herself, proudly looking about but keeping her eyes most attentively on the two sturdy fair-haired boys who sat with their mother and father on the settee across the room. Silas Jordan, short, partly bald, with a pleasant, good-natured face and courteous manners, was forty years old, just a year older than his still attractive, rather buxom yellow-haired wife Helen. The Jordans owned one hundred and fifty acres of excellent riverfront land half a mile from the Ellerbys' acreage, had settled there about three years ago after Silas Jordan lost his South Carolina tobacco crop in a field fire set by renegade slaves. Bobby Jordan, not quite thirteen, was tall and gawky, towheaded, and, as Arabella had already mischievously discovered, blushed easily whenever he talked to a girl. Ashton, a year older, with long light-brown curls and sensitive features, was quite reserved and prim, an excellent scholar at the Lowndesboro Academy for Young Gentlemen.

Now the sounds of "Greensleeves" filled the large drawing room as old Lucien, in his customary buckskin and moccasins, led Sybella gallantly out onto the floor, bowed to her, and then took her in his arms and began to dance a slow and stately measure to the charming old tune.

"Isn't he simply marvelous, Father!" honey-haired eighteen-year-old Lucy Williamson leaned over to whisper to her heavy-set, morose-looking gray-haired father. "It's like something out of a storybook to see him dressed like that, as they must have been in the days of the Indians long before Alabama became a state."

"Yes, Daughter, he's a remarkable man indeed," Edward Williamson agreed. "And he certainly has the best plantation in the entire state. But then, I think I've got the best overseer. His son Henry was telling me before we went in to dinner that he's made young Luke his overseer and Thomas, the nigger who used to be in charge, is now the assistant. Well, that's just as it should be."

"Please don't say such things, Father. You know I don't hold with slavery." Lucy's exquisite heart-shaped face clouded with distress, and she looked down at her folded hands in her lap. She wore a pretty sky-blue silk frock with puffed sleeves and shoulders, high neckline, the skirt descending to her dainty ankles, with soft cloth slippers which matched the dress. To her father's left, coppery-haired fifteen-year-old Maybelle archly eyed Mark Bouchard who stood beside his older brother Luke across the room, whispering to him but without taking his eyes off the flirtatious red-haired girl.

"You mean you don't like Amos Greer, Lucy. I don't take to him too much myself, but he gets cotton out of my land and that's all that matters. And I mean to put money away for you and Maybelle, so you girls won't have to want for anything when I'm gone," her father declared. Then, seeing how disturbed she still seemed, he added jocularly, "Now you just forget plantation business, Lucy, and enjoy yourself, hear?"

The strains of "Greensleeves" had ebbed away, and old Lucien drew back from his smiling daughter-in-law and made her a courtly bow, amid the applause of the watching guests. "Thank you, Sybella dear," he murmured. "You've made me feel young again. And I'm sure you're woman enough to keep my son feeling that way—I surely hope you will, for now that he's well, I'm just a little afraid he may do what the devil did."

"And what's that, Father?" Sybella, in her turn, curtsied to her father-in-law.

"Oh, surely you recall the story of how, when the devil was sick, the devil a monk would be. But when the devil was well, the devil of a monk was he," Lucien smilingly explained as he led Sybella back to her settee. "And now I shall make my excuses and retire. Let the young folks enjoy their party."

"It wouldn't have been possible without you, Father.

31

And don't you worry about Henry, we've made up and he knows how I feel about him."

"If he doesn't, he's a fool, my dear. Good night, and thank you again for humoring an old man." Lucien bent to take Sybella's hand and bring it to his lips, and smiled and nodded at her as he turned to take his leave of the guests.

Henry watched his father leave the drawing room, not without a look of grudging admiration at the still erect carriage of the old man. Then, moving to the center of the room, he clapped his hands and announced, "And now, ladies and gentlemen, we'll have the quadrille. Gentlemen, choose your partners. I want everyone to have a chance to dance with everyone else tonight. All of you who are neighbors of mine, this is the evening in which we welcome you to Windhaven and offer you the full extent of our hospitality." As he finished, he turned to look back at James Cavendish and Benjamin Harnesty, and gave them a covert wink which they acknowledged with knowing smiles as they began to whisper to each other.

Then, walking over to the settee, he bent to Sybella and graciously demanded, "I think, Mrs. Bouchard, that you owe me the very next dance. I was jealous of my father there, you know."

"He's the only one you'll ever have to be jealous about, Henry dear," Sybella twitted him as she swiftly rose to accept his invitation to the dance. He nodded to the two Jamaicans, who began a lively quadrille, a jaunty tune from the Carolinas which the slaves themselves were wont to play after the harvest had been brought in. Leading her out onto the middle of the floor, he nodded pleasantly to his guests, while Sybella watched him, her eyes intent upon his face as if divining his true mood. She saw, from the corner of her eye, Frank Ellerby take his wife by the hand and lead her onto the floor, and observed also the indifferent look on the handsome matron's face. Edward Williamson had led gentle honey-haired Lucy out to share the quadrille with him, while Silas Jordan was accompanied by his buxom Helen.

32

The irrepressible Arabella, stroking the folds of her pretty new dress in a self-conscious attempt to preen herself—a gesture she had sometimes seen Sybella make—looked over toward the settee where Bobby and Ashton Jordan sat. With all her might, she wished that either one, or better still, both, would ask her to dance. After all, what fun could there be in a party that was reserved just for the grownups? And Mother had taught her some of the simple dance steps, and she was quite sure she could do as well as those boys.

To her delight, gawky Bobby Jordan now left his older brother and came toward her. Putting a hand to his heart, he stammered, "Miss Arabella, would you honor me, m'am, please?"

"Why, I'd be just delighted, Bobby!" It was all Arabella could do to keep from springing out of her chair in her delight. She had to remind herself that she was only a few years away from being grown-up herself and so she must act that way if she expected a good-looking boy like Bobby to pay attention to her. "You shall have my very first dance, Bobby Jordan," she declared, with as serious a look on her pretty face as if she were a vaunted belle of the ball dispensing her favors to a swarm of ardent suitors.

"Will you dance with me, Daughter?" Edward Williamson turned to his elder daughter, who was staring down at her folded hands. "Please, honey, don't look so upset. I declare, ever since your mother died, it's been hard on me seeing you fret and look so lonesome."

"I miss Mama too, but it's not that," Lucy murmured. "It all seemed so different till we came here, Papa. And I'm sure that even our slaves feel the same way, ever since you hired that dreadful man. I'm sorry, Papa, I didn't mean to spoil your evening. And it was awfully thoughtful of you to bring Maybelle and me here to see this beautiful house and, best of all, to meet old Mr. Bouchard. I do admire him so."

"So do I, Daughter. But you kbnow," he added with a speculative twinkle in his eyes, "the best way I know for a pretty girl like you to get over her lonesomeness is having some fine young man make a fuss over her. And unless I miss my guess, Luke Bouchard has got his eye on you right now. Why don't we go out and dance, and I'm sure he'll ask you for the next one."

"Papa, you mustn't embarrass me like that!" A blush suffused Lucy's pale carnation-tinted cheeks as she gracefully rose and took her father's offered arm.

Maybelle, who wore a green silk frock not unlike her older sister's, leaned forward, all her attention now directed at swaggering Mark who had continued to eye her while standing talking with Luke. Glancing quickly around to make certain that her father wouldn't notice, she gave him an almost imperceptible nod and crooked her forefinger, then swiftly leaned back and, with the attitude of a very prim young lady, folded her hands in her lap and waited.

"Say now, Luke, I think I'll have me a dance with that pretty red-haired filly over there. Didn't you see her sign to me to come on over?" Mark boastingly asked Luke.

"To be honest with you, Mark, no." Luke was watching the graceful girl who now faced her father on the dance floor, each bowing low to the other in the stately form of the quadrille.

"I get it. You like that Lucy, don't you? Well, that's fine with me. Personally, I think Maybelle has a lot more spirit—that's what I like in a filly. Just like breaking in a new mare—it's always more fun when she wants to give you a battle," the youth declared as he strode toward Edward Williamson's younger daughter.

"Mind if I have this dance, Miss Maybelle?" he grinned at her.

"La, I sure don't, not one little bit, Mr. Bouchard." Maybelle fluttered her eyelids at him as she coyly rose and tendered him her soft little hand. Mark caught his father's eyes and, with a mocking wink, bowed to kiss Maybelle's hand, much as his own father might have done. Henry Bouchard frowned and turned back to Sybella: "That young whippersnapper is getting just a mite too big for his breeches, Sybella. Maybe he'd mind if you gave him a talking-to."

"Oh Henry, I thought you and Mark had patched things up by this time! He's your son, after all, and don't forget," she couldn't help her swiftly malicious counter, "he sets such store by you that he tries to take after you in many ways."

"I suppose I had that coming, Sybella," Henry Bouchard sighed. "Very well, I'll talk to the boy in a nice fatherly way. I've kept my word so far—I mean, Celia is your private maid now and I'll not bother her."

"I shouldn't take it kindly at all if you did. But did you notice, Henry, Luke is watching that pretty Lucy Williamson dancing with her father!"

"She's pretty enough, but much too tame. I've no doubt she's a blue-stocking, shuts herself up and reads books the way Luke does."

"And what's wrong with that? Hasn't Luke learned enough out of his books and out of his work on the land to have earned his promotion to being your overseer, Henry?"

"All right, all right, Sybella. Let's not get into a family argument. It's our housewarming. I want everybody to be happy. And that means both of us, my dear." Then, as he took her hand and lifted it in one of the quaint flourishes of the quadrille, he whispered, "I'll come to your bedroom tonight, dearest Sybella. You'll see that I'm not thinking of Celia at all or anyone else."

There was a pause now, as the first part of the quadrille came to an end, and the couples bowed to one another. Sybella, disengaging herself from Henry's arms, moved over to Arabella, who had not yet let go of Bobby Jordan's hand. "Darling," she said gently, "it's really past your bedtime now. Be a sweet girl, thank young Master Jordan for the dance and excuse yourself to everyone."

"Oh, no, Mama," Arabella pouted, her large eyes widening and filming with sudden tears, "can't I stay up late just this once? It's the first real party I've ever been to—please, Mama!"

Sybella put her arm around the little girl's shoulders, bent and kissed her. "Precious, you mustn't try to grow up too fast. If you had all the fun now, there wouldn't be anything left for the many tomorrows ahead of you, don't you see, Arabella? Now you've already made a wonderful impression, so don't spoil it. Make your apologies to everyone and say good night."

Luke, who stood beside the Jordan boy, turned to his sister: "If you leave now after that very first dance, dear, you'll have made a perfect impression. You'll really have been the belle of the ball, and they'll all be thinking about you."

"Do you really think so, dear Luke?" Her quivering lips had curved into a radiant smile.

Luke nodded, "Oh yes, Arabella. And besides, once you've gone, it won't seem the same without that pretty dress and the very pretty young lady in it. Everybody will be remembering it all night long."

"Oh, Luke," the little girl impulsively exclaimed, "I just love you!" She flung her arms around him, standing on tiptoe to proffer her mouth, and he teasingly kissed her on the tip of her nose. "Now that's the way to be a young lady, Arabella. Good night, dear sister."

Sybella's eyes met her stepson's in a look that conveyed all her gratitude and admiration. Smilingly, she followed Arabella as the latter, her pout replaced by her most grown-up mien, curtsied to the men and said her good nights. "That's my darling," she whispered to Arabella and gave her a kiss, leading her to the open door of the drawing room. "Now off you go to bed. And be careful not to wake Fleurette. In the morning, bright and early, you can tell her all about the dance."

"You were very nice to her, Mr. Bouchard," Lucy Williamson murmured to her handsome partner. Her father had relinquished her to Luke and gone back to the settee, enjoying a cup of punch which Matthew brought him on a tray.

"She's a charming little minx, Miss Williamson, and, as Mother so often says, her only problem is that she can't wait to be grown-up."

"I suppose that's true." The girl's face grew pensive.

36

"When Mama was alive and we were back in Georgia, I loved being her little girl even though I was older than Maybelle. We were all so close then. Mama loved to play charades and to make up stories for Maybelle and me to act out. But—but it's different now. And it's been terribly hard on Papa. I guess maybe that's why he's so busy with his land and the crops, trying to forget his grief over Mama."

"I know how you feel, Miss Williamson. My mother died soon after I was born, you see. Sybella's my stepmother, but I've been lucky because she's always treated me as if I were her very own flesh and blood."

"You know, it's—it's strange, Mr. Bouchard. I'm sure you're not much older than I am, but you're so wise and kind and gentle—and Papa was telling me that your father just made you overseer over all this land. It must be a terrible responsibility."

"Yes, but I want to work it just the way Grandfather planned, not to take everything but to give it and share it, not to overwork the land but to be grateful for what it yields as well as for those who work on it."

The music had begun again, but Lucy Williamson stared eagerly at the young man who faced her. "Would you mind awfully much if we didn't dance this next measure, Mr. Bouchard? I—I'd enjoy talking to you a lot more—but now I'm being awfully rude as a guest—"

"Of course you aren't, Miss Williamson. Please, won't you call me Luke? I'm not all that old, you know." He smiled gently.

"I will if you'll call me Lucy."

"It's a bargain. Maybe you'd like to see Grandfather's library. He was born in France, you know, and of course he has many books in that language, like Voltaire and Moliere and Corneille."

"Oh yes, I'd just adore seeing them. At the school, I've already had two years of French, so I can read a little."

"I'd be happy to lend you any book you'd like. I'm sure Grandfather would want you to enjoy it. Come along now."

37

Sybella had gone back to Henry, not without noticing that her stepson and Lucy Williamson had just left the drawing room. "I'm so glad Luke fancies that sweet girl," she confided to her husband. "I know how lonely she must be to come to a new home and to have lost her mother."

"True enough, my dear, and I see that Mark is smitten with that flirtatious Maybelle. Not a bad idea, our two boys starting their courting of the girls whose father has some land I've got my eye on as well as on his extremely efficient overseer."

"Henry, please don't try to manipulate things. If our sons are going to fall in love, let them do it of their own accord, not because it'll get you more land, more slaves. And why would you need an overseer now that you've named Luke to take charge of Windhaven?"

"A man can't get too much land, the way things are. Father keeps saying there's going to be a panic because old Andy Jackson wouldn't renew the charter on the Bank of the United States. He might just be right, you know. And if that happens, there'll be very little money anywhere, and land will be all that matters. But let's not talk about business matters, my darling. You don't know how delicious you are in that new gown. And the music's beginning again."

"Why don't I dance this one with poor Mr. Williamson, who's all by himself over there on the settee? And you can dance with one of the other women, as a good host should do to make everyone feel welcome."

She saw his eyes brighten and saw him turn toward Wilma Ellerby, who had returned to the settee with her husband, sitting with her face turned away from him and a look of disdain on her provocative features. Noticing that, she whispered to him, "Don't forget, my darling, you promised to come to me tonight when the party's over."

CHAPTER FOUR

Lest Sybella think that he was more than ordinarily interested in Wilma Ellerby, Henry Bouchard purposely approached Silas Jordan's wife and, bowing in his most gallant manner, asked her to be his partner for the next dance. Sybella, with her most gracious smile, extended her hand to Edward Williamson, whose morose face brightened, and led him out onto the floor. James Cavendish, noticing Wilma Ellerby's continued indifference toward her husband, hesitantly approached the attractive young matron and beamed with pleasure when she accepted his invitation. Benjamin Harnesty then approached flirtatious young Maybelle Williamson, who had gone back to sit down but continued to chat with Mark. Clearing his throat, he asked: "Miss Maybelle, I'd be mighty honored if you'd favor me with this next dance, unless you're already spoken for."

Mark Bouchard gave the former surveyor a furious look, but Maybelle, secretly fascinated by this apparent duel for her favors, reached out to pat Mark's wrist and to whisper, "La, Mr. Bouchard, don't be so jealous! You shall have the very next dance, I promise!" Then, rising, and giving the dazzled older man her most provocative smile, she huskily murmured, "I do declare, Mr. Harnesty, you've such a way with you I just can't resist your invitation. Of course, I'm really not as old as you think, sir, I'm just a little past fifteen, you know. But if you still want to dance—I don't see why I can't."

Glancing back over her shoulder, she cast Mark a teasing smile as he glared at her. *He'd pay her back for flouting him like that, the little vixen! Two can play at that game as well as one. And then that little speech about being just a child—he'd be willing to wager, if he could get her to bed just once without her father's being the wiser, she'd have as many tricks as a young New Orleans whore.*

Accordingly, he seated himself on the settee she had just quitted, and when the liveried majordomo approached with a tray of freshly made punch, he beckoned, seized a glass and, his eyes still following Maybelle as she and her partner began to bow to each other in the formal prelude of this courtly dance, downed half his glass at a single gulp in a defiant gesture. He saw her glance back at him and make a charming little moué, then turn back attentively to reply to something Benjamin Harnesty was whispering to her. At the same moment, she almost brazenly pressed herself against the older man, and Mark's fingers tightened around his glass as a lustful rage began to swirl through him.

Helen Jordan, whose widely flaring pink marcelline gown with its high-necked bodice and long, puffed sleeves made her seem plumper than she actually was, had also observed her host's preoccupation with Wilma Ellerby, and consequently did her best to gain his attention by favoring him with her most demure smile and a question: "My gracious me, Mr. Bouchard, I've never seen such a magnificent house! You must have lots of slaves to look after it and all the land you have."

"Yes, it's quite a responsibility." He turned to look at her appraisingly. Her widely oval face, the dainty pug nose and the generous, sweet mouth seemed somewhat insipid to his taste, but his calculating gaze had already stripped her flouncy gown from her and determined that even though she was nearly forty, her figure was still appealing. "Actually, Father has much more

40

land than I do. He originally bought six hundred and forty acres, while I have about two hundred and twenty-five, you see. Though mine, of course, is quite some distance away from Father's, so that young Luke won't be looking after it—I'll do that myself till I can appoint my own overseer. As to slaves, well, I've nearly fifty, and Father has nearly that many. Of course, because he has more land than I do, I've lent him a good many of my field hands. If I were you, and you talk to him again, I wouldn't mention the matter of slaves—he prefers to call his freed men."

"I see. Well, I suppose before Alabama became a state, it was possible to free the slaves, wasn't it?"

"That's quite right, Mrs. Jordan. But we've all learned from the Nat Turner Rebellion what can happen when you give the blacks liberty. They're better off working under discipline than having to fend for themselves."

"That's what Silas says. Of course, we only have about twenty, because you know that Silas lost a great deal back in South Carolina. And although I feel sorry for the blacks who have cruel masters, I still can't forgive those awful niggers who set fire to our fields. Silas managed to catch one of them and shot him out of hand. But do let's talk about pleasant things. Your little Arabella is so sweet, and I was so happy to see Bobby dance with her just like a little gentleman. Ashton, I'm afraid, is more of a scholarly type, and he hasn't started to notice girls yet even though he's older."

Henry Bouchard cynically thought to himself that this was exactly the case with Luke and Mark, and had to admit to some surprise at the way his sobersides of an elder son had seemed to take to Lucy Williamson. "Yes, Mrs. Jordan, Bella's quite the flirt of the family. I'm going to have to keep a close watch over her as she grows up or I'll have all the boys for miles around beating a path to our door."

"I want to thank you, too, Mr. Bouchard, for being such a nice neighbor and ginning Silas's cotton for him

41

and storing it. It's very neighborly, I must say, and I think it won't be long before we get used to Alabama ways. We did hate to leave our beautiful house in South Carolina and all our wonderful friends."

"It's my pleasure, Mrs. Jordan," Henry Bouchard declared. "I hope this tune isn't too lively for you? At our next party, I intend to hire some real musicians out of New Orleans, not just have music furnished by two slaves. They're not too bad, though."

"I should say they aren't! Oh my, I haven't had this much fun in years, Mr. Bouchard."

"Well now, I'm glad you're enjoying yourself. And of course I want you and Silas and the boys to spend the night. We've plenty of rooms on the second floor for our good neighbors. And you'll enjoy Mammy Clorinda's famous breakfast."

"My gracious sakes, I declare I ate so much supper, I shouldn't dare to think of breakfast or I won't be able to fit this dress, and it's tight enough already—oh dear, that was an awfully unladylike thing to say—do forgive me!"

"I can forgive a beautiful woman anything, dear Mrs. Jordan," Henry Bouchard said as, the dance ending, he gallantly led her back to the settee, then shook hands with her husband and repeated his invitation to stay the night.

After a pause, the two Jamaicans resumed with the fiddle and the harmonica to play a Creole waltz which was all the vogue in New Orleans, and this time Silas Jordan escorted his flushed, happy wife onto the floor, while Sybella Bouchard accepted the invitation of James Cavendish to dance. Maybelle Williamson walked over to where young Mark stood, still glowering, and whispered, "I do hope you're not mad at little me, Mr. Bouchard. Maybe, if you don't feel like dancing, we could go somewhere and chat."

"That's a capital idea, Maybelle!" He grinned wolfishly as he took her arm and, glancing back to make certain that no one was watching, quickly escorted her out of the drawing room.

In the library, Luke Bouchard opened the largest cherrywood bookcase and took out a handsomely bound atlas of France, profuse with pen-and-ink sketches which depicted the countryside, the ports, the teeming cities of his grandfather's native land. Taking it over to an ornate escritoire, he opened it to the section detailing the province of Normandy, while Lucy Williamson, her eyes shining with interest, bent beside him to study the illustrations. "Grandfather was born in that province, you see, Lucy," he explained. "He was born in the little village of Yves-sur-lac, and his father was a count."

"And he gave it all up to come here and begin his life all over again, Luke?"

"Yes, because he knew that there would be a revolution in France and that titles wouldn't mean anything anymore. Besides, even if there hadn't been a revolution, Grandfather loved people too much to want to set himself above them in any way."

"Then he actually was a nobleman, wasn't he, Luke?"

"Not quite, Lucy. You see, he had an older brother, who would be the heir to the title. His father and mother and his brother died after he'd come here. He'd already dropped the 'de' of his name to prove that he wasn't the least bit interested in the aristocracy. But this house was built exactly like the old château in Yves-sur-lac."

"It's such a beautiful country, I know I've always dreamed of traveling and seeing France and Italy and Germany too, Luke." She straightened, looking at him, and then blushed adorably as his eyes met hers.

"I'd like to travel too, Lucy, but mainly in this big new country. There's so much of it still unexplored, a whole continent. Grandfather spent most of his life right here when there weren't very many other whites, only the Creeks and the blacks to help him work his land. And there must be so many other Indian tribes throughout this country, where the white man hasn't come yet, and I only hope that the people who do come to settle there will have the same feeling for the

Indians that Grandfather had for the Creeks. After all, they were the very first on the land, they owned it, and now here in this part of the country it's been taken away from them and they've been driven out to wander, to starve and to die."

The girl stood listening to him, her face rapt with interest, then nodded eagerly: "I only wish Papa felt the same way you and your grandfather do, Luke. Of course, back in Georgia he worried a lot about the Indians too, and he didn't like them. And he thinks that the blacks ought to be glad they have white masters to direct them and make them work and take care of them, because otherwise they couldn't shift for themselves."

"My grandfather's slaves were bought in Mobile, and the first two he had were given to him by the Creeks when he married the old chief's daughter. But he freed them right away. In fact, even today those who work on his land are free, but of course the laws still won't allow them to own property or to marry under their own names and to live the way we do. It's a terrible shame, and I only wish I could do something about it. But as long as I'm overseer now, I don't feel that they're inferior to me; I feel they're valuable workers who are helping make Windhaven prosperous and strong, and I think they have a right to the fruits of their labors just as much as we do."

"Oh, Luke, I—I'm so glad you feel that way! Back where we are, Papa has an overseer, Amos Greer, and he hates the blacks—he always calls them niggers, and he's so free with the whip it makes me want to cry sometimes."

"Grandfather never lifted a whip to any black, and I shan't either, you can depend on that, Lucy. I think I can get more out of my workers by praising them and by giving them rewards when they do an especially good job than I ever could by being brutal to them."

"It—it's like a breath of fresh air, being here and meeting you, Luke, and meeting your wonderful grandfather too. I'm so very glad I was able to come tonight with Papa."

"I—I'm glad you came too, Lucy." As he turned away from the atlas, his hand brushed hers, and she gasped, and they looked at each other for a long moment, her face coloring as she again met his gaze. Then, as if embarrassed by this show of emotion, Luke quickly turned back to the atlas and began to turn the pages: "Here's Italy, Lucy. There's some beautiful country there along the Mediterranean. And you know, they're building steamboats now, and they can cross the ocean in only a few weeks when it used to take months on a sailing ship. Maybe one day, before you know it, you'll be able to see all those places."

"I—I surely hope so, Luke. And I hope, too, that when I do, it'll be with someone whom I care for very much and with whom I can share all the lovely things we'll see together."

She had spoken impulsively, and then in the silence that followed, was suddenly aware of how much of her inner self she had revealed, and turned away, her exquisite, gentle face suffused with blushes.

In her role as gracious hostess, Sybella smilingly agreed to Benjamin Harnesty's request to be his partner in the next dance. Frank Ellerby had gone over to sit next to James Cavendish, after the latter had finished dancing with Sybella and thanked her, and the two men were soon engaged in earnest conversation.

Noticing this, Henry Bouchard approached the settee on which Wilma Ellerby was seated, and bowed to her. "Perhaps you'd favor me with this dance, Mrs. Ellerby?" he hazarded.

"It's mighty kind of you, Mr. Bouchard. But this room is getting a bit stuffy, don't you think? I'd so much rather take a little walk and ask you some questions about this wonderful house—that is, if you don't think I'm being too forward, sir."

Their eyes met, and Wilma Ellerby gazed searchingly into his sun-bronzed face. He sent a quick glance toward Sybella, and saw that she was gaily chatting with Benjamin Harnesty, and then softly replied, "It would be my pleasure, Mrs. Ellerby. And you needn't apologize at all. The fact is, I rather prefer forward women to the dull, tame variety."

Her large, cat-green eyes widened at this riposte, and her small, overripe mouth curved in a sudden amused smile as she rose to accept his arm. "And I, sir," she murmured under her breath for only him to hear, "feel the same way about dull, predictable men."

Though it was mid-January, the night air was not unbearably cool, and there was a full moon in the cloudless sky. Henry Bouchard led Wilma Ellerby toward the white-trellised little gazebo which fronted the attractive garden of phlox, roses, geraniums, daisies, marigolds and hibiscus. Honeysuckle vines, twining themselves like ivy around the latticework of the gazebo, ornamented it with their delicate tubular red, yellow and white flowers. The young matron seated herself on the low bench and exhaled a sigh of pleasure: "Oh, I declare, this is absolutely delightful, Mr. Bouchard!"

"You aren't too chilly without a shawl or cloak, Mrs. Ellerby?" he inquired as he seated himself close to her, his left arm stealthily moving round her supple waist, his eyes fixing on the enticing cleft of her firm full bosom.

"Oh no, gracious me, no. Besides, I've this fichu—and it really isn't too cool. What a beautiful night, Mr. Bouchard!"

"But your house and its view of the river are just as enviable, my dear Mrs. Ellerby."

"Oh, won't you call me Wilma? I feel I've known you ever so long, I really do." She turned to him with a confiding little smile, glancing down to notice the positioning of his arm, and with a soft little laugh, pressed closer to him, her lips invitingly moist and slightly parted.

"I'd never want to come between a happily married wife and her husband, my dear Wilma," Henry Bouchard made a token show of observing the proprieties.

"Then, sir, you're not as perceptive as I'd have

46

thought. I shouldn't say that Frank and I are happily married."

"Oh? I feel somewhat awkwardly out of place, my dear Wilma, if I've forced you to mention something you'd rather not have me know," he ventured, still studying her upturned face, while his arm tightened slightly round her waist.

"It's really no secret. It certainly isn't so far as Frank is concerned, I'll have you know. But I thought when we talked at supper that you understood."

"That you aren't happy with him?" he drew her out, and the quickening rise and fall of her breasts began to make him quiver with anticipation. The zestful danger of a flirtation with the young matron in the face of Sybella's awareness of Wilma's far-from-modest attire had quickened all his predatory instincts, like those of a hunter who senses that the chase is soon to begin and that the quarry is not unwilling. "Well," he said generously, "perhaps it's because you miss Charleston. I'll admit there's more social life there and doubtless more convivial people than you will find in this little part of Alabama."

"It's not that," Wilma Ellerby looked away, twisting her fingers in her lap and frowning. "I was born in Boston, you know. My mother had died and my father's business as a dry-goods merchant was going very badly. Mother had really been the guiding light in the venture anyway, and my father's heart wasn't in it after her death. And then Frank came along and I knew he was a gentleman and very wealthy, and I was concerned about poor Father's money problems, so I said yes to Frank. Oh, at first I didn't miss Boston so much when Frank brought me to Charleston. But you see, well, I thought Frank would take over his father's auctioneering business. Instead, all of a sudden, he insisted on becoming a farmer and buying land and raising cotton, which is something I never dreamed of his doing."

"I see."

"No you don't, Henry, not at all," she turned to him again, her eyes filming with sudden tears of self-pity. "I don't know what got into him to make him break with his father, who was terribly disappointed when Frank told him of his decision. But it changed Frank overnight, and he's become so cold and distant, wrapped up in working the land and seeing that his slaves produce the finest cotton, that's all he ever talks about. And not once has he offered to take me back to Charleston for a ball or anything like that. That's why I was so thrilled when you and your wife invited us here for your housewarming, Henry."

"Well, you have to give Frank a little time." Again he was being opportunistically generous. "You can't really expect much of a yield on your land for the first couple of years, and I suppose Frank's concerned. He has made quite an investment, and I've ginned his cotton for him and I'm hoping to get a fair price when I take it to Mobile in the next few weeks."

"Not only that, he's spent so much money on slaves and seed and things for the house, now he begrudges me even this pretty gown. Even though he's only thirty, he's beginning to act like an old man already, and I'm still young and I haven't had much fun, I can tell you," she pouted.

His arm had tightened possessively round her waist now, and his right hand came up to tilt her chin as he brushed her lips with his, then her eyelids. "Don't cry, Wilma," he huskily murmured, "things will be all right, you'll see."

"No they won't. I declare, I'm so upset. Certainly you must have seen how Frank has been ignoring me practically all evening. Why, he's not even jealous. I don't think he cares about me any more. And—and—I think he does it to punish me, just because I feel I'm still attractive—"

"You certainly are, Wilma. You're very beautiful in that gown," Henry Bouchard interrrupted. Then, both his hands stealthily moving to the sides of her swelling breasts, he kissed her boldly on the mouth. With a little moan of pleased surprise, Wilma Ellerby hugged him to her, returning his kiss with ardor till at last she broke away, her face flushed. "Oh my, what must you think of me! We shouldn't, Henry. I wouldn't want to get Sybella angry—she's such a lovely person, so thoughtful. It's only that I feel so lonely and abandoned, Henry."

"Now you mustn't feel that way at all, Wilma dear," he consoled her, his fingers still pressing against the sides of her heaving bosom. "I'm sure that once Frank gets the planting work over and done with, he'll have more time for you."

"No, I don't think so. Leastways, we've been married four years, and he really doesn't seem to care for me too much—that way. You—you know what I mean, Henry dear? Of course, he was the first man I ever had, you see, but he's become so distant, and he doesn't seem to like it when I show him the least affection. I can't think why."

"I can't either, because if you were my wife and liked to have me with you, I'd certainly make love to you, Wilma," he muttered as he took her lips again. Shivering, Wilma Ellerby closed her eyes and hugged him tightly as she parted her lips and savored the titillating excitement of another man's kiss.

The blood was pounding in his temples when at last he released her, aware of the dangers. They could so easily be discovered in this compromising situation, and besides, hasty lovemaking outdoors wasn't what he really wanted from the young matron. Gently, he reassured her: "I think we'd best go back now, Wilma, before we're missed. But there'll be other times for us to meet, when it won't be quite so risky."

"Oh I do hope so! Dear Henry—you're so understanding and sympathetic!" she sighed as she began to pat her curls back into place and smooth her rumpled gown. As she rose, she turned to look out at the distant quadrangle where the slave cabins were. "How beautiful it is out here, how quiet and lovely with all those beautiful flowers!"

"Sybella planned the garden, and Thomas looks after it. Yes, it is attractive, isn't it?"

She put a hand on his arm and murmured, "That's where the slaves live, out in those little cabins out there near the fields, isn't it, Henry?"

"Yes, it is."

Her eyes lowered, she murmured, "I oughtn't to tell you this, but I'm worried that maybe Frank—well, you know there are lots of nice-looking nigger girls—well, maybe he's visiting one of them back at our place and that's why he doesn't seem to have time for me."

"Well, of course, I don't know about that, Wilma, but I can tell you that a plantation owner sometimes has a little diversion with a slave girl. But that doesn't mean he doesn't love his wife. I—er—I myself haven't done that, you understand. But I know about other slave owners in these parts, and it's not what you would really call an affair. After all, a slave is just a piece of property, and there isn't any emotion and certainly no love in the matter. You mustn't distress yourself with such thoughts. Come along, I'll get you another glass of punch."

Mark Bouchard had led Maybelle through the back of the house, circled the separate kitchen where Mammy Clorinda still presided, then circled the garden and approached the slave quarters. The largest cabin of all was just beyond the garden, designated for the overseer, who had been Thomas until Henry Bouchard had elevated his elder son to that post. It still belonged to Thomas, since Luke would remain in the château and defer his studies for the time being at the academy. To the left of this cabin was a large shed in which tools, sacks of fertilizer and grain, harnesses and straps and garden tools were kept, and it was to this shed that Mark led the flirtatious teenaged girl.

He paused in the door of the shed to gesture toward the rows of smaller cabins which formed a compact quadrangle, with a kind of wide court where the slaves gathered for their barbecues and singing, or, on Sundays to take the sun, to gossip and sing songs. "See over there, Maybelle? We've got about thirty-two cabins for the slaves. Over on my father's land, he's got almost as many. We've got house niggers, but we've got lots of prime field hands too for the cotton."

"My daddy says he's got the best overseer in Alabama," Maybelle boasted, glancing nervously around into the darkness which was lighted only by the flickering lanterns in the cabins beyond and the bright rays of the full moon overhead. "Are you still mad at me, Mark?"

"Not now, no, honey. Come on inside. We don't want these niggers to see us. Don't want anybody snooping around when a fellow gets acquainted with his girl."

"Who said I was your girl, Mr. Bouchard?" Maybelle conquettishly bridled, but she gave only token resistance when he drew her into the darkened shed.

"I say so. You know you were looking at me all through supper and in the drawing room too. And then you tried to get me jealous with that stupid fat Mr. Harnesty, didn't you?"

"Land sakes, I did no such thing," Maybelle demurred, petulantly stamping her foot and dragging her wrist free. "I think I'd better go back right now."

"No you don't, Maybelle!" oung and virile, he moved to stand in front of the door, confronting her, his face flushed in anticipation. "What you need is a real man to teach you not to play tricks on a fellow. I'm speaking up for you right now, and you'd be right smart to pay heed. One of these days, when Grandfather's gone, I'll own at least half of this plantation. I'll be a real catch for any girl then."

"Well, I like that! You certainly do fancy yourself, don't you, Mr. Bouchard?" Suddenly she found herself leaning against the shed wall, her arms pinned to her sides.

"You should be real nice and beg my pardon for making me so jealous, hear?" said Mark.

"Please—I didn't mean any harm—my gracious, can't you take a joke?" Maybelle was beginning to wonder why she was alone in a dark shed with Mark Bouchard. "After all, it's only the first time I've visited you, you know htat. How do you expect a girl to make up her mind the first time?"

"Because I'm telling you to, that's why, Maybelle! You certainly wouldn't take up with that Harnesty fel-

51

low; he's old enough to be your father and then some. Tell me now, are you sweet on any other fellow? If you are, you'd best forget about him. I'm the one you're dealing with now, Maybelle girl." And his lips drew close to hers.

"Please—let me go—I'll be your girl—but you're not very nice to force me this way—please, Mr. Bouchard—"

"Call me Mark."

"Mark—I—I'll kiss you all right, only please be nice!" the flustered girl begged, more and more alarmed at finding that she had completely lost control of her flirtatious little maneuver to arouse Mark's interest.

"All right. Put your arms around my neck and kiss me right on the mouth and do it nice, because you're my girl now."

With a little shiver of pleasure, Maybelle circled his neck with her slim arms and tendered her mouth, her eyes closed, her young bosom rising and falling. His hands lowered to her enticingly rounded, resilient hips, squeezing them possessively through her two petticoats and muslin drawers, as he crushed his mouth on hers.

"You'd—you'd better let me go back now, please, Mark," she pleaded, suddenly ashamed of her hot response to his lovemaking. "I'm scared—Daddy'll skin me alive if he finds out about this."

"No he won't, Maybelle. He'll be glad that Henry Bouchard's son is taking an interest in his younger daughter, you can bet on that. He's beholden to my dad, don't you ever forget it. Why, if we were to go and tell him now, he'd be right happy to hear how things are working out for us."

"But I'm a good girl—please Mark—it's not right to t—touch me like—that—"

"You know you like it, Maybelle. Come on, over here, let's get ourselves nice and comfy," he urged as, again seizing her by the wrists, he led her, half-reluctantly, toward a nearby bench and pulled her down atop his lap. His left arm gripped her waist like a vise.

"No, Mark! I want to go back, do you hears? Please,"

She struggled frantically, but Mark's hand had already found her intimate bare flesh. She cried out.

The door swung open and Thomas stood framed in the opening. "Something wrong here?" he asked.

"Who the hell's that?" Mark Bouchard angrily swore as he straightened, leaving an embarrassed Maybelle to plunge her tearful face into her hands.

"It's Thomas—is that you, Mr. Bouchard?"

"You're damned right. What the hell business is it of yours what I'm doing in here? You're not even the overseer here any more, so get back to your cabin and let us be!"

"I can't rightly do that, Mr. Mark, sir," Thomas's voice was low and apologetic. "Miss Sybella told me to keep my eyes peeled and make sure everything was all right during the party. I don't think she'd like to know that you'd taken one of the young ladies out here in the dark, sir."

"Why, you—, I'll have my father trice you up and whip the hell out of you, see if I don't!" Mark sprang to his feet, his fists clenched, his eyes glittering with fury. Maybelle profited by this diversion to hurry out of the shed back to the château. "There, goddamn you, see what you've done? I'll tell my father about this, you can depend on it. Now get the hell back to your cabin where you belong, nigger!"

"I meant no harm, Mr. Mark, you know that. Only, seems like to me the young lady's a guest and her pappy wouldn't much like to know what was going on."

"So you've set yourself up to spy on your betters, have you? I don't care whether my mother told you to snoop around or not, you had no damned business breaking in on Maybelle and me. All right, I'm going back into the house. I don't want to see your ugly black face around again, you hear?" Rudely shoving by the patient Ashanti, he strode back to the château.

Thomas sighed and shook his head. "That boy is sure growing up too fast for his own good," he lamented half-aloud. "And I'd feel lots happier if he would take more after the old gentleman than his father, 'deed I would."

CHAPTER FIVE

Henry Bouchard did not go back to the drawing room at once, but directed himself toward the kitchen where Mammy Clorinda and her two young scullery maids, both Kru girls in their late teens, were tidying up after the elaborate supper which had been served to the guests at the housewarming. As he entered, the stout black woman, in her red calico with white apron and a red bandanna tied around her head, hastily arose from the table where she had been directing the work of her two girls and enjoying a sip of Madeira from a nearly emptied decanter which Matthew had brought back to the kitchen. "Law's sake, Mistuh Bouchard sir, Ah sho didn't 'spect you so late—Ah hopes ebbrythin' was all right tonight?"

"It was one of your best suppers, Mammy Clorinda," he chuckled, eying the empty cut-glass goblet from which she had been drinking. "So much so that I'm going to overlook your indulgence in my best Madeira. In fact, you deserve it, and with my compliments."

"Thankee, suh, thankee!" From the sigh which the cook exhaled, it was obvious that she had feared punishment for daring to partake of her master's wine. "Now, is dere anythin' Ah kin do for you, suh?" Besides givin' you a nice, swift kick where you needs it, she thought.

"There is indeed. I promised three gentlemen some fine bed wenches, Mammy. There's that Mr. Harnesty

55

and Mr. Cavendish, and old Mr. Williamson. He's a widower, you know, the one with the two daughters."

"Yassuh, Ah knows who you means, mastuh, she said, hiding a frown."

"Well, then, the two bachelors are sharing the first room in the right-hand wing of the second floor, just off the stairway, and Mr. Williamson has the room right across the hall from theirs. Two of the wenches will go to the room on the left, and the third girl will go into the room at the right, understand me?"

"Yassuh." She bobbed her head in a parody of enthusiasm, her earrings dancing in the broadly pierced lobes.

"What about these two girls here? Think they can service a guest?" His eyes scanned the two suddenly trembling young Kru girls who were scraping the pots and pans, and one of them dropped the scraping spoon with a noisy clatter, her eyes wide and shadowed with apprehension.

"Dey ain't nebbah been busted before, mastuh. Ah don't rightly know effen dey'd know how to please a nice white mastuh. But I 'spects Matthew, he could pick dem out hisself, he know de gals out in the cabins purty well by now, suh."

"That's fine. You have him pick out three of the best-looking nigger girls, tell him to rub them down good so they won't have any musky smell to them, put on white shifts and slippers, and go on up and take care of my guests. Have him tell them they're not to leave until the men fall asleep, and they're to mind their manners or I'll take a whip to them myself."

"Yassuh, right away, I'll go get Matthew. He's most likely clearing up the dining room right now, suh."

Henry approached the two young girls, frowning. "Turn around, put your arms down at your sides and stand up straight," he ordered.

The girl who had dropped the spoon, tall, slim, began suddenly to whimper.

"Shet yoah mouf, Nancy gal, Ah's shamed of you," Mammy Clorinda sharply reprimanded her, trying to protect the girl from the white man's anger.

Biting her lips, the frightened girl managed to control any further outcry as Henry Bouchard, pursing his lips with the air of a connoisseur viewing a work of art, walked round her and contemplated her slim body from every angle. Then he peremptorily demanded, "So you've never had a man yet, girl?"

"Nossuh, mastuh," Nancy faltered.

"High time you were getting used to it. Mammy, why don't you marry this one off to one of the best field hands? I'd like to have a few more babies on the plantation; they'll be worth money one of these days if what my father says is true. Now let's have a look at the other one—look up at me, girl!"—this last bitingly, to a darker-skinned, comely girl of medium height with splendidly ripe haunches and bosom, who had been staring down at the floor and twisting her fingers distractedly.

"Dat dere's Lucille, mastuh," Mammy Clorinda volunteered. "Ah knows mahself she's mighty sweet on Sammy, who works out in de fields, suh."

"She's almost too good for him, this one." Henry Bouchard appraisingly reached out his hand and patted Lucille's hip, then brushed his palm against one swelling, round full breast, at which the girl started with a stifled gasp of shame. "Look sharp now, don't give me a look like that or I'll put a whip to your bottom, you black bitch!" he growled. "Tell you what, Mammy, just have Matthew take two girls from the cabins; let Lucille service old Mr. Williamson. Mind you now, he's in the room directly to the right. Don't make any mistake about it. He's the most important guest I've got and that's why I'm going to give him a special treat."

"Oh, mastuh, please, please doan make me do dat!" Lucille suddenly knelt down, flung her arms around Henry Bouchard's legs and gazed up at him tearfully, her lips trembling pathetically. "Please, mastuh! You kin whup me, but please don't make me do it, Ah nebbah had no hankerin', honest Ah didn't, mastuh!"

"Stop your sniveling, you stupid little bitch! You should be honored. Mr. Williamson's a fine gentleman, and he's got two beautiful daughters and a nice plantation, and he's a good friend of mine. Now you stop that blubbering and go with Matthew and get yourself fixed up so you won't pester Mr. Williamson with that nigger smell of yours, hear? And at breakfast tomorrow morning, if he tells me that you didn't please him, I'll have you triced up in the shed and I'll whip that big bottom of yours bloody, you understand me?"

"You better do wut he says, chile," Mammy Clorinda commiserated. "Look, chile, just like de mastuh said, it's a real honoh foh you to please a fine gennelmun lak dat Mr. Williamson. It sho nuff is. 'Sides which, once he's busted you, den you kin marry up with Sammy and he'll pleasure you real good, you'll see, gal. Now git up off the floor and you go find Matthew and tell him wut de mastuh said, you heah me? If you doan, Ah's gwine whup you mahself after Mistah Bouchard done finished with your black hide. G'wan now, git!"

Dolefully, tears running down her cheeks, the pretty Kru scullery maid got to her feet and, with a last despairing glance at the scowling face of Henry Bouchard, hurried out of the kitchen to find the majordomo.

"Ah's sorry Lucille was so uppity, mastuh suh," the fat cook apologized. "Now 'pears lak to me if you is gwine hab bed wenches foah youah guests from now on, suh, Ah'd bettah hab a little talk wid Matthew and hab him pick de purtiest gals to please dem."

"That's an excellent idea, Mammy. See to it." There was a sudden rumble of thunder in the distance, and Henry Bouchard frowned again. "Looks as if we're going to have a storm. Well, it's a good thing I asked the guests to stay overnight. That reminds me, Mammy, be sure you make plenty of your fine hot biscuits for breakfast tomorrow, with lots of honey. And there's still plenty of that sweet ham, isn't there?"

"Dere sho nuff is, mastuh. You doan hab to worry none about mah kitchen, Ah promises, mastuh."

"No, I think I've found out by now that buying you down in New Orleans was a piece of luck for us, Mammy. I never had such good vittles till you came to cook for us."

"Thank you, suh." Her broad face beamed with pleasure as she bobbed her head again.

With a last glance at the still-frightened Nancy, Henry Bouchard turned and strode out of the kitchen. As soon as he was gone, Mammy's smile vanished. She walked over to Nancy and took her into her arms. "Ah knows how you feel, baby," she said softly, "Ah knows. But there ain't nothin' we can do. Maybe someday things'll be different . . ." Her eyes went cold. "Ah just hope Ah'm around when de bleedin' starts . . ."

Out of an impulse, Henry paused at the door of the study before returning to the drawing room, noted that the door was partly open, and entered. Old Lucien sat in a high-backed chair beside the window, gazing out toward the river at the tall red bluff where his beautiful young Creek wife and their infant son had been buried so long ago. His gnarled hands grasped the scrolled arms of the chair as he stared out into the darkness.

"Father, I thought you'd gone to bed, but knowing your habits, I thought I'd just take a chance and see if you were still up."

"Come in, Henry. That dance took the wind out of my sails, I don't mind telling you. So before I went to bed, I thought I'd just sit here quietly and look out over the river."

"I understand, Father. Were you pleased with the party?"

"Oh yes!" The old man turned to smile at his son who now stood beside him and put his hand on Lucien's shoulder. "It brought back memories when I was just a boy and my father and mother used to have gala parties in the old château back in Yves-sur-lac. And the costumes—you wouldn't believe how women's fashions have changed in all that time, Henry."

"For my part, they wear far too much," Henry Bouchard chuckled. "But it appears that Luke has at last found someone to be interested in, that Lucy Williamson."

"He couldn't have made a better choice, in my opinion. She's a sweet, gentle girl. In some ways, she reminds me of my poor Priscilla—your own mother, Henry."

"I know, Father. You've told me how good and sweet she was."

Lucien Bouchard turned to look up at his son, his weather-beaten old face quizzical, lighted only by the filtering rays of moonlight through the windowpane. "These last few years, Henry, I've had plenty of time to think over the past. One can never predict what the future will bring, though one can at best plan for it. Now you, my son, have some of the traits of my brother Jean, selfish, ambitious, even despotic at times. And yet your mother was a warm-hearted, demure young woman. Luke, who in so many ways reminds me of my own idealistic self, is your son by that unfortunate girl Dora. Yet if you were to judge breeding the way one does in horses, one would never have suspected that her stock would have produced such an honorable, quiet and sober young man, much more mature than his years."

"You're not very flattering to me, Father, but then you really never have been," Henry's voice had an edge to it.

"Don't misunderstand me, Henry. I never pretended to be a saint, and I certainly never expected you to be one. It's only that perhaps I was brought up by a different code, one that I tried to make you understand when you were a boy, but which you never seemed to favor. I willingly admit that our circumstances are different. I had the advantages of being brought up in a gracious home with a sympathetic mother and an honorable father who cultivated the arts and tried to be just and fair with the peasants who tilled their land. You were born on this Alabama frontier, where there were few white neighbors, where you could hardly be expected to have the advantages of music and books and the gentle things of life."

"That's just exactly it, Father. The world has changed for all of us. Remember, almost a third of all the inhabitants of this state of Alabama are black slaves. And don't forget how that crazy Nat Turner showed that slaves will turn against their masters, no matter how kind they are. They're property, Father, and while in your day it was all right to free them and

60

to work with them, because there weren't any other whites around, and only the Indians for your neighbors, that doesn't hold true today."

"You want me to start preaching again, don't you, Henry? Well, you know my feelings. Men, no matter what creed or color, should be treated like men, not beasts of the field."

"That's all very fine-sounding, Father. But don't forget that men are not much different from beasts of the field except perhaps for opportunities and education and the skill to profit from all of it. Men enjoy women, and it's much easier if the women are nigger slaves because they're property and their feelings don't matter. And best of all, a man doesn't get involved bedding a nigger girl down as he does one of his own kind. Well, I'll leave you here with your memories, Father. I've got to see about my guests' bed wenches."

"Your guests' bed wenches?" Lucien Bouchard incredulously echoed.

"Of course. Matthew will bring up a girl apiece for Mr. Harnesty and Mr. Cavendish, and one for old Mr. Williamson—after all, he's a widower and I'm sure he'll appreciate it."

"My God, Henry, do you realize what you're doing? You'd make Windhaven no better than a whorehouse!" His voice was choked with anger and dismay and his fingers dug into the arms of his chair as he stared at the cynical face of his son.

"Don't get upset, Father, you might have a stroke. As it happens, one of the girls, Lucille, is one that I myself bought in Mobile, and the two others that Matthew will pick will probably be daughters of field hands I bought also, so they're not yours. As you will recall, Father, because you've considerably more acreage than I have, I sent over a good many of my field hands to stay right here on Windhaven."

"Now you're talking like that lawyer of a father-in-law of yours, my son! It's damnable, do you understand? Slaves or not, they have feelings and emotions. How do you think a virginal girl must feel to know that, because her parents were born into slavery, she must, under the penalty of the whip or worse, give her

61

body to any man designated to her and, more than that, seek diligently to pleasure him? I wouldn't expect that even of a young novice in a New Orleans brothel."

"Father, you're making a mountain out of a molehill. And they are my slaves, as I told you. So I've a perfect right to do what I wish with them. Besides, I've a purpose."

"Oh, of course, and I know what your purpose is. You're greedy to acquire the land which old Williamson and those two other men are holding, and you're trying to soften them up so they won't suspect your conniving. Leave me here to my memories, Henry. I only pray to God it were in my power to free every black man and woman and child on Windhaven and on your land as well. Mark my words, one day all those states which have enacted laws preventing the liberation of slaves will regret the tyranny they have imposed upon people brought here against their will and forced into a bondage which is so piously justified by the politicians as by the preachers. Leave me now!"

Henry stared hard at his father, then shrugged and left the study. When he reached the drawing room, he found it nearly empty except for Sybella, who was chatting with Helen Jordan as her husband prepared to usher Bobby and Ashton up to the room which had been prepared for them. There was no sign of Maybelle Williamson, nor of Lucy and her father, and the Ellerbys had already gone to their guest chamber, while the two bachelors were eagerly awaiting the arrival of the promised bed wenches.

Sybella turned to see her husband standing nearby, nodded coolly at him, and concluded her remarks to Helen Jordan: "I'll see you at breakfast, Helen. I've so enjoyed having you and your family here. And I do hope you'll stay through Sunday—it's so nice to have friendly neighbors one can discuss things with."

"You're very kind, Mrs. Bouchard. I'll see you tomorrow, then. Now you really must excuse me, I have to look in on the boys and see that they're all right." She gave a soft, pleased little laugh. "I'm sure that Bobby won't be able to get to sleep, not only being in a strange bed but with all the excitement of dancing with your lovely Arabella!"

With a cordial nod, she turned and left the room, and Henry Bouchard moved toward his wife and took her hands in his. "A wonderful party, Syb darling, wasn't it?"

"You seemed to find it so, Mr. Bouchard," she archly countered, giving him a studied look. "Did you enjoy your little rendezvous with Wilma Ellerby?"

He flushed angrily and scowled. "She wanted to see the house, that's all."

"She wanted to see you, you mean," Sybella corrected. "I'll admit she's a very attractive woman, but if I were you, Henry, I shouldn't make a fool of myself over her. Helen Jordan thinks there's trouble between Frank and Wilma Ellerby and I shouldn't care to have you involved in it, apart from the obvious reason."

"She's not adjusting to plantation life, that's all. A high-spirited young woman who was born in Boston and married a man she expected to stay in Charleston where at least there's some social life—naturally she'd be unhappy."

"You know, Henry, my father says that when a man tries to be devious, he's at his most transparent."

"And what is that supposed to mean?" he said, glowering.

"Only that you needn't try to invent excuses for flirting with her, that's all, dear. Perhaps I should have worn just as low-cut a gown as she did; you might have paid more attention to me tonight. Yes, I know very well you've got designs on Frank Ellerby's land, but don't try to tell me that you expect to get it by having an affair with his wife."

"Now see here, Sybella," he exploded, "that's unworthy of you!"

"Yes, perhaps it was just a bit catty, dear." She smiled knowingly. "But you see, I know you better than you think I do. I don't mind your noticing that other women can be attractive—you wouldn't be very much of a man if you didn't, Henry. But I'd never want to find out that you sneaked behind my back to make love to a neighbor's wife or, for that matter,

63

amused yourself with one of the servants as you tried to do with Celia."

"Damn it, woman, won't you ever forget that? I think I've paid enough for the attempt anyway."

"Yes, I rather think you did at that, Henry. Now come along to bed." She tucked her arm in his and gave him a provocative little smile. "If it helps any, you can pretend I'm Wilma Ellerby tonight when you make love to me. Maybe that will get her out of your system."

"Good God, Syb, you're incredible!"

"I'd hoped you'd still remember that, darling. I told you on our wedding night that I had a most unmaidenly interest in lovemaking, and I still do. Or are you forgetting so soon that evening when we planned the housewarming? Now don't look so angry. Come along and help me undress, and see if I'm not still just as nice in bed as ever that Wilma Ellerby would be."

"I plan to do just that, you vixen!" Henry Bouchard drew her close to him, darting his tongue tip against her dainty ear, his hands groping for her round full breasts.

"Not till we're in the bedroom, Mr. Bouchard, if you please," Sybella primly demurred. "The difference between Wilma Ellerby and myself, I rather like to think, is that she flaunts so much of her person out in public but is probably only an *allumeuse,* a tease. Whereas, my dearest husband, once we're alone together, I'll deny you nothing. Now take my hand nicely, as a devoted husband should, and lead me to our privacy."

Once inside his bedroom, Henry Bouchard impatiently pulled her to him, and Sybella, with a happy little laugh, arched to him, locking her arms round his neck, letting him feel the ardent pressure of her delectably contoured body through the high-necked, long-skirted brown silk frock, her chemise and two petticoats. His hands roamed down her body as she demurely loosened his cravat and waistcoat, all the while enthusiastically returning his fiercely demanding kiss.

"Mmm, that was nice, husband," she huskily murmured when he at last ended the kiss and released her, his face flushed and eyes sparkling. "I'd feel very feminine and very much wanted if you'd be sweet enough to be my lady's maid tonight."

"Yes, yes, Sybella!" he hoarsely agreed as with fumbling fingers he loosened the frock and drew it up over her head and let it tumble to the floor.

"Oh, no, if a maid did that, she'd be dismissed on the spot, Mr. Bouchard! Pray pick it up, drape it neatly over the back of that chair," she tauntingly instructed. He compressed his lips, glared at her, then, with a sigh, stooped to retrieve it and draped it carefully over the chair near the door.

"Very much better. Haste makes waste, you know, Henry," she twitted him.

"You'll pay for that, you heartless vixen," he muttered as he divested her of her chemise, then swore under his breath as the knots of the drawstrings of her petticoats refused to yield. "There!" he said at last as he watched her daintily step out of them, retrieved them and laid them on the chair seat, his eyes glowing to see her naked in drawers and hose and elegant new shoes.

"Those too, unless you want me to keep my stockings on, the way you did the last time, Henry." The corners of her moist lips twitched as she suppressed the teasing smile.

"This time, I want you all naked, all mine," he said, moving behind her, his hands straying round to cup and knead her satiny warm breasts. Sybella gasped with delight, closed her eyes, tilted back her head. "Oh, that's very much better than any lady's maid, darling!" she whispered.

"I mean to try to give you full satisfaction," he said, kissing her nape, then her dimpled bare shoulders. His hands descended to the waistband of her coquettish drawers, and husked her of that final veil; then he knelt down to remove first her shoes, then carefully drew off each silken stocking. Naked now, Sybella raised her sculptured arms above her head, bending one knee, just as a female slave might present herself on the auction block, but she did not voice the thought

65

that at once leaped into her mind, *He must have seen Celia this way when he bought her. I'm going to make him see just me and no one else, not ever again, if I can.*

"Do I please my lord and master?" she asked in a cajolingly soft murmur which he could scarcely hear.

"Damn you, you know the answer to that, Sybella!" he replied as he hastily undressed. Then, stepping to her, he took her by the shoulders and turned her to face him. "Don't you?" he repeated as his mouth came down on hers and his hands gripped the base of her curvacious buttocks.

Sybella moaned softly as her left arm crooked round his shoulder, her right hand stroking his flank, then moving between their shuddering bodies till his convulsive gasp betokened the agonizing excitement of her bold caress.

"Yes, Sybella, yes," he feverishly muttered as he lifted her by the buttocks and bore her, her pliant arms clinging tightly round his waist, to the bed. And as she nimbly arched herself to receive the brunt of his cohesion, Sybella knew that for now, at least, she had banished the wraith of Wilma Ellerby from their embrace.

Wilma Ellerby had taken off her red marcelline frock and lace fichu, and stood before the mirrored dressing table in only her white silk stockings which rose just to her lower thighs and were gartered in blue satin elastic, and reached back to unknot her thick bun of shimmering light-brown hair till it tumbled below her shoulders. In the mirror she could see her husband lying in bed in only his underdrawers, his head pillowed on his hands, staring morosely up at the ceiling.

"Well, Frank, go ahead and say what's on your mind," she challenged, as she turned to face him, her slim hands stroking her alluringly svelte hips.

"What's there to say, Wilma? If you mean your leaving the drawing room with Henry Bouchard, I was well aware of it."

"Oh, I'm sure you were," she strode toward the four-poster bed, hands on her hips, her green eyes insolent and narrowed. "Don't lie there feeling so sorry for yourself, Frank Ellerby! If you must know, I didn't compromise your honor. And you don't really have to be jealous of Henry Bouchard. All he did was happen to notice that I'm still a good-looking woman—which is something you've been failing to do ever since we came to Alabama. I don't understand it at all, Frank. Don't I please you anymore? You seemed to be quite taken with me when you met me in Boston."

He turned his face away and closed his eyes, uttering a weary sigh. "Things happen to a man, Wilma," he at last replied. "We were both infatuated with each other at the time. Maybe we've discovered that each of us is lacking something to make it a perfect marriage."

"Well, sir, I can't think why!" she angrily flashed. "Haven't I always met my obligations as a wife? Back in Charleston, you were willing enough to have me share your bed. And then, out of a clear sky, you tell me that you're coming here and taking up cotton-raising, of all things! When you could have had a perfectly fine and honorable position in your father's auctioneering firm. And now all you do is stay out in the fields and hobnob with that nigger foreman George. You seem to prefer his company more than you do mine, sir, and I tell you I can't take much more of it!"

"Please keep your voice down, Wilma," he said softly, still keeping his face averted.

"Not only that, you actually dare to invite that nigger in to have supper with you. Don't you have any respect for your own wife, Frank Ellerby?" Her voice trembled with anger and self-pity. "Now that we've met all our neighbors, don't you think they'll find out how friendly you are toward that nigger? Why, even old Mr. Bouchard who's kept that freed nigger Thomas as his overseer all these years finally gave in and saw what was right and let his grandson Luke be made overseer here at Windhaven. The least you could do, it seems to me, is hire some capable white overseer from Natchez or Huntsville."

"I really don't care to discuss it, Wilma. I'm rather tired tonight. Please come to bed."

"Oh yes, I'll come to bed. For all the good it'll do me, too, you might just as well be in another room.

Well, I'll tell you one thing. If this keeps up any longer, either I'm going to leave you and go back to Boston or else—" She paused and took a deep breath. "Or else I'll find myself a man who understands that a woman has needs of her own sometimes." She turned back to the dressing table, made a movement as if to remove her stays, and then, thinking better of it, her face sullen and bright tears sparkling in her eyes, leaned over to blow out the candle on the little table beside the bed. Then, pulling back the covers, she got into bed and turned on her side away from him.

Breakfast was over, and Sybella had taken Wilma Ellerby, Helen Jordan and Lucy and Maybelle Williamson to inspect the kitchen and then the garden. Ashton and Bobby Jordan had asked to see the Windhaven stable, a low, sturdy wooden-frame building to the right of the slave cabins, where Jimmy, a lanky young Kru slave, who had been a groom for a New Orleans owner before Henry Bouchard bought him, showed the boys around the stalls and told them about the pedigree of the mares and stallions and geldings quartered in them.

Old Lucien Bouchard had breakfasted with his guests this morning, and then excused himself to go back to his room, sensing that his son and the other male guests wanted to talk business. Luke accompanied his grandfather back to his room and stayed to chat with him, but young Mark eagerly listened to the conversation of his elders as Edward Williamson turned to Henry Bouchard and, with a chuckle, declared, "I must say, Mr. Bouchard, you're a right neighborly host."

"I take it you enjoyed Lucille last night, eh, Edward?"

"Matter of fact, I did, sir, though I confess I'm a little surprised you sent me a virgin. That girl hadn't been busted at all—didn't you know that?"

"Of course I did. But nothing's too good for a neighbor with the two loveliest daughters this side of Mobile." Henry Bouchard grinned broadly. "Have some more coffee. Can I send out for more biscuits and honey for you gentlemen?"

"No, no, we're stuffed now," Benjamin Harnesty shook his head and patted his paunch.

"Well, gentlemen"—Henry Bouchard leaned back in his chair with an expansive smile—"I've a notion the price of cotton will go up a bit this year, from all I've been able to gather. You gentlemen will soon be starting your new crop, I've no doubt."

"Oh yes, my overseer's getting the field hands into shape already," Edward Williamson said.

"Well, I plan to go to Mobile soon and of course I'll ship all of your bales downriver and get the best price I can. If you've no objection, I'll act as your factor and just take what you owe me for ginning and storage off the total receipts," Henry Bouchard suggested.

"I've no objection at all. You're a smart cotton man, everyone around here knows that, Mr. Bouchard," James Cavendish said. "And by the way, Benjamin and I want to thank you for those sweet little black gals you had visit us last night. They were most satisfactory, sir."

"I'm glad to hear that. But Edward, you didn't finish telling me about Lucille. Did she give you any trouble at all because it was her first time?" Henry Bouchard leaned forward, his eyes bright with concupiscent interest.

"Well, sir, she peeled down right smart enough when I told her to, and for a time there she was sort of tearful. But I cuddled her and talked gentle to her a bit, and after I had to hurt her just a little bit, I'd no reason to complain." The widower's face creased in an embarrassed smile.

"Well, that's fine. It's not a bad idea to let these little bitches have a touch of the whip once in a while to let them know who's master, though."

That's true enough, Mr. Bouchard. At least that's my overseer's theory, and from the cotton he's been giving me every year since I started with him, I've really no reason to complain about his methods. Understand, I'm a peaceable man and I don't like to see people hurt needlessly, but there are plenty of shiftless niggers who can't work any other way except having the whip put to them to teach them their duties."

69

"That's exactly what I've always thought, Mr. Williamson."

"You know, Mr. Bouchard," Williamson went on as he took a last sip from his cup, "Amos Greer is something of a sporting man himself, and he's given me a pretty good idea. Might make some money off it quite apart from cotton this year."

"Oh? What's that?"

"Well, sir, he tells me that the last owner he worked for used to put on fights between his champion nigger and all comers, winner take all. Now mind you, I've heard about a Louisiana sugar cane planter who used to put his champion in a pit and then his neighbors would send down their best fighters, and it was a fight to the finish. I mean death, sir. Of course I wouldn't go along with anything that brutal, you understand. But Mr. Greer tells me I've got a field hand by the name of Davey who can whip his weight in wildcats. So I've been thinking that maybe there might be some other planters in these parts who'd like to see a good knock-down fight and wager a little something on the side, just for the interest of it."

"Yes, that's a capital idea!" Henry Bouchard's face was alight with excitement. "You know, after I get done at Mobile I might just go to New Orleans and see if I can't pick me up a real fighting stud. After all, when you're paying from a thousand to two thousand for a topnotch field hand, and you have to pay for his keep and wait a year or two before you really get good cotton production out of him, you might just as well earn yourself a dividend while you're at it. Yes, I might just do that. And now, gentlemen, shall we go back to the ladies?"

CHAPTER SIX

It was a week after the housewarming at Windhaven, and old Lucien Bouchard and Luke sat in the study to discuss the new planting for the coming year.

"You'll be biting off a mighty big job, boy, handling all the acres on this plantation. Still and all, you'll have Thomas to help you, and he has a real instinct for the land."

"I know that, Grandfather. So far as I'm concerned, I don't care anything about having the title of overseer. I'll look to Thomas to fill in all the things I don't know yet," Luke replied, smiling.

"As you know, I let about a third of my acres go fallow last year, so you'll want to lay off the rows with the scooter plow and drag all the grass, weeds and stalks into the furrows. Then you'll use a two-horse plow to draw two good furrows over the vegetable matter, so that the sods can be well plowed out about a fortnight before you plant."

"Yes, Grandfather."

"You'll have a much better stand that way, and the plants will be much more vigorous. You see, Luke, imperfect seeds die out as soon as they get old, and only the hardy ones can survive." The white-haired old man chuckled. "That's somewhat like men, Luke. The tough and the hardy ones survive, like me. Though I don't say that I'd guarantee much of a harvest if I were to be planted myself."

71

"I never think of you as being old, Grandfather. Certainly not your mind, anyway."

Lucien Bouchard patted his grandson's shoulder, then in a gruff voice declared, "You'd better not say that in your father's hearing. He's consigned my ideas to the limbo of antiquity. But no matter. Just remember, your second plowing ought to be done with a sweep next to the bottom, with a mold board next to the plant, to dirt the young cotton. You'll plow the balance of the row under the turning plow to keep up the bed."

"Thomas has told me that already, Grandfather."

"Good, good! Picking ought to begin as soon as a field hand can gather fifty pounds a day. You see, the oil in the cotton is soon evaporated by the sun, wind and rain, and you lose a good percentage of weight thereby. Make sure the hands pick as free from leaf as is consistent with good work. Some of the smaller planters aren't too careful about how much leaf they get into their cotton, and then they complain at Mobile when their bales are weighed and appraised."

"Yes, Grandfather."

"I'd like corn and beans and yams on about a third of the acreage that's already been worked for cotton, Luke. It wouldn't hurt, either, to put in a good orchard at the south end of the fields. That'll be good for the soil, too."

"I understand, Grandfather."

Lucien Bouchard leaned back in his chair and smilingly nodded. "You'll do just fine, Luke. In a way, it's going to be a contest between you and your father. You see, he'll supervise his own acreage, and he's chosen two good black foremen. They're his slaves, though if I owned them they wouldn't be. What I'm afraid of is that one of these days he'll want a white overseer, someone like Amos Greer who runs the Williamson holdings. I pray I never live to see such a man drive the blacks on Windhaven land, Luke. He represents all that is evil and avaricious."

"But maybe Father will be able to hire a humane kind of overseer," Luke suggested.

"The danger is that your father is himself a driving, ambitious man. So naturally when Edward Williamson told him how much production Amos Greer was getting out of his field hands, it was bound to appeal to him. And he'd never let you take over his own acres, I'm certain of that."

"I'm going to spend a good deal of time with Thomas out in the fields, till I learn everything he knows, I promise you, Grandfather."

"I know you will, Luke. Tell me, honestly, will you miss your schooling?"

"Not really, Grandfather. You've got a really wonderful library here, and I like the feeling of working on the land, of planting things and watching them grow and knowing that I'm helping to produce food and clothing for other people."

"Then you have the same feeling that I did back in Yves-sur-lac. It's a good feeling, Luke, the very best there is. Not just because you own the land, the way a miser piles up golden coins so that he can hide away in a dusty attic and clink them one against the other to see the size of his fortune. Not that at all, Grandson. But rather how those coins of harvest from thriving land can pass across the seas and bring back goods we need here to strengthen our own economy, goods that will create work for the people across the ocean just as they do for the people here. All of us working together in harmony and understanding and blessing the land which blesses us in its turn if we use it wisely—yes, that's the secret."

He was silent a moment, reflectively nursing his chin and staring out of the window toward the bend of the river. "But this issue of slavery disturbs me most of all, Luke. You know, you've heard me talk of James G. Birney, the mayor of Huntsville."

"Yes, I have, Grandfather."

"He was the man who was instrumental in getting the Alabama legislature about fifteen years ago to allow slaves to be freed by their owners, and to have that made a part of the state constitution. Of course, with the hue and cry over the Nat Turner Rebellion that

73

created such a bitter feeling, such a vengeful spirit in all the slave-holding states, such constitutional allowance is only mere theory now. But Birney has another idea. He's become an agent for the American Colonization Society. The purpose of that group, as I've heard it, is to purchase slaves or to take blacks who are already free and send them back to Liberia. There seems to be a little interest in it, because the planters and the politicians say that it will remove the troublemaking freed men from their midst and also because it won't terminate the property rights the planters already hold over their slaves. I only hope there are enough sensible men to give that notion furtherance. I myself support it. In the North and in the East, men work for wages, many of them black. I only wish we could see that in the South. A hard-working black who spends from sunup till sundown in the fields ought to be able to have his freedom as a man, as a worker, to be paid honest wages for his toil, to be able to buy his own little shelter and the clothes and the things he needs for his family, to have savings in a bank and to leave a legacy to his children that will provide for them till they in turn are old enough to earn their own livelihood."

"That's the way it really ought to be, yes, Grandfather."

"But you see, Luke, you and I are dreaming again. And I'm sure that if your father were here with us now, he'd scoff at such an idea. More than that, he'd probably be very angry with me for filling his son's head with daydreams that won't come true."

"I don't look upon them as daydreams, Grandfather. Maybe one day I can make those dreams come true for them in my own way."

"That's what I pray for, Luke." Lucien Bouchard reached out to grasp Luke's hand across the table. "I want to tell you something in all confidence, my beloved grandson. You've heard me say there's bound to be an economic setback for this part of the country in the next few years. I'm quite certain of it. The shifting of specie away from the Bank of the United States is going to cause a number of bank failures. So many of the planters are doing business on credit, in expectation of crops. Yes, maybe the cotton market will go up this year, but it can also plunge downward overnight, based on what will happen overseas. And so, I've written Antoine Rigalle, with whose banking house I've kept most of my money, to place some $75,000 in the Bank of Liverpool. This will be money for the future, if anything should happen to your father. Of course, he will inherit Windhaven under the terms of my will. You as his elder son will naturally be the prime heir, after that, and of course he has his own account and his own profits. But that money, Luke, is really meant to be a stake for your own future, perhaps one day to save Windhaven from financial disaster. Or, if in the years ahead you seek some new frontier just as I did when I was a young man, it will be there to help you make a fresh start. That, too, is part of the joy of having held this land: ever since the Creeks gave it to me, it has provided handsomely for all of us."

"But you began with almost nothing, Grandfather."

"Yes, I know. But never fear, you won't even have to think of it, since you're the sort of young man who will shape his own destiny. Unlike your father you don't place profits and money above all else. Come now, let's ask Mammy Clorinda to give us a little lunch."

It was the afternoon of the first Friday in February, on an exceptionally warm day, that Henry Bouchard decided to pay a call on Edward Williamson. In his trim linen frock coat, he rode out to the fields where Luke was conferring with Thomas on the plowing of some fifteen acres which had not yet been cultivated for cotton.

"Luke, how'd you like to ride with me over to Williamson's place?" he asked. "Maybe you could get some pointers from his man Greer. I'd like to talk business with Williamson anyway, and you could look around the place and keep your eyes open and maybe learn something useful."

"I'd like that very much, Father," Luke said, think-

75

ing that he might see Lucy again and renew their friendship.

"Well then, go tidy up and dress in your best. After all, you're my heir and I don't want Williamson to look down his nose at you. Not that he had better dare it anyhow, seeing that he owes me a good $2000 for seed and ginning and storage," Henry Bouchard maliciously added.

As Luke nodded and hurried back into the red-brick château, Henry Bouchard glowered down at Thomas, who had taken a hoe and begun to chop some of the weeds in the furrow nearest him. "Seems like you were a little impertinent to Mark last month," he said in an unpleasantly harsh tone. "The boy told me the day after the housewarming how you'd walked in on him and Miss Maybelle and forgot your place."

"Mr. Bouchard, I didn't forget my place. Your wife asked me to keep an eye on things outside, and I knew young Mr. Mark had taken Miss Maybelle into the shed. I didn't think it was exactly proper for them to be alone together, young as they both are."

"I see. So you're setting yourself up as a judge of white folks' behavior now, are you, Thomas? Yes, it seems to me you are forgetting your place. It's true that my father freed you, as he did your father before you, but you still can't own any property or have any say on this plantation, not while I'm alive, anyway. Don't you go forgetting it. He wanted me to have you whipped—well, I won't go that far, but don't let me catch you trying to act like a white man with my boy, you understand me?"

"Very well, Mr. Bouchard. I'm sorry if I offended either of you."

"That's a little better. Now go back to your work." Henry Bouchard abruptly tugged at the bridle, his mare rearing and whinnying in protest as the sharp bit pained her, and then wheeled her back toward the château.

Half an hour later, Luke and his father dismounted in front of the Williamson house as a middle-aged, nearly bald slave hurried out to take the reins of their horses and lead them to the little wooden shed which served as stable.

"The house isn't much, Luke," Henry Bouchard disparagingly commented as he gestured toward it with his riding crop, "but he managed to wangle some really fine land along the river and he got it dirt-cheap. The only smart thing about Williamson is that he had sense enough to hire Amos Greer. One of these days, I might hire him away, too. Or, better still, in case Williamson doesn't make a go of his land and pay off his debts, I might wind up owning everything. Naturally, that's in the strictest confidence."

"Of course, Father."

The Williamson house was only one story high, built of wood and brick, with a small portico over the heavy oaken door. The windows were made of wood, opening like doors inward, and in bad weather they were closed and bolted, their ugliness concealed by curtains.

"He doesn't have glass the way we have at Windhaven," Henry Bouchard boasted with a contemptuous curl of his lip. "He uses French doors, you see. And of course you don't dare open them in summer or you'd have mosquitoes and bugs swarming in. But I didn't come here to see the house. If I ever do take over the property, I'll burn it to the ground and build something really outstanding, something like Windhaven, you'll see." He ascended the two stone steps to the door, lifted the knocker and hammered at it resoundingly. "Where the devil's his footman? Well now, it's about time," as a frightened-looking elderly Negro opened the door and regarded the scowling visitor with trepidation, his eyes darting to the riding crop in Henry Bouchard's hand.

"Ah's sorry Ah didn't come sooner, mastuh suh," he falteringly apologized. "Does you wish to see Mistah Williamson, suh?"

"Yes, of course, you fool. Where is your master?"

"He—he out at de shed wid Mistah Greer, suh, he watchin' dat runaway Benjy git hisself whupped, suh. Effen you'll come in, Ah'll go tell the mastuh you is heah, suh."

"Very well. Come on in, Luke. You, nigger, are the young ladies at home?" Henry Bouchard demanded as he entered the modest living room and looked disdainfully around.

"Yassuh, dey's bof at home, suh. Miss Lucy, she come home a mite earlier from de young ladies' school down de road a ways, 'n Miss Maybelle, she jist now come home from dere, suh."

Henry Bouchard glanced back at his son, a mocking smile on his lips. "What's your name, nigger?" he then demanded.

"Obadiah, suh."

"Well then, Obadiah, suppose you go tell Miss Lucy that Luke Bouchard is here to see her. Then you can take me out to see your master. I've business with him anyway. Now be quick about it!"

"Yassuh, yassuh, right away, suh!" the elderly Negro hurried from the room.

"I'm sure, Luke, you don't want to watch a runaway slave being punished. But I want to see this overseer in action. So you may as well pay your respects to Lucy Williamson, and when you've finished lollygagging, you can come looking for me. I want to take a quick look at Williamson's cotton fields anyway."

"As you say, Father," Luke said patiently.

Obadiah hastily returned, bobbing his head and forcing a smile of greeting to his quivering lips. "Miss Lucy, she say she be in directly, suh. Now Ah takes you to de mastuh, suh," he announced.

Henry Bouchard slapped his riding crop against his thigh. "Good. Now don't forget what I told you, Luke. Be sure to pay the young lady my respects, of course." Then, with an ironic chuckle, he followed the footman out of the house and along the left side out to a large, sturdy wooden shed. It stood in a clearing beyond which, some fifty feet distant, were two rows of a dozen cabins facing one another. To the left of the shed was a still larger cabin, evidently that of the overseer. It was nearly dusk, and Henry Bouchard could see, huddling before the cabins, several elderly and very young black women, as well as little children clinging to their hands. Beyond the cabins lay the already well-furrowed cotton fields which fronted the river and extended to the east as far as a meandering, sluggish little creek which was a kind of boundary line.

As Henry Bouchard approached the shed, with Obadiah having suddenly stopped behind him, there came a sudden sound like a pistol shot, followed by a low gurgling cry.

"Oh, Gawd hab mercy on a poah sinnah!" Obadiah moaned, his trembling hands covering his wrinkled face. A chorus of groans and sobs rose from the tearful, huddling female slaves who stood in the doors of their cabins and stared helplessly at the shed. Once again the sharp crack of a whip on human flesh was heard, and with it a strident, agonized cry: "Aaahhhrrr—oh, Lawd, hab mercy, mastuh, *please!*" from the victim.

The door of the shed had been left open, and as Henry Bouchard entered, he saw Edward Williamson standing to one side of it, arms folded, eyes intent upon the punishment being meted out to the unfortunate runaway. In the very center of the shed, a heavy, upright log had been solidly fixed into the ground, with a narrow plank nailed to the top to form a crossarm. His wrists drawn up high above his head and roped to the crossarm, wearing only a pair of tattered cotton breeches, his back, sides and shoulders streaked with angry weals, a wiry, ebony-skinned Kru in his mid-thirties writhed against the rough-barked post. His sides heaving, his bare toes scrabbling at the ground, he turned his contorted face back over his shoulder and uttered an agonized shriek as the sadistically grinning overseer raised his cowhide whip again.

Amos Greer was thirty-four years old, towheaded, with a stubbly beard and sideburns, heavy jowls, the broad broken nose of a pugilist, thin lips and pale blue eyes with hardly any lashes or brows above. His father had been a Massachusetts whaler and his mother a Baltimore tavern wench who had borne him without benefit of clergy and left him in a basket on the steps of an orphanage six months later. At thirteen, he had

79

been apprenticed to a chandler, a sadistic pederast who, failing on several occasions to entice him into his own sexual aberration, had unmercifully flogged and starved him. Six months later, Amos Greer, pretending to acquiesce to his master's unnatural lust, had broken his skull with a candlestick and run away to Charleston with fifty shillings stolen from his master's till.

In Charleston, he had found work as a stableboy in a disreputable inn where a plump blond indentured maid initiated him into manhood. A few months later, after the maid had been given a public flogging of a dozen lashes and a month's imprisonment for having picked the pockets of a drunken patron of the inn, Amos Greer bought her indenture from the innkeeper after she had been freed. The cost was twenty-five pounds, most of which he himself had taken from the drunkard's purse and conveniently hidden the rest in the maid's room where it was found by the constable after the indignant patron had made his complaint.

For the next year, Amos Greer became a panderer of the tricked maid's carnal services, and frugally saved the money she was able to earn for him until he had accumulated a hundred pounds. This done, and having constantly cozened her into prostituting herself so that they could eventually earn a sufficient stake for their marriage, Amos Greer brought an Indian trader to the squalid room he and the girl shared on the outskirts of the city. He drugged the trader's rum with laudanum and, having sent the girl out for more rum, first robbed him of his money and then left the room. In a nearby tavern, where he stopped for a mug of rum, he encountered a night watchman to whom he guilefully avowed that he had seen a known thief and whore lure the Indian trader into her room and that he suspected foul play. A few hours later, having purchased a horse and saddle from a livery, he was on his way to the town of Walterboro. Some months before, a crony he had met in the same tavern told him that there were extensive tobacco plantations in that thriving area, and young Amos Greer—who had been given the name of David Blessing at the orphanage—had determined to change his life as impulsively as he had just changed his name.

Because he was sturdy and well-developed for his teens, he found work at once, curing tobacco leaves at a small plantation owned by an elderly, hard-working Englishman with a shrewish wife and two ne'er-do-well sons. Though his wages were small, Amos Greer was shrewd enough to see that he could learn a great deal about the running of a plantation, and for the next three years he quelled his predatory instincts sufficiently to gain the post of assistant overseer and the gratitude of his employer.

Six months later, however, the Englishman died of smallpox, and the widow and her sons decided to sell the plantation and return to England. Amos Greer was almost immediately offered a similar post by a neighboring tobacco planter, a bachelor in his early fifties. He might well have risen to the post of overseer, for his superior was as old as the planter and beset by spells of rheumatism. But two years after he had gone to work for Tobias Bentley, the latter married a flighty nineteen-year-old Charleston blonde out of a desire to have a son and heir. Julia Bentley, soon discovering that her elderly husband was impotent, began to play the role of Potiphar's wife to the towheaded young assistant overseer. Unlike the biblical Joseph, Amos Greer did not take long to succumb to Julia Bentley's blandishments. A month later, when the aging husband discovered his young wife's infidelity, he was sufficiently philosophical to blame himself and to be content with discharging Amos Greer without further reprisal.

His next post was as a foreman on a somewhat larger cotton plantation where sea-island cotton was being successfully grown, the profitable long-staple variety which had been imported from the West Indies. Here Amos Greer thoroughly learned his trade, remained for five years and rightfully earned the post of overseer at the then munificent salary of $750 per year. Here, too, he learned to use the whip with an expertise which cowed the most defiant field hand and compelled many an attractive black slave girl to come to his cabin at night and satisfy his brutal lusts. But one night, after a drunken brawl with his older assistant overseer over the favors of a comely Fulani girl both coveted, Amos Greer killed his subordinate and fled to Georgia. There he worked on another cotton plantation, as an assistant, on land owned by a neighbor of Edward Williamson. And after the death of Williamson's wife, when the bereaved planter decided to move to Alabama with Lucy and Maybelle, he had made Amos Greer too good an offer to refuse.

Now, pausing, Amos Greer drew back the cowhide whip, his lips curving to bare strong yellow teeth as he prepared to resume the punishment. Edward Williamson glanced around and recognized his visitor, beckoned to him. "Afternoon, Mr. Bouchard. He's just about done with Benjy now. Second time this ornery nigger took into his head to run away. I think this time he'll be cured of it."

The sickening thwack of the cowhide as it curled around the writhing Kru's waist punctuated the planter's words, and Benjy jerked convulsively at the post, then sagged, his body shaken by a convulsive spasm.

"That'll do, Greer," Edward Williamson curtly ordered.

"I'll have him branded next, Mr. Williamson. Then we'll wake him up with the pimentade. Davey, you lazy black bastard, get that ladle ready."

Davey, a towering Hausa, standing at one side stirring an iron pot full of the syrupy caustic mixture, nodded, his eyes rolling to the whites. Amos Greer tossed the cowhide to the ground, strode toward an iron brazier filled with glowing coals, tugged a heavy cloth glove out of his pocket and put it on his right hand, then grasped the wooden handle of an oblong branding iron and approached the moaning slave. Brutally, palming the Kru's head with his left hand, he jerked back the tortured face and deftly pressed the red-hot end of the iron onto the Kru's forehead. There was a horrid sizzling and a frenzied shriek, and when

Amos Greer drew away the branding iron, the letter R stood out on the blistered flesh.

"Douse him with pimentade, Davey, and plenty of it. Then leave him here to think things over. You can cut him down after supper and give him something to eat and drink. Tell him the next time he tries running off, we'll hamstring him and brand him on the backs of both knees—understand, nigger?"

"Yassuh," the tall Hausa field hand mumbled, bobbing his head, his eyes again rolling to the whites as he came forward with the dripping ladle and poured it down the welted, bleeding back of the unconscious runaway.

"How very nice to see you again, Luke!" Lucy Williamson's somberly shadowed blue eyes brightened as she came forward to greet the tall young man. "Please excuse me for keeping you so long, Luke. When Obadiah told me you and your father were here, I—I had to change. I didn't want you to see me in the old dress I wore to Mrs. Sedley's Seminary for Young Ladies." Indeed, she was wearing the same attractive sky-blue silk frock she had worn at the Windhaven housewarming, and as Luke's eyes met hers, she colored exquisitely.

"Father came over to talk business with your father, Lucy. I'm very glad he asked me to come along, I wanted to see you again, you know."

"That—that's very nice of you." She looked down at the floor for a moment, then nervously bit her lip. "I—I suppose Obadiah took him out to the shed. Oh, it's just dreadful what that horrible man is doing to poor Benjy!"

"What do you mean, Lucy?"

She looked up at him, her eyes suddenly shimmering and wide with tears, her lips trembling. "He said he was going to have that awful Mr. Greer whip and brand Benjy so he'd never run away again. You see, Benjy had a wife, Martha, and the first time they both tried to run away, Papa let Mr. Greer whip them both. Then he persuaded Papa that Martha wasn't a good wife because—well—because she would make up to other men, so Papa sold her to a slave trader a few weeks ago. That's why Benjy ran away again; he was going to try to find Martha, he said. Oh, I wish to God there wasn't such a thing as slavery, Luke!"

She burst into tears, covering her face with her hands. Distressed for her, Luke could only hold her gently and murmur, "I know, I know, honey. Don't fret yourself so. Try not to think of it. I only wish I could help."

"Oh, you do, just—just by being here—oh, what a silly fool I am, acting this way to a guest—please, Luke, would you like—could I show you my garden? Maybe if I see the flowers, I'll think of lovely things and not spoil your visit—"

"Of course, I'd love to see your garden, Lucy."

She led the way outside and around the side of the house nearest the river. The air was warm and moist with the promise of rain, and the soft shadows of early twilight touched the clump of oak trees far beyond at the riverbank.

"I planted these myself, Luke." Lucy turned to him with a tremulous smile. "Mama always loved yellow roses so, they were her favorites of all the flowers."

"They're beautiful, Lucy."

She turned back to the bed just as a butterfly hovered over the row nearest her and settled on the tallest stalk. "Oh, look, Luke!" she breathed.

He stood beside her, raptly watching the butterfly hover over the rose and then as swiftly take flight and disappear into the darkness. Their eyes met, and as he reached for her, Lucy Williamson uttered a little sob and came into his arms. She trembled as he gathered her to him, pressing his hungry lips upon her face, her neck, her mouth, with all the pent-up passion of first love. And Lucy knew then she would never want—or need—any man but Luke Bouchard. . . .

CHAPTER SEVEN

A few days after Henry Bouchard's visit to the Williamson plantation, old Lucien went down to the fields to talk to the faithful Ashanti, Thomas, the son of Ben and Ellen.

"Good to see you out here in the fields again, Mr. Lucien." The wiry, soft-spoken freed man grinned and tipped the wide-brimmed hat he wore for protection against the already hot afternoon sun. "You know, that grandson of yours, Mr. Luke, he's a fast learner. Maybe he's young yet, but he loves this place so and all the blacks feel the same way about him."

"I'm glad, Thomas. So long as I'm alive, I'll do everything in my power to see that you and the workers are fairly treated. You know, of course, that in my account at Mobile I have a ledger entry showing that each of the men who has been here with me has money coming. By the unfortunate laws we now have, they can't own it, but it's mine to give them as I choose. And I've made my will with Sybella's father, the lawyer, so that I'm sure my wishes will be carried out. Now I've an errand for you to do, if you can spare the time in the next day or so, Thomas."

"We're coming along fine with the chopping and hoeing, Mr. Lucien. No trouble at all. The ground isn't as stiff as we were afraid of, and we should have a fine crop come fall."

"That's good news. Henry will be going to Mobile in

another week or two, and he's going to bring back a good bull and a few cows and some steers for meat for the workers as well as for ourselves. Perhaps he'd better buy a few pigs too. I'm partial to good fresh pork."

"So am I, Mr. Lucien," Thomas grinned.

"I know you'll be glad about this errand, Thomas. You'll have a chance to see your sister Disjamilla and her husband, Eisquayaw. And I want you to take some wagons of supplies to the Creeks who are left at their new home near Tuskegee."

Thomas's face sobered and he nodded sadly. "They won't be there much longer, I'm thinking, Mr. Lucien. There's only about eighty of them left all told. And I hear tell the goverment's going to move them to the west pretty soon, just like they've moved so many others."

"Yes, I know." Lucien fell silent, remembering his old friend Nanakota's proud self-inflicted death so that he might end his days on the land which the Creeks had once ruled so well. "You'll take some money to the new *Mico*, Turintaka. You'll tell him that it's the customary share of my profits, the share I first promised old Tunkamara and Nanakota after him."

"Yes, Mr. Lucien."

"When the government moves them, they'll be given certificates entitling them to so much land in the new country. But you and I know that many of the Creeks were robbed of those certificates by greedy, unscrupulous men. Ask Turintaka to send a courier to me as soon as he receives word when he and his people will be moved. I want to be sure that they aren't tricked out of their rights. What a pity the government wouldn't allow me to let them live here peacefully on my land—I've certainly more than enough for the comforts of my family and myself, and there are many acres that would have made a pleasant little village for them."

"Their mistake was to be born with red skins instead of white, Mr. Lucien, I'm thinking." Thomas uttered a heavy sigh.

"Yes, my old friend, just as yours was in being born

86

black. But I'll say this to you, only your father, Ben, could be any closer to me, and both of you are fine good men I've been proud and fortunate to know."

They shook hands solemnly, and Thomas turned away to blink his eyes, muttering that for February the sun was exceptionally warm. Lucien hastened to add, "Spend a few days with your sister, Thomas. You'll be wanting to see your niece and nephew again, too, won't you?"

The Ashanti's face brightened as he nodded with an eager smile: "Yes, my sister is very proud of Manoka and Shonanoy. Manoka is twenty-one now, a tall fine young man who would have been a great warrior for the Creeks in the old days. And his sister, who is three years younger, is a real beauty. It is said that she is betrothed to Nisquame, who is one of the beloved men in the Creek village." Then he sighed again and shook his head. "When I visited them there two months ago, my sister and her husband were not well. Disjamilla told me that the Indian agent was to send a doctor to the village, but I do not know whether this was done. And when I think of what Econchate was and see now the poor lodges of the Creeks, I weep for them."

"As I do, Thomas. Yes, Nanakota said to me, just before he died, that he was afraid that no one would remember the rich strong life of the Creeks, their culture, their reverent ways and their beliefs in their god Ibofanaga, the Giver of Breath. I told him that I would remember and that I would teach my children to remember as well. Alas, only my grandson Luke cares to remember. What gladdens me in this is that he does not remember for my sake, but because he is concerned with all men and the good that is in them."

"He must learn also to be on guard against the evil that is in so many," Thomas said softly. "I will go to the storehouse in the morning and have the wagons loaded, Mr. Lucien. I will take one of the freed men, Tom, with me."

"That is good. Before you leave, come to the study and I will give you the money you will give on my behalf to the *Mico*. And tell your sister and her husband

and your nephew and niece that I wish them well and that I pray for their safe journey to the west when the time comes. Assure them that I will do everything in my power to provide them with food and clothing for the journey, and money too if more is needed."

But when Thomas returned from the Creek village near Tuskegee a week later, it was with a heavy heart. Both Disjamilla and her husband Eisquayaw had died, and the *Mico* had told him, "They were stricken with the fever, and they were both weak from hunger." And when the Ashanti had asked how this could be, the *Mico* had bowed his head and solemnly replied, "It is not because our blood brother did not send food enough for all of us. It was because lying men who told us that they worked for the government came one night and robbed our storehouse and then told us we would be paid for the goods they had taken. But they gave us nothing in return except lies, and we are too few and too weak to dispute their lying words on the battlefield. It is well that Nanakota did not live to see this shame and treachery which have fallen upon the once proud Creeks. Yet we must accept it, if it is the destiny which Ibofanaga wills us to endure."

"If that's the case, Thomas," Lucien assured the Ashanti, "we must see to it that Manoka and Shonanoy are brought here to Windhaven to live. I do not think the present law will prevent my giving shelter to your niece and nephew. If need be, I will have them enter into a contract with me for work on the plantation, and that will keep the authorities from sending them on with the poor betrayed Creeks to the reservation chosen for them. It will be a sorry day for Alabama when they leave the boundaries forever. If white men had only learned how to deal with them honorably and to learn from their culture and their industry, perhaps this nation would be even stronger than it is."

Lucien Bouchard at once dispatched two letters, one to the Commissioner of Indian Affairs in Washington, the other to the legislature at Tuscaloosa, protesting the reprehensible treatment accorded to the Creeks. In it, he indignantly declared: "You have compelled them to sign a treaty and they have honorably kept to the terms of it. Yet by such theft and roguery—there are no more precise terms to describe what happened to the supplies which were furnished by me to these peaceful Indians—you have as much as broken the treaty and proved that the white man does not keep his word. These Creeks, because of such a treaty, are virtually wards of the United States Government: it is like turning orphans out into the wilderness after first having piously promised to safeguard them from all adversity."

Both letters were formally acknowledged, with promises to investigate the "regrettable and unfortunate occurrence." Yet no further news of any such investigation ever reached the valiant white-haired founder of Windhaven who, since his first days at Econchate, had always kept his word to the friendly Creeks.

Mark warily followed his father into the study and, at Henry's gesture, sat down. "We've had our differences, Mark," he told the surly youth, "but here's a chance for you to be of service to both of us. I've agreed to let Luke become overseer here at Windhaven, and because he's the elder son, that's only natural. But you've as much at stake in Windhaven as he does, so far as I'm concerned. Besides, I think you've got more gumption and more energy in driving ahead to get what you want." His lips curled in an ironic smile as he added, "I haven't forgotten how you scored on me with Celia."

"You know I'm sorry about that, Pa." Mark uneasily shifted in his chair, his face reddening.

"Never mind, it's water under the bridge now. You won't be sixteen till next September, but in many ways you're more of a man than that dreamer Luke."

Mark straightened in his chair, permitting himself a pleased, self-conscious grin. "Well at least, Pa, I've been to bed with a wench and Luke hasn't."

"So you have," his father drily observed with a grimace. "And I also notice that you've taken to calling

89

me 'Pa' instead of 'Father'—no, to be honest with you, I like that much better. You've got spunk and you're not afraid of me. Luke is certainly respectful and devoted, I don't gainsay that at all, but he's let Grandfather shape his thinking for him. Now this is a time to make money, not fool around with other crops when we know that prime cotton is going to get a pretty good price this year. And I might as well tell you I've got ideas for picking up more river land."

"Like Mr. Williamson's, maybe, Pa?"

"Precisely. Incidentally, I notice that you took a shine to that saucy little redhead at the housewarming, that Maybelle. Not a bad idea, boy. You could do worse than match up with her. You see, if anything happens to old Ed Williamson, his two daughters can't inherit his property. It would have to go to probate and be handled by an executor. On the other hand, if you were to marry Maybelle, you could take it over if anything happened to him—do you catch my drift?"

"I'm way ahead of you, Pa."

"Of course, he's in pretty good health and he's not really old, and besides I wouldn't hear of your marrying till you're sixteen anyway. But just give it some thought. Now then, how'd you like to come along to Mobile and then New Orleans with me next week?"

"Gosh, I'd like it fine, Pa!" The youth's eyes sparkled.

"You know, I went over to Ed Williamson's place a couple of weeks ago, and I saw this nigger slave Davey he's so riled up about. He thinks Davey will coin him a mint by fighting all comers. And from the conversation we had, I found out that he's got gambling fever."

"Oh?"

"I'll tell you what that means. He's a widower, and I had a little talk with Amos Greer on the side when he wasn't around to hear me. Greer says that Williamson hasn't had much truck with the wenches on his plantation, which means he's hankering. That was one reason I sent him up Lucille at the housewarming. Now in New Orleans, there's a fellow by the name of Pierre Lourat, one of the biggest slave dealers there, and he

90

has a string of fancy girls. If I took Ed Williamson down to meet him while maybe I pick up a big husky nigger who can whip the daylights out of his Davey, I might just get him in deep enough to move in on him · even faster than you'll be able to become his son-in-law."

"That's real tricky, Pa. I give you credit, you're always thinking ahead."

"You have to in this world if you don't want to be taken by your next-door neighbor. I don't think your mother will put up too much objection to your dropping out of school for a week or two. Besides, you're not really the type for book learning anyway. We'll leave that to Luke. And if he should happen to mismanage Windhaven now that he's overseer, even his grandfather will have to admit that the boy wasn't really ready, that all he had was a lot of highfalutin' notions which might have worked in the early days, but not today when there's competition from all the other planters moving into Alabama. All right, then. I'll talk to your mother about this. Just don't say anything to anybody else."

Mark Bouchard rose from his chair, a broad grin on his face, and held out his hand to his father to signify the end of their uneasy truce—and the resumption of Henry Bouchard's favoritism toward his younger son.

Henry Bouchard had been delighted with the business transacted in Mobile, as had Edward Williamson. The latter's four hundred and fifty bales of 182,-000 pounds of prime cotton had netted almost $30,000. From this, with the widower's grateful consent, Henry Bouchard had deducted the $2000 owing him as well as his factor's commission of $3000. The sale price had been 16½ cents per pound, a slight increase over the previous year and one which convinced old Lucien's only son that his father's gloomy prediction of a financial crisis had been unduly pessimistic.

James Cavendish's forty-five bales had netted $2984.95 and Benjamin Harnesty's forty bales $2653.20; each of these bachelor planters owed Henry

Bouchard $1000 for ginning, storage and seeds and tools, so that the steamboat trip to Mobile carrying his three neighbors' cotton had earned him the sizable amount of $7000—a sum more than ample to purchase a superb fighting black who could best Williamson's Davey and with enough left over for his sybarite enjoyments in glamorous New Orleans.

The packet from Mobile brought Henry and Mark and Edward Williamson into a harbor so crowded that old Lucien would never have recognized it. A good part of the port allocated to steamboats was being extended, for new companies were being chartered for navigating the Mississippi and western waters, opening an inland communication by turnpikes of railroads with Nashville and then across to the Atlantic. Abreast of the city, alongside the levee, lay scores of arks, Kentucky boats, forty to ninety feet long and ten to fifteen wide, made of rough planks pinned together with wooden bolts. These usually floated down the stream in pairs.

Their huge oars were fashioned out of straight trees, and five or six men acted as steersmen on each ark to guide it into its proper channel. There were bushwhacking keelboats and flatboats from Kentucky, built of massive timbers. Some of them were family boats, fitted with compartments for ladies and their servants, and in the same bottom and under the same roof, with quarters for cattle, horses, sheep, dogs and poultry. These boats were navigated from the roof which covered the cabin and manned by burly Kentuckians and Tennesseans. From their poles, one could see hams, ears of corn, apples, animal skins, and whisky mugs, primitive advertising signs which told would-be buyers what wares they could find aboard. A pall of black smoke floated down the river from the steamboats which hissed and puffed their way to their mooring. As their packet made its way toward the levee, Mark and Henry and Edward Williamson could see the celebrated Grampus towboat, which had two large four-masted ships grappled to her side, two brigs at a cable's length behind, and, still farther in the rear, two schooners and two sloops.

The levee was vast, extended now to three miles and bordered by tiers of merchant shipping from every part of the trading world. Once a shipmaster had chosen his berth, he could load or unload without shifting a line, a facility derived from nature that no other port in the world could rival. Along the entire extent of this line, situated below the levee some four hundred feet distant, stood a range of storehouses, cotton presses and shops connected by well-flagged sidewalks. Floundering through the pond of water in the middle of what might be called a street, there were hundreds of light drays, each drawn by three or four mules, laden with cotton. Crowds of laborers, sailors, bargemen and draymen, and gangs of slaves were already busy at work.

"By God, Ed," Henry Bouchard exclaimed, his face aglow, "what a pity we can't ship our cotton direct to New Orleans! I do believe it's the greatest port in the world, and there's nothing to rival the excitement and the pleasures one can find here. Mobile's all very well for business, but you'll soon see that when it comes to amusing oneself, it can't hold a candle to New Orleans! Why, they're even lighting the streets with gas now, and the city surveyor says that by April streets will be paved and sidewalks bricked as far as Claiborne Street and to the Elysian Field and the Second Municipality. Now then, we'll find a fancy rig to take us to the Orleans Hotel. Mark my words, we'll have much larger hotels before long, with all the people who come to New Orleans!"

"Doubtless it's the slave trade that's bringing them, don't you imagine, Mr. Bouchard?" Williamson turned to his companion.

"Of course it is. And you'll find that prime niggers bring higher prices here than in Mobile, and of course you'll find more fancy wenches." He gave the widower a wink. "In spite of these damned abolitionists who are spreading around the country, we're thriving on slavery, sir, and we mean to keep on with it. Just let the Federal Government try to ban it, you'll see secession."

"That won't be so easy," Williamson commented. "Remember the Nullification Crisis three years ago, when South Carolina, under Andy Jackson's own Vice President John C. Calhoun, protested against the high taxes which made goods from New England so much more expensive to the South? He said that if any state of the Union regarded the Federal law as unconstitutional, it was entitled to nullify it. And Jackson said that no state had a right to secede and that nullification would mean insurrection and war. Why, old Andy actually ordered a man-of-war to Charleston Harbor, got his Congress to pass a bill authorizing him to use Federal force, and South Carolina had to give in. No, secession won't be easy under our form of government. But then, Mr. Bouchard, I'm reasonably certain that sensible people, even in the North, will learn that in this part of the country slavery is the only possible way to get good labor. Why, man, no Southern gentleman would soil his hands with work that we put the niggers to doing, and even if he did, there wouldn't be money enough in the world to pay him for it."

"My feelings exactly, Ed," Henry Bouchard chuckled. In an expansive mood, he had told his widower neighbor that he himself would stand the cost of the trip to New Orleans as well as the expenses of their nocturnal entertainment. Also, during the trip from Mobile to New Orleans, he had cleverly talked of Pierre Lourat's gambling parlors, and had been rewarded by seeing a flicker of interest in Edward Williamson's eyes.

As they carefully made their way along the wide gangplank to the levee, Henry Bouchard turned to his planter neighbor and said, "There's bound to be a carriage in which we can ride to our hotel. The dray is too commonplace for merchants like yourself and myself, my good friend Ed. Besides, all these people will make way for a carriage while they'll ignore a dray—ho, you there, driver!" He suddenly cupped his hands to his mouth and bellowed out as he saw an open carriage driven by an old Negro wearing a tall black stovepipe hat and listlessly flicking his whip at the piebald mare drawing it. "Watch your footing, Mark, it's slippery here. Good! Driver, to the Orleans Hotel as quickly as you can!"

Then, leaning back, he sighed with anticipatory pleasure. "We'll dine tonight at Moreau's. I've never had better red snapper and turtle soup. I came here four years ago to find the French architect who would undertake building Windhaven, you see, and he was the one who introduced me to this superb restaurant. There's a dessert of rich cake with fruit soaked in wines and cognacs to top off one of the best meals you ever had. And while we're ordering, I'll send a nigger boy over to Pierre Lourat's auction rooms on Chartres Street to tell him that we'd like to see him and to hold in reserve some of his fanciest slaves." Leaning toward the widower, he muttered, "Now that you've had your crops sold for you and you've money in your pocket to treat yourself, Edward, why not buy yourself a pretty wench to comfort you on those lonely nights back at your plantation?"

"Oh no, I couldn't do that." Williamson flushed. "I'm afraid Lucy would never forgive me for something like that. That's one reason, though I'll admit I've been tempted many a time, I haven't pestered any of the likely black wenches on my place. I've had to leave that to Amos Greer, who has no scruples in the matter, though I envy the rogue. Why, he has only to lift his cowhide, and a girl will hurry to his cabin and do her utmost to pleasure him."

"Oh, look, Pa!" Mark pointed to a group of Negro women and quadroons carrying on their bandanna-wrapped heads a whole table or platform laden with cakes, apples, oranges, figs, bananas, pineapples and coconuts.

"Of course, my son," Henry Bouchard benevolently explained. "This part of the levee is opposite the market house, and those niggers are servants from the fine houses sent here to buy delicacies for their masters' and mistresses' tables. God, what a crowd—sailors, riverboat men, slaves, sea captains and pirates too, I'll warrant! There's adventure and excitement here for the

95

taking, Edward! You'll soon be glad you came, I promise you that!"

A few hours later, after enjoying the sumptuous repast, Henry Bouchard, Edward Williamson and young Mark stood in the elegantly furnished auction room which had once borne the sign of "Maison Duvalier" and now was known as "Maison Lourat." Old Armand Duvalier, once a French privateer who had flown the skull and crossbones for a time and then become a blackbirder, had succumbed to an attack of river fever eight months ago. His young manager, now twenty-five, had inherited not only the auction rooms but also the several profitable bordellos which had brought his patron enormous revenue.

"We meet again, *mon ami*," the young Creole smilingly bowed to Henry Bouchard and his son, then shook hands with Edward Williamson. He wore a black frock coat with a high cravat and ruffled silk shirt, seemed even taller than he had been when Henry Bouchard had visited New Orleans in November 1831 to commission a competent architect to build the château of Windhaven. Yet his dark, glittering eyes, his ripe, moist mouth, and the flaring nostrils proclaimed Lourat still the expert sensualist: under that façade, as Henry Bouchard knew only too well, was the shrewd cunning of a profiteer and the dexterity of a murderous swordsman. Indeed, the manager of the Orleans Hotel, on having learned that Henry Bouchard was a friend of Lourat's, had volunteered the information that only two weeks ago the mercurial young man had fought no fewer than three duels on a point of honor and rapiered all three of his adversaries to their deaths.

"I have brought along my friend Edward Williamson this time, Pierre," Henry explained. "I've told him about your gambling rooms, and he's just come from Mobile with a very tidy profit on his cotton. I'm sure you'll be able to find suitable amusement on his first visit to New Orleans."

"I shall personally see to it, *M'sieu* Williamson." Pierre Lourat bowed courteously. "But when you sent

96

your messenger from the hotel to announce your presence in the Queen City, I purposely held off from the auction block several particularly choice offerings. Two are wenches, two are magnificent field hands, but perhaps something more than that. One especially, a pure-blooded Mandingo named Djamba, was himself a monarch of his country until he was betrayed into slavery. He has exceptional intelligence to couple with his great strength. He is proud and I do not think that handling him with the whip is advisable. One can appeal to his intellect and achieve far more."

"Who ever heard of a nigger with brains?" Edward Williamson sneered.

Pierre Lourat looked at the planter, his face coldly impassive. "Why, as to that, Mr. Williamson, I seem to recall a few. I could mention Toussaint L'Ouverture and Jean-Jacques Dessalines, both of whom were born slaves and yet rose to leadership, even over the vaunted whites."

"True enough, Pierre, but Toussaint died in one of Napoleon's prisons and Dessalines was so despotic a ruler that he was murdered," Henry Bouchard riposted.

"There have been white leaders who have met a similar fate, history will tell you," the slave dealer coolly countered. "Do you remember Charles Stuart and our own Louis XVI? And even those who brought about the downfall of our lamented monarch, Robespierre and Danton, were themselves destroyed. Leadership is no guarantee of longevity. One must depend on one's wit, one's brain, and for me, my needle-sharp rapier." With this, he patted the elegantly tool-worked basket grip of the blade which swung at his left side. "But let us speak of more pleasant things, gentlemen. As you see, there are few buyers in the auction room, because I had it closed to all except a very select number of my favorites as soon as I received your note. And now, if you will take your seats in these comfortable Empire chairs, I shall have my mulatto maid Caroline bring you some little cakes and Madeira so that you may be at your ease to appraise the merchandise I shall offer."

He clapped his hands and a pretty, teenaged light-colored girl wearing only an almost transparent white linen shift, high-heeled slippers and dark stockings which rose to mid-thigh and were held there with purple rosette garters, came forward with a tray on which were plates of sugar and honey cakes and a decanter of the rich, strong white wine made on the islands off the northwest coast of Africa.

Next, Pierre Lourat gestured to a sturdy black attendant dressed in red livery, as he took his place before the large rectangular platform at the forefront of the room. From an antechamber, the attendant now led a tall young woman with oval face, great mournful dark-brown eyes and deeply dimpled chin, clad in a red velvet wrapper, barefooted, her wrists shackled with silver gyves between which was a foot-long chain. The attendant led her up the little flight of steps at the side of the platform and stood beside her, awaiting his master's sign.

"This one is Emmy, an octoroon of twenty, the mistress of one of our better-known merchants whose business judgment, alas, did not match his eye for beauty. When he was wiped out at one of the banks which failed through President Jackson's manipulations, he blew out his brains and left sizable debts. Emmy is therefore my property to sell, since I was one of his principal creditors. Let me hear a bid, gentlemen."

"A thousand dollars!" came from a squat little planter who sat in one of the loge chairs slightly behind Mark, Henry and Edward Williamson.

"Oh come now, *M'sieu* Duclos, you can't expect to get such a treasure for a niggardly sum like that!" Pierre Lourat disdainfully took out a scented kerchief and delicately sniffed at it, patted his mouth then pocketed it. "Emmy spent three years with her esteemed patron, and I can tell you that he explicitly rhapsodized over her capabilities in bed. However, I think that if you see her as nature made her, totally unadorned, you will want to amend your bid."

With this, he made an abrupt gesture, and the

liveried attendant stepped beside the submissive octo-roon and whispered into her ear. She shivered, then nodded, and one heard the clink of her silver chain as with her own hands she undid the wrapper to stand naked before the six men who witnessed this private sale.

"*Mordieu!*" A wealthy dandy dressed in green frock coat and matching wide pantaloons, with an enormous cravat in the center of which gleamed a diamond stick-pin, lifted his ivory-headed walking stick and brought it down on the floor to mark his excitement. "Two thousand dollars!"

"A little better, Charles, but still by no means what Emmy is worth. Tell yourself that at twenty and with three years as the *petite maitresse* of the most demand-ing master—her very docility tells you that he knew how to enforce his wishes!—she can amuse you for many years before her beauty begins to fade, and you can teach her what she does not yet know."

"Three thousand, then!" the dandy hoarsely shouted.

Henry Bouchard stared covetously at the beautiful young octoroon. Her fettered hands protectively cov-ered the most intimate part of her nakedness as she stood with bowed head, her blue-black, shimmering hair streaming to her deeply hollowed waist. Pierre Lourat made another gesture, and again the liveried at-tendant approached the submissive octoroon to whisper to her. Then, very slowly, she raised her hands to cover her face, as tears rolled down her cheeks, and Henry Bouchard as well as his precocious young son gasped aloud to see that she had been completely depi-lated, and the lips of her vulva delicately tinted with rouge.

"I'll bid three thousand!" the dandy cried, pounding his walking stick on the floor of the auction room.

"You could afford her, Ed," Henry Bouchard leaned over to whisper to his neighbor. "Go to four thousand, I'm sure you'll get her. I'd buy her myself, except Sy-bella wouldn't give me a moment's peace." He scowled, remembering his disappointment with Celia.

"My God, you don't know how I want to," Edward Williamson groaned, "but Lucy would look upon me as if I were a pariah. She still mourns her mother, the poor darling. But I tell you, I'll certainly go to one of Lourat's bordellos when this is over, I'm that roused! I can imagine what pleasure that bitch's former master had in breaking her in—she'd have been about seventeen then."

"That's true. Well, perhaps you're right. Besides, you'll want to keep some of your money for the roulette wheel and *vingt-et-un*, I fancy," Henry Bouchard whispered back, without taking his eyes off the trembling, silently weeping naked girl.

But it was the squat Duclos who finally purchased Emmy with a bid of $3800, the Creole dandy reluctantly giving her up after his final offer of $3500 had been exceeded by the other man. The liveried attendant replaced her wrapper and led her out of the auction room back into the antechamber, where Duclos himself hurried to claim his prize.

Next came a strapping young Hausa of twenty, grinning and good-natured, clad only in a breechclout, who already spoke a little English and had, according to Pierre Lourat's dossier, worked for a year on a Louisiana sugarcane plantation. "I may say, gentlemen, that to survive without a single blemish or even a lash mark indicates the strength and the obedience of this top-quality field hand. Let me hear your bids!"

The Hausa went for $1800 to the same man who had purchased Emmy, and who then left the auction room after his two new slaves had been clothed and suitably shackled to his orders.

"Next, a superb Fulani girl of eighteen," Pierre Lourat announced. "Her name is Jitarda, she is still a virgin, and she was purchased as a maid for Mademoiselle Eugenia St. Croix, of whose betrothal you may have recently read in the social news column of our leading journal. It appears that the estimable and virtuous *demoiselle*, discovering that her father had arranged for her marriage to a wealthy but most notorious rake, decided not to put temptation in his path and so insisted that Jitarda be sold. The money will be used to embellish her already formidable trousseau. Meanwhile, you gentlemen have an opportunity to obtain a truly exquisite specimen, She too speaks a little English. Note the flawless and very light-brown skin of this girl. There is always a premium on a Fulani, because the breed makes for perceptive and at the same time docile slaves. For those of you who are not acquainted with this breed, I may say that the Fulani is a pastoral and nomadic people of mixed negroid and Mediterranean stock found throughout the Sudan from Senegal eastward. Their most attractive girls were in great demand among the Arabs, the sheiks as well as the wealthiest slave dealers themselves, because of their beauty. But let Jitarda's loveliness speak for itself."

Once again he clapped his hands and the attendant led from the antechamber a tall, light-skinned girl with high forehead and highset cheekbones, bright inquisitive brown eyes, the nose slightly broad but almost straight enough to be taken for Caucasian, with full ripe lips, her black hair almost like that of an Indian girl's, but bound in a thick braid almost to the waist. Pierre Lourat had had her presented in a blue silk shift with dainty sandals on her shapely feet. Like the octoroon, her wrists were shackled with silver with a long chain between them.

It was the Creole dandy who purchased Jitarda for $2350, and it was Henry Bouchard who adroitly—and to gain Pierre Lourat's gratitude for thus increasing his profit—topped the original bid twice but not by so much as to extinguish the dandy's obvious desire for the girl.

After he had departed with his prize, only one other bidder remained besides Edward Williamson, Henry and Mark, a Louisiana planter's agent who had come to New Orleans to find prime field hands. He had let the Hausa go because he believed the price too steep, but as the liveried attendant now led out the last slave of this private auction, he rose from his chair and stroked his short pointed beard, his cold gray eyes scanning the magnificent physique of the Mandingo whom Pierre Lourat now introduced.

"This is Djamba, gentlemen. As I've said, a pure-blooded Mandingo from the village of Mopti near the Niger River. Twenty-three years of age, and a prince of his tribe. I may tell you that when he was brought back on the slaver, my captain took exceptional care of him and quartered him in a separate cabin in the hold. We didn't want him to come down with fever or get into a fight with any of the sailors—he's a proud one, as you can see. We brought along a Gullah girl whom the missionaries had taught to speak English, and she speaks his native tongue well enough for him to understand her. So on the trip to New Orleans, she taught him enough to understand the commands of his new master. Now then, here he is, see for yourself!"

Henry's eyes gleamed as the attendant brought out a young man with a dark, coppery-tinted skin, six feet three inches tall, with magnificent thews and broadly developed chest, a proudly erect head, vigorously muscled shoulders and arms. He, like the Hausa, was naked but for a breechclout, and his wrists were equally shackled in silver, but with a far shorter chain than was provided for the slave girls.

"I'll start with fifteen hundred," the bearded agent said, raising his hand.

Henry rose from his chair and approached the platform. He stared at the expressive, haughty face of the tall Mandingo, the strong jaws, the firm incisive mouth, the broad but well-made nose, the keen eyes and the broad forehead. But most of all he stared into Djamba's eyes, and there was a pride and quiet self-knowledge in the Mandingo's gaze which attracted him. No, it wasn't just nigger arrogance; he knew that well enough and he knew how to punish it, too. This one was different, this one was proud because he had the right to be, because he'd been a leader. Well, here was just the fighter to smash Williamson's Davey into a bloody pulp.

"I'll double that bid," he said in a loud clear voice.

"It's too rich for my blood, sir." The agent shook his

102

head and rose from his chair. "Well, Mr. Lourat, I'll be back tomorrow to see your regular lot. Maybe you'll have something special for me, but not at these prices. I bid you a good evening and thank you for your hospitality."

"My thanks to you, Mr. Shepard." Pierre Lourat gave him a mocking little bow. Then, to Henry Bouchard, he said, "My congratulations, *M'sieu* Bouchard. You've bought yourself one of the finest slaves I've ever had the privilege of showing on the block."

CHAPTER EIGHT

The tall Mandingo stood staring at the man who faced him, their eyes still unwavering appraising the other. He had understood enough of the conversation between Pierre Lourat and Henry Bouchard to know that this man had bought him, though he did not know why. And this man who had bought him was strong, he knew that also, and capable of anger and hatred, perhaps even of treachery. Well he knew what treachery was. Only, before, he had been powerless to avert it, because he had not guessed how vindictive a scorned woman could be. But this time, he did not think a treacherous woman would have anything to do with his fate. Louala, the plump, friendly girl who had visited him in the hold during the voyage from Africa, had told him that the white men would sell him to work in the fields in this new land and that he must work hard and obey or they would lash him cruelly with their whips. If he did what they wished, they would feed him well and perhaps give him a woman for his bed at night.

There was something in the look of this white man who had bought him which he could not quite understand. No, it was not fear—though if he wished even now, he could reach out and strangle this man with his two strong hands, just as he could break the spine of that strutting young white man who had spoken to these other masters about him, Djamba. He lis-

105

tened now, while these two men spoke to each other, and he tried to understand them so that he might have some further clue to his destiny in this strange new land across the great ocean.

"It's said that the Mandingo descended from Coptic or even Arabian nomadic tribes many centuries ago," Pierre Lourat was explaining to Henry Bouchard. "They were warlike, and for many years they ruled much of Africa. But when the Spaniards and the Portuguese came centuries ago in search of slaves, the tribes separated and sought to escape, and thus they lost much of their power. Yes, Djamba was a prince of his tribe, that's what Louala told my captain. How he came to be captured—well, even Louala couldn't learn that, because Djamba wouldn't tell her. He just stared ahead and said, 'It was because a lioness proved to be a hyena.' Well, perhaps he'll tell you the story himself once you train him to your work at Windhaven, *M'sieu*."

It had been four months ago to this very day that he had edged forward on his belly, sucking in his breath as his strong right hand gripped the haft of the iron-headed spear. He had stalked the lean, black-maned lion for over three hours, following the spoor left by the killer beast which had thrice within the last moon raided the village of Mopti, whose newly elected king he had just become. It had been mid-afternoon and the sun beat scorchingly down upon his sinewy, bronzed body, naked save for a loincloth made of a zebra skin and the strong sandals which his beautiful young wife Itulde had fashioned for him with her own soft hands.

The trail had led more than three miles from the branch of the Niger River which wound just to the north of his village, seeking out this predator that, grown old and fearful, now dared to strike down women and children as his prey and then flee for safety. He, Djamba, must prove his valor to his tribe. Surely his brother, fat, slothful Bulwayo, would never do so. A mirthless smile curved his lips at the thought. Nay, likelier that Karmida, that beauteous shrew whom

106

his brother had taken to wife, would herself have taken up the lion spear and followed the murderous beast than Bulwayo, two years younger than himself but already an old woman, his mind clouded with fears, superstitions, whimpering hesitations.

It was good that there had been no doubt about a succession, when, last year, their father, old Murbaya, had died of the black flux. He had ruled the Mopti for thirty years, and his deeds were as valorous as those of any tribal kings the Mandingos had ever known . . . aye, as valorous even as those of Mfumbe, who ruled the warrior Zulus more than a thousand miles to the south. Old Jabkri, the *bokono*, who foretold the future by reading the *du*, the magic lots, had proclaimed at once that he, Djamba, being the elder son, must ascend the throne, and that the magic lots foretold that he should rule first as prince regent for a year until his title of king was assured by the gods.

His senses sharpened as he heard a soft coughing roar beyond and above him. He lay on a grassy knoll, behind which towered a huge baobab tree. Scarcely a hundred feet beyond, a small ridge of irregular and jagged rocks rose perhaps twenty feet above the ground. The fearful villagers called these the Caves of the Dead, for once, many moons ago before even the oldest villager now alive could now recall, it was said that an army of the Ashanti tribe had silently crept along this pathway toward the Niger intent on massacring the inhabitants of the little villages along the river so that their ambitious king might extend his sway. Then, with a great howling of wind and rolling of thunder, demons had poured forth from the Caves of the Dead, dispersed and slain them.

Djamba smiled at the recollection, for such stories were for the children, the old women—yes, and for his brother too. There was no doubt that this was the best way to prove his right to the crown of the Mandingos. In the year following his father's death, he had felt himself unworthy of taking beloved old Murbaya's place. He had been more like a moonstruck youth, content to stay in his hut and to make love to Itulde, whom he had wed on the very day when Jabkri had proclaimed him prince regent and the rightful heir to the throne of the Mopti.

He moved forward a little now, shading his eyes from the sun with his cupped left hand, and thought he saw movement out of the nearest cavelike aperture in the rocks beyond. The thing to do would be to entice the beast to leap down upon him so that he could plant the spear into the soft earth and impale the killer. At eighteen, he had killed his first lion, and five thereafter, till the day of his father's death. But this last year had been one of comfort, peace and contentment with his lovely bride. All that concerned him was her barren-ness, for her mother and grandmother before her had been as fertile as the swift eland. Nor was it for lack of trying, as he lay upon the lion's skin which served them both as bed and thrust his fierce manhood deep into Itulde's soft, tightening loins till she drained him of all his seed with that sweet, husky-voiced, shudder-ing way she had of announcing her own delight.

True enough, she was only nineteen, but then there were wives in Mopti who had borne two or three or even four sons by that time. For all he knew, Karmida, his brother's wife, might even now be with child. If aught should befall him to cast him down from the throne, if Itulde should die barren, then it would be Bulwayo who would wear the crown in his stead, and that must not be!

He knew that Karmida hated him, and had ever since the night, only a month before his coronation as prince regent, when he had gone down to the river to offer a prayer to the river god Lagosti to give his father back his strength and health. She had crept through the trees, silent as the adder gliding along the earth, and touched him. When he had whirled, she had smiled at him, loosened her garment and murmured, "Will you not look with favor upon me, Djamba? I could not sleep, so I came to tell you that my thighs hunger to house your manhood."

But even if he had had the slightest lust for her—and he had not—he could not then have taken her, not

108

with his father's grave illness weighing upon his mind. He had told her that, and her smile had turned to a look of hatred, and she had turned back along the trail and vanished. Then, two months after his marriage to Itulde, she had cozened fat Bulwayo into marriage. Oh, she was plump and comely, but her eyes were shifty and her mouth could pour forth venom as well as honey. But what she had done worst of all was to rouse his lethargic brother into thinking that he was a man when everyone in the village knew that Bulwayo was a coward, terrified not only of his own shadow but of the dung beetle which might crawl across the threshold of his hut.

Once again he heard the coughing roar and inched forward toward the ledge of rock. His body glistened with sweat and the sun dried him almost instantly. From afar, he could hear the cawing of a crow. Yes, he must wait till the beast showed itself, then provoke it into the death leap. Although it had often tasted human blood, its victims had been women and children, so the black-maned killer would surely not be brave enough to seek him out in combat unless it were certain of victory. Had it killed strong warriors, that would be another story.

As he lay there waiting, Djamba thought to himself how curious it was that in the past few moons Karmida had been gentle and kind to his wife. Itulde had fallen ill just after her monthly time and Karmida had insisted upon nursing and feeding her. Itulde had told him this and he had been puzzled and wary. Perhaps, after all, she was content with his brother and with the importance of being wife to the next in succession to the Mandingo throne. Perhaps wisdom had come to her, and surely it should, for she was four and twenty, older than his brother and himself, and indeed old for a woman taken in marriage for the purpose of being fruitful. For a moment his mind dwelt upon the obscenity of the two of them coupling, then rejected it. For he did not even believe that Bulwayo was any more a man in the embrace of love than at the hunt or by the council fires. . . .

109

In his hut, Bulwayo lolled upon the zebra skin, munching upon kernels of dried corn, as Karmida knelt beside him her face crafty, her eyes heavy-lidded. "What does my lord and husband think of what I have done?" she seductively murmured as she put forth a hand toward his loincloth.

Bulwayo, who lay upon his back, stretched and yawned slothfully. "A fine notion if it works. Yet Djamba may have already planted his seed time enough into the womb of Itulde to get her with child. Even should Djamba be taken by the slavers, his child, not I, would be king. This is our tribal law, woman."

"Have no fear, my noble husband," Karmida smiled even as her words dripped the acid of sarcasm. "She is not with child. I have given her ergot, each time before the curse of woman is upon her. And these past weeks I have fed her the datura, the powder that is made by crushing the plantain weed. She will not conceive, my husband."

"You have done well, Karmida. And the Arab has promised you much gold?" Bulwayo put one pudgy hand to the back of his head and propped himself up to regard his kneeling wife, his thick lips curling in a smirk of pleasure.

"Yes, much gold, oh my husband."

"Then he would give as much again for the wife of Djamba, since a female slave as comely as she would be welcome in the harems of the sheiks or in the great palaces of the lords of the East."

"You speak with great wisdom, as befits one who shall be king of the Mopti," Karmida purred. "The Arab and his men camp in the forest to the north of our village. I myself will go to him and tell him that he must pay me also for Itulde, once Djamba is taken. Then you need fear your brother's taunts no longer, and I, I too, shall be avenged."

"Why do you hate my brother so, woman?" Bulwayo asked, his beady eyes narrowing.

"I hate him because he is king and my husband is not," Karmida lied. "I will do honor to my husband as king of the Mandingos of the Mopti, I will exalt him."

110

Then, leaning toward him, she whispered, "Will my husband permit his worthless wife to please him in the way he desires most of all?"

Bulwayo sucked in his breath and nodded, his tongue nervously wetting his quivering lips.

Karmida sinuously moved forward on her knees beside him. Her deft fingers loosened the loincloth, caressed his hairless testicles. She bent her head, her lips nuzzling the dormant tip of his weapon. Bulwayo whimpered like a woman and closed his eyes as his body tautened.

"Lie still, oh my husband, oh my king to be," Karmida crooned, as she continued her lascivious ministrations. . . .

Another wearying hour had passed, the black-maned lion still skulked in its protective cave. Djamba ground his teeth with mounting anger at the cowardly beast. Well, he must provoke it now before darkness fell, for otherwise it might well escape and come back to kill again and again. He began to crawl forward. When he reached the end of the grassy knoll, the ledge lay perhaps fifteen feet beyond. Straining his eyes, he could just make out the head of the beast in that shadowy entry of the nearest cave.

His left hand brushed something and he glanced momentarily at it. It was a sturdy plantain. For the moment, his eyes flickered back to the ledge above and beyond, and then he turned his head to stare at the weed, as a terrible comprehension gripped him. Datura—it was known by the witch doctors in every village as a creeping poison that would make a woman's womb reject the seed of her mate. Now he knew with terrible certainty why Itulde had fallen ill, why she was still barren. That evil bitch Karmida had put the poison into the food she had brought his lissome young wife. His fingers dug into the haft of the heavy spear and his eyes blazed with anger. He could see it all. It was Karmida's revenge because he had spited her by his rejection. She had married his fat worthless brother so that she could scheme, so that she could make Bulwayo share her ambition to be queen of the Mopti. Well, when he returned from the hunt this sundown, the entire village should know of the treachery of his brother's wife. They would beat her and stone her and drive her forth into the jungle. Even Jabkri would pronounce such a sentence without hesitation.

Then he heard the coughing roar louder than ever; and as he glanced up again, he saw that the lean, gaunt, black-maned beast had emerged from the dark aperture of the cave into the dimming sunlight, crouching there on the edge of the ledge, its baleful yellow eyes staring down at him, its long tufted tail whipping back and forth.

He knelt quickly, calling out in a hoarse, thirst-parched voice a Mandingo's taunt to a cowardly enemy: "Ho, spawn of hyena dung, do you show yourself at last?" And as he called, he swiftly dug the wooden haft of the spear into the soft earth, then gripped it with both hands. His biceps rippled, as with all his strength he dug the haft down as far as it would go.

With an angry roar, the lion sprang through the air and for an instant Djamba's heart was in his mouth. He crouched, his hands gripping and angling the shaft as the beast came down upon him, straight down upon the head of the spear. A maddened, coughing, gurgling sound ripped from the beast. In its death throes, its left paw struck Djamba a glancing blow on the shoulder, the dew claws tearing the flesh. But the iron head of the spear had found the heart, and the black-maned killer lay on its side, the wooden haft cracked off by its weight.

Djamba staggered erect, seized the broken haft, and with all his might tugged the bloody blade free. Then, with a shout of triumph, he made his way back to his village, heedless of the gash in his shoulder.

The wiry, black-bearded slave trader, Mougar ben Ali, chuckled with contempt at the ways of infidels and savages. By the beard of the Prophet, whenever one could evoke jealousy and hatred among *giaours* and blacks alike, a diligent and imaginative true believer could come by a handsome profit. Today's work alone

112

would bring him much gold after he had delivered the coffle of shackled slaves to the Portuguese captain whose ship lay at anchor off Conakry on the Guinea Coast, only two weeks' overland journey from here. Then he could return to his own little villa in Port Said and there enjoy the fruits of his leisure with some delightful young handmaiden whom he would buy for himself. Perhaps it would be one of the young Fulani virgins, or again a buxom Ashanti wench just out of puberty.

This happy prospect would come about because of the simple accident of family hatreds, he cynically thought to himself. That stupid woman Karmida from the village of Mopti had already secretly come to his camp to tell him how he might surprise and enslave Djamba, the announced king of that village. Mougar ben Ali had pricked up his ears at this news, for a strong Mandingo male, and above all a young king who had slain a lion with a spear, would fetch a staggering price from the Portuguese slaver. Yet, having already made his bargain with the woman, she had returned to him only an hour ago to urge him to abduct also a comely Mandingo girl. Not a virgin, true enough, but young and a great beauty—and the wife of this selfsame king Karmida was delivering up to him. Praise to Allah that there was envy among the infidels and savages: it made for good trading!

Mougar ben Ali beckoned to his lieutenant, a swarthy pockmarked Bedouin named Ishmael ben Nurali, who had for ten prospering years served him well in the capture of prize slaves whose taking called for more skill than a mere raid in force upon a native village. He spoke swiftly, and the Bedouin listened, and then turned to his three strong, crafty Senegalese bearers. Long ago, these three had themselves been slaves, captured in a raid on their own village by a rival Arab trader whom, in the course of hostile competition, Mougar ben Ali himself had slain. He had freed the bearers on condition they would work with him; they had sworn on the bones of their fathers to serve him and to do what was ordered of them. Thus

113

they looked aside as to the treachery of delivering their own black brothers into bondage; and they were as ruthless as the stalking leopard on the trail of a valuable prize. The Bedouin instructed them how best to over-power and take Djamba prisoner as he returned to his village after the hunt for the killer lion which had terrorized the village of Mopti.

Mougar ben Ali had allowed Karmida to play an im-portant part in this capture of Djamba and his woman. He had told her to hurry back to Mopti to tell Itulde that Djamba had been severely clawed by the black-maned lion and might not live. Then, when Itulde would hasten toward the Caves of the Dead in search of her mate, two other skillfully trained bearers would seize her and add her to this long, shackled coffle which already numbered over two hundred men, women and children destined for the cargo hold of the Portuguese slave ship and thence either to Havana, Mobile or New Orleans for sale as human cattle, cost-lier by far than their animal counterparts, certain to suffer more than those dumb brutes who would eventu-ally be slaughtered for food. For these human slaves were to feed other, crueler appetites by far than mere hunger.

It had pleased the Arabian slave trader to let Kar-mida go back to her village without telling her that by nightfall, when all in Mopti should be asleep, his raiders would fall upon them and take many more slaves—her, first of all. Thus he would get back the few gold coins he had given this treacherous Mandingo bitch, and Allah himself would applaud such a just punishment for her act of betrayal against her brother-in-law and his young wife.

The three brawny Senegalese had waited behind thick hedges along the path on which Djamba trotted back toward Mopti. They saw how proudly he had held aloft the bloodied spearhead fixed to the broken haft which he had taken from the heart of the black-maned lion, and they knew they must take him by stealth. One of them, creeping out from the hedge be-hind him, struck Djamba a fierce blow across the back

114

of his skull with a club made from baobab wood, felling him to the ground. His two companions bound the young Mandingo hand and foot, then trundled him back to the camp of their master. Meanwhile, the other two bearers lay in wait for Itulde.

Djamba's young bride, thinking only of her husband's agony, not even thinking to question Karmida's news in her own devotion and love for Djamba, had sobbingly hurried toward the path near the river to follow her husband's trail on to the Caves of the Dead. It was easily, swiftly done. One bearer clapped his hands over her mouth, his companion twisted her arms behind her back and expertly bound her wrists with a rawhide thong. Then both men lifted her and bore her back to the camp of Mougar ben Ali, taking care to place her in their master's hut so that the young Mandingo king would not see her and perhaps try to kill the raiders in his attempt to save her.

When the jackal barked at midnight near their camp, Mougar ben Ali and his aide Ishmael ben Nurali exchanged a smile. "It is a good omen," the Arab said as he gave the sign to his men. Thirty bearers with spears and muskets crept toward the sleeping village. Karmida, in betraying Djamba out of her lust for power and vengeance, had unwittingly let the wily slave trader know that few warriors guarded the village, for the Mandingos of Mopti lived in peace under their young ruler. So there was no fear of a pitched battle; the watchful sentry at the edge of the village who might have sounded the alarm was at once silenced by an assegai flung out of a thicket into his broad back.

An hour later, some twenty men, as many women and a dozen children, wrists shackled behind them and united on that communal chain, were herded back to Mougar ben Ali's camp. Among them was Karmida. Her fat young husband Bulwayo had had a spear thrust through his belly and he had died like a coward, weepingly begging the Senegalese bearer to spare his life. Karmida had been a little startled at this, but realized that it was even better: now she would be queen of the

Mopti. But when the slavers' men had dragged her out of her husband's hut and bound her to the others, she had shrieked aloud, "No, no, not me! Why do you chain me? Did I not give you Djamba and Itulde to earn my freedom?" And so the men and women of Mopti spat at her, knowing what evil she had done.

She had shrieked so loudly that the bearers had had to gag her, and when they reached the camp they took her out of the coffle and flung her down before the hut of Mougar ben Ali. Her maddened, tear-blurred eyes fell on Itulde, who lay there inside the door, bound and gagged. And the wife of Djamba saw the betrayer of her husband and herself come now to her own justice.

"In the morning, let that one be pegged out and given the whip, to bridle her lying and treacherous tongue," Mougar ben Ali had decreed. "For her I reserve the auction block at Port Said. Who knows, I may even decide to keep her as my own concubine. Has not the Prophet said that verily those who dig a pit for others shall fall into it themselves?"

Late that night, he had come out of his tent, stripped Karmida naked and savagely violated her. "This is part of your payment, treacherous Mandingo bitch," he had growled at her, partly in Arabic, partly in the *lingua franca* which was the universal tongue to many tribes. "I'll pay you well, better than gold. Tomorrow, when you're pegged out, I'll have Burbo, an artist with the lash, make you wriggle like a houri in that paradise which Mohammed promises the faithful. But this is payment of a kind as well, to show you what a man, not a weakling like your Bulwayo, does to a bitch who has ideas beyond her station!"

And at dawn, when the slavers began to prepare for the trek which would end at the harbor where the Portuguese ship awaited them, two of the bearers hammered four thick wooden pegs into the ground, and forced Karmida down on her belly and held her while they corded her wrists and ankles to spreadeagle her. One of them contemptuously squatted to tear away her gag, and Karmida began to babble: "Have mercy! I do not deserve such punishment, not after what I have done for you, oh Mougar ben Ali! You will earn much gold from the captives I have shown you how to take—why do you then have me whipped?"

Burbo, the giant Senegalese whose whipping artistry Mougar ben Ali had cited to Karmida, stared greedily down at the handsome plump naked victim offered to his talents. Striding into one of the nearby tents, he emerged with a long braided black leather whip affixed to a short, heavy, thick wooden stick. The whip itself was fully six feet in length, with knotted tip. Drawing the long lash back, Burbo made it crack ominously in the air several times over the stretched, shuddering naked body, and Karmida, turning her contorted face back over her shoulder, uttered a piercing scream: "Oh, not with that—oh have mercy!"

Burbo eyed his master questioningly. "Twenty, but don't cut the skin. I wish her to suffer, but not to be permanently marked," Mougar ben Ali pronounced sentence.

With superb virtuosity and expert cruelty, Burbo plied the braided whip across the sufferer's buttocks and upper thighs, never once cutting the skin, but inflicting dark, angry weals all over it. He took care not to crisscross any of the marks, which would assuredly have cut the skin and drawn blood. Yet by the time he had finished, Karmida lay convulsively jerking and twisting, bathed in sweat, half-fainting, her throat raw from the prolonged, inhuman shrieks which the lash had torn from her.

And that long inland trek to the port of Conakry had been an indescribable hell for young Djamba, shackled at the very head of the line in this coffle of captured slaves. His beautiful young wife Itulde had, by the slaver's order, been made the very last in that tragic processional of over two hundred destined for the slave ship. Mougar ben Ali was considerate enough to his victims, pausing several times during the torrid days of the march for a rest so that they might have water and food. But the burning sun, the ever-deadly tsetse fly and snakes like the deadly mamba, the puff adder and the cobra, which lurked silently in the thick-

117

ets of heavy grass through which the captives had to march, took their inevitable toll. By the end of the fortnight, thirty-four men, women and children had died. Yet Mougar ben Ali was not displeased, for he foresaw that the profits gleaned on those who had survived would more than compensate him for his loss.

It was little comfort for Djamba to learn that his treacherous sister-in-law, Karmida, who had arranged for Mougar ben Ali to abduct him and Itulde, had herself become a slave and that Bulwayo had been slain. For Djamba resented the shackles of servitude, he who had always been free, and most of all he agonized over the fate of his beautiful young bride. Others along that chained line passed down to him the news of Karmida's treachery and her subsequent fate, and told him how, often at night, when Mougar ben Ali rested in his tent, two of the Senegalese bearers dragged her into the tent to serve as the Arab's concubine. They did not harm Itulde, but Djamba was tortured by the thoughts of how he and his wife would be separated once they were aboard the slave ship and how they were certain to be separated forever when sold.

And then came the fateful day when they were marched aboard the Portuguese vessel, while Mougar ben Ali and the captain of the slaver settled their business with a transfer of gold to the Arab. He had decided to take Karmida back with him to Port Said, and by now the plump handsome wife of Bulwayo had been thoroughly cowed by her master. Frequent whippings had made her comply to his most lecherous desires. He had discovered early her talent for the servile way in which she had gratified her fat, almost impotent husband Bulwayo, and he took perverse delight in compelling this ambitious traitress to serve him in just such manner.

And then, the worst horror of all, on the seventh night of the voyage to that far-off land, Djamba had witnessed the cruel, unjust punishment and tragic death of his beautiful young wife. Just after sundown, Manuel Arrigar, the boatswain, a coarse-bearded Portuguese ruffian in his early forties who had made many

118

voyages with the same captain, had gone down to the women's section of the hold with bowls of rice and stew, but with his mind bent on satisfying his lusts. He knew that it was forbidden to take the maidenhead of a young and comely Fulani, Ashanti or Mandingo, since this would be to diminish their value, but this rule did not apply to the married captives. And his greedy eyes had already studied the shapely brown-skinned body of young Itulde from the very first moment that she had been brought aboard the ship.

He had retained the largest bowl of stew for Itulde, and moved to her now at one end of the hold as she crouched in the corner, weeping pitifully for the loss of her husband and the ruination of their lives. She wore only a loincloth, and her round, high-set breasts with their wide, dusky-coral aureolae had already inflamed him. He licked his lips as he moved toward her, a leer on his ugly face. Since he spoke several African dialects and knew her to be a Mandingo, he addressed her in her own tongue: "Here, dark-eyed gazelle, see what I have brought you! It's because you've found favor in my eyes."

In the same tongue, Itulde, lifting her face and staring at him with revulsion, exclaimed, "Touch me not, white jackal! If my man were here, he would tear you to pieces as he has done with the lion!"

Manuel Arrigar burst into jeering laughter, set down the bowl, then seized Itulde and crushed her against his panting chest, as his lips slavered over her neck and shoulders. What satiny, smooth, warm brown skin the bitch had! He was almost tempted to buy her from the captain, but he knew this could not be. But who was to know if he were to enjoy himself for a few moments with her, since she spoke no Portuguese and could not complain of the assault?

She fought desperately, but to no avail. The other women, staring dully or with curiosity, did not dare intervene. Three of them had already been flogged at the mast for having struck their captors at the moment of being brought aboard the vessel, and they were afraid.

Shackled as she was, weakened by sorrow and the

long, exhausting trek to the slave ship, she could not withstand his ferocious rut. In her agony, she shrieked out the name of her husband, and Djamba, who with the other men had been shackled on the other side of the hold, heard her piteous cries. He began to hammer on the door with his fists, cursing and crying out in his Mandingo tongue. Hearing the clamor, the second mate, Felipe Luna, a burly, one-eyed rogue feared for his cruelty to helpless blacks aboard the vessel, came down the wooden steps into the hold, a belaying pin in his right hand, and bellowed for silence.

Meanwhile, as her ravisher glutted himself upon her, Itulde dug her fingernails into his cheeks and raked them to draw blood. With a bellow of rage, the brutal boatswain wrenched himself out of her and staggered to his feet, put a hand to his cheek and stared at the blood on it. "I'll teach you to mark me, you African sow!" he roared. Seizing her, he forced her out of the hold and up to the wooden post at the back of the poopdeck which was used for flogging rebellious slaves. In a trice, he had her wrists gripped in the iron shackles fixed into the top of the post. Then, seizing a leather cat-o'-nine-tails, he moved behind her and swept the cat across her juttingly rounded satiny buttocks. Itulde writhed, jerking at her fettered wrists, her head flinging back, her eyes mad with suffering as her mouth gaped in a shrill cry of pain.

Felipe Luna had struck Djamba several times on the back and shoulders as he tried to silence the rebellious young Mandingo ruler. But Djamba, who continued to hear his wife's cries of agony in the foul embrace of her ravisher, had paid him no heed. With an angry curse, Luna raised the belaying pin and struck him viciously across the top of the skull. Djamba's eyes rolled in their sockets, and he fell unconscious to the floor.

After Manuel Arrigar finished the flogging, Itulde's naked body hung limply from the post. He seized a bucket of brine and doused her with it. She came awake, shrieking again in torment as the brine bit like acid into the bleeding welts left by the flogging. Then again, in his unspeakable rut, the boatswain ravaged her as she writhed helplessly before him. When he had finished, he unshackled her and let her sprawl, moaning feebly, to the deck.

Luna had unshackled the unconscious Djamba and, calling for another member of the crew to aid him, had dragged the young Mandingo up to the deck. They revived him by dousing him with a bucket of brine, and when Luna menaced him with the belaying pin and shouted to him in the jargon which served as communication between slaves and slavers, Djamba stared uncomprehendingly at him. Momentarily, he could neither hear nor speak. But his eyes strained toward the poopdeck, just in time to see his young wife lying sprawled on the timbers, and tears rolled down his cheeks.

Itulde slowly raised herself to her hands and knees, her body aflame, her loins aching from the bestial violation of the boatswain. Before anyone could intercept her or suspect her intent, the young wife of the Mandingo ruler ran toward the rail, clambered atop it, poised herself for a moment, then flung herself into the ocean.

A shout of alarm rose, but it was too late. A triangular black fin cut the water swiftly as a giant shark marked its prey. As the crew crowded against the rail to watch, they saw Itulde's naked, brown-skinned body suddenly jerk, then disappear, and heard her last shrill cry of agony.

Djamba saw too, and speech came back to him as he weepingly called out her name, the tears pouring down his cheeks as four men held his arms lest he try to follow his martyred wife.

The captain of the vessel had shown strange kindness to him then, as if regretting the cruelty of his seamen. He had Djamba taken to a small cabin near the hold, and sent in the young Gullah girl, seen to it that food and drink and care for his hurts were provided. And now he stood on this platform, still the proud Mandingo, but neither ruler nor husband, the slave of this strange, glowering man who could not take his eyes from him.

At least he was alive, and a man could be proud of that if he put his life to good usage. What the future would hold he could not tell. There was no *bokono* to read the *du* for him now.

Henry Bouchard turned to Pierre Lourat. "Keep him for me, Pierre. The three of us will enjoy a little of your special hospitality before we take the slave back to Windhaven."

CHAPTER NINE

"Mama, do you think Papa'll bring me back a nice present from New Orleans? Maybe some earrings or a pretty new dress?" Arabella anxiously asked her mother as Sybella, a knitted woolen shawl over her neck and shoulders as protection against the cool late afternoon air, pruned her geranium bed.

"I'm sure he'll bring you something, dear. But you're still a little too young for earrings, Arabella."

"But I'll be eleven in April, Mama," Arabella petulantly countered.

"I know why you want those earrings. You've had your first taste of being a grownup when you danced with that nice Bobby Jordan at the housewarming. Yes, that's it. But I told you, darling, you mustn't try to grow up too fast. That would spoil all the fun. And it's much too early for you to be thinking about having a young gentleman friend. Maybe in five years we'll talk about things like that."

"But by then Bobby Jordan will have got another girl and he won't like me anymore." Arabella's pert face clouded.

Sybella laughed softly, squatted down and grasped her daughter's wrists as she stared lovingly into the girl's suddenly misty dark-brown eyes. "You little dickens," she gently chided, "I see I'm going to have to give you your first lesson in dealing with boys. You mustn't ever want to throw yourself at a fellow, Arabella dear. It's much better if you let him think you're very, very special and hard to get. He'll be lots more interested in you, you'll see. And I'm pretty sure that Bobby Jordan isn't going to forget you soon. Why, after all, it's only a few weeks since we had our party, now, isn't it?"

"Why—yes, but—"

"Besides, I don't know any other pretty girls your age who live around here whom Bobby would be likely to meet. So I think the best thing for you to do, Arabella, is to just go on and let yourself grow up day to day, and one of these days, before you know it, if Bobby really likes you a lot—and I'm pretty sure he does—he'll come visiting by himself to call on you and court you."

"Oh, do you really think so, Mama?" Now she was wide-eyed with excitement and an exquisite flush suffused her dimpled, creamy cheeks.

Sybella nodded. "I'm sure of it. Now, see if you can find any weeds over there in the beds of daisies and marigolds."

"All right, Mama." Arabella reached out to hug and kiss her mother, then moved down the neatly arranged rows of flowers, each bed set off by a low lattice. "Just the same," she couldn't help adding, "I hope Papa brings me something nice. And something for Fleurette, too."

"Now that's a nice thought for a big sister to have for her little sister, dear," Sybella smilingly approved. Straightening, she called, "Why, here's Thomas, and he's got something—what is it, Thomas?"

The Ashanti tipped his straw hat with one hand as he came forward. "Found this little coon hiding in a log near the creek. His mama and little brothers and sisters, they're all dead. Dick, he's one of the new slaves Mr. Bouchard bought for hisself down in Mobile last year, he told me he never seen a coon before and he was scared 'cause he thought it was going to bite him, so he took a stick and hit it and the little ones."

"Oh how dreadful!" Sybella cried.

"Yes, Miz Bouchard. I gave him a good talking-to,

124

made him feel mighty ashamed. Then I found this little one—'pears to me he's no more than two weeks old."

"Oh, Mama, could I keep him for a pet? Fleurette and I would take real good care of him, we would!" Arabella exclaimed, staring at the tiny ball of grayish fur which Thomas cradled in his arms.

"Well, I don't know, honey," Sybella said doubtfully, glancing toward Thomas for help.

"When you git them this young, Miz Bouchard, m'am, you can train 'em to be nice 'n gentle. Like I said, this one's about two weeks old. Now you kin feed him by twisting a rag and dipping it in milk, 'cause that'll remind him how he used to suck on his mammy. I'll git a basket from Mammy Clorinda, and have her put some old rags in it for a bed. Also, beggin' your pardon, Miz Bouchard, the first couple of weeks you have to rub your finger on his tummy so's he'll piddle proper. His mammy showed him how to do that herself with her tongue when she was alive, you see."

"But won't it claw or bite, Thomas?" Sybella frowned uneasily.

"Not if you git it tame right off, Miz Bouchard. Now when it's about a month old or so, you jist have Missy Bella let it go out of the house and go where it wants. It'll be tame enough to know where its food is and to come back to a nice home like Windhaven, you can depend on that." His wrinkled face broke into a reminiscent grin. "My daddy got me one to play with when I was about twelve, I remember. 'Course, I was so busy helpin' him and growin' up I didn't take proper care of it and it finally ran away to shift for itself. But, no, m'am, it won't claw or bite Missy Bella if it's treated right from the very start, I promises you that."

"Oh, I love it—what a cute little black face it has! And its tiny little tail, it's got rings on it already!" Arabella gleefully clapped her hands again.

"It'll grow about twelve pounds, maybe up to sixteen or so, when it's got its full growth, Missy Bella," Thomas told her. "We're coming into better weather now, so it'll be jist fine if you let it out every day, maybe a couple times in the morning and afternoon, or just before you go to bed. It'll get used to Windhaven, you'll see. Not going to be anything around here going to harm Missy Bella's little coon. I'll tell all the field hands to watch out for it if they see it come out to the fields. Most likely, it'll start to climb trees and take itself a nap in the crotch of a nice big oak."

"Well, I guess it'll be all right, if you say so, Thomas. And I think it would be very nice for the children to have a pet. Especially Arabella here." Sybella gave her older daughter a whimsical glance. "Might take her mind off boys and such for a spell."

"I'm going to name him Bobby!" the little girl decided.

"Oh no, you aren't, young lady!" Sybella laughed. "That's hardly fair to Bobby. You know, it would be like pretending that Bobby is already your pet and you've got him wrapped around your little finger. And as I've already told you, you're far too young to start thinking such notions. Remember, it's all right for a woman to have a hold on her man, but she's smart if she doesn't let him see how she's doing it. And I'm sure that if Bobby Jordan ever heard that you named your little raccoon after him, he wouldn't take too kindly to it."

"Hmm," Arabella scowled and creased her forehead as she strove to find another name. "Well, how about Timmy, Mama?"

"That's all right, I think. Yes, it'll do very nicely. All right, Thomas will get the basket from Mammy Clorinda, and after you've helped me weed my garden, we'll go back to your room and see how it likes its new home."

A little later, while Sybella stood in the doorway and watched with mingled amusement and maternal pride, Arabella industriously knelt beside the basket, carefully lowering the milk-soaked cotton rag to the raccoon's mouth. Fleurette, kneeling on all fours on the other side, breathlessly watched the feeding process, and emitted squeals of pleasure when the tiny animal clasped its furry paws against the rag to keep it pressed against its eagerly sucking mouth.

126

At least, Sybella told herself, the introduction of Timmy into Windhaven would perhaps halt Arabella's impatience to be old enough for courting.

Up the marble steps and down a narrow corridor thickly carpeted with red velvet, Pierre Lourat led the two planters and Mark Bouchard, opened the door of the last room at the end and smilingly inclined his head to invite them to precede him. There were half a dozen round walnut tables with scrolled legs, covered with green velvet, at which elegantly dressed Creoles and more conventionally attired wealthy American merchants sat to take part in the games of roulette, baccarat and *vingt-et-un*.

There were even several attractive, stunningly gowned women at the tables, encouraging their escorts, and one, Henry Bouchard noticed with some surprise, piling her own chips on a *carré* for roulette.

"You are welcome to watch or to play, as you choose, gentlemen," Pierre Lourat smilingly declared. "Allow me first to offer you some champagne." He snapped his fingers, and from the far end of the room, a charming young chestnut-haired woman approached, bearing a tray on which were Venetian goblets filled with a sparkling golden liquid. She was about twenty-one, tall, with round, demure face and enormous hazel eyes, *retroussé* nose with delicately flaring wings, and a small, provocatively ripe mouth. Her hair was gathered into a thick chignon which fell below the nuque and gathered into a net made of silver threads; her rose-colored silk gown, which left her shoulders entirely bare and revealed the top of the wide cleft between her sumptuously round breasts, was modish with its flaring skirt and puffed sleeves.

As she approached the two planters and the gaping youth, she managed a pretty, deft curtsy while holding the tray steady, and then straightened, without tipping any of the goblets.

"Good evening, *messieurs*," she greeted them in a sweet, clear voice.

"This is Charmaine." Pierre Lourat reached for one

of the goblets and handed it to Henry Bouchard. "The best French champagne, imported from Paris." He then offered another goblet to Edward Williamson and a third to Mark Bouchard.

"Why, it's extremely cold! How delightful!" Henry declared, surprised.

"That is because we have ice at times, *M'sieu* Bouchard. Yes, it's quite a luxury, since it came from Maine on a sailing vessel and part of the cargo was lost before it could dock here in New Orleans. Understandably, what was left commanded quite a high price. We conserve it by keeping it in a zinc-lined box in the cellar. Others, I am told, sprinkle it with sawdust and keep it in a dry well. And of course it's available only during the winter season. But it does bring out the bouquet, does it not?"

"Tremendously exhilarating." Williamson had drained his goblet at almost a gulp and replaced it on the tray which Charmaine stood holding, her eyes detailing each of the trio and sending roguish glances to each one, as if she meant to intimate that she found all of them irresistible.

"To your very good health, *messieurs*," Pierre Lourat sipped from his goblet and inclined his head as he gave the toast. "Now, what's your pleasure?"

"I—I'd like to try my hand," Williamson nervously stammered. "But as for money—you see, Mister Bouchard has just given me a draft from the Mobile trading house where he arranged for the sale of my cotton—"

"Say no more. Your credit is good here so long as *M'sieu* Bouchard vouches for you. Now, would you care to try the wheel? Or perhaps *vingt-et-un*?"

"In that case, the wheel." Williamson's dry lips had begun to twitch and he nervously wetted them with the tip of his tongue.

"Certainly, *M'sieu* Williamson. If you will follow me, I'll find a place for you. And you, *M'sieu* Bouchard, and your handsome young son, would you care to join your friend?"

"I'll watch for a spell, Pierre," Henry decided.

"Let me try my hand just once, please, Pa," Mark pleaded.

"Well, I'll advance you a hundred dollars. If you lose, don't come back to me for more. I suppose it won't do any harm to know something of the vice of gambling—seeing that you are already acquainted with women and appear to have enjoyed that vintage champagne," his father said drily. Taking out his purse, he handed Mark several banknotes issued by the major Mobile bank which handled the principal accounts of the cotton trading house. "There you are."

"Thanks, Pa. I'll see if I can't win for you, and I'll split my winnings—fair enough?"

"Fairer than what happened with Celia," Henry couldn't help riposting. Mark sent him an angry look, flushing hotly, and then strode after Edward Williamson, whom Pierre Lourat ushered to an empty chair at the table where the handsome woman appeared to be as earnest a gambler as her male companions.

As the planter seated himself, a stocky, florid-faced man in a green frock coat and rumpled cravat angrily rose from his chair on the other side of the woman with a hoarse exclamation: "That cleans me out! That damned wheel can't be honest!"

The owner of the establishment swiftly moved beside the angry loser and, in a soft voice that reached only the latter's ears, said, "*M'sieu* Carver, your remark was indiscreet, don't you agree? If you mean to imply that either my croupier or my wheel is dishonest, I shall demand satisfaction of you."

The man's puffy, scowling face turned scarlet, and his eyes widened. "I—I didn't mean any harm, Mister Lourat," he stammered. "It's just that I've had a bad losing streak. No offense meant."

"Then in that case, none taken. I grieve that you lost so much tonight, *M'sieu* Carver, but perhaps another night you will break the bank. Allow me to offer you some champagne, and, if your choler has not disturbed your appreciation for my accommodating *filles*, it would be my pleasure to offer you whomever you desire to be your companion for the night. And of course, *ça va sans dire*, there will be no charge whatsoever—it will be my pleasure."

"Well, sir, at least you're a gentleman. Very well, I'll accept. Damnation, at least I'll have some enjoyment out of this wretched night," the man grumbled, though obviously appeased, and began to grin fatuously as Charmaine approached with her tray of goblets filled to the brim with the sparkling wine.

Williamson found himself seated at the right of the mature but still beautiful woman who had a single stack of chips before her and now, tapping the tip of her forefinger against her dainty little Grecian nose with just the hint of a dimple, was deciding on the next number to play. The tall, gaunt-faced, moustachioed croupier, in a long black frock coat, his eyes impassive, waited for the players and encouraged them with a pleasant, *"Faites vos jeux, messieurs et madame!"*

Mark, having exchanged his banknotes for a small stack of chips, placed one of them on the square of the green velvet cloth which sectioned off with white dye the numbers 16 through 19, then leaned back and unabashedly stared at the attractive woman. Her dark-brown hair was drawn up over her high-arching forehead to give full display of her sensitive oval face, and pinned in a mass of tiny curls at the nape of her slim neck. Her cheekbones were high-set and her mouth was sensual, small but full. Her red taffeta gown bared creamy shoulders and its bodice just hinted at the valley between proud, round, thrusting breasts. There was rice powder on her cheeks and her lips were moist. Suddenly she turned to look at Mark, her dark-brown eyes soft and warm, and a faint little smile curved her lips as she murmured, *"Bon soir, m'sieu."*

He was about to reply, when the croupier's voice rose above the murmur of conversation round the table, *"Rien ne va plus!"* as the wheel was spun. Mark cleared his throat, flushed hotly, his nostrils dilating at the strong scent of the woman's perfume as well as the nearness of her creamy bare shoulders.

"Tiens, you've won, *m'sieu,"* she uttered a soft little laugh and gestured toward the table. Mark turned to

see the croupier shoving chips toward him. *"Le numero dix-sept a gagné, m'sieu,"* the croupier explained.

"You've brought me luck," Mark said huskily. He reached toward the white-dyed squares and this time placed three chips on the same *carré*. "I'll stick to this for the time being."

"You are quite a handsome fellow, *m'sieu,* and you make up your mind quickly," the woman murmured to him as she reached out to put two of her chips on the same square.

Once again the wheel was spun and Mark won again, to his great delight.

Charmaine now moved toward the table, paused behind him and to his right and in her sweet voice asked, "May I serve *m'sieu* another glass of champagne?"

"Yes, and the lady will have one too," Mark exclaimed as he reached for two goblets and handed one to the woman beside him. Then, with a grandiose gesture, he tossed two chips onto the tray. "It's for you," he said to the girl.

"M'sieu is generous. *Merci bien."* She dropped him a dainty curtsy and then moved round the table.

"My name is Mark Bouchard," he murmured to the woman as he lifted his glass toward her.

She clinked glasses with him. "And mine is Louisa Voisin, *M'sieu* Bouchard," she answered in almost a whisper.

Henry, standing off to one side, smiled grimly as he watched his precocious son's progress as both gambler and *bon vivant.* Then he looked over to Edward Williamson, and frowned to see that the latter's pile of chips had dwindled by a good half. His eyes narrowed and glistening, his face taut, his lips compressed, the gray-haired planter leaned forward, his fingers fumbling with the chips as he made his bets, haphazardly placing several chips on this square, others on another well beyond the first stake, and then several on the word *"Noir"* designated on one of the dye-marked squares. Again the croupier spun the wheel, and the ball settled on the red and a number covered by none of Williamson's chips. The inexorable rake drew the chips off the table, and Edward Williamson shook his head and leaned back with a groan of exasperation.

Half an hour later, Mark had won three hundred dollars, and, pleased with his first success, decided to call a halt to his evening's play. Again he beckoned to Charmaine to bring more champagne for himself and his fascinating neighbor.

"You've really brought me luck, Louisa! You aren't married, are you?" he whispered, staring hungrily at her shoulders.

She lifted a little lacquered fan, opened it and hid her smile, but her eyes danced with amusement as she contemplated him a moment. Then she shook her head: "Oh no, *M'sieu* Mark. Is that your father standing over there talking to *M'sieu* Lourat?"

"Yes, it is. Why, do you know him, Louisa?"

For an instant, her eyes grew veiled, as she glanced swiftly toward the stocky black-haired man who was earnestly whispering to the Creole dandy. Then, shrugging her beautiful bare shoulders, she replied, "I don't think so. New Orleans is such a big city, one sees so many people in the course of a year it's hard to remember." Then, after a significant pause and lowering her voice, she murmured, "But I don't think I should forget someone like you, *M'sieu* Mark. You're handsome, young, you make your own decisions quickly and you've much force and strength."

"Louisa—I mean—I think we're going to stay here a few days—I'd like to see you again, maybe take you to dinner or something?" he blurted, nervously glancing at his father, who was still intent on his conversation with the owner of the gambling room.

"That can be arranged. Understand, I don't let just anyone come to visit me. But if you wish to get in touch with me, you've only to tell *M'sieu* Lourat. He'll get word to me, you see. Shall we say, he is a business associate of mine. And now I must go. Thank you for the champagne and your nice compliments, *mon joli gars*." As she rose, Mark Bouchard awkwardly rose to his feet, almost stumbling backward and righting himself with an effort, his face turning crimson with annoyance at his own clumsiness. Her soft little fluted laugh made him scowl, but that quickly vanished when she leaned forward and gave him a swift, stinging kiss on the chin, whispering, "Till we meet again, *mon cher*."

As she walked toward the door of the gambling room, Pierre Lourat excused himself to Henry Bouchard and moved toward her. "I'm glad you were here tonight, *ma belle*. I've just thought of a way in which you can help reduce the size of your account. Why don't you wait for me in my office till my guests have finished their gambling? I think we've something mutually beneficial to discuss."

"As you say, Pierre." Her eyes lowered, her lips tightened, and then, her head high, with a last long glance back at the table where Mark still stood goggling at her and touching the place on his chin she had just kissed, she sent him a dazzling smile and left the room.

Half an hour later, Edward Williamson abruptly rose to his feet, his face ashen-pale, his eyes haggard. Pretty Charmaine approached, offering the tray of champagne-filled goblets, and he seized one and downed it almost with a single gulp, putting the goblet back on the tray with a trembling hand. Then, unsteadily, he made his way to Henry Bouchard and Pierre Lourat. "I'm wiped out, Henry. I owe this gentleman five thousand dollars. Will you see that it's taken out of the draft on my cotton?"

"Of course, Ed. I'll go to Antoine Rigalle's bank in the morning and negotiate these drafts from Mobile—I've got to take my commissions out of them anyway. Don't worry, you've still a tidy sum left to take back with you," Henry Bouchard said, grinning.

"And now, gentlemen," the Creole smoothly rejoined, "may I offer you diversion at *Les Extases*? It is one of three *maisons de joie* which I maintain for the entertainment of admired and discriminating clients such as yourselves."

Henry Bouchard's eyes glittered with concupiscent anticipation as he nodded. "It'll be my treat, Ed. You

133

know the old saying, unlucky at cards, lucky at love—perhaps an hour with one of Pierre's delightful wenches will inspire you to a winning streak tomorrow night."

"Yes—maybe it will. I'd like to try to recoup my losses in any case." The gray-haired planter fumbled for a kerchief and wiped the perspiration off his deeply creased forehead.

Mark Bouchard now joined his father and Edward Williamson, swaggering with adolescent satisfaction after his encounter with Louisa Voisin. He had been just in time to hear the Creole offer his father and the widower an amorous partner for the night, and now brashly interposed, "Pa, I'll pay for my own girl—I won back your stake and enough to pay my own way, if you've no objection."

Pierre Lourat eyed the youth, his face blandly deferential. "Perhaps, *M'sieu* Bouchard, your son is one of those fortunate few who are lucky at both cards and love, *n'est-ce-pas?*"

As his father gave him a sour look, Mark emptied his pockets of chips and handed back the original stake of a hundred dollars. "There, we're even, Pa. Give the rest to Mister Lourat and have him pick a real looker for me—like that girl who was at the table with me just now."

"Your son has excellent taste, *M'sieu* Bouchard. Come along then, gentlemen. I'll send you off in a carriage to *Les Extases* with a note to Madame Julie who is in charge of the establishment. She'll see to it that you have no reason to complain of Pierre Lourat's New Orleans hospitality."

"Thanks, Pierre," Henry chuckled and clapped the Creole on the back so vigorously that the latter winced. "I'll drop over to your auction rooms tomorrow as soon as I've had a chance to cash these drafts. I'll pay you for Djamba and my friend Ed's debt of honor."

"There's no rush at all, *mon ami*."

"Henry—if you don't mind, could you get the balance in cash for me?" Edward Williamson suddenly

134

put in, his voice hoarse and shaking. "I'll be back tomorrow night to see if I can't get back what I've lost."

"Of course, if you want it that way, Ed. But now, let's not think of sordid money matters, let's surrender ourselves to the pleasures of the flesh, as one might say, eh, Pierre?" Again Henry Bouchard dealt Pierre Lourat a hearty buffet between his shoulderblades, and the Creole stiffened, his eyes hard with anger for a tiny moment. Then, with the affable smile of a complaisant host, he smoothly replied, "Ah, but it is somewhat more than pleasure. That is why I have called my little rendezvous *Les Extases* . . . the ecstasies. Madame Julie will make certain that you understand the difference, I assure you."

In his private office, just off the auction room where Djamba had been displayed, Pierre Lourat sat at his desk and, opening a silver snuffbox, took a pinch and delicately patted it into his nostrils. Across from the desk, in a cherrywood chair with a stately, high back and deeply scrolled arms, the dark-haired woman who had been Mark Bouchard's neighbor attentively eyed the Creole's every studied move. Finally, an impatient frown lining her high-arching forehead, she leaned forward to demand, "And now, are you going to tell me what you meant about settling my debt to you, *M'sieu* Lourat?"

Sniffing fastidiously, the Creole now reached for a glass of Bordeaux, meditatively sipped at it, then set down the glass and smiled at the beauty before him. "Gently, *ma chérie*. It was quite fortunate for both of us that you decided to pay me a visit and that I allowed you credit enough to play at the table tonight. I see that you made a conquest of young *M'sieu* Mark Bouchard. Doubtless you have your own motives, *ma belle*. And I have mine."

"You're a devil, Pierre! But I've no choice—"

"Oh, but you do, *ma jolie*," he suavely interposed. "You could always enter one of my *maisons de joie*. Even though you're approaching your thirty-ninth birthday—forgive me, but in my business I must always be accurate about the age and condition of merchandise—"

"How dare you insult me so!" She half-rose from the chair, a furious blush suffusing her powdered cheeks.

"I didn't mean to offend you, *chérie*. Now, sit down like a good girl and I'll tell you what I've in mind. When your estimable father, Philippe Entrevois, died of fever three years ago, his banking house was in deplorable condition. He was a sentimentalist, your father, which is not to his discredit in the least, except insofar as it cast you into a state of, shall we say, elegant poverty. Now with a beautiful woman, that's a condition which can easily be altered for the better."

"Please spare me your histories, *M'sieu* Lourat," she said.

"I'm afraid I must refresh your memory on a certain part of these histories, as you call them. Now as it happens, Antoine Rigalle is not only a dear friend but also an esteemed client. Having never married, he understandably visits my establishments of Venus quite frequently. And, being one of the most solvent and respected bankers in all New Orleans, it's only natural that, as we became friends, he would confide in me, not only as to the monetary dealings of his rivals but also concerning their private lives. That, *ma belle*, is how I happen to know that you, his daughter, have a trace of *sang nègre* in your aristocratic veins. It appears that your esteemed father's grandmother was a beautiful West Indian black who so bewitched Philippe's grandfather that he manumitted her and wed her quite legally."

"Must you eternally remind me of that?" She turned her face away from him, closing her eyes and compressing her lips, her magnificent bosom heaving with sudden emotion.

"Yes, it seems I must. The debtor's plight is not yet viewed sentimentally by our New Orleans courts. The archaic law provides that, where the taint of black blood is found in the wife or the daughter or even the son of a man who dies before his creditors can be satisfied, that survivor may be sold into slavery, the

136

proceeds being awarded to the creditors. I knew this, and that is why I offered you a post as a kind of aide to me. Not only did I settle a regular stipend on you, but I also obligingly paid many of your extravagant expenses for clothing and the exquisite furnishings of the apartment in which you live. Nor was I ungentlemanly enough to suggest that you pay me back by joining the staff of the very accomplished young ladies under the supervision of Madame Julie."

"Thank you for your kindness, *M'sieu* Lourat." Her voice trembled with shame and rage.

He held up a placating hand. "Do not be vexed with me, *ma belle*. Your talents and your beauty befit you for a much more suitable and profitable role, and that's what I'm getting to at the moment. You know that all I've asked of you these past three years is to visit the gambling room and to encourage my fatuous patrons to be more daring than usual. And thus far you've done rather well for me. Only this time, as I began to tell you, we can combine our motives in this partnership, each for the other's profit. And unless I misunderstood what Antoine Rigalle once told me, you will have a chance for your revenge."

"Revenge?" she echoed, mystified.

Pierre Lourat nodded. "I saw you stare at Henry Bouchard when he was talking to me. Yes, you met him and his father Lucien at the counting house of Antoine Rigalle, about nineteen years ago. Rigalle, you see, had learned something of the story from his old patron Jules Ronsart, who knew Lucien well. So, wanting to learn more about your mother and father, I sent one of my men to Mobile to search through the old records of births and deaths and marriages, *tu me suives, chérie?*"

"Have done with it, I beg of you!" Her voice was faint and quivering.

"Very shortly. It appears that your mother was one Edmée de Bouchard. Apparently, she had married old Lucien's elder brother, who was killed in the slave revolt in Haiti. To escape Port-au-Prince, your mother willingly sold herself under indenture to a French sea

137

captain, who brought her to Mobile. There old Lucien Bouchard met her and purchased her indenture, only to set her free and provide for her occupation as a seamstress. She then married your father. Thus, although your lamented mother had not a trace of impurity to her, you do because of your father's blood lines. Then your father took a quadroon mistress to his bed a few months after your mother's death. From that union, there is your half sister Rosa, who is nearly eighteen. Thus, for her sake as well as your own, *ma chérie*, I urge you to use your wit and your beauty to avoid the auction block or the fate of a *putaine*."

The woman bowed her head, covered her face in her hands and sobbed softly. Recovering after a moment, she said dully, "Yes, my mother told me about Lucien Bouchard. And I do remember meeting his son in Rigalle's counting house. And now his grandson seems to be enamored of me."

"But that's perfect, don't you see?" Pierre Lourat slyly chuckled as he leaned forward across the desk. "Henry Bouchard doesn't recognize you, and of course my having suggested that you change your name from Louisette Entrevois to Louisa Voisin will aid our profitable little deception. I did that also to save you from the civil authorities, just in case they wished to pursue the matter of your father's outstanding debts. Now old Lucien, though he is still alive, rarely comes to New Orleans. He must be well into his seventies by now, I think—yes, I'm sure of it."

He stopped to sip his wine as the woman fidgeted, then resumed: "Henry Bouchard, to all practical purposes, will inherit a great deal of river-front land, which produces the best cotton in the state of Alabama. I've made inquiries about the Bouchard family, you see, as well as about your own, *ma belle*. There's an older son, Luke, but from what I'm told he's a dreamer like his grandfather. So it will be young Mark, the pride and the strength now of the Bouchard line, who stands closest to all that valuable estate. If you were to intrigue him into marriage, you would have a powerful hold upon the Bouchard fortune in due course. Come, don't look at me like that. You're still damnably beautiful and you know it. No one would take you for a woman approaching forty, believe me, not even I myself, and I know something of women, as you may well believe." He chuckled cynically.

"Let your half sister Rosa pose as your slave. Use her if need be to entrap this lustful boy—oh yes, I saw how he could scarcely keep his eyes from your bare shoulders and how his fingers twitched to husk that taffeta gown from you. Compromise him, offer him Rosa if need be, promise him the delights of a harem once he weds you, and the marriage can be performed here in New Orleans before his father's any the wiser—or old Lucien too, for that matter. Then I'll personally write off all the debts your lamented father incurred, clear your name forever, and you will be your own mistress and, one day, the queen of one of the richest estates in all of Alabama. Now, is that so dreadful a prospect?"

"No. No, it isn't, Pierre. Lucien loved my mother, she told me so. But he was such a prig, such a virtuous saint, he always held it against her because she married his brother Jean. Didn't he understand her parents wanted her to be a countess, and that she would have been his loving sweetheart all the same? Yes, you're right." Her lips had tightened into a sadistic grimace. "Nothing would suit me more than to pay them all back, those lordly Bouchards. Mark asked if he could see me again very soon. I told him to get word to you, and you'd arrange it."

She rose from her chair, and Pierre Lourat came from around the desk to kiss her hand as he said admiringly, "There are going to be hard times ahead, *ma chérie*. Get yourself married to Mark Bouchard, and one day you and I will be able to control that valuable property which will mean much more than specie or even jewels."

As she opened the door to go out, the suave Creole mockingly added, "Never forget, *ma jolie*, just in case you're tempted to cross me, that in a court of law you and Rosa have a bloodline almost exactly the same—

139

which means you and she are octoroons, hence liable to sale at auction should you both be left entirely destitute. A word to the wise, eh, *chérie*?"

Babette, the slim, olive-skinned, black-haired nineteen-year-old *fille de joie* whom Madame Julie had sent to an upstairs room with Mark Bouchard, lay whimpering on the rumpled bed, burying her tear-stained face in the pillow. Her robe lay on the floor, and on her buttocks and thighs and lower back there blazed the angry striations left by Mark Bouchard's leather belt.

"Stop your sniveling, you pretty little bitch, and turn over, unless you want a little more," the youth, naked but for his boots, menaced her as he brought the belt down once again across the tops of her lithe, long thighs.

With a piteous wail, Babette hastily rolled over on her back, holding up her clasped hands to petition mercy. "*Plus, plus du fouet, je t'en prie, m'sieu*! I'll do anything you wish, oh please, no more!"

"That's more like it," he sniggered as, flinging down the belt, he mounted her and brutally possessed her.

CHAPTER TEN

It was well past midnight when Louisa Voisin dismounted from the carriage in which Pierre Lourat had thoughtfully sent her to the little house on Eglantine Street, just off Royal. He had acquired the house nearly four years ago when its elderly merchant owner had lost it to him on a turn of the wheel in a desperate all-or-nothing stake. The Creole dandy had occasionally used the charming little house with its inner courtyard facing a lavish garden as a *maison de luxe* for several of his most accomplished girls. But when the daughter of Philippe Entrevois had gone to him and implored him to help her escape the inevitable consequences of her father's bankruptcy, the wily entrepreneur had installed her and young Rosa in the house and engaged her services to lure wealthy men to his gambling tables and to induce them to take greater risks than they ordinarily would by tempting them with the promise of her still maddeningly desirable body.

Although she had played the role of *demi-vierge* with consummate artistry these last few years, the ironic fact was that she was still a virgin despite her mature age. When she had been seventeen, Philippe Entrevois had arranged for her betrothal to the son of a rival banker with whom he was on the friendliest of terms. It had been a calculated maneuver to form an alliance between their two houses for the sake of greater financial strength to his own house—but the young man had contracted yellow fever and died a week later. Louisette—to give her her real name—had then been sent to a private Catholic school for young ladies in the suburb of Gretna, where she remained until shortly after her eighteenth birthday. It had been part of Philippe Entrevois' careful plan to build as impeccable a background for the daughter of Edmée de Bouchard as he could manage, in order to spare his daughter the disgrace of being described as a "*femme de couleur*." To that end, he had even gone so far as to circulate the contrived story that Louisette Entrevois had actually been his stepdaughter, not his own daughter by Edmée, and that the latter had been impregnated by her own husband just before he was murdered by Haitian rebels.

Of course Philippe Entrevois had counted on the fact that after so long, there would be few persons alive who would remember the actual facts: that he had met Lucien Bouchard's first sweetheart in Mobile, working as a seamstress after Lucien had bought her indenture from Jabez Corrigan, captain of the vessel which had brought Edmée from Haiti to Mobile, possessed her one night as a master would a slave so as to purge himself for all time of the effect she had had upon him, and then manumitted her. But Edmée had told her young daughter the story of Lucien's devotion back in Normandy and how she had married his older brother Jean to secure the title. Thus Louisette understood only too well that Philippe Entrevois was her true father and that his grandmother had in truth been a black of surpassing beauty but unequivocally a black slave.

Her life indeed might have been altered if the planned marriage between herself and the banker's son had come off; then she would have been secure, the wife of a handsome young man whose own blood lines for generations betrayed no such damning taint as hers. And she had been mildly curious over what would have been expected of her on the wedding night, since Maurice, her affianced and intended, had already managed to stir her senses with his ardent kisses and

142

caresses. At the finishing school, however, though it was strictly supervised, Louisette was seduced by her wanton roommate, a nineteen-year-old blonde, Vivienne Monrier, who had already experimented with all the sensual vices and whose elderly uncle and guardian had finally sent her to this school in the vain hope that the holy sisters would ameliorate her nature.

Consequently, her own pronounced carnal senses having been feverishly awakened by Vivienne's expert tutelage, Louisette Entrevois no longer sought marriage as the perfect escape from the deadly secret stigma of her lineage. Several times, her concerned father urged her to consider a suitable fiancé, but Louisette found this or that wrong with him and put her father off year after year. After her mother's death, she was shocked when Philippe Entrevois went to one of the famous quadroon balls and arranged with the mother of a strikingly handsome girl named Diana to provide for them both and to install his young mistress in a charming little cottage on Rampart Street. When Rosa was born from that union, Philippe Entrevois took Diana and the baby into his own house, ostensibly as his slave housekeeper and her illegitimate child by an unknown father. This only served to estrange Louisette all the more from her father and to make her determined not to offer her own virginal body to the thoughtless rut of a virile man.

Since Philippe Entrevois had never had a son and his wealth had seemed stable enough to assure her of security even in the event of his death by the terms of his will which he had once confided to her, Louisette had sealed her resolve never to marry. Yet the sudden financial failure of his banking house and the subsequent shocking awareness of her perilous status before the inexorable law had made her turn to Pierre Lourat for an immediate salvation. And now, he who held all the cards had determined to play them, and she was still pale and trembling from the harrowing realization of what must be done. But now, the corroding catalyst of hatred had been added to this devil's brew: Edmée, in revealing to her the association she had had with

143

Lucien Bouchard, had painted him in the worst possible colors and, self-pityingly, had portrayed herself as the luckless, despoiled victim of a prudish, selfish man's inordinate lust.

Doffing her pelisse and dainty bonnet, she went down the hallway to the room which young Rosa occupied, knocked lightly, and entered.

There was a startled cry as her half sister awoke, propping herself up on an elbow and blinking her eyes to accustom herself to the darkness, broken only by the flickering of the little candle in its porcelain holder which the older woman carried in her left hand. "Oh—I—I was asleep, *ma soeur*," the girl faltered.

"I'm sorry to have wakened you, dear Rosa. But we must talk. It's very important, dear. No, no, lie still, I'll sit here in this chair. There, I'll set the candle down on the night table."

Rosa, who bore the surname of Bonhomme, which her real father had bestowed upon her to strengthen his fabrication of her birth, was four months away from her eighteenth birthday. Of medium height, with gentle, heart-shaped face and extraordinarily large, limpid dark-brown eyes, a soft sweet mouth with tremulous lower lip, she was already excitingly endowed with a nubile, ripening figure. Her glossy jet-black hair fell in a thick sheaf almost to her waist, intensifying the pallor of her pale skin with only the faintest overtones of ochre, a tint which betrayed her origin. Her white silk nightshift emphasized the succulent, high-perched rounds of her firm bosom, hugged the lissome waist which flared into alluringly rounded hips and upstandingly curvaceous buttocks and beautifully rounded, soft satiny thighs. In a soft, melodious voice, her exquisite face taut with anxiety, she stammered, "Please tell me—please, Louisette, what's wrong?"

"Shh, darling. Now first, you must always call me Louisa. Even between us from now on, *tu comprends*? You know very well that *M'sieu* Lourat has had me change my name so that the authorities won't do anything to us because of what happened to poor Papa's bank."

"Yes—I—I'd forgotten. But it's so late—what's happened—oh please, I'm worried—"

"Now there's nothing to worry about, darling," the woman gently reassured her, reaching out to caress Rosa's quivering cheek. "This concerns us both, sweetheart. But I'm going to have to ask you to be a very good girl and to do something very brave for me, your Louisa. Louisa, you will remember, won't you, Rosa dear?"

"Yes—yes, of course I'll remember—tell me, what is it, please tell me!" the young octoroon insisted, sitting up now and clasping her hands in anguish.

"You remember the story my mother told me about the man whom she loved and who let her marry his brother, Rosa? The man who bought her as an indentured slave in Mobile and used her like a slave so shamefully?"

"Yes, *ma soeur*, you've told me."

"You mustn't call me sister, not ever again! Be very careful of that," Louisette Entrevois said between her teeth, her eyes narrow and cruel as they fixed on the frightened young girl's anxious face.

"I don't understand—what do you wish of me, L—Louisa?" Rosa faltered.

Louisette Entrevois bent down and kissed Rosa tenderly on the mouth, her hands stroking the soft bare arms, crooning to the girl as if in truth she were the latter's mother and not sired by the same progenitor. "Don't make me be angry with you, I don't want to be cruel to my darling one," she breathed. "Now listen very carefully. That man, old Lucien Bouchard, has a grandson named Mark. He's just a boy, but he'll be the heir to the rich Windhaven plantation and fortune. Pierre Lourat has ordered me to make him fall in love with me, do you understand? Enough so that he'll marry me, young though he is."

"Yes, I think I understand that. But how am I to help, Louisa?"

Louisette Entrevois stepped back and shifted the candle on the night table so that its flame illumined her own exotically lovely face. "You're going to have to

145

pretend that you're my slave, darling. And when Mark comes to visit me, as he will tomorrow or the next night, I'm certain of it, I'm going to tell him that if he marries me, he can have you as his bed wench. And I'm afraid I'll have to prove what I say by letting him make love to you."

"Oh no, Louisette, *par pitié, pas ça!*" the young octoroon shrank back, a hand to her mouth, her eyes enormous and shadowed with fear and revulsion.

Louisette reached out and slapped her half sister's cheek so cruelly that the red mark stood emblazoned on the ivory skin, drawing a strangled cry of pain. "You must, do you understand? Don't worry, it'll only be the one time, I promise you that. He'll be so crazy about you, he'll think that he can have you every night once he marries me, and me into the bargain, that he'll do just about anything. Don't you understand, Rosa? If we don't do what Pierre Lourat says, both of us may have to end up in one of his houses, taking on any man who has the price to enter it. Do you know what that would mean? You, my sweet little half sister, a virgin, entertaining some drunken planter from a surgarcane plantation, or some riverboat ruffian who doesn't know what a well-bred lady is like? And I—I too would have to submit to that horror. No, Rosa, you must do this for me. Once I can make Mark Bouchard marry me, then we both can live in style, never have to worry about money again, never be in debt to anyone, least of all Pierre Lourat. Please, my sweetheart, say you'll do it for me!"

"Oh please, please, I can't—you know that I've never been with a man—please—"

As the girl burst into tears, Louisette seized her by the shoulders and rolled her over onto her stomach. Then, rucking up the silk shift, and pinning Rosa down with her left palm against the small of the girl's supple back, she began to spank the girl's naked buttocks with all her might. Rosa sobbed and squealed, kicking and twisting, but Louisette Entrevois restrained her and continued till at last Rosa cried out between sobs,

"Aiii! *Assez, je meurs, arretez, par pitié*—ooh—*oui—oui, je ferai tout ce que vous voulez!*"

Louisette Entrevois straightened, panting, her eyes glistening, and then swiftly began to undress. When she was naked, she clambered in beside the still sobbing octoroon, and gently turned Rosa over to face her, her hands stroking the vividly splotched buttocks as she drew the girl to her. "Don't cry, little one—there, there, it'll be fine, you'll see! Now I'll love you, to make up for the spanking—you're going to be my little slave, aren't you, you're going to be obedient, it'll make us both free! Yes, yes, kiss me, there and there—*je t'aime, ma petite* Rosa!"

"It's good to see you again, Antoine!" Henry Bouchard strode into the private office of the Creole banker with eagerly outstretched hand. "By God, life certainly agrees with you here in New Orleans. You don't look a day older than when I saw you last and you recommended father's fine architect, that fellow Maurice Arnaut."

It was true. Antoine Rigalle had just turned fifty-one, and his hair was silver-gray, but he was still tall and supple and quick of movement, just as he had been twenty-four years ago on the occasion of their first meeting, when young Rigalle had been a clerk in the counting house of old Jules Ronsart. Both Ronsart and the wonderful Arabian palomino which the former had purchased from Lucien Bouchard to give the founder of Windhaven a stake in this new world had long since passed to their eternal reward. And under the astute management of the clerk who had become Ronsart's successor, the House of Ronsart and Rigalle—as it was now called by way of the former clerk's graceful tribute to his old employer—had prospered and become perhaps the most solid of all private banks in the entire Queen City.

"If it's a question of compliments, *mon ami*," Rigalle energetically shook Henry Bouchard's hand, "I'll say the same for you. The exception is that I hardly see a

147

single gray hair in your head whereas, alas, mine has not a dark one left."

"I also remember how you suggested that we enjoy an evening at *Les Extases*," Lucien's son slyly countered, "and this time I've taken your advice before I called on you. Though from what Pierre Lourat tells me, you old devil, you're still a celebrated and frequent guest at the establishment. So you've never married?"

"No, perhaps because this business is such a demanding mistress, what with President Jackson's shifting of currencies and his outspoken distaste for the Bank of the United States. He's a man of the people, and he's caught the popular feeling that too large an institution will favor the very rich. Still and all, *mon ami*, we've plenty of wealthy residents in our fair city, and of course as a private banker, I wholeheartedly endorse the partiality our homespun President shows for private enterprise. But now, sit down and let me pour some sherry for you and ask you how I may be of service. The Bouchard account, needless to say, continues to grow and merits our utmost attention here. And I say that not just out of friendship for that wonderful father of yours, Lucien. By the way, how is the old gentleman?"

"Still as spry as ever and still lecturing me against the evils of acquiring land and slaves, I'm afraid, Antoine. Ah, that's capital sherry, though I'm not usually a drinking man this early in the day. Well, I'd like to put part of this draft of mine into my account here and have the rest in cash. I've bought a prime field hand from Lourat, and I need a little money for expenses." He drew the Mobile draft for his cotton out of his inner waistcoat pocket and laid it before the Creole banker. "Now here's one made out to Edward Williamson, my good neighbor. He'd like all of his in cash, if that's possible."

"*Mais certainement*, only I'm sure you're going to advise your friend to be very careful with so much money in his possession. There are still thieves and rogues afoot at night, despite our patrols and our new gaslights along the main streets, you know."

"I rather fancy my friend is going to take all of that money directly to the gambling room. Last night he dropped five thousand dollars on Lourat's wheel." Henry Bouchard laid down another draft. "You see, he's already endorsed it. And of course I'll vouch for him, but the Mobile house is one you know to be solid enough to honor."

"But of course. You've others, *M'sieu* Henry?"

"I have three more, made out to James Cavendish, Benjamin Harnesty and Frank Ellerby. Since they are in debt to me for the cost of their seed and my having ginned their cotton for them this last season, I'll tell you what cash I want taken out, and then you can give me drafts on your house made out to them for the balance. Here's the total amount of their indebtedness, I've written it down on a separate bit of paper for you. And here is also a paper which all of them have signed authorizing me to act as their factor in the matter."

"Quite proper, quite legal. And they're all on the same Mobile house, so we'll have no problems whatsoever. Well now, since it's near the lunch hour, why don't I turn these drafts over to my chief clerk, and you and I will enjoy some really beautiful *courtbouillon*."

"Now that's a dish I'm not familiar with, Antoine."

"It's one of the finest Creole culinary inventions, I assure you, *mon ami!*" The banker kissed his own fingertips in an effusive gesture to designate the superlative. "One uses red fish, cooked in an iron pot. You chop onion and then brown it in a flour and oil roux, and then you add a mixture of chopped green pepper and celery, tomatoes, parsley, thyme, allspice, bay leaves, garlic, salt, pepper, lemon and flour. Let the pot simmer for half an hour and then drop in the fish slices. A quarter of an hour later you add a glass of fine strong claret. Then your *courtbouillon* is ready."

"You're making me hungry already, Antoine!" Bouchard laughed.

"Now, just because New Orleans is a seaport, you mustn't think that we have only fish as our dining specialty, ah no, *jamais de la vie!* This restaurant,

Duchamps, quite new and really superb, features grillades, which are veal rounds simmered in a tightly covered iron pot over a slow fire in a mixture of their own juices, with butter and flour and the usual tomato, green pepper, onion, parsley and garlic combination. Or again, with cooler weather like this and an appetite such as that sturdy body of yours indicates you surely have, *mon ami*, you might enjoy a chicken gumbo to start with, then a taste of our great pompano *en papillote*, which is a most delicately flavored fish baked in a paper bag to conserve its flavor. First of all, of course, the chef covers the fish with a sauce made out of cream, shrimp, crab flakes and spiced egg yolks, and bakes it all for ten minutes in a hot oven. Thus the bag is puffed up like a balloon when it emerges from the oven, and that is why we call it *en papillote, comprenez?*"

"I can see that we shall never get back to the office this afternoon. But let's go before you think of other recipes that will make me want to sample everything this new restaurant has to offer a hungry man," Henry laughingly declared.

Mark, who at his father's request had waited in the carriage outside the counting house, joined Antoine Rigalle and his father at lunch at the delightful little restaurant which the Creole banker had recommended. As they ended it with the strong coffee that was mixed with chicory and a dollop of hot milk, a favorite brew of New Orleans diners, Antoine Rigalle smilingly asked, "Well, gentlemen, what are your plans for this evening? If you've nothing better to do, I might offer you dinner at Moreau's and then a visit to *Les Extases* as my guests."

"Why, that would be most attractive, Antoine." Henry Bouchard glanced at his son. "Have you any other plans for yourself, Mark?"

"If you don't mind, Pa, I—I'd like to see someone I met last night."

Henry chuckled. "That very attractive woman you sat next to at the roulette table, I'll be bound. Am I right, boy?"

Mark scowled at his father and uncomfortably shifted in his seat. "I'm not exactly a boy, Pa, if you don't mind. That little filly Babette didn't think so, anyhow."

"Yes, and that reminds me," his father gave him an equally inimical glance. "Madame Julie took me aside just before we were leaving and complained of your high-handed bedroom manners. Babette wasn't used to being treated like a nigger slave-girl, Mark. In future, you've only to tell the proprietress of such an establishment your particular likes and dislikes, and she'll see to it that you have a girl who's used to rough handling, understand me?"

"You're a fine one to talk!" the youth scornfully retaliated.

Before Henry Bouchard, his face florid with anger, could counter, Antoine Rigalle suavely interposed as peacemaker: "*Messieurs*, it distresses me to see two such fine gentlemen at odds over so intimate a matter. Moreover, I can understand your son's fancy for bending a pleasure girl to his will. I confess that I myself at times, having neither plantation nor slaves, indulge myself in the fantasy of being a sultan in a seraglio who commands a beautiful slave girl to attend him and, finding her reluctant or passive, attempts to quicken her responses with just a touch of the lash. Never, I assure you, to mar the soft satiny skin or to leave permanent marks, just enough to make her caper and twist like a charming ballerina intent upon dedicating her delicious choreography to your special pleasures. I might suggest, *mon ami*, that you and your stalwart, vigorous young son will find girls especially trained in catering to these foibles at the house of Madame Norcier, on the Esplanade. If you like, I should be privileged to give you my card of introduction to that discreet and very amiable patroness of the goddess of clandestine love."

Henry's eyes glittered, and, giving his son a swift, glowering look, nodded. The Creole banker drew a card out of his waistcoat pocket, scribbled a few words of introduction on the back, and handed it to him.

"Thanks, Antoine. I might visit her after I've stayed a spell with my neighbor Edward Williamson. He's bound and determined to get back what he lost last night at Lourat's wheel," Henry Bouchard declared as he tucked the card away. Then, grudgingly, he glanced at Mark and muttered, "If you like, you're free to keep whatever appointments you've in mind. And I suppose you'll be wanting a little money for your evening's pleasure."

"I earned it last night, Pa, and if you like, I'll go back to the gambling room tonight and do just as well."

"No need for that," Henry Bouchard hastily replied. Opening his purse, he handed the sullen youth several banknotes. "Just don't let me hear any complaints from Madame Julie, if you please."

"I'm not going there, Pa. Thanks for the fine lunch, Mister Rigalle. Er, if you don't mind, Pa, I'd like to go back to the hotel and freshen up a bit, and then I have to get in touch with someone."

"Ah, youth, youth, irrepressible youth!" the banker chuckled, shaking his head with a rueful look on his handsome face. "We've a proverb, we Creoles: *si jeunesse savait, si viellesse pouvait*—if youth but knew, if age but could." He rose, threw some banknotes down on the table and graciously gestured at the hovering waiter. "A superb repast, *mon vieux*. Be sure to tell *M'sieu* Duclos of our high opinion of his culinary skill. As for me, *mes amis*, I shall go back to the counting house and make sure that your drafts have been handled as you directed."

"I'll go back with you then, Antoine. Williamson will be wanting that cash so that he'll have his courage bolstered for tonight's play," Henry Bouchard ironically smiled.

A handsome quadroon in her early forties, wearing a bright orange bandanna, a green cottanade dress with high neck, puffed sleeves and billowing skirt to the ankles, white lisle stockings and silver-buckled shoes, admitted Mark Bouchard to the exquisitely furnished

152

sitting room of the two-story house on Eglantine Street. The first floor itself was only a façade, the entrance leading up a narrow stairway to the second floor with its two sitting rooms, three bedrooms and the *chambre de bain*. At the back of the first floor was the kitchen, and a kind of dumbwaiter set off in the wall just outside, by which the cook could hoist by means of a pulley rope the delicacies she prepared for the residents or guests above.

The quadroon ushered Mark to an ornately upholstered settee and, graciously inclining her head, inquired in a soft, melodious voice, "May I bring *M'su* a glass of wine? My name is Diana. I shall tell *Mam'selle* Voisin that you are here to see her. It won't be long, *M'su*."

"A glass of wine, by all means," Mark jovially replied, looking around with interest at the handsome tapestries on the wall and the mock fireplace with its marble mantelpiece, the teakwood tabouret on which a costly Sèvres vase regally sat, the entirety evoking an aura of aristocratic elegance and wealth.

"At once, *M'su*," Diana again respectfully inclined her head, and disappeared.

Mark, after having left his father and Antoine Rigalle, had gone directly to the gambling room of Pierre Lourat and there invested half of the hundred dollars Henry had given him, playing the black or the red on each turn. Shrewdly, he had resisted the impulse to play two coins after having lost one, and was content with the ratio of two coins won for one gambled to end after some forty minutes of play nearly two hundred dollars ahead. He had then gone to a nearby tailor's shop and purchased a redingote of bottle-green cloth, with a black velvet collar, added a pair of light-gray trousers, selected an elegant lingerie cravat, chamois gloves and black silk top hat. Finally, he had invested ten dollars in a malacca walking stick with knobbed head, sturdy yet flexible. When he saw himself in the tailor's mirror, inside the curtained dressing room at the very back of the shop, he grinned at his

153

reflection and muttered to himself, "Boy am I, Pa? You're dead wrong about that!"

A moment later, the handsome quadroon entered the sitting room with a tray on which was posed a tulip-bulb-shaped Venetian glass filled with dark red wine. She set the tray down on an enamel-topped table beside the settee and quietly asked, "May I take your redingote and hat, *M'su*?"

Mark turned red with embarrassment, conscious that in his adolescent eagerness to see the mysterious, exotic beauty with whom he had made a rendezvous, he had forgotten to remove hat and overcoat. Clumsily getting to his feet, he frowned as he snapped at the woman, "Why didn't you take it when I first came in, nigger? I ought to tell your mistress you're a lazy slave, that's what I ought to do."

The quadroon straightened, her eyes respectfully lowered, so that he did not see their sudden furious glow; nor was he aware of the tightening of her jaw muscles as she docilely and softly replied, "Forgive me, *M'su*, I thought only of telling my mistress that you had arrived, for she was eager to see you."

This placating and guileful answer completely erased the youth's anger, born out of his having been made aware of how schoolboyishly he had behaved. "Yes, of course! Here you are—take them away, and tell me if she'll be here soon."

"I am here now, *M'sieu* Bouchard," the woman's thrillingly husky voice murmured from the doorway, and Mark Bouchard goggled at her as, without taking his eyes from her, he shoved the redingote and hat toward Diana, who collected them and swiftly left the sitting room.

Louisette Entrevois had prepared herself with exceptional skill for this meeting with her adolescent suitor. She had combed out her hair and sheathed it in a silver net which caressed her creamy back to just below the shoulderblades. Her voluptuous figure was accentuated and even boldly displayed in the low-cut magenta silk peignoir which descended to her slim ankles, was belted with purple satin to emphasize the suppleness of

154

her waist and the sensual flare of her hips. There were three silver buttons below the bodice, beginning just under the thrusting globes of her bosom. She had touched the lobes of her dainty ears with the perfume stopper, as well as the cleft of her breasts and her slim wrists which were just visible where the filmy puffed sleeves ended.

"So nice to see you again, *M'sieu* Mark," she came slowly toward him, and even the gauche youth could not fail to sense the degree of intimacy with which she had changed from using his surname to his given name, still less the warmly admiring look in her dark eyes. She extended her right hand to him, and for a moment Mark Bouchard reached for it. Then, remembering his father's more sophisticated behavior at the housewarming, he suddenly brought it to his lips and planted a rather loud kiss on the back. With a throaty little laugh, she deftly turned her hand and gently brushed his lips with her soft moist palm, then drew her hand away as she murmured, "Please drink your wine. It was sweet of you to send word that you wanted to take me out to dinner. But it's chilly out, and there's a threat of rain. I don't really feel like dressing, so why don't I have my housekeeper Diana prepare a little supper for us?"

"Yes—I—I'd like that, Louisa!" he blurted. "Go ahead, sit down, please do."

"Thank you, my dear Mark." Once more fixing him with her soulful eyes, Louisette Entrevois let him perceive how eagerly attentive she was to his presence as she moved to a nearby straight-backed chair and felinely seated herself, leaning slightly forward to let him glimpse the tempting creamy cleft of her bosom.

Still bemused, he reached toward his glass of wine and tried to sip it as a gentleman would, watching her all the while, his face reddening again under her sweetly smiling scrutiny. "You're—you're very beautiful, Louisa." His voice was hoarse and edgy. As he shifted in his chair, his elbow bumped the malacca cane which he had propped against the arm, knocking it to the floor. With an imprecation under his breath, he stooped to retrieve it.

"Diana forgot to take it. Do forgive her, she hasn't been very long in my service," Louisette Entrevois purred as she rose and came toward him, reaching for the stick. "Unless of course you brought it along to beat me into submission, *mon cher*?"

He shuddered, his face turning brick-red as her slyly malicious remark touched all too unerringly the secret core of his sexual proclivities. "My God, no!" he exclaimed as she took the stick from his unresisting fingers. "You—you aren't a slave, you're—you're a fine lady, Louisa!"

"That's a lovely compliment, dear Mark. There now, it's safely in the corner. But of course, every woman, no matter how much a lady she is, has just a little of the slave in her—that is, when she finally meets the man who she knows will be her true master. And I have the feeling that even though you're young, you're quite wise in the ways of women."

Momentarily at a loss for words, Mark seized his glass and downed the rest of the wine, then set it back with a clatter on the enamel-topped table. "I—I'm old enough," he finally answered, prompted by his sudden angry recollection of his father's jibe at the restaurant that noon.

"But of course you are, my dear one," Louisette murmured. "Quite old enough to lead your own life and to decide what you want and when you want it. You must never let anyone tell you otherwise, believe me." She clasped her hands together and rose, her eyes lifting to the ceiling as if she were enacting the role of one of Corneille's great tragediennes. "*Hélas*, if only I, a weak woman, could take my own advice and do what a man could do and be free for all time! No, Mark dear, only a man of strength and vision can give a dependent woman the freedom her soul yearns for, believe me."

"What do you mean, Louisa?" He rose from the settee and moved toward her, his face suddenly anxious and perturbed. "Has someoody made you un-

156

happy? Tell me who. I'll break his neck for him, I promise you!"

"Oh no, darling—but how sweet of you to offer yourself as my gallant rescuer and knight," she whispered, linking her soft arms around his neck and moving close to him, her lips only inches from his. Once again he breathed in the tantalizing scent of her perfume, recognized it from the night before, felt his virility harden and throb with sudden excitement. "You see, dear, when a girl's father dies, and if he leaves debts, she's liable for them. Why, did you know that she could even be sold on the auction block as a slave?"

"I thought only niggers—I mean—slaves—" he hoarsely stammered, clenching his fists to hold back the impulse to cup her swelling breasts, so maddeningly near.

"If only that were true—and of course, I'm not a slave and I'm white, as you can see."

"Why—yes, Louisa—you—you've got wonderful white skin—you're so very beautiful—Louisa—can't I help in some way? Tell me what to do to make you happy! I—I want to I—love you!"

She put a hand to her soft quivering mouth to stifle a feigned sob, her eyes searching his, and then murmured, "Oh, Mark, you don't know how much I want you to love me too! I'm so much older than you are, and a man of your experience may find it impossible to believe—but I swear to you on my mother's grave that what I'm about to tell you is the truth—I—I've never had a man, not ever, in my whole life. And I'd so like to be yours, Mark, but I could never give myself to a man unless I was his wife."

His jaw dropped, his throat was suddenly choked, as the erotic spell of her perfume and the nearness of her and the tantalizing white satin of her shoulders and the shadowy cleft of her bosom which the peignoir just concealed wrought their sensual power upon his precociously virile senses. "M—marry you—you mean—you mean you'd marry me if I asked you, Louisa? I—I don't know—I don't know if Pa would let me—I'm

157

practically sixteen—I mean—damn it to hell, Louisa, I do want you, and I'll try like hell to marry you if it'll make you happy and get you out of your trouble. If it's money, maybe I can get some from Pa before we leave New Orleans—"

"Oh, my sweet lover"—she put a finger to his lips and shook her head—"yes, you really are my gallant knight. But I couldn't take money from you, that would make me one of those fancy girls on Rampart Street. I'll wait for you, Mark. If I thought for a moment you really meant it when you said you'd marry me, I'm sure I could persuade Papa's creditors to wait—how long would it be, my darling?"

"Well, September—I think—I don't know why Pa wouldn't let me—hell, my mother wasn't much more than that when she got married, I'm pretty sure—sure I will, Louisa!"—casting caution to the winds, Mark Bouchard seized her by the shoulders and buried his lips in the hollow of her swelling breasts.

With one soft hand she carressed the back of his head, while with the other she gently pushed at his cheek, whispering, "Oh no, my darling, we mustn't—it would be so easy for me to yield to you, you're so strong and masterful, but I told you, I'm still a virgin—let's wait till our wedding night, my sweet young lover!"

"Louisa—I have to—I want you so—" he groaned.

"I know, I know," she whispered back, cupping his flushed cheeks with both hands and kissing him lightly on the tip of his nose. "I know how wrought up I've made you, and it's all my fault. But I've a young slave girl, a beautiful octoroon named Rosa. She'll do whatever I tell her to, and if you'd like right now, she'd go to bed with you. Then you could pretend it was I—and when we're married, darling, because she is my slave, you can have her whenever you tire of me. Would you like that?"

"My God—Louisa—yes—yes—I'm crazy for you—I have to—and you're sure it would be like that when we get married? You wouldn't mind if I took her

158

to bed once in a while, Louisa darling?" he gasped incredulously.

"Of course I wouldn't. Come along now, quickly. Diana is preparing supper, but you've time to meet Rosa and to relieve yourself—I know what strong men like you want, my darling, that's why I'll be such a good wife for you. Come along now!"

She led him by the hand out of the sitting room and down the corridor to a bedroom door, already partly opened. It was dark inside, but Mark Bouchard's straining eyes could make out a shadowy form on a large four-poster bed. There was the sound of muffled sobs, which strangely stimulated his already whetted desires.

Louisette Entrevois whispered, "Take off your clothes and go to her, my darling. I'll have supper ready when you've finished. Then we can chat about our future together. Hurry now, pretend it's I, if you like, it'll only prove how much you love me!" And then aloud, in an imperious voice, she commanded, "Rosa, my slave girl, you're going to service my future husband, so make sure you please him or I'll have you thrashed, do you understand me?"

Mark could wait no longer. Already he was taking off his clothes, panting with lust, as Louisa slipped quietly out of the bedroom and closed the door behind her.

She smiled secretively to herself. Rosa wouldn't dare tell her mother Diana about any of this. Just before this clumsy boy had come calling, she'd reminded Rosa once again of what could happen to them both if Pierre Lourat decided to collect their father's unpaid debts and used them as salable assets. Besides, Rosa was young, and just one breaking-in wouldn't really hurt her, wouldn't spoil the very special kind of love the two of them had for each other. And of course, once Mark Bouchard went through with his promise to marry her—as she was going to make certain he would, with Pierre Lourat's help—there'd be no need for either of them to service such a young, thoughtless brute. . . .

By the time Mark had stumbled out of the little house, slaked with passion, food and wine and the seductive promises of coveted Louisa, Edward Williamson had lost nearly every banknote from the thick sheaf which Henry Bouchard had handed him. All that he had left was $1600, plus the almost obsessed resolve to return the next night to attempt to recoup all that he had thus far lost.

CHAPTER ELEVEN

"Look, Thomas, isn't he getting big and fat?" Arabella exulted as she carefully cradled the baby raccoon in her arms and rocked it to and fro. She put a finger to its mouth and joyously giggled as its pink tongue emerged and eagerly licked her finger. "He likes me lots, Thomas, doesn't he?"

"Me too," Fleurette chimed in, gleefully clapping her hands as the little animal turned its comical black-masked face toward her and uttered a little squeal.

It was just after lunch on Saturday of the week which Henry and Mark Bouchard were spending in New Orleans. The tall, wiry Ashanti stood in the door-way of the room which the two sisters shared, a warm smile lighting his usually sober features. "He sure does take to you, Miss Bella," he agreed. His long associa-tion with the field hands had led him to adopt, at times, their dialect and their slurring speech. But more than that, ever since Mark had stormed at him for eavesdropping on the latter's tryst with Maybelle in the shed and Henry had reprimanded him for taking too much on himself, Lucien's former overseer had uncon-ciously begun to adopt a more deferential manner with the members of the household.

"Why, he must have put on at least a pound just since last week, don't you think so, Thomas?" Arabella said.

"At least that, Miss Bella. Now you remember, in

161

another week or two, it'll be time to let him go inspect outdoors for himself. You train him that way, he won't ever turn on you or bite or claw. 'Course, when he grows older, you'll have to watch he doesn't try to chew the buttons of your dress or nibble at your hair if you bend down and let it fall into his face. But I think he's going to make a mighty loving pet for you and Miss Fleurette, and that's a fact."

Sybella, who had just come from the kitchen where she had gone to discuss with Mammy Clorinda the menu for tonight's dinner and tomorrow's meals, now appeared, and Thomas respectfully moved aside with a smiling "Afternoon, Miz Bouchard, m'am."

"The same to you, Thomas. I rather expect Mr. Bouchard and Mark to be back by tomorrow, as I'm sure he'll want to see how his fields are being prepared."

"They're fine, Miz Bouchard," Thomas earnestly assured her. "This morning, I rode over to talk with the foremen, John, Fred, Douglas and Peter, and they've been working right smart. All the hands are doing just what Mr. Bouchard had the foremen plan for them to do. He'll be able to start his seeding just the way he wants it soon as he's back, m'am."

Sybella shook her head and frowned. "What I'm most afraid of, Thomas—and mind you, this is just between ourselves—is that my husband seems to want to take over other smaller holdings which are located quite a distance apart. He's going to spread himself too thin, and he's certainly going to have to hire at least one overseer if not several—and you know as well as I do, the way he feels about it, they'll be white."

"Yes, m'am." Thomas looked down at the floor, his face suddenly grave. "But then, if they're all like Mr. Luke, there's nothing to worry about. He gets along just fine with everyone. Even the field hands who don't speak hardly a word of English at all like him a lot and say he's a good master. One thing about it, for sure, Miz Bouchard, he'll never use the whip. If a man's doing wrong—why, just this morning, I saw him step down into one of the rows and pat Jasper on the shoul-

162

der and take Jasper's hoe away from him and then show him, nice and smiling as you please, m'am, how you ought to chop to break up the soil and get those weeds out good. And Jasper took to it like he'd been born with the knowledge, once Mr. Luke showed him. Now that's a better way than the whip, I'm thinking."

"That's because he has Grandfather's heart, and I don't care how old-fashioned that is, I'm grateful for it, Thomas. Now then, shall we take Timmy out for a walk and show him what to expect around Windhaven, Arabella and Fleurette?"

"Oh yes, Mama!" Arabella excitedly retorted, reaching for Fleurette's hand. "Come along, honey, we'll go walk along with Timmy and see if he likes it."

Gently, the black-haired girl set the baby raccoon down on the floor and, turning back to cluck at it and to beckon to it, led the way. Sybella and Thomas watched, exchanging an amused look, and then the Ashanti suddenly murmured, "Miz Bouchard, could I bother you for just a minute? I'd like to ask you something."

"Of course, Thomas." Raising her voice, she called, "You go on ahead, girls, I'll be there in just a second." Then, turning back to the Ashanti, she nodded: "Say what's on your mind, Thomas. You know that I shan't ever break your confidences."

"Thank you, Miz Bouchard. I'm grateful to God that my daddy Ben was given by the Creeks to old Mr. Lucien. I know he felt that Mr. Lucien looked on him as a man, looked to him for help and that's why my daddy did everything he could to make things right. And I feel the same way. But, begging your pardon, Miz Bouchard, I wonder what you'd say if I told you I'd like to marry that purty l'il yeller gal Celia."

"Celia, my maid? Why, Thomas, that's right, you never have married."

"No, m'am. And I know I'm along in years, past forty, but I'm still in my prime, I can still do a good day's work in the fields, you know that. You see, Miz Bouchard, I heard that—well, excuse me for mentioning it, but—"

"You're trying to say that you know Celia's pregnant. Yes, that's true. And it's good and decent of you to tell me that you want to marry her. Personally, I think it's a wonderful idea. But of course, since my husband bought Celia in New Orleans, technically she belongs to him as a slave. I don't have the right to dispose of my husband's property under the law, Thomas. If I did, I'd say yes in a minute."

"Thank you, Miz Bouchard. Maybe, after Mr. Bouchard gets back, you might sound him out and see if he'd go along with the notion? I'd be mighty good to Celia. She's such a sweet girl, and from what Mammy Clorinda has told me, she still feels she isn't wanted in this house. You know how it is."

"Yes." Sybella's lips compressed, remembering the lovely young girl's frightening and shameful introduction to Windhaven. "Well then, Thomas, you have my promise that I'll speak to him when I think he's in a proper mood." Then, with a flash of her irrepressible wit and spirit, she added, "I think I've been married to him long enough to be able to change his moods for the better once in a while. And now let's go see how Timmy is making out, shall we, Thomas?"

Henry Bouchard, who was not really a gambler, had accompanied Williamson to the elegantly furnished salon to watch his neighbor attempt to recoup his heavy losses on the wheel. Out of curiosity, he essayed a few hands of *vingt-et-un* with indifferent success, while he watched his neighbor first play $200 on the red and lose, then a similar amount on the black and lose again. He saw that the widower's eyes were glazed and his face pale and damp with sweat, and out of compassion was about to urge him not to play with such desperate abandon. If Williamson lost his last $1200, he would have gambled away every penny earned on his cotton for the past year, and there could be no doubt that such a loss would plunge him into financial difficulties.

Then his eyes narrowed with a calculating glint: those difficulties could well work to his own advantage.

Even though he knew his neighbor to have put away another $20,000 in savings from earnings the two previous years, this week's disaster would force him to walk a precarious financial tightrope in the management of his house and acreage. There was Amos Greer to be paid; there was seed to be bought and cotton to be ginned again this fall; there were taxes and of course the living expenses of Williamson's two young daughters.

And so, when he saw his neighbor shove $400 worth of chips onto the square which designated black, Henry Bouchard kept his own counsel and beckoned to Charmaine for a glass of champagne, drinking a silent toast to the eventualities of circumstance. Those four hundred acres of prime land and that sturdy house might well be within his reach for a pittance; let there be a drastic lowering of the cotton price this fall and increased expenses in the production of that cotton, and Edward Williamson could very easily go into serious debt which he himself would be willing to assume—in return for a first mortgage on all of that desirable property.

Indeed, he watched the wheels turn, heard the clattering of the little ball as it whirled round and round, capriciously stopping, then leaping to another slot, and with all his might he willed Edward Williamson to lose—and lose indeed he did.

Now, as if the man were acting under an unseen compulsion, he shoved his remaining chips onto the square marked *"Rouge,"* and leaned back with a groan, clenching his fists and shivering as, with hollow eyes he watched the croupier spin the wheel. There was a chorus of sighs from the other participants around the table as the wheel halted and the little ball lay in a black slot. What Henry Bouchard had consciously wished had come true.

For a long moment there was silence, and then the widower stumbled to his feet, shoving back his chair, and staggered toward the door of the gambling room, his eyes unseeing, his face a twisted mask of despair and torment. Henry saw Pierre Lourat move toward the planter, saw him whisper into Edward Williamson's ear, saw Lourat put his arm around the older man's shoulders and lead him away. Cynically, he thought to himself: *That Creole is a genius, and he's deadly, too, that's why no one dares question the honesty of his wheel or his cards. He'll send Ed to one of his houses, let the poor devil have a night of pleasure with one of the fancy girls to take his mind off what's just happened. That's the best way. And when we go back tomorrow, I'll be his helpful friend and offer to stand by him all through the year so that he won't have to worry about any sacrifices. And maybe Mark will get sweet enough on Maybelle to marry her and then that Williamson land will one day be Bouchard land. One day, before not too much longer, by God, I'm going to own more acres than Father does—yes, and I'll make more money than he ever knew how to do!*

Mark had pleaded a bad headache this Saturday afternoon and begged off accompanying his father to the gambling salon in the evening. Henry had chuckled, with almost a paternal I-told-you-so look on his face, as he'd twitted the boy: "That's what comes of burning your candle at both ends, Mark. Well, at least you've got it out of your system, so that when we go back to Windhaven, I'll expect you to be on your best behavior, understand? I've let you act like a man, the way you said you wanted to, haven't I? You had a taste of gambling, you've had champagne, and you've bedded at least one wench I know of and quite likely two, eh, Mark? You don't have to tell me, but I'll bet that handsome brown-haired jade you met at the table early this week showed you up for the fledgling you really are. Now if I'd been there in your place, I'd have had her eating out of my hand—don't look at me like that, you young pup! Don't forget I'm your father and you're not yet sixteen, for all your sowing your wild oats this week! Very well then, go sulk in your room and have a good night's sleep. Just see to it you're wide awake and ready to board the steamboat tomorrow noon!"

This time, Mark had not replied to his father's taunts. He had glowered, then averted his face and

166

mumbled something unintelligible, and his father had clapped him on the back and gone down the corridor, in high good humor at having at last bested his belligerent young son.

But it was not the aftereffects of his week-long dissipation which had silenced Mark Bouchard's always volatile tongue. It was the sickening knowledge that—though how, he could not quite fully understand—he owed a gentleman's debt of honor to Pierre Lourat, a debt of nearly $6000 . . . and that he had gambled away that sum through the urging of Louisa Voisin, whose fiancé he had ardently agreed to become.

Yesterday, Friday, a messenger had come to the hotel just before noon with a letter in her own flowery hand, in an envelope scented with her haunting perfume. She had asked him to visit her at once, and he had quickly dressed and taken a carriage to the little house on Eglantine Street.

She herself admitted him to the sitting room, took his hand in hers and kissed him passionately on the mouth, then murmured, "Do you still feel the same about me as you did the other night, my darling?"

"Oh yes, Louisa! More than ever, I want to marry you, you know I do! And Rosa—she was wonderful to me the other night—she's so young and nice, oh, not like you, of course, Louisa!"

"My dearest, my husband-to-be, Mark darling," she murmured, giving him another kiss that made him shudder with a sudden fierce longing for her. "I must be truthful with you. You see, I told you that Papa died in bankruptcy, and that my slave Rosa and I and the housekeeper Diana would be at the mercy of Papa's creditors. Well, you see, *M'sieu* Lourat, who was a dear friend of Papa's, came forward and assumed his debts, so that we wouldn't be thrown out into the street and Rosa and Diana sold on the block as slaves. But I have to pay him back somehow, you see. I work for him, in a way—I didn't really want to tell you, but I must, because you're so fine and good and honest, Mark."

"I told you I'd see if I couldn't get money for you,

167

Louisa—" he stammered, his senses swimming from the nearness of her in the filmy peignoir which reeked with that exotic perfume.

"Let me finish, darling." She put a finger to his lips, then brushed them with a palm, and her eyes sent him a message of tender promise. "I work for *M'sieu* Lourat as a kind of hostess, shall we say. It means, in short, my dear, that I am in the gambling rooms, that I circulate among the tables and urge *M'sieu* Lourat's clients to play for higher stakes. From all of this, he gives me a very small commission, which he credits against Papa's debt. But there's still a great deal left, and it's been three years and now that I've met you, I want so much to be free. You don't know how I'd love to marry you, go live with you in your fine house and be a wife and sweetheart to you, and Rosa likes you too—she told me so the other night after you made love to her so handsomely."

At these words, Mark Bouchard uttered a groan of lust, grasped her voluptuously rounded hips with his hands and pressed himself ardently against her, panting, "Louisa, Louisa, I want that too, you don't know how much! Tell me what I can do to get you free of him!"

"Well, you tried your hand at the roulette wheel, and even if you did it only as a lark, you won, you remember. Suppose you were to go there this afternoon, and I'd go with you, to bring you luck? You could win, and perhaps from your winnings you'd have stake enough to go on playing for even higher stakes. And maybe, if both of us were very lucky, darling, you could free me once and for all from the clutches of that heartless Creole—you know he sells slaves as well as he does pleasure girls, and you don't know how I've dreamed of being free of such a man all these unhappy years, my darling!"

"I—I don't know, Louisa," he hesitated, nervously biting his lower lip. "I haven't too much money with me, perhaps a hundred dollars or so. That wouldn't be enough to win big at the wheel, Louisa."

"But *M'sieu* Lourat knows that you're a Bouchard,

darling. Your father's credit is beyond question with him—he's told me that, you see. You could buy a good number of chips to start with on your father's credit, and then as you win, you'd pay that back at once and have enough left over to play for my freedom—my freedom to be your wife, and my wedding present to you will be my slave Rosa for whenever you want her, darling."

His chest heaved, he flushed, and already he could remember the darkness in that wide comfortable bed, the sobbing plaints of the young octoroon who had endured him, making him believe that she was actually enamored of his virile, selfish passion.

"All right! After all, Pa's poked fun at me long enough about not being a man. I'll show him what kind of a man I am!"

"My darling, my wonderful husband-to-be," Louisette Entrevois whispered, cupping his flushed cheeks in her soft hands, kissing him gently on the mouth, then insinuating just a flick of her nimble tongue to whet his desires to unbearable pitch. "Oh no, sweetheart, there'll be time enough for that when we're married. I want to save myself for our wedding night—it'll be wonderful then, you'll see. Now we'll have Diana fix us a bite of lunch, and then you will visit Rosa—she wants to see you again and wish you her own luck before you go off to set us all free, darling."

He wolfed down the food which Rosa's unsuspecting mother had prepared in the kitchen, then swiftly undressed and hurried into the darkened bedroom. But this time, Rosa, clad only in a short white silk shift which scarcely descended to her knees, had softly whispered, "Let me pleasure you my own way, master, please! Then, after you've set us free, you're to come back this afternoon and Rosa will love you good!"

Bemused, entranced by this harem-like prospect in which he would command the embraces of these two voluptuous women, one so mature and worldly wise, the other so virginally shy yet obeisant, Mark Bouchard stretched out on the bed while Rosa

169

crouched over him, titillating him with fingers, lips and tongue until at last he had cried out in rapture under her perverse erotic blandishments. . . .

She helped him dress, fondling and caressing and kissing him, praising his sturdiness and his wonderful abilities as a lover, whispering that she could hardly wait till she was his bed slave as she would be when he married her dear mistress. And then Louisette Entrevois and Mark Bouchard had gone off in a carriage to the establishment of Pierre Lourat, entered the gambling salon where the Creole dandy, impeccably dressed, greeted the young scion of the Bouchard fortune.

Mark seated himself before the wheel, having first explained to Pierre Lourat that he had only a little more than a hundred dollars with him, to which the Creole had assured him, "But one does not need to mention money when two gentlemen deal with each other, *M'sieu* Bouchard. You have only to tell me what credit you wish, and I will instruct my croupier to honor your request. Let me have Charmaine serve you and *Mam'selle* Voisin my very best champagne."

With Louisa Voisin beside him, in the same red taffeta gown she had worn that first night he had met her, Mark Bouchard faced the croupier with a heady exhilaration, certain that he could not lose. From time to time, he glanced toward his voluptuous companion, who squeezed his elbow, gave him meaningful smiles, communicated her pleasure at his bravado with those limpid, dark eyes.

At first it had gone well. Within half an hour, using only his original stake, he had won nearly a thousand dollars. Then a streak of bad fortune wiped that out, and, apologetically stammering, he turned to Pierre Lourat, who clapped his hands and called, "Jacques, whatever *M'sieu* Bouchard desires, I agree to it."

"*Bien, M'sieu* Lourat. How many chips does *M'sieu* Bouchard wish to buy?" the croupier inquired of the flushed, excited youth.

"Well, say a thousand dollars to start," Mark Bouchard replied.

Once again he had begun to win and then, inexplicably, whether he played red or black, chose a *carré* in which he would win if any of the four numbers chosen was designated by the capricious ball, or staked all on a single number, he lost repeatedly.

"*Pauvre chéri*, you've had bad luck, but it'll change, I know it will."

But after two hours, Mark loosened his cravat, his face sickly pale and damp with sweat. He tried to speak but could not; and when he rose from his chair, he sent Pierre Lourat an agonized look of supplication.

"Come now, *M'sieu* Bouchard, there's no reason to look so tragic, the world isn't lost. It's a debt of honor, and you have only to sign this note agreeing that you or your father will pay within a reasonable amount of time. I'm sure that somehow you'll be able to induce your estimable father to make good a debt which you incurred in his name."

And then, even as Mark, listlessly scrawling his name on the sheet of paper which the gambler placed before him, stared hopelessly at that now motionless wheel which had plunged him into the depths of despair, Pierre Lourat had suavely added, "Louisa tells me that you are much smitten with her and that you have done her the honor to propose marriage. It's quite possible, *M'sieu* Mark, that if that marriage comes about, I shall be pleased to tear up this note you have signed as my wedding present to you both."

There was, then, still the leavening of hope for Mark; he told himself that it was more probable for him to induce his father to agree to a marriage with so beautiful and desirable a woman than to part with all that money which had surely not been his to lose.

CHAPTER TWELVE

The Mandingo slave Djamba had been returned to the quarters just behind Pierre Lourat's auction room on Chartres Street to await the disposition of his new master. On the fateful Saturday evening when Edward Williamson had lost the last of his cotton money to the roulette wheel, Henry Bouchard had taken his leave of the slim Creole dandy and directed that Djamba be brought over to the Orleans Hotel, where he and his son and Williamson were staying, by ten o'clock the following morning, so that they would have ample time to board the steamboat which would sail shortly after noon. "Well, Pierre, I must thank you for a memorable week," Henry Bouchard jovially declared. "I shall certainly tell my neighbors what admirable hospitality you offer visitors to New Orleans and what prime slaves of both sexes you have for sale."

Pierre Lourat bowed, his face bland and expressionless. "It has been my pleasure, *M'sieu* Bouchard. I only regret that your friend had such bad luck."

"Well, it wasn't for me to advise him; he's a grown man, Pierre. Though I myself wouldn't have flung away the chips he did trying to double after a loss. But then, I don't have gambling fever—leastways, not when it comes to games of chance. I'd rather have the odds stacked in my favor, such as land and slaves. Those are things you can hold on to and increase the value of just by waiting."

173

"Very true, *M'sieu* Bouchard. My esteemed late patron Armand Duvalier taught me that when I was a very young apprentice," Pierre Lourat smiled. "Let me wish you a pleasant journey back to Windhaven, and hope that I'll have the pleasure of entertaining you again very soon." He extended his hand with a gracious smile and Henry Bouchard heartily shook it.

"You say this slave Djamba speaks some English, is that right, Pierre?"

"Yes. The girl who tended him during the voyage from Africa was most diligent. She'd been promised a reward if she instructed him well—I arranged for her sale to a very pleasant old gentleman who lives near Natchez and will most likely employ her as his favorite bed wench. Her duties are certain to be light, since I'm afraid the dear old gentleman is hardly so demanding as you or your sturdy son, *M'sieu* Bouchard." The Creole winked knowingly and Henry Bouchard burst out laughing at the lewd innuendo. "She'd been told that if she failed her duties, she'd be sold to a sugarcane plantation here in Louisiana, and that's a fate most sensible slaves try to avoid. No, you'll be able to communicate with him without too much difficulty, I'm sure. Do you plan to make a field hand of him, may I ask?"

"I'm not yet sure. He has tremendous strength, and I'm sure he could exceed any quota set for any of the niggers I now have working on my acres these days," Henry Bouchard replied. "Can you think of any other skills he might be able to offer?"

"He's quite courageous and proud—but you saw that for yourself on the auction block. Now I remember that Sumara—that was the Gullah girl who tended him on the vesssel—learned that he was skillful with animals. His tribe kept a herd of cattle to supply meat when the hunt wasn't successful. According to Sumara, Djamba once slowed down a big bull that broke away from the pens and was running through the village, subdued it by talking to it and gentling it till one of the villagers could get a rope around its neck and drag it back. And of course he's killed lions with a spear—

174

many of the Mandingo warriors must do that to prove their manhood."

"I see." Henry Bouchard reflectively nursed his chin. "You know, I'd thought of putting him up as a fighter against Ed Williamson's strong nigger Davey. He'd been boasting how his man could take on all comers and he was willing to bet heavily on the outcome. But after watching him at your gambling salon, Pierre, I've a feeling that he'll be back before long to try to get back his money. That means I'll use Djamba some other way. Of course it could be picking cotton, but we've a pretty good stable at Windhaven and while I've got a smart young nigger boy Jimmy handling it at the moment, maybe Djamba could work there for a spell. I've a black stallion, Midnight, that's been giving Jimmy a little trouble, a skittish horse that doesn't take too kindly to a rider. Yes, I might just see what Djamba can do with Midnight. Well now, if your business ever brings you upriver our way, Pierre, be sure to stop at Windhaven. I'd like to return the hospitality—though of course I can't begin to offer you the selection of bed wenches that's in your own stable," he grinned.

And so the two men had taken leave of each other without Henry's learning of the debt which Mark had incurred by playing on his father's credit. Nor had Pierre Lourat any intention of revealing that secret at this time: he had already learned from Henry's chance comments about Williamson that the latter would be plunged into a precarious financial situation . . . and by now he had inferred that Henry Bouchard, who preferred to gamble on land and slaves instead of with chips and cards, might well seek to aggrandize his own holdings by taking advantage of the widower's plight. That would mean even greater prosperity for Windhaven, and in turn by his own engineering of an alliance between Louisette Entrevois and young Mark Bouchard, he was sure to derive a most advantageous profit.

He permitted himself one closing question as he shook hands with Lucien Bouchard's ambitious son:

"Do you wish me to shackle Djamba when I have him delivered to your hotel, *M'sieu* Bouchard?"

"No, I don't think it'll be necessary. The captain will put him in the hold, and there are plenty of stevedores around to make sure he won't escape. It wouldn't do him much good anyway if he did try—a nigger as good-looking and powerful and young as that would be picked up on sight. Somehow, I have the notion that I can get more out of him by gentling him than by using the whip and irons."

"That's very shrewd of you, *mon ami*. It's the same thing with a woman in most cases, though there are those who secretly long for just such domination," Pierre Lourat remarked . . .

"We'll be in Mobile this evening, stay the night at an inn, and then the *Orion* will bring us back to Windhaven by nightfall." Henry Bouchard stood beside Edward Williamson at the rail, looking out onto the crowded levee. "Cheer up, Ed, it's not the end of the world. Why, with that prime four hundred acres of yours, and Amos Greer getting your niggers to increase their quota every year, you'll have that money back by next fall, if you don't take it back from Pierre Lourat before then."

Williamson heaved a sigh and shook his head, staring apathetically at the slaves, sailors, commission men and vendors who seemed to move in an endless procession. "I just went crazy, I guess. I always used to like to play cards for a good stake, but my poor wife didn't hold with gambling and she only allowed me a sociable game when I had guests at the house. It wasn't just the trouble with the Indians that made me decide to leave Georgia, you see, Henry. I wanted to make a fresh start, because I missed Helen so. I didn't want to be reminded of all the happy times we'd had out there struggling to build something for the future." He sighed again. "Of course, I wanted a son to carry on after me, but after Maybelle was born, the doctor told me that Helen probably wouldn't ever be able to give me another child. Don't misunderstand, I loved her more than I ever loved any other woman—that's another

176

reason why, to this day, I couldn't think of bedding down with a black wench in my own house, and surely not with Lucy around—she's so set against slavery it sometimes worries me, Henry."

"She'll get over it. All she has to do is to marry some nice fellow, and she'll be so wrapped up in him she'll just take the niggers around the house like pieces of furniture and not even notice them."

"No, sir, you don't know my Lucy. She's sweet and gentle, but she's got a mind of her own on lots of things, and that's one of them. Mostly, she just can't stand the sight of Amos Greer. And yet I don't dare get rid of him. I'd never find another overseer who could get the cotton out of the land the way that man can."

Henry Bouchard pursed his lips, a speculative look coming into his eyes. "Well, if ever you do decide you don't want him any longer, I'll be glad to take him off your hands. You see now, some of my land is in dibs and dabs, and it's not all together. As it stands now, I've got to rely on good nigger foremen, but there's a limit to what they can do. And of course they don't have the brains of a white man. I have to put the fear of God into them and stand over them and call them in every so often just to make sure the field hands know what my orders are. Now a fellow like Greer, with plenty of guts and energy, wouldn't have any trouble making a tour of the various parcels of land and seeing that things were done right, not that man."

"If I get rid of Amos Greer right now, after what's just happened to me in New Orleans, Henry, I'd be ready to sell out and call it quits." Williamson laughed wanly. "I'm not really much of a farmer. My father was a good one back in England, and because I was his only son, I guess I just got into it because it was expected of me. He had a worse time with the Indians than I did, but he managed. And then back in Georgia I had a fellow by the name of Dan Denton, a hard-driving overseer who knew all about tobacco and indigo and cotton and how to keep the niggers in line. But when I decided to pull up stakes after Helen's death, Dan told me he'd already got another job lined up, and so we shook hands and that was it. Amos Greer came along just about then—he'd been working for a neighbor of mine who was in pretty bad health. No, I'd better hold on to him for a spell yet, Henry."

"Just as you say, Ed."

"I'd been hoping to keep enough ahead of the game to build my own ginning shed this summer," the older man went on. "But after last night, I'll have to abandon that project. It means I'm going to have to turn to you to get my cotton ready for the market, Henry."

"I'll be glad to. And I won't even raise my rate from last year, Ed. Nothing's too good for a friend and neighbor. Well, enjoy the sights. I'm going down to the hold and talk to Djamba, just so we both can get off on the right foot when we're back at Windhaven."

He turned to Mark, who eyed him uneasily, and said, "Keep Ed company and try to cheer him up, Mark boy. Say now, you look a mite peaked yourself—remember what I told you about burning the candle at both ends, eh?" And with a booming laugh, Henry Bouchard made his way down into the hold of the steamboat.

Williamson turned to the youth, a wan smile lighting his somber features. "He rides you a good deal, I can see that, Mark. Never mind. You've all your life ahead of you and you'll be your own master before long, I'm thinking. At least be grateful that you don't have my worries. How different things would have been for me if Helen hadn't died!"

"I was sorry to hear that you lost so much money, Mr. Williamson. But, like Pa says, you'll more than make it up with this year's crop. I guess you can look at it as if it were a kind of fling—something like the one I had."

"You've a real sense of humor, Mark." Williamson's laugh was short and grim. "The night I saw you, you didn't do too badly. And you're the age when a fellow can go to bed with a likely wench and wake up in the morning with no conscience to bother him. All I could think of was that I wallowed like a rutting dog, and I

178

was hoping that, if there is a hereafter, Helen didn't find out that the man she married, who wouldn't ever do more than take a hasty glance at a comely filly, behaved as if it was his first time, with some fancy girl."

"You oughtn't to downgrade yourself so much, Mr. Williamson. It's not as if your wife was alive and you were cheating on her. A man's got to have his fun, specially when he hasn't got a woman of his at home, I'm thinking."

"Lord, boy, you've got a head on those young shoulders. I envy you your youth. You're in a time when you're just feeling your muscles and finding out how much fun you can have before you get all weighted down with responsibilities."

"I'll be sixteen in September. And if you want to know something, I'd just as soon settle down with a girl I liked a lot and maybe have my own land and work it so nobody could tell me what I could do," Mark Bouchard countered. "Maybe I'm talking out of turn, Mr. Williamson, but I took a shine to that Maybelle of yours."

Williamson managed a half-hearted grin. "Well, if it's any comfort to you, Mark, she rather took a fancy to you. When we got back home after that big housewarming of yours, all she could talk about was what a cocksure, high-handed fellow you were. Now I know my girls, and when Maybelle gets riled up about a fellow and starts telling me she can't stand him for dirt, I know it's just the other way around, if you get my meaning, boy."

Mark kept the polite smile on his lips, though inwardly wincing at the paternal "boy" with which his own father so often exasperated him. Besides, it rubbed salt in the raw wound of his guilty knowledge of the outcome of that Friday afternoon session at the roulette wheel. Yet, at the same time, it had just reminded him also of his father's hint that an alliance with Maybelle would be very useful.

"Why, now, Mr. Williamson, I do hope your daughter didn't feel I wasn't showing her the proper respect. The fact is, she's a real handful and no mistake. A man

179

could do a lot worse than take himself a wife like your Maybelle."

Then, as he saw the man's eyes regarding him attentively, he lowered his own and, clearing his throat in the pretense of humility, added, "Sure, I know I'm too young to be talking about a thing like that, Mr. Williamson. But Mother got married when she wasn't hardly more than my age, you know, and I'd take it most kindly if, when I get to be sixteen this September, you would think it over that maybe I could be the right man for your Maybelle. I'd sure be mighty pleased if you would, Mr. Williamson."

"Well, now, Mark, as you say, it's just a little early to be talking about a solemn thing like marriage, and my girl's about a month younger than you are. But let's see how things work out, shall we? In the fall, if you're still in the same mind—and that saucy redhaired minx of mine hasn't set her cap for some other fellow—why, we'll talk about it then."

"That's very kind of you, sir." Mark grinned and shook the planter's hand. "Mighty kind of you indeed, and you can depend on it, I'll treat Maybelle right."

He could scarcely conceal his exultation. *By God, this might just be a way out of trouble! If Pa won't let me marry Louisa Voisin—and I'd sure much rather be hitched to her than Maybelle because then I could have Rosa whenever I wanted to—then maybe he'll be pleased enough that I took his advice to get myself a hold on old man Williamson, that he just might hand over the six thousand dollars as a kind of wedding present. Then I could pay that Mr. Lourat back—and I'll bet I could still sneak off to New Orleans whenever I had a mind to and have some fun with both Louisa and that sweet piece of slave meat Rosa.*

"Yassuh, he jist fine, suh. Jack and me, we jist brought him in a l'il cornpone and water, and he didn't give no trouble. Ah'll unlock de hold foah you now, suh. He sho nuff a mighty big nigger, dat one!" the gray-haired black freedman whose blue cap marked with the white letters, ORION, proclaimed him a mem-

180

ber of the steamboat crew, respectfully touched the bill of his cap and hurried over to the door of the hold which he unbolted and drew open. Henry Bouchard curtly nodded, then entered as the door closed behind him.

The Mandingo sprang to his feet from the wooden trunk on which he had been sitting. He wore only a pair of cotton trousers and heavy work shoes, his gleaming brown muscular body naked from the waist up, and Henry Bouchard was again impressed by the magnificent muscles of his new slave.

"Afternoon, Djamba." He smiled coldly. "You know I'm your new master, don't you?"

"Yes," came the single word, as Djamba's alert dark eyes studied the planter. But there was no insolence in that gaze, nothing from which Henry could take umbrage. Moreover, he was in an exceptionally genial mood over the events of this past week. No doubt about it, Sybella was still a mighty fine bedful for a man, but it never did any harm to enjoy a little variety, and certainly not the experienced kind Pierre Lourat offered a discriminating client. Those bitches had sweet little tricks he wouldn't even dream of asking Sybella to try on him, and the best thing about it was, they were white.

"That's good, Djamba. The man who sold you to me tells me that you killed lions back in Africa."

"Yes, massa," Djamba noncommittally answered. His unwavering look continued to study the man before him, and here in the darkened hold of the steamboat it was as if two adversaries, each respecting the other, had begun to take the other's measure.

"You can understand what I say to you?"

This time Djamba contented himself with a nod and his lips curved in just a semblance of an affirmative smile. He stood, arms at his sides, relaxed, yet the tremendous vitality and power of him was unmistakable. It was like a force contained, the true unleashed atavism of it controlled by the Mandingo's superb self-discipline. And it was an attitude which impressed Henry far more as to the veracity of Pierre Lourat's statement that this man had been a ruler of his tribe, than anything else could have done.

"Good. You're going to work for me at a big plantation called Windhaven. Maybe someday I'll make you fight other slaves to show how strong you are, Djamba. But for now, I'm going to let you work in the stables. I have many horses, some of them not yet tamed. I'll see how well you do with them."

"It will be as you say, massa." Djamba's voice was resonant yet soft, once again with the suggestion of contained power.

"You will have plenty to eat, and, if you are a good slave, I'll see that you have a woman at night. Would you like that?"

Djamba lowered his eyes. The white man's words recalled his grief for young Itulde. He closed his eyes a moment, a spasm of anguished memory crossing his features. Then, in an expressionless voice, nodding his head, he answered, "If massa wishes, Djamba will obey."

"That's fine!" Henry said. "That girl who took care of you on the ship taught you very well, Djamba. We'll get along fine together, you and I." Then his face hardened and his eyes narrowed: "But you must always remember that whatever you are told to do, you will do it. Otherwise, I will punish you. Remember that, Djamba. I am told that you were the ruler of your people back in Africa. Here at Windhaven it is I who rule. You will obey me as those people in your village obeyed you—do you understand me?"

"I do, massa."

"Very good! Now, this evening, we will come to Mobile. The men here will take you off this steamboat and take you to another one on which we will go to Windhaven tomorrow morning. They will bring you food and water, and they will not put ropes or chains around you if you do not try to run away."

"There is no place for me to run, massa." Djamba's eyes, unafraid, were steady.

"That's it exactly! No, there's no place to run away to, not when you're a slave, Djamba. If you remember

182

that, we'll get along fine. Now I'll leave you. Do you want more food or water?"

"No, massa, thank you."

Henry Bouchard's eyes widened. He had not expected such docility or such intelligent communication from the Mandingo. He thought to himself, *The black bastard is certainly a quick learner, and that Gullah girl must have been a damn good teacher. I'll bet he plowed her furrow many a time before they got to New Orleans.* Then, with a satisfied nod, he turned on his heel and left the hold.

CHAPTER THIRTEEN

"Lawsa mercy, but dat dere nigger's sure a sight for mah old eyes!" fat Mammy Clorinda rolled her eyes and clucked her tongue while the two Kru kitchen girls, Nancy and Lucille, simultaneously giggled and unconsciously rubbed their fingers against their thighs.

Henry Bouchard and his son Mark had returned to Windhaven just in time for lunch, and the former's first act had been to send Jimmy, the young stableboy, after Thomas with orders that the former overseer come at once to the kitchen.

Sybella had been with Arabella and Fleurette, all three of them enjoying the little raccoon's antics, and she had come to the landing of the second floor when she heard voices. "Welcome back, Henry darling!" she affectionately called, and then caught her breath at the sight of a towering, sturdy young slave who stood docilely just behind her husband and her son. At the sound of a woman's voice, Djamba looked slowly up, beheld the handsome, auburn-haired mistress of Windhaven. In her no-nonsense blue cotton dress with its flaring skirt, her shimmering hair rumpled from her frolicking with her daughters—all three of them had pretended to chase little Timmy round the room—she was suddenly aware of her mussed appearance. A slow blush suffused her cheeks as Djamba continued to fix her with his dark, intense eyes. Yet even at that distance, Sybella sensed that here was no ordinary slave,

185

and that there was nothing offensive or insolent in his demeanor.

Henry had looked up too, waved his hand and called, "I'll be up directly, Syb. Got myself a prime new hand in New Orleans, and I'm taking him out for Mammy Clorinda to feed him. Thomas will get him a cabin and settle him down. Are the girls all right?"

"Just fine, Henry darling. We've been playing with their new pet. It's a baby raccoon."

"A raccoon?" he scowled. "What the devil—well, we'll talk about that when I see you. Tell the girls I brought some presents for them. I've got a little doll for Fleurette and an ivory comb, a real Spanish comb, for Arabella."

Old Lucien Bouchard too had heard the sound of voices from his room on the first floor, and had come out to welcome back his son. Still erect and walking slowly but with unerring step, he had come toward the wide foyer at the entrance to the red-brick château, just in time to hear his son speak of a Spanish comb. At about the same time, Jimmy hurried back into the house, breathless from having run on his errand for the master: "Thomas, he say he go right to the kitchen, massa!" he exclaimed.

"All right, boy, you can go back to the stable," Henry Bouchard dismissed him. "Father, good to see you looking well as ever! I tell you, you're going to outlive all of us."

"You were never very good at flattery, Henry, so don't start now at your age," Lucien drily retorted, the ghost of a smile on his lips.

"And you still haven't stopped lecturing me, Father, old as I am," Henry Bouchard wryly countered. "This is Djamba. A full-blooded Mandingo, and from what Pierre Lourat tells me, king or prince or something like that of his entire tribe. First I thought of matching him against Ed Williamson's Davey—but poor old Ed gambled away every cent he made on his cotton last year, so I don't think he'll be wanting to arrange any fights for a while. Djamba"—this sharply to the silent Mandingo behind him, and without turning his head—

"this is my father, Lucien Bouchard. You'll take orders from him just as you will from me, and the woman above you is my wife and you'll obey her too."

"I will, massa," Djamba murmured.

Then Henry bade Mark greet his mother and tidy up for lunch, and after a cordial leavetaking of his father and the promise that he would meet him in the study later to tell him about the trip to Mobile and New Orleans, headed for the kitchen with Djamba following him as a trained dog follows its master.

Lucien Bouchard stood there, watching the tall, powerful slave walk quickly after his son. He remained there for a long moment, and many thoughts crowded back out of the limbo of the past, evoked now like friendly, companionable ghosts after so long by his son's words, by the sight of the sturdy, superbly muscular Mandingo. *A Spanish comb for Arabella, my son said. Ah, I once bought a Spanish comb in Mobile for my young wife Dimarte, and I buried it in the ground beside her grave and perhaps it is still there. How the cycle of life renews itself and continues, and how much of what is old becomes new again, and will be old and then again new throughout all our days! And that slave, that tall, handsome, fearless slave who reminds me a little of Ben in the days when both of us were young and learning to know each other as men, not as slave and master. But will that day ever come again for Windhaven? Not with Henry and perhaps still less with Mark, I fear. Only with Luke. Yes, it was as the owl foretold just after my last birthday. As the owl foretold. . . .*

"This is Djamba, Thomas," Henry Bouchard said. "Let him eat all he wants, and if you can talk his language, explain to him that for the time being he will be under your orders. I'd like to see what he can do with horses, especially that ornery Midnight. So take him out to the stable with you, then pick a cabin for him. Don't let any of the wenches near him yet—I'm not sure whether I'm going to breed him, though he's for

187

sure prime stock and you don't mate stock like that with just any nigger wench."

"I'll take care of it, Mr. Bouchard, sir." Thomas's voice was low and deferential.

"That's about all, then. How are the fields coming along?"

"I've been over to see all your foremen, Mr. Bouchard, at least two-three times a week. They're hoed and chopped pretty good now. You can be putting in your seed whenever you're ready."

"And Luke?"

"He's taking hold real good, Mr. Bouchard. You'll be proud of him. Gets along fine with all the field hands."

"Yes, I suppose he would." There was an underlying contempt in Henry's voice, but Thomas did not acknowledge it in any way, standing patiently waiting beside the tall Mandingo. Henry Bouchard ordered Mammy Clorinda to prepare some lunch for Sybella and himself and to have one of the girls bring it up on a tray and to be quick about it. And then he went back up the stairs to the second floor to Sybella.

"Mammy, get Djamba some pone and any meat you can spare and maybe a little soup," Thomas urged.

"Yassuh, ah kin see dat big nigger kin take lotsa feedin', dat foah shuah!" the fat cook cackled. "You gals, you done heerd what Thomas said, so jist you shake youah stumps or Ah'll take a switch to you, heah?"

Again Nancy and Lucille giggled, not so much out of fear of Mammy's threat—for by now they knew that the cook was the very soul of kindness—but rather out of a spellbound fascination at the towering young man who patiently waited. Mammy Clorinda eyed them sharply, then glanced back at Djamba and began to laugh till her enormous bosom jiggled: "Hee, hee, hee, doan dat beat all! Ah knows wut you gals has got on youah minds, doan think Ah doan! You is figgerin how you'se gwine sneak off to his cabin when it gits real dark and hab him mess wid you, ain't dat right?"

"Oh no, Mammy Clorinda, I wasn't thinking that at

all," Lucille gasped. She bit her lips and lowered her eyes, suddenly agitated.

"Ah knows, chile." Mammy Clorinda's voice was low and gentle. "You's a good gal, Ah knows that right well. Doggone shame de massa up and had you pleasure dat ol' Mistah Williamson. But dat wut a slave has gotta git used to, chile. Dey ain't no other way nohow. Now you be sweet 'n git dis yeah big nigger somepin good to eat, you heah?"

"Why—yes, right away, Mammy," Lucille faltered.

Thomas turned to study the newcomer, his sober face kindly and concerned. Tentatively, he asked in Ashanti, "The master called you a Mandingo. Is it so, my brother?"

In the same tongue, though haltingly, Djamba replied, "It is so, my brother. I was of the Mopti near the River Niger. I was to be their king, but my brother and his treacherous wife betrayed not only me but my people, and we were taken into bondage."

"You are strong and young, you will have a new life here. I myself am free, for old Mr. Lucien, the man with the white hair, who dresses in the soft skin of the deer, believes that all men are brothers and should not be slaves."

"It was he, then, whom I saw come out to speak to the man who bought me?"

"Yes, that was he. And the man who bought you is his son, but he does not hold with his father. He believes that those with black and brown skins are born to be slaves and to serve him and to do his bidding. But his wife, the mistress, she with the hair of the color of fire, she is good and kind. She has kept many slaves from having felt the whip when the master is angry with them. And then there is the older son, whose name is Luke. He has been made the overseer of this place, and he works on the land with his hands just like the slaves, and he, like the old man with the white hair, believes that all men are brothers. I will help you all I can, Djamba, so that slavery will not be too harsh for you."

The Mandingo held out both hands and Thomas

189

gripped them. Then Djamba said slowly in the Ashanti tongue, "Nothing that happens to me here can be as terrible as that which has already taken place. To have my brother sell me into slavery, to see my own young wife bound and made to follow in the coffle of the slaves marching to the great ship that brought us across the seas. And then to see her beaten because she would not let the men in that ship dishonor her, so that in her shame she flung herself into the waters to die honorably—nothing, my brother, can destroy my soul and my courage more than that."

"You are called Djamba. In your tongue, I know that it means 'the proud warrior.' I, Thomas, tell you this. You must learn to humble your pride, you must conquer within yourself the fierce instinct to fight those who would tyrannize you. Yes, in this new country, there are already many whites who rule those who have the misfortune to be their slaves with cruelty and hatred, a hatred born out of fear that one day the slaves will rise up against their brutal masters. But I tell you, Djamba, that here at Windhaven there are many who are good and kind and who do not look upon you with scorn or fear. And I myself will be your brother in the days of your new life with us, to help you all I can to understand this."

Mammy Clorinda and her two kitchen girls watched open-mouthed as the Ashanti and the Mandingo again clasped hands and stared into each other's eyes. Then, with an apologetic little laugh, Thomas turned to them. "Now then, Mammy Clorinda, show Djamba what kind of vittles a good worker can expect from you here at Windhaven."

Both Lucille and Nancy had outdone themselves in serving the young Mandingo, while the fat cook chuckled and shook her head in ribald amusement. "You gals better not fuss round dat dere nigger so much, less'n you wants to get busted good," she teasingly warned. And then, rolling her eyes expressively again, she muttered, half to herself, "Lawsa mercy, effen Ah wuz 'bout ten years younger 'n shed me some of mah babyfat, Ah'd make a fuss mahself!"

When he had had his fill, Djamba turned questioningly to Thomas, who nodded: "Come now, my brother, I'll show you the horses we keep here at Windhaven. Some are for working, some for riding. And there is a new one whose name is Midnight, whom you will find to be as strong and proud and spirited as yourself. Perhaps he will understand you better than he does young Jimmy, who, for all his skill, has not yet managed to train him to be ridden by a master."

In the Ashanti tongue, Djamba responded softly, "Perhaps, like myself, he finds it hard to believe that once he was free and now must serve another. You are kind and wise, my brother. You will help me learn this hard lesson, as I must."

Thomas led the way to the low, sturdily built stable, made of hewn oak and pine, the chinks thoroughly covered with an improvised cement made from the rich red clay so prevalent in the fertile section of this new Southern state. The lanky young Kru stableboy, Jimmy, bobbed his head and grinned at the sight of the former overseer, and hurried to open the two wide doors by drawing away the narrow plank which served as bolt between the broad wooden handles. It was plain to see that the size and height of the new slave greatly impressed him, judging from his nervously uneasy glances at the silent, poised Mandingo.

"Jimmy, this is Djamba. The master just brought him from New Orleans, and I'd like him to help you with the horses. He's going to see what he can do with Midnight."

"Yassuh, Mistah Thomas suh," Jimmy hastily yet respectfully agreed. "Now effen all ob dem wuz lak Dulcy, Miz Bouchard's mare, wouldn't be no trouble for dis yeah nigger! But dat Midnight, he a real debbil hoss, dat foah shoah!"

The stable had been neatly sectioned off into twenty stalls, ten on each side, amply wide and with piles of hay, buckets of oats and water for the working mules used in the cotton gin, several pack ponies, and the mares, geldings and stallions. At the far back of the stable, there stood a light four-wheeled phaeton, with two seats facing forward and its separate front seat for the coachman. Thomas and two slaves who were expert carpenters had just finished it after a month of work, devoting what time they could after their daily chores were done.

"When you get a chance, Jimmy, see if you can't polish up those wheels some," Thomas told the stable-boy. He walked over to inspect the phaeton, Djamba slowly following him and alertly observing the horses and mules in the stalls. "And you just might smooth down these two little seats at the back, Jimmy; that'll be where Miss Bella and Missy Fleurette will ride with their mamma and papa once the weather gets a little warmer."

"I'll do that right off, Mistah Thomas suh!" Jimmy eagerly agreed. "See, dat ornery Midnight, he heah us comin', he already startin' to kick up his heels!"

At the very last and largest stall to the right, not far from the phaeton, a magnificent black stallion with a white star on its forehead snorted, kicked fretfully at the door of its stall, then whinnied, its eyes bright and suspicious at the sight of the tall newcomer.

"Ol' Mistah Lucien, he comin', Mistah Thomas suh!" Jimmy suddenly piped up, turning to point at the entrance of the stable. It was true. The white-haired founder of Windhaven, after having heard his son Henry's brief report about the purchase of a slave of unusually prime quality, had come out to see for himself.

"Afternoon, Mr. Lucien," Thomas smilingly greeted the one man of whom his dead father Ben had once said, "He's the only man I know, my son, whom I'd willingly call master."

"And to you too, Thomas, and Jimmy. This must be Djamba about whom my son Henry was just telling me."

"Yes, Mr. Lucien." Thomas touched the hand of the Mandingo, murmuring something in the Ashanti tongue.

Djamba turned and stared at the wiry old man, who

192

wore the necklace of bear claws around his neck, that symbol of fortitude in the wilderness which he himself had taken to prove to the hostile Creeks that he, like they, could endure hardship and great danger. Their eyes met, and there was a long silence between them, as the young stableboy uneasily glanced at Thomas, then back at the two men, races and ages apart and yet in this moment of meeting somehow communing without words.

"You are strong and proud, Djamba," Lucien Bouchard gently said with a quick smile. "That is good. This land is new to you, I know, but I hope that you will one day call it home."

"Yes, massa."

Lucien Bouchard approached the Mandingo and held out his hand. "I will be your friend here, as I know Thomas is already, Djamba. Will you take my hand in friendship?"

For a moment, Djamba did not move, but his eyes narrowed as if he were trying to read into this strange old man's very soul. Thomas, beside him, murmured again in the dialect which Djamba fluently understood; then, with a nod and an almost shy grin, the muscular young black held out his hand and Lucien clasped it.

"That is good. Thomas will see that no one treats you badly, Djamba. Now, my son tells me you have great skill with animals. But I do not think you had a horse as fine as this in Africa where you came from."

Djamba watched him intently, almost as if he were memorizing Lucien Bouchard's features. Then, without turning his gaze, he murmured something to Thomas, who translated: "He says that he had oxen in the village where he was chief, and that he and the hunters would set traps for wild antelopes when they did not come close enough to be killed with the spear or the bow and arrow."

"Perhaps an antelope would be swifter than Midnight, but I'm not sure of that." Lucien Bouchard smilingly shrugged. "Thomas, you were only a very little boy, perhaps still a baby, when I first met Charles Weatherford, who built a trading house on the first eastern bluff below where the Coosa and Tallapoosa met. He was the first man to lay out a race path, and he would go into Georgia and steal ponies and horses and train them so that he could gamble with the Indians on the speed of this or that animal."

"I seem to remember just a little. Wasn't he the father of the man who led the Creeks against General Andy Jackson?"

"The very same, the very same. Now you see, some of the horses Charles Weatherford stole were from the Spanish around Mobile. Many of them came originally from Mexico, and had been bred with wild ponies and horses from Florida and Georgia as well. Midnight must surely be from such interbreeding. In some ways, he reminds me of my wonderful Arabe. The long forelegs, that strong chest and barrel, the firm withers and above all that spirited head with that defiant look in his eyes—yes, there's the wild mare and the Spanish stallion from generations back."

"We found him nearly a year ago just beyond that forest to the southeast, didn't we, Mr. Lucien?" Thomas put in. "Lord knows how long he'd been living there or what happened to the rest of the herd he ran with."

"Alas, perhaps they vanished as the Creeks have vanished from the land, Thomas," Lucien Bouchard sadly replied. "But I'm glad you found him. And I hope his spirit will never be broken—just as I hope that for Djamba too."

As Lucien Bouchard spoke, the Mandingo slowly approached the stall in which the great black stallion still snorted and pawed in its straw. It reared back, snorting a warning, but as Djamba slowly stretched out his arms, palms upward, Midnight halted. Its bright brown eyes considered the Mandingo, who did not move his hands but continued to stand facing the magnificent stallion. Then Djamba spoke, unintelligible words, soft and soothing, some with a quick sibilance to them, and Midnight tossed its head, then approached the door of the stall, snuffling and bobbing its head out toward his outstretched palms.

194

"Ah nebba thought anybody could git dat close widout Midnight's kickin' up a real fuss," Jimmy breathed incredulously.

"Quickly, Jimmy, some sugar if you have it, or a carrot will do," Lucien Bouchard whispered to the stableboy.

Jimmy hurried over to a small wooden trough which stood between two of the pony stalls, took out a large, irregular-shaped cone of brown sugar and broke off a small lump, then hastened back to put it into Djamba's right hand, hastily backing away even as he did so. "I tried dat once, Mistah Lucien—ah means massa—" he nervously confided in a hoarse whisper, " 'n he lak to near take mah hand off, dat Midnight did!"

"I've told you, Jimmy, you needn't call Thomas or me master, not ever, unless, of course, my son Henry is around or one of the other planters. Now then, let's watch and see what Midnight does," Lucien Bouchard said.

Once again Djamba spoke in the dialect with which he had first addressed the stallion. Midnight whinnied, tossed its head, then warily approached, drawing back its lips to bare its powerful teeth, Djamba smiled and nodded. Almost daintily, the stallion nipped up the lump of sugar, crunched it, whinnied again, then bobbed its head as if in gratitude.

"Wal, Ah declare, doan dat beat all!" Jimmy gasped, shaking his head in disbelief.

"I think, Thomas," Lucien Bouchard smilingly declared, "Midnight has found a friend, and so has Djamba."

CHAPTER FOURTEEN

Two weeks after his return from New Orleans, Mark Bouchard composed two letters, not without painstaking thought and effort. One of them was addressed to Mademoiselle Louisa Voisin at the address on Eglantine Street; the other to Pierre Lourat at the auction rooms on Chartres Street. Since the distance between Lowndesboro and New Orleans was under four hundred miles, the cost was ten cents per letter. The letter to the exotic woman who had enticed him with the beautiful teenaged octoroon promised that he would soon speak to his father to arrange marriage between them; the letter to the Creole gambler urged the latter to keep the secret and be patient until such time as Mark Bouchard could broach this important project with some hope of paternal approval. Having learned the schedule of steamboats up and down the Alabama River, Mark managed to be at the loading dock of the Windhaven plantation just when the *Orion* docked briefly, made his way up the gangplank and hastily handed the two sheets of paper (folded and closed with sealing wax, the addresses scrawled on the back) to the captain and held out two silver dollars. "I'd take it kindly as a favor if you'd get these sent down to New Orleans, Captain. And here's enough to pay the postage and to drink my health into the bargain," he offered.

"Be glad to, sonny," the steamboat captain said, ignoring Mark's frown at the belittling term. "Ah ha, I see one of them's to a lady. Now I remember you, you and your pappy came up with us from Mobile couple weeks back, ain't that right now?"

"Yes, that's right." Mark glowered. "Are you going to take them or not?"

"Now don't get techy, sonny. 'Course I'll take them. You paid me mighty handsome, didn't you? Just you stop worrying, they'll get there, maybe in a week or so. All right now, if that's all the business you've got with me, sonny, mind getting back down on the dock? Want to get up steam and get to Mobile on time." He winked broadly at the irritated youth. "You ain't the only fellow's got a gal down yonder. Well, seein' as how I'm going all the way on to New Orleans myself this trip, I might just look this little lady up myself, you understand. Now mebbe she might just take a fancy to a full-grown man—no offense meant, sonny. Just my little joke, you know."

With an angry glare, Mark stomped down the gangplank to the dock, watched as it was pulled up, and the shrill blast of the steamboat whistle and the chugging of the paddle wheels announced its departure. *Stupid old fool*, he thought to himself, clenching his fists and staring after the departing steamboat. Then he turned slowly back toward the red-brick château, the prey of fretful anxieties. If he had his choice, he'd much rather marry that fine lady Louisa and have her tasty slave girl thrown in as a bed wench. Not that Maybelle, that little red-haired spitfire, wasn't a tasty armful, not by a long shot. But the important thing was that Pierre Lourat would keep his mouth shut about that $6000 and be patient enough to wait until he could straighten this out with Pa and find out just how the land lay. Because when it came to hard cash, Pa was a particularly tough and ornery customer. As he reached the château, he brightened. Pa had wanted him not to miss the chance of getting Maybelle to consider him as a husband, and while he waited for just the right time to tell him about Louisa Voisin, he could be sparking Maybelle a little and let old man Williamson know that he was serious about the girl. That would please Pa too, seeing that he was doing something Pa had told him to do.

Well, he'd go back to the Academy next Monday, but from some of the remarks Pa had made on the trip back home, it was pretty plain that he didn't hold much with book learning, and that was just fine with Mark. Let Luke work in the fields all day and stay up late at night reading those silly books Grandfather had in the library all he wanted to, he didn't really know what life was all about yet. Mark grinned to himself with the smug look of a man who had just figured out how to eat his cake and have it too. Why, here he'd bedded a fancy girl and a cute little octoroon bitch all in the same week, eaten like a king and drunk champagne, and taken his turn in the gambling room like any fine gentleman, and Luke hadn't done any of those things, though he was nearly four years older.

Henry Bouchard's first impulse on seeing the little raccoon had been to kick it, but he had restrained himself on discovering how delighted both Arabella and Fleurette were over the new pet, and how pleased Sybella herself appeared to be that her precociously flirtatious older daughter now had something to think about besides boys and the next housewarming party. Moreover, he had good-naturedly reflected to himself that he was quite willing to endure the presence of a tame raccoon in exchange for not being asked about the diversions which had kept him a week in New Orleans. Nor did he think it necessary to tell Sybella that he had had Mark initiated in a house of pleasure. He did, however, tactfully suggest—one night after he had come to her bed and quite satisfactorily made love to her—that there was really no need for his younger son to continue at the Lowndesboro Academy. "You can see for yourself, Syb, honey," he had murmured as he caressed her still youthfully firm breasts, "how restless the young scamp is up at that school. I think if he worked on the land and maybe rode horseback and saw to some of the smaller chores around the plantation, especially on my own holdings, he'd feel himself to be more useful. You know how a boy is when he's beginning to approach manhood, honey. And of course he's bound to be envious of Luke, now that Luke's overseer."

"Well, Henry, if that's what you think best, I certainly shan't stand in the way," she had agreed, in a voice rather huskily soft with the unexpected luxury of passion given and taken between them as in their first days of marriage. Indeed, she had hoped that this renewal of their union would bring them another child and perhaps not only solidify their marriage but also prove to him that there was no need for him to seek his carnal pleasure elsewhere. She understood well enough that many a neighboring planter visited the slave cabins to have both release from carnal yearnings and to sire offspring who would be the more valuable because they were their own. Indeed, she had even shocked him a little this very night—to her secret delighted amusement and the happy recollection of their very first time together—by saying, "You know, my darling, that a wife isn't really very different from one of your black slave girls. She can pleasure you, and usually a great deal more because she loves you and isn't afraid of you, and she can also breed." He had silenced her with a greedy kiss and made her shudder with sensual response in his ardent taking of her.

However, even though both Arabella and Fleurette shared Timmy, who each day was growing more and more inquisitive and beginning to wander around the fields from daybreak, when the little girls let him out, until nightfall when he would return, it was Fleurette who declared, "You get to play more with Timmy than I do, Bella. I do so wish he was all mine. Maybe Thomas can find one just like him, just for me, maybe, Bella?"

And when Arabella, once again acting like the grown-up young lady she yearned to be, had responded, "I should say not, Fleurette! Daddy wouldn't let us have two, he doesn't even like Timmy around as it is. And besides, Timmy just likes me better than he likes you, that's all," Fleurette burst into tears and ran to her mother's room for consolation.

"There, there, don't cry, sweetheart," Sybella had crooned as she cuddled the sobbing little girl in her arms, "we'll see if Thomas can't find you some other kind of pet you can take care of all by yourself. It wasn't nice of your sister to tease you like that, honey. Now I'll tell you what, I'll ask Thomas if he can't whittle you a nice wooden horse or maybe a bird. Would you like that?"

"Why—yes, Mama," Fleurette had sniffled, blinking her eyes to clear them of the tears and hugging Sybella with an impulsive eagerness, "but I'd lots rather have something just like Timmy. Please, could I, Mama? Daddy wouldn't mind, would he, not really?"

"We'll see, Fleurette. Now then, my big girl isn't going to cry over how silly her big sister has been, is she? Let's go down to the kitchen and see if Mammy Clorinda can't find my sweetheart something specially nice to eat for lunch, shall we?"

It was the second week of March, and the field hands were busy planting the seed for the new crop. Luke and his grandfather spent many hours on the acres that stretched far behind the château, and the founder of Windhaven walked along the rows with his grandson following him, pausing to chat with the workers, most of whose names he remembered and for all of whom he had a warm smile and gracious words of encouragement. Luke had seen to it that his grandfather's instructions for the diversification of crops had been carried out, and already some of the snap bean plants were beginning to push up through the rich soil.

"If we don't have too much rain this year, Luke, the crops should be abundant. There'll be enough to feed all the workers as well as ourselves," Lucien observed with a satisfied nod after he had completed his tour of inspection. "What saddens me is that I can do so little for the Creeks. Of course I'm still sending supplies every month, but there are so few of them left, and they don't know from day to day when they'll be told to leave the state. Promise me, Luke, that if anything

201

should happen to me, you'll see that they're dealt with fairly, and that the greedy speculators who follow them like a flock of buzzards won't steal their land certificates away from them. Most of all, make sure that when the orders are given to move them, Thomas's niece and nephew are brought here and given a home. If necessary, to satisfy the rigorous laws, you may have to register them as slaves—and since their mother was black, that at least will help to verify the fiction of their reason for being here. It would be cruel to send them on to the far West."

"I promise I'll do everything I can for them, Grandfather."

"I know you will, Luke. Now, even though a great deal of the money in my Mobile account which I allocated to those good friends was wiped out, there's still enough there to pay for such clothes and tools and other things they'll need on their journey West. Once again, as I say, if I shouldn't be here to see to it myself, use the money to buy provisions and useful tools for them. Giving them the money outright might be unwise—because of President Jackson's financial policies, it's quite possible that any currency from this part of the country might not be recognized or have the same value where they're going. Also, there's the danger that it could be stolen from them—you understand, Luke."

The youth nodded.

"Well then, Luke, I think we've put in a good day's work. My old bones are beginning to feel it, I can tell you. Let's go back by way of the little creek. It's such a pleasant view there too, and maybe we'll find Arabella and Fleurette out looking for Timmy."

As they neared the far side of the fields and the hill which bordered them, old Lucien halted and turned to Luke: "Let me stand here a minute, my grandson. I would commune with the spirits of those others who were dear to me, as well as my beloved Dimarte."

Luke, understanding, moved quietly away and walked on slowly toward the rows of slave cabins. He saw Thomas there, talking earnestly with two young Gullahs, who were nodding eagerly. The shadows of the setting sun had touched the well-spaced furrows where the crops would grow, making the earth seem still richer in that subduing shadow which mingled with the last warm rays. He could see the men working in the fields, many of them looking up at the old man who stood so erect, facing the hill, hands clasped as in prayer, head bowed, his lips silently moving. He understood that Lucien Bouchard was paying tribute to the memories of courageous young Amelia, the bondservant whom that old man had long ago saved from death at Econchate as a suspected conspiratress in the assassination of the *Mico* Tunkamara; to the little child Etienne who had died of river fever while Ben's and Ellen's child Thomas, stricken with that same malady also, had survived; and to the gentle English girl Priscilla who had died giving birth to Luke's own father, Henry.

And when Lucien Bouchard slowly turned to come toward him, Luke could see that ineffable look of anguish on his grandfather's weatherbeaten, wrinkled face; could understand that in this timeless moment of communion, his grandfather had reached back through the long distant years to recall the abiding love and faith which both those young women had so willingly given, love and faith so strong that even in their brief span they had strengthened this indomitable old man and intensified his courage against adversity.

He waited till the old man came to him, and did not speak, waiting for him to break this reverent silence. Then at last Lucien sighed deeply and said gently, "My days are numbered, Luke, while yours have scarcely begun. Sometimes a man is impatient to know what destiny holds in store for him. I know that when I was back in Paris and attending the university, I had all those fine youthful dreams about freedom for all mankind and justice and truth and honor which would not be achieved by the point of a sword or the barrel of a musket. Sometimes I've asked myself what would have happened if I had stayed in France and tried to cope with the horrors of a revolution born out of hatred and oppression. Instead, I sought a new land for a new beginning. Could I have been a coward in believing that no man could halt the whirlwind of that agonized revolt against feudal aristocracy?"

"No one could ever call you a coward, Grandfather."

"Not in the physical sense, perhaps, Luke. But even the bravest man is sometimes helpless against such terrible enemies as bigotry and prejudice. You see, I gave up my birthright of aristocracy, only to find that after all these years here in this new country there are already signs of another kind of harmful aristocracy—those who seek to be richer than their neighbors in the possession of land and slaves, who look upon laboring with one's hands as unworthy, fit only for their black inferiors. What I fear most is that one day in your own time, Luke, there may be just such a revolution against the oppression which this new aristocracy is certain to breed. If it happens, then yours will be the choice of how to cope with it without sacrificing those ideals in which you steadfastly believe and without which your life cannot satisfy you."

"But you know that I do not hold with slavery anymore than you do, Grandfather."

Lucien Bouchard stopped and put his hand on his grandson's shoulder. "I know that, my grandson. Those workers out there in my fields are freed men, yet if I were to tell them today to go find employment elsewhere, where would they go? How would they survive? On your father's land, there are only slaves, and our neighbors have black slaves also. Soon the land will be barren. And then they will be driven to make their profits through the trading and breeding of slaves, and there is the tragic evil. And with more slaves there will be even stricter laws enacted to keep these slaves in bondage lest they revolt against their masters. The revolution in France came about because the multitudes of poor and oppressed peasants could no longer endure the rigorous laws and taxations imposed upon them by the nobility who thought that their arrogant rule was conferred upon them by right of birth and destined to be immortal. You see, Luke, men study history in the fine universities and in the handsome books in their libraries, but they do not always profit from the lessons history has to offer us. Think of that, my grandson, and think how helpless one man can be, however strongly he may believe in justice and honor, if the world goes mad around him."

"Why, Grandfather, I should think a man would first try to survive and then to find a frontier where he could put his own theories into practice, just as you've done."

Lucien Bouchard smiled and shook his head. "Your answer is exactly the same as mine when I was at the University of Paris, Luke. And as you grow older, you'll see that you must change and adapt those fine theories to reality. Sometimes you'll have to compromise, yes, even to survive. But there's one thing I'd say to you, one thing I've learned in my long life. And it's simply this: life is empty without the sharing of love, love far beyond the physical aspect which is nature's way of perpetuating us all. Love is a sharing and a giving, not a taking. And I, more than most men, have been blessed with its abundance. I loved three women in my life, those three who are with me always, even now. It was willed that my time with each should be all too brief, and yet each in her own way gave me wisdom and courage. And each of them had the constancy that would have endured a lifetime if God had granted it; yet in a sense, He did, since I remember each so well with my own faithful constancy. May it be His will, Luke, that the woman you choose will stand by you and match you in your devotion to her. That's my prayer, my grandson." Then his eyes brightened and he added cheerfully, "Look there, near the creek, Arabella and Fleurette have found their pet! He's crawling inside that hollow log, the rascal, and now he's sticking his head out and looking at them."

"There's something in that ravine just ahead of the creek, Grandfather—why, it's a little rabbit, and it looks as if its leg is broken!" Luke exclaimed.

The ravine was near a patch of wild clover which extended for about a dozen feet and was about a yard

205

away from the very last row of corn which old Lucien had designated to be planted in this distant portion. A crude snare had been dug near the edge of the clover patch, but so clumsily contrived that when the rabbit's hind paw was caught, the frame had toppled over. In the ravine, the little white rabbit squealed and struggled, a piece of the cord still trailing from its paw. Its leg had been broken between the first joint and paw, and now as the two men approached, it lay on its side, its terrified eyes rolling up at them, its mouth open, its sides heaving.

Arabella and Fleurette, having heard the rabbit's squeals, now hurried toward the ravine. Arabella cradled Timmy in her arms, while Fleurette tried to keep up with her, glancing up at her sister with a look of reproach on her face.

"Oh, it's a little bunny!" Fleurette exclaimed, squatting down and holding out her arms to it. "It hurt its leg, oh poor little bunny!"

"If I can set the leg, Luke, it would make a fine pet for the little one, don't you think?" Old Lucien quizzically eyed his grandson. "Arabella seems to have appropriated Timmy all to herself, judging from the way Fleurette's looking at her."

"I'll give you a hand, Grandfather. I'll hold its head and front paws," Luke offered.

"Poor frightened little thing," the old man murmured. He glanced hurriedly around in search of a piece of wood; then he uttered an exclamation of satisfaction as he saw a sturdy, straight twig lying in his path, and slowly stooped to retrieve it.

"This will do for a splint, Luke. And I think my kerchief will bind it firmly. You hold it while I set the leg."

As the rabbit saw the two men step down into the shallow ravine, it squealed again and tried to drag itself away. Luke gently cupped its head, murmuring soothingly to it, while old Lucien swiftly and mercifully snapped the joint back into place. The rabbit fought savagely at that twinge of pain, but Luke held it firmly as Lucien pressed the twig against the joint and then wound his kerchief tightly round it, deftly knotting it. "There now, there now, it's all over," he said.

Thomas had come to the edge of the fields and squatted down on the edge of the ravine. "I guess it was Danny who set that snare, Mr. Lucien," he volunteered. "He and Arthur were just telling me they had a hankering for rabbit stew, and they'd seen a couple of rabbits over near that clover the other day."

Lucien lifted the little rabbit into his arms and stepped out of the ravine, his face aglow with its gentle smile. "Do you suppose you could build a hutch for it, Thomas? Maybe in the stable. Horses love to have a pet around, I've observed. And we'll let Fleurette name it and keep it for her very own." He turned to the little girl. "Would you like that, Fleurette? Then you won't mind so much if Arabella tends to Timmy. It'll be your rabbit, not hers."

"Oh yes, Grandpa, I want the little bunny! It's so pretty and soft and white!" she exclaimed, clapping her hands and jumping up and down. And this time it was Arabella's turn to sulk and, to show that it really didn't matter, to hug Timmy closer and to look down at it and whisper to it, "That's all right, Timmy, you like me better anyway, you know you do."

"Sure, Mr. Lucien, I'd be glad to. And it's real easy to feed it, too, Miss Fleurette. Now you take that clover there, or carrots and carrot tops or lettuce or anything green, it'll get fat and sassy, you just watch."

"That's what I'll call it— I'll call it Sassy!" Fleurette decided. "Can I watch you make the bunny a place to stay, can I?"

"Of course you can, honey. Come along and we'll see if maybe you can't help me make it," Thomas chuckled as he carefully took the rabbit from Lucien and moved toward the stable, the little girl happily skipping along beside him.

It was twilight now, and on the other side of the fields and beyond them, the red bluff stood in its darkened majesty. Lucien turned to stare at it, a hand to his squinting eyes as if to clarify his vision. He said softly, almost as if to himself, "Seeing my father's gamekeeper kill a man for having snared just such a rabbit as that one brought me here. Now the cycle is complete. It is a sign that all my roots are here, all my hopes and dreams."

CHAPTER FIFTEEN

A month afetr Mark Bouchard had written to his inamorata, the *River Queen* halted its journey to Montgomery to stop long enough at the loading dock near Windhaven Plantation to drop off a packet of letters for Lucien and Henry, and Louisette Entrevois' reply to Mark. There were also some supplies from Mobile which Henry Bouchard had ordered, and Thomas supervised the unloading of these, then brought the packet of letters into the château.

Old Lucien's letter was from Antoine Rigalle, enclosing a current accounting of the former's negotiable drafts and accrued savings, as well as a personal note from Jules Ronsart's aging successor. The note reassured Lucien that his wish to have $75,000 withdrawn from his personal account and transferred to the Bank of Liverpool had been carried out, with the name of Luke Bouchard as joint owner. If at any time Lucien's grandson wished to draw upon that sum, he had only to express that request in a formal letter which would bear a recognizable signature. For Lucien Bouchard had already arranged the recognition of his grandson's signature and had had the lawyer Grover Mason draw up a document attesting to Lucien's wish that, in the event of his death, Luke would then be free to demand the entire principal amount.

But there was a postscript to this personal note which greatly troubled Lucien. In it, Antoine Rigalle remarked that the daughter of the late Philippe Entrevois, now grown to womanhood and as yet unmarried, was apparently in the employ of the slave dealer and gambler Pierre Lourat, who apparently had either paid off her late father's pressing debts or satisfied the creditors as to eventual payment in full. Moreover, Rigalle wrote, this attractive woman had changed her name to Louisa Voisin and could often be seen at the theater or the opera in the company of Pierre Lourat, together with a beautiful young octoroon girl named Rosa. It was the Creole banker's strong suspicion that Rosa was the child of Philippe Entrevois as a result of his union with a strikingly beautiful quadroon with whom he had established a permanent liaison after his wife's death. Lucien sat in his study rereading the note, staring out of the window and frowning with apprehension. He well recalled how, some nineteen years ago, when he had taken Henry to New Orleans, Philippe Entrevois and his lovely daughter had paid a visit to the counting house. Still more vividly, he recalled how Henry had praised the girl's beauty and expressed the hope that he could find a wife like her, and he remembered his scathing answer to his son.

Was it possible that Henry had met and visited the daughter of Edmée de Courent, that tantalizing young girl with whom he had believed himself to be so deeply in love back in Normandy? The years seemed to fall away as he closed his eyes and remembered Edmée's sensitive oval face, the soft tremulous lips, the sweet voice. She had been only eight years old when he first saw her and already was fascinated by her piquancy and femininity. And in the decade to follow he had watched her grow to young womanhood, desirable, provocative, and, as he had then thought, possessed with a keen intelligence which would understand and share his dreams. Instead, she had been only a shallow opportunist, preferring his brother Jean to him because such a union would bring her the title of countess, and at the same time unexpectedly and shamelessly proposing that she be his mistress even though she would still be his brother's wife. Because of her, because of his indignation over the death of that little poacher who had been killed for trespassing on a nobleman's estate, he had left his home and crossed the ocean to find a new start in a wilderness ruled by people called savages, yet whose laws and culture often showed that they were perhaps even more civilized than those who would hunt them down and seek to drive them from the land forever.

No, he told himself, Henry wouldn't be that much of a fool to have an affair with Edmée's daughter. Certainly if Antoine Rigalle knew such damaging gossip about the woman who now called herself Louisa Voisin, all of New Orleans would know it too. What a strange quirk of fate it was that, having fled France and believed that he had put Edmée away from him forever, she had come to Mobile as an indentured bondservant. He had freed her, slaked his youthful desire for her in a single night of unreasoning passion, hoping then that she would never again cross the orderly pathway of his life. And yet her daughter now appeared again upon the Bouchard horizon, doubly threatening because Philippe Entrevois had had the black blood of his grandmother in his veins.

He crumpled Rigalle's note, his cheeks twitching with anger, thrust it into his jacket pocket. No, there was no need to pry into his son's affairs. Doubtless Henry would continue to be unfaithful to Sybella by visiting the elegant bordellos of New Orleans whenever he had the occasion, but at least he appeared to have learned the good sense of not openly flaunting his transient passions with any of the slave women and girls who toiled on his own holdings, not since that dreadful quarrel with young Mark last November. And besides, knowing Henry's aversion to those he considered his inferiors by race and skin and menial status, Lucien was quite certain that Henry would have remembered his warning about Louisette Entrevois, though it had been so many years ago.

What concerned him even more now was his anxiety over the fate of Thomas's niece and nephew. Last week, Thomas had ridden to the Creek village near Tuskegee and returned to report that the government had as yet set no definite date for the moving of those abandoned outcasts to the West. He had even suggested that Thomas urge Manoka and Shonanoy to leave the village and come here to live at Windhaven. But they had refused, telling their uncle that they wished to remain with their people to the very end. Both of them were planting corn and taking care of the sick and the children of the desolate little village. Once again Lucien felt his helplessness in the face of the stringent, impersonal laws which had been legislated for the purpose of making these once noble people virtual pariahs. But no man-made law would ever make him break his pledge, the pledge he had given to both old Tunkamara and Nanakota and to the new *Mico* who had succeeded both those wise and kindly Creek leaders.

For Henry, there was a statement from Rigalle's bank concerning his own private account, and also a letter from Pierre Lourat, which courteously expressed the latter's pleasure in being able to extend hospitality to him and also the hope that Henry was satisfied with his purchase of Djamba. In addition, the Creole asked whether Henry could give him an accurate appraisal of Williamson's financial situation, to determine the extent of credit that could justifiably be allowed him. He had, Pierre Lourat explained, paid a visit to New Orleans just last week, spent two nights in the gambling room and come away a loser by $4000. At the time, Pierre Lourat explained, Williamson had asked to be allowed credit, since he did not feel disposed to carrying so much cash with him when he visited New Orleans. There was, however, no reference to Mark's indebtedness.

The news put Henry into an excellent humor. He at once replied to Pierre Lourat's letter by disclosing the amount he knew to be in Williamson's account, adding that his neighbor owned four hundred acres of prime cotton land, that the weather thus far had been ideal for a bounteous crop and that there was every indication that the good price prevailing in Mobile last year would be maintained this fall. "I should not hesitate to

212

declare him quite responsible, and I am certain that his luck must change for the better," he concluded.

As he laid down his quill pen and shook sand onto the paper, he smiled broadly, pleased with himself. That endorsement, he knew, would be a virtual *carte blanche* by which Edward Williamson could be led to plunge his entire fortune on the spin of the roulette wheel. Once that fortune had vanished, it would be child's play to offer solicitous concern and friendly aid to his neighbor, perhaps even suggesting that, in exchange for a mortgage on the land, he would be ready to advance Edward Williamson such funds as would be needed. And by adding those four hundred acres to his holdings, he would surpass his father's acreage and acquire in addition prime slaves, to say nothing of being easily able to induce Amos Greer to serve him in the capacity of overseer once the latter's impoverished master could no longer afford his services.

Mark, who had gone out to the fields with one of his father's black foremen to see how the work was being done and to begin his own apprenticeship, was startled late that same afternoon to find his father riding up on a roan gelding and, as he dismounted, calling to him: "Mark, here's a letter for you."

"A—a letter, Pa?" The youth's voice stuck in his throat as his father strode toward him.

"Judging from the handwriting, it's from a woman in New Orleans. I can guess whose it is." To Mark's relief, his father gave him a broad wink. "Most likely that fancy piece you sat next to in the gambling salon, isn't that right, boy?"

Mark's heart had begun to pound, and a flush suffused his face as he falteringly extended his hand for the letter. "Well, yes, I guess so. I—I wrote her some time back, Pa."

"You never told me whether you bedded her or not. It appears you must have, and she's probably asking to see you again. Go ahead, read it." Henry Bouchard grinned knowingly, hands on his hips, enjoying his son's schoolboyish embarrassment and confusion.

Mark glanced nervously around. They were a few

yards away from the last row of cotton plants on the boundary of Henry Bouchard's original acreage, and only a few slaves were working, not close enough to hear what was said. "If—if you say so, Pa," he stammeringly assented and, breaking the wax seal, opened the letter.

"Well, what does she say? Does she want you back in bed with her, boy? I'll give you this, you've got good taste, because I noticed her myself. Come to think of it, you and I have already found our tastes to be the same, haven't we?"

Mark gave his father a sudden furious look, but went back to reading the letter, for his anxiety over its contents outweighed his irritation at his father's taunt.

It was a short letter:

Mon cher époux Mark:

That is how I already think of you, my very dear one. I know that you have not forgotten your promise, for I have your beautiful letter and I keep it next to my heart always. You said that you would become sixteen in September and that you would then come to New Orleans to keep your promise of freeing me from *M'sieu* Lourat. The days drag on wearily for me, since I still must work to earn my livelihood and to pay—though only in a very small part, as you well know—Father's heavy debt.

When you talk to your father about me—as I know you will—he may say that I have no dowry to bring you. The fact is, my beloved, I have some jewelry which my father gave my poor mother, and which I have fortunately been able to keep in spite of my unpleasant financial situation. *M'sieu* Lourat does not know this, or he might have asked me to turn over the jewelry to him as a partial payment on that debt. And of course, as you know, my dear one, I shall bring you Rosa as your slave when you are my husband.

Summer is always unpleasant here in New Orleans, but I am condemned to remain here until you have freed me. Do not keep me waiting too long, dearest Mark. I send you a thousand kisses, and the promise that I will be a loving, dutiful wife.

Always your

Louisa

"Well, well, is she hungry for you, boy?" his father's voice broke in upon his reverie, which the closing words had evoked. "She—she'd like to see me again, Pa, yes, if that's what you mean," he blurted.

"Well now," Henry prodded sarcastically, "I suppose you'd like to be off to New Orleans again? Not quite so quickly, boy. I let you out of school to teach you to be useful around here, and you're going to learn everything the foremen know, so that you can properly take your place by next year sure. Maybe after the harvest this winter, when we're ready to take our cotton down to Mobile, I'll take you along so you can visit your lady love."

As his father's mocking gaze surveyed him, Mark realized that there would be little point in putting off the subject of marriage. Taking a deep breath, he nervously began, "Pa, what would you say if I wanted to get married in the fall, right after my birthday?"

"I'd say it wasn't too bad an idea. You've got hot blood in you, don't think I don't know it. Settling you down with a decent girl might steady you, I've no doubt about that."

"What I meant—well, Pa, the fact is, Louisa says she loves me, and I feel the same way about her."

"The devil you say! She's too old for you, to begin with. And a fancy girl in a gambling room isn't my idea of a proper wife. You don't know anything about her."

"Yes I do, Pa," Mark defiantly answered. "She—she's got some jewelry that's worth a lot, and she owns

215

an octóroon slave girl, Rosa. She says that if I marry her, I'd own Rosa too. And—and she's even prettier than Celia, Pa."

The glint of erotic interest shone in Henry Bouchard's narrowed eyes. "So you've got it all worked out, have you, boy? I can see what you're thinking. You'd marry this woman and then you'd have her octoroon bitch to play with when you'd a mind to, is that it?"

Again Mark's face crimsoned and he lowered his eyes. "Well, what's wrong with that? You—you bought Celia down there so you could go to bed with her, didn't you, Pa?"

"Just remind me of that once again, Mark, and I'll smash you for it! I let you off pretty lightly for treating your father that way—a lot of men would have thrashed you bloody for knocking me down the stairs and breaking my leg, don't you forget it!" Henry Bouchard's voice rose angrily, till the slaves nearest them covertly turned to glance their way.

"Damn it, I—I apologized for that, I thought you'd forgotten it, Pa." Mark's voice had the whine of self-pity in it now as he shifted on his feet and swallowed nervously.

"I'll never forget it, but as long as you behave yourself and don't get too big for your breeches, we'll get along," Henry Bouchard growled, irritatedly swishing the leather riding crop he held in his right hand. "Now you know what I said to you a while back about that Maybelle Williamson. It'd be a sight better if you started sparking her, boy. Ed Williamson's been down to New Orleans again, all by himself, and lost a lot more money. If he keeps that up, he's going to have to mortgage all he's got. And if you married Maybelle, it'd be much easier to take over. I've told you I've got my eye on that land of his, and his overseer too. Besides which he's got some topnotch field hands I could use on my land. Some of my own lazy niggers are getting old and they don't do a full day's work anymore. I've been thinking of selling some, but I don't feel like buying any new ones, not if I can latch on to Ed Williamson's batch."

"But Maybelle's too flighty, Pa. I—I don't love her, not the way I do Louisa." Mark Bouchard's voice shook in his sudden desperation. The awful secret of the gambling debt loomed like the merciless sword of Damocles over him, as his eyes fixed on the riding crop in his father's hand.

"Love!" Henry contemptuously spat out the word. "What does a boy like you know about love? A man gets married to breed sons, to have a woman to run the house and to entertain guests, a woman he can show off with pride because she's from a good family. That Louisa of yours, I'll wager, is certainly old enough to be your mother and getting to the age where she'd never be able to give you children. Now Maybelle is young enough to breed a litter for you."

"You married someone you wanted to, though, Pa!" his son sulkily countered. "Why can't I do the same thing?"

"Because this Louisa of yours doesn't own land I want, and not too much else, I'm thinking, that's why. Don't look at me like that, you young pup! I don't give a damn if you take her to bed when you feel like it—and that'll be when the crop's in a long time from now. But marrying her? Is she the sort of wife you'd be proud to show off to all the neighbors, a fancy piece whom you found in a New Orleans gambling den? Not hardly. Now that's enough of that talk. And don't let me catch you writing to her that you're longing to marry her. Understand me?"

"I—I—" Mark's face contorted with his mounting fear. "Look, Pa, I—I have to marry her—she—she's going to have a baby."

Henry stared open-mouthed at his son for a moment, then burst into raucous, jeering laughter. "Well, I'll say this for you, boy, you've proved yourself more of a man than your milksop of an older brother, and that's for certain! First Celia, and now this Louisa of yours, so I take back what I said about her being too

217

old to bear a child. Well now, that's my sap in your veins, and I can't fault you for that, can I, eh?"

Mark stood his ground, his face flushed, breathing quickly as he prayed that his father would accept this last-throw gambit.

"Well, if it's done, it's done. Damn it all, boy, I'd have imagined that fancy piece would have known the tricks to keep your seed from bigging her, at any rate! A fine mess you've got yourself into. Well, since that's the way it is and you're so set on marrying her, I'll write to Pierre Lourat and let him give me some further particulars on the lady. If that's what she is, to be sure. Besides, how do you know it's yours?"

"She—she said she hadn't ever had another man before, Pa—no, don't look at me like that—I swear it's the truth—I mean—when I took her—"

But Mark's anguished fumbling served contrarily to abate his father's sudden suspicion. "By God!" he laughed again, slashed at his boot with the riding crop. "You young devil, you've certainly a way with females for all you've hardly been weaned yet! All right, then. You'll have to marry her, I suppose, if the child's yours. Perhaps it's not so bad after all. The way Ed Williamson keeps losing his money, maybe I can get that land and those slaves and Amos Greer without your being tied down to that skittish Maybelle of his. All the same, you're not to marry her until September. Even at that, our neighbors are going to raise their eyebrows when they hear that a sixteen-year-old boy has taken himself a woman who's deep into her thirties, if I'm any judge."

"I—I don't give a damn what anyone thinks, Pa."

"No, that's quite evident already." Again Henry sent his son a furious, sardonic glance. "I suppose she could use a little money. I'll write Rigalle tomorrow and have him give the lady a draft for five hundred out of my account. You can send along a note telling her that we'll both be down in September. I'll want to have a talk with my prospective daughter-in-law; after all, it's only reasonable."

"Th—thanks, Pa," Mark stuttered, as an almost

218

nauseating wave of relief swept through him. He thought to himself, *I've got to sneak a letter off to that Lourat fellow and let him know that Pa's agreed to my marrying Louisa. Maybe he'll cancel that I.O.U. before Pa finds out about it—he's just got to!*

After that interview with his son, Henry Bouchard angrily strode out into the fields in search of Djamba. Last week, his original plan to pit Djamba's fighting skill against all comers had been crystallized by a chance meeting with Boysden Marley, a middle-aged cotton planter who owned sixty acres of river-fronting land about a dozen miles downriver from him. Marley, a widower with twenty slaves and a reputation for drinking and siring innumerable offspring from among five comely black female slaves (including his wife's own maid, the knowledge of which had driven his meek, self-effacing, childless wife to an overdose of laudanum), had boasted, "I've got me a hulking big black Angola buck, Matty, and he can whup any nigger in this country, and I'll put my money on it!" To this boast Henry had responded that he had recently acquired a Mandingo who could give good account of himself, but a formal match had not yet been arranged. Well, Henry thought to himself, now was as good a time as any to make that defiant big black slave of his earn his keep.

He found Djamba working the horses with Jimmy, the Kru stableboy, and beckoned to him. The Mandingo came obediently: "Yes, master?"

"Remember I told you I might fight you against somebody and see if you're as good with your fists as you were killing lions?"

Djamba nodded. "Yes, I do, master."

"That's good. Because I'm going to try to arrange a match between you and a nigger Boysden Marley thinks the world of, says he can lick anybody in the county. I'm going to bet lots of money on you, Djamba, and you'd better not lose."

"I hear what you say, master. But I have never fought a man in that way. I do not know this man you say I must fight. I do not hate him—"

219

"You're my slave nigger, Djamba," Henry interrupted, "and you'll do what I say, or I'll have you tied up and whipped. I'm going to send word to old Marley that anytime his nigger's ready for a showdown, you'll be there to challenge him. Now get back to your work."

"Yes, master." Djamba lowered his eyes and waited till Henry had turned back to the house. Then he shook his head sadly and went back to the horses.

Later that same afternoon, Boysden Marley and Matty, a wiry, tall, muscular Angola in his late twenties, with heavy chest and solid, ripplingly muscled thighs, rode up on horseback, and Jimmy hurried to take the reins. Marley, in a dirty brown waistcoat, soiled white breeches and dusty boots, hawked and spat, then growled, "Nigger, go tell Mr. Henry Bouchard that Boysden Marley's here to see him about that fight."

"Yassuh, ah gwine tell him right off, massa." Jimmy touched his hand to his head as Djamba came out of the stable. "Djamba, you min' tendin' Mistah Marley's hosses while Ah goes fin' Massa Henry?"

"I'll do it, Jimmy, go on," Djamba nodded.

"Huh!" the widower planter sneered, looking Djamba up and down, "mebbe you're the nigger Bouchard was boastin' so about. Whut you think, Matty?"

The Angola, a sneer on his angular, flat-nosed face, sniggered. "He sho nuff big enuff, Massa Marley suh, 'n Ah betcha he jist as dum' a nigger. Ah kin whup him, suh."

"You better back that up in the ring, boy, 'cause I'm callin' on that buck's master right now to fix things," Boysden Marley growled.

Jimmy came hurrying back. "He home, massa, he says you does come in direc'ly, suh!"

"Good. Matty, stay here, size that nigger up fer yerself. I'll be back in a jiffy," the planter directed as he followed the Kru stableboy.

"Yassuh, Ah be heah. Doan know effen disyeah dum' nigger be, though. Look lak to me, Ah kin jist look mean at 'im, he'll take off into de woods," the

Angola cackled, then hawked and spat at Djamba's feet in imitation of his master.

Djamba remained silent, folding his arms across his powerful chest. "Cat got youah tongue, boy?" the Angola jeered. "Or does you do youah bes' wohk wid de gals in bed at night? Yeah, dat's it—betcha youah massa's wife mebbe hab you come poke her—hey—oww—ouff—ahghghrrrrr!"

At the reference to Sybella, Djamba's eyes had blazed. Leaping at the Angola, he smashed his right fist into the man's mouth, breaking two teeth and felling Matty to the ground. Groaning, the Angola stumbled to his feet and aimed a savage kick at Djamba's crotch, but the Mandingo sprang to one side, caught Matty's ankle and wrenched it savagely. A shrill, agonized scream was torn from the wiry slave as he fell headlong, whimpering.

"Ma laig, you done broke ma laig. Gawd, niggah, you done huht Matty bad, whafoah you do dat to poah Matty?"

"You never again speak of my master's wife, or I'll kill you." Djamba bent over the cringing, whimpering black. "Never again open your evil mouth to say such a thing. I will know of it if you do."

"Yassuh, ow, oh mah laig! Ah's sorry, Ah woan say it nebbah no moah, Ah promises—oh, Gawd, Ah huhts so—"

"What the devil—Matty, you clumsy nigger, get up—" Boysden Marley, followed by Henry Bouchard, had just come out of the house.

"Ah cain't nohow, massah suh, mah laig's done broke bad." The Angola lifted a hand over his face as if to ward off a blow. "Dat niggah got mad wid me, he done broke ma laig!"

Henry Bouchard turned to the Mandingo. "How did it happen, Djamba? What the hell possessed you to hurt Mr. Marley's nigger? For sure we can't have a fight now."

"No sir. He said—he said bad things about—about your people, master," Djamba stolidly retorted.

Henry Bouchard whirled, his face purpling. "Damn

221

it, Marley, I thought you trained your niggers. There'll be no fight—and a good thing too, you'd lose your shirt if you bet against my Djamba. Now get your nasty-mouthed nigger off this property."

It was Djamba who helped the still whimpering Angola to get astride his horse. When they had ridden off Henry Bouchard eyed the Mandingo with sullen respect. "No sense fighting you if you'd spoil the other owners' niggers. Guess I'd better let you do what you do best around here, Djamba."

Djamba bent his head. "Thank you, master. I go back to work now," he said.

And when Henry Bouchard had stalked back into the house, Djamba said to himself in his native tongue, "I am black and I was a king, and the master's woman would be such a queen as the greatest king who ever lived would be honored to have. I cannot help desiring her, because she is good and beautiful and wise and I have a man's lust of the flesh that yearns for her. But it will never be. I respect her, I honor her, and only in that way can I show the desire I have for her, even if the day should come when she has no mate."

Not quite an hour before Henry had brought Mark's letter to him, a phaeton drawn by a coal-black mare with a tall young Fulani slave as coachman halted in the driveway near the château. Lucy Williamson handed down a basket of freshly baked cornbread to him as he dismounted and came round to take it from her and then offer his other hand to help her down. "Thank you, Moses." She gave him a radiant smile. "I'll try not to stay too long. I don't want to get you into trouble with Mr. Greer. Although I don't see how you ought to, seeing as how I told Papa I wanted you to drive me over here to Windhaven."

"No'm, but Ah'd sure be mighty grateful, Missy Lucy, if, when we got back, you'd jist tell Mistah Greer dat anyhow, effen you doan mind." The handsome, high-cheekboned face of the Fulani was taut with concern. "He tol' me Ah wuz to stay at de stable 'n polish de harness all week long."

"Never mind, of course I'll tell him. Now I'll just

222

leave Zora's basket of cornbread with Mrs. Bouchard and have a word or two with Mr. Luke, and then we'll go right back, Moses."

"Yessum, thank you, Missy Lucy," the Fulani touched his forehead in thankful acknowledgment. He had made the mare's reins fast to a hitching post, and went over to her now, stroking her withers and crooning to her as Lucy Williamson ascended the stone steps and took hold of the knocker to announce her presence.

The door was opened by Matthew, who bowed and smiled warmly as he greeted her. "Dis yeah is sho a pleasant surprise, Miz Lucy m'am! Step right in, make yourself to home."

"Thank you. Is—is Mr. Luke at home?"

"Bless you, Miz Lucy, no, he out in de fields. But I'll have him fetched for you in a jiffy. Here, lemme take youah basket. Oh, Mizziz Bouchard, heah Miz Lucy come callin'!" The footman turned as Sybella Bouchard came down the wide stairs and into the foyer.

"Why, Lucy dear, how nice to see you again! But you mustn't wait so long—good gracious, this is your first time since the housewarming, isn't it?"

"Yes, Mrs. Bouchard." Lucy's lovely cheeks were stained with a vivid blush as she extended the basket. "Papa's housekeeper Zora makes a simply wonderful cornbread, so I asked her for some, to thank you for having Papa and Maybelle and me over that time."

"What a sweet notion, Lucy! Thank you so much. Matthew, would you take this into the kitchen and have Mammy Clorinda heat it up just a little bit when we have our supper tonight? Now then, Lucy, won't you come in?"

"I—I'd love to, honestly, Mrs. Bouchard, and I hope you don't think I'm forward—the fact is—well, I wondered if I could have a word with Luke." Now Lucy Williamson's blush was more vivid than ever, and she lowered her eyes before Sybella's smiling scrutiny.

"I'll send someone to bring him in. He's out with Thomas not too far away from the house, my dear, and

223

I don't think you're being forward at all. Speaking as his stepmother, and just between the two of us, I'm awfully glad he likes such a sweet girl as you."

"Oh Mrs. Bouchard, you'll turn me vain with such a compliment!" the girl protested.

"That's not so. You've much too sensible a head on your shoulders, Lucy. Now if you'll excuse me for a moment, I'll have someone get word to Luke that you're here. While you're waiting, dear, might I offer you a glass of nice cool milk?"

"Oh no, thank you, Mrs. Bouchard. I'll wait right here—I want to get back home as soon as I can. You see, I sort of borrowed one of Papa's slaves to drive out here, and I don't want him to get into trouble with our overseer."

About ten minutes later, Luke, in open-necked shirt and cotton breeches, came forward to greet Lucy. Sybella had tactfully disappeared to leave the two young people alone.

"Why, Lucy, it's wonderful to see you again. I—I've been meaning to come over and visit, but you know my father's made me overseer and I'm busy working with Thomas getting the planting all finished. The land here, as I once told you, is used for other crops besides cotton, and it takes time and care to make sure that everything is done right."

"Oh, Luke, I—I do wish you'd come to see me when you can—oh dear, what must you think of me? As I told your stepmother, I'm being forward again. But—well, I'm so worried about Papa. You know, he's gone off to New Orleans by himself to gamble, I know he has, and he's lost heavily. I can tell from the way he talks and looks. Just like a ghost, Luke. All he can think about or talk about is going back down there and winning back all his money. And Mr. Greer is getting meaner to the slaves than ever, and Papa doesn't seem to be around or to care what's happening. I'm so afraid!"

"There, you mustn't worry, Lucy." Luke took her hands in his and quickly kissed them.

"Oh, Luke! I'm behaving just like a ninny, coming

224

over here to cry on your shoulder—but I don't know what to do."

"Lucy, I don't have the right to say anything like this yet, but I've been wanting to ever since I met you at the housewarming. Don't you know how I feel about you?"

"Yes—I—I know, Luke." She bowed her head, and he could feel her hands tremble in his and see the glint of tears on her long lashes.

"I love you, Lucy. I'd want nothing better in the world than to have you love me too, enough to marry me. Then maybe I'd have the right to talk to your papa and Mr. Greer and see if I couldn't be of help and maybe get the slaves better treatment."

"Oh Luke, yes—I want to marry you, too—" She impulsively put her arms around him and offered him her sweet eager mouth.

"I'll come calling on your father just as soon as I can, Lucy dear," he promised. "Please don't cry any more. Or else I'll be thinking you're crying at the thought of marrying me."

"Oh no, oh my dearest, how could you ever think that!" was her tremulous answer as, tightening her arms around him, she kissed him with rapturous fervor. "Do be quick and come talk to Papa, won't you, please, Luke? Now I've got to get back. Otherwise that awful Mr. Greer will whip Moses just because I borrowed him for an hour or so. Good-bye, my dearest, my very dearest Luke!"

CHAPTER SIXTEEN

Shortly before noon, the day after Lucy's visit, Luke Bouchard saddled his chestnut gelding and rode off to the rambling one-story wood and brick house with its gloomily shuttered windows. A teenaged Hausa hurried from the nearby stable and Luke handed him the reins, asking, "Where can I find your master, boy?"

"He in de house, massa. He wid Mistah Greer, suh, right now, suh."

"Thank you. Take care of Jemmy for me, and if you've time, you might give him a rubdown. Here's for your trouble." Luke handed the astonished young slave a silver dollar.

"Why, massa, doan need you pay me none foah carin' foah youah hoss, massa," the Hausa protested.

"I'm not your master, and I want to pay you for your work. Keep it and buy yourself a treat. Go ahead," Luke gave him an encouraging smile.

"Yassuh. Thank'ee, massa." Then, rolling his eyes nearly to the whites, he added fearfully. "You won't tell Mistah Greer you done gimme dis, will you, massa?"

"Of course I won't. It's just between ourselves. He's a good horse, and you might give him half a pail of water to drink, no more."

"Ah sho nuff gwine take good care ob him, massa, doan you worry none." The Hausa grinned and bobbed his head as he led the gelding away.

Luke stepped to the door and knocked on it with his fist, for there was no ornate knocker as at Windhaven. In a moment, old Obadiah opened the door and effusively greeted the young man. "Come in, suh. Massa, he in de study wid Mistah Greer. Ah'll tell him you'se here to see him, suh."

"Thank you." Again Luke smiled warmly. The old black glanced back, an admiring look on his wrinkled face, as he made his way down the hall to the study and, knocking timidly, waited for his master's order to enter, then stammered, "Mistah Luke, he heah to see you, massa suh."

"Well, have him come in right now. Amos, I guess we've about finished our business, haven't we?" Edward Williamson, his face drawn, his clothes rumpled and his cheeks stubbled with thick gray beard, looked dully up at the heavy-jowled overseer. Amos Greer, in boots, breeches and half-buttoned cambric shirt, stood with his legs planted apart, in a swaggering attitude, holding a coiled cowhide whip. "Just about, Mr. Williamson. Now you know what I told you about that quota. Cotton's going to bring a good price this fall, so I'm going to make those black bastards work their tails off to get it to market for you on time and make you money again."

"I don't know, Mr. Greer." Edward Williamson dubiously shook his head. "You know, flesh and blood can do just so much."

"That's where I beg to differ with you, Mr. Williamson." Amos Greer's pale blue eyes glittered with an undisguised contempt. "There's not a nigger out there who can't pick three hundred pounds from sunup to sundown if he puts his tail into it. And I aim to see that he does just that, or else he'll be in the shed feeling this cowhide perk him up a mite."

"But you've got the women out there too, in the hot sun," Williamson protested, half-raising a trembling hand in an ineffectual gesture of disapproval.

"Hell, Mr. Williamson, those aren't fancy bed wenches I've got picking cotton, you know. They've got strong arms and strong legs just like the bucks, and

228

they'll do a day's work or they'll answer to me for it. Anyhow, I've only set them two hundred fifty as their quota."

"But that sounds like a terrible amount of work, Mr. Greer."

"For you and me, Mr. Williamson, sure it does. But these lazy niggers don't know anything but work, that's all they're good for, and then you've got to spend half your time showing them how you want it done. Only with this—" He lifted the vicious-looking cowhide. "—I reckon they'll learn a little faster than if I just talk a blue streak. No sir, you've got to be firm with them, let them know what you want and what'll happen if they don't produce. That's the only way to make money with cotton these days."

At this moment, Luke Bouchard entered through the half-open door and stood, glancing uneasily at the glowering overseer.

"Come in, Luke. Glad to see you, boy." Williamson put both palms on his desk and lifted himself with a visible effort. "How's your father and the old man?"

"Quite well, thank you, Mr. Williamson. I didn't mean to intrude on you."

"Mr. Greer was just going. We were talking about quotas for cotton picking, you see."

"Yes sir."

Amos Greer smirked at the youth, looking him up and down with even more outright insolence than he had shown his own master. "They tell me you're doing my kind of work over at Windhaven for your daddy, Mr. Bouchard." Into the "Mister" he put a deliberate sarcastic emphasis.

"I'm learning as I go along, Mr. Greer," Luke Bouchard mildly replied, refusing to be drawn into open hostility with this man for whom he had immediately taken a strong dislike. "But of course, mine's a different situation. I'm working with freed men, you're dealing with slaves."

"I didn't know there was a difference, Mr. Bouchard," again Amos Greer dragged out the formal appellation.

"A considerable one, to my mind, Mr. Greer. My grandfather freed his slaves from the very outset, and while it's true they can't own property or money, they serve him as loyal workers. I personally happen to think he gets more work out of them that way than by driving them with force."

"I don't want to seem downright rude, Mr. Bouchard," the overseer drawled, "but someday I'd like to put a little side bet on what you and I can get done, you name a time like a month or two. I'll bet you my niggers raise and bale at least three times the cotton yours do, no matter what you call them."

"I'm not interested in any contest whose purpose is the degradation of human beings into mere beasts of the field," Luke stiffly retorted.

"By God, you're mighty fancy with your fine language!" Amos Greer sneered. "I never had much schooling, never had much time for it, too busy earning my daily bread and such. But any time you want to talk about producing cotton and making money on it, come around and see how I work."

"Thank you, I'd rather not."

"Why you—" the overseer muttered under his breath, then caught himself and forced a hypocritical smile to his thin lips. "You'll excuse me if I get back to my niggers. I'll be back at the end of the week, Mr. Williamson, and tell you how we're doing with the new system."

"Very well, Mr. Greer," Williamson agreed. "But I beg of you, if you've punishments to inflict, do see to it that they're—well, I don't want my daughters to see or hear such things, you understand me?"

"Sure. Don't you worry, I'll just lock them up nice and tight in the shed and if they yell too loud under the cowhide, why, I can always gag them, can't I? Good day to you, Mr. Bouchard."

Williamson leaned back in his chair, helplessly shrugging, then bowed his head and put his hands to his face for a moment. Recovering, and in a quavering, apologetic tone, he temporized: "Please excuse Mr. Greer, Luke, if you will. He's a rough, direct man, and

230

it distresses me to be beholden to him, but the fact is he has made money for me."

"I understand, Mr. Williamson. You don't seem well, sir. Could I get you a glass of water?"

"Oh no, thank you, you're most kind. It's just that I've had some wretched luck lately. It's a lonely life, this, and it has been ever since my wife died. I thought that by coming to a new home I could put all that behind me and make a fresh start for the sake of my girls. I'm afraid I've botched it, though, Luke."

"Not so far as your girls are concerned, Mr. Williamson. And certainly not Lucy, sir. In fact, that's the reason I've come to see you. Perhaps I picked a bad time."

"Oh no, I'll be quite all right." He forced a wavering smile to his trembling lips. "I think I can guess that you find my elder daughter appealing. She has the gentleness of her mother, and perhaps when I'm around her, I can remember the happy days the two of us had back in Georgia. Yes, Lucy's a fine girl."

"She is that and more, Mr. Williamson. I've come to ask you if you'd consider me worthy of marrying her, sir."

"Why, Luke, nothing could please me more than to hear what you've just told me!" Edward Williamson rose, his palms again on the desk to steady himself. "I don't mind telling you I like you a good deal, Luke. You take after your grandfather, and he's a wonderful old man. Don't think I didn't catch the difference between your way and Mr. Greer's way just now, but as I said, I have to sink or swim with him now. Still and all, someday, if I can ever straighten out my affairs, you and I might talk about the way you'd handle the fields if you were in charge."

"It wouldn't be my right to presume to do that at all now, Mr. Williamson. As it stands, Mr. Greer would rightly look upon me as an intruder, and I'm afraid I'm young and inexperienced in comparison. And, too, I've had a good deal of book-learning which he doesn't particularly favor."

"No, that's very evident, of course." Williamson

231

smiled bitterly. "Just the same, to get back to a far more pleasant subject, yes, by all means, you've got my approval. I daresay you've had some talks with my daughter on this subject already?"

"Yes, sir, she was kind enough to visit Windhaven yesterday and to bring some of your housekeeper's delicious cornbread to my stepmother."

"Zora will be happy to hear that your stepmother enjoyed it, Luke. She stepped in when my wife died and she's been cook and housekeeper ever since. A fine upstanding woman, part West Indian and part white and a widow these past eight years. Her man, Jonas, was my stable groom back in Georgia, you see."

"Yes, sir."

"She's been kind to the girls, and there's times when I've thought of marrying her, except that it wouldn't do. And I've been careful not to trifle with her affections, shall we say, just because of all that, you understand."

Luke nodded, somewhat uneasy at the planter's personal revelations.

"But to get back to you and Lucy, Luke. If it's my consent you're after, you have it and with my blessing. I know that my Maybelle happens to be setting her cap for your half brother Mark." The older man chuckled drily. "But it's only right and fitting that Lucy be the first to marry. And I'll tell you right off, Luke, I feel a great deal better in my mind, now that you've come to tell me what's on yours, because with my bad luck and all, I've been worrying about what might just happen to my girls."

"I'm sure it can't be as bad as that, sir."

"Bad enough. I've been gambling in New Orleans, Luke, and it's like a fever. All I can think of is going back there and winning just to prove I can, and winning big so I can wipe out my losses and have something extra to leave the girls when I'm gone. I know it's damn foolishness, but it's just like going crazy for hard spirits or a wench you can't get out of your mind. Never mind, it's my problem and I didn't mean to foist it on you, Luke."

"I wish I could help you, Mr. Williamson."

"I know you do, Luke. You're a fine honest young man, and it does my heart good to know that you'll be looking after Lucy. When did you two plan on tying the knot?"

"That's whenever the both of you find it suitable, sir."

Williamson seated himself again, leaned forward, his eyes intent on the youth. "Do it as quickly as you can, then, Luke. I've watched Lucy pine for her mother, and I know she's not happy about my overseer. If you'd take her away to Windhaven, you're close enough so that you both could come over and visit me whenever you liked. But she'd be in your safekeeping, and she'd be happy, I know."

"We'd go to Mobile, Mr. Williamson. Grandfather was a Catholic and my father professes the same faith. I hope that's not objectionable?"

"Of course it isn't, Luke boy. I'm Church of England myself, but it's a long time since I've set foot in a church or heard the Good Book read. Maybe I will when it's read over me. No matter. Now, why don't I have Obadiah call her in so you can tell her the news, Luke?"

Just before supper on the following day, an angry Henry Bouchard entered his father's study to find Lucien at his escritoire, pen in hand, with several already filled sheets of paper lying beside him. Lucien Bouchard laid down his pen and turned at the sound of his son's footsteps.

"You've heard the news, Father, about Luke's wanting to marry that older Williamson girl?" *Sly fox,* he thought, *snatched her daddy's land right out from under our noses.*

Lucien frowned. "Yes I have, Henry, and I'm quite in favor of it. She's a fine, sweet girl, and in my opinion she'll be the perfect wife for him. I was just writing to my friend Antoine Rigalle, asking him to engage the best rooms in the Orleans Hotel and to see to it that they have a most enjoyable honeymoon during their week in New Orleans."

"I understand my dear son plans to take the Williamson girl to Mobile maybe the end of next week and be married there, then go on to New Orleans."

"Yes, that's true, Henry."

"I was thinking I might go to New Orleans myself and have a talk with the woman my son Mark seems to have become involved with."

"I don't understand, Henry. I know you took him along with you, and I supposed that if you wanted to initiate him, you'd have arranged it at one of the more respectable houses of pleasure."

"It wasn't a question of a whore, Father. No, that son of mine went and got a woman with child, so he's going to have to marry her. It appears she has an octoroon slave and a small dowry in jewelry."

"How could you let that happen to him, Henry? Isn't he a bit young to be thinking of marriage? I could understand the infatuation for a pretty girl for hire, but not a serious complication like that."

"Well, when I took Ed Williamson and Mark along to Pierre Lourat's gambling rooms, Mark tried his hand at the roulette wheel. As a beginner, he did rather well, I must say. But he was seated next to a most handsome woman—even I could see that—and apparently they had a rendezvous or two, and the next thing I know he's had a letter from the woman telling him that she's going to bear his child, and besides, he really wants to marry her."

"An unescorted woman in Pierre Lourat's gambling rooms? I think it would be well, Henry, for you to investigate her background before you agree to such a marriage. It sounds as if she's simply an adventuress."

"Her name's Louisa Voisin, Mark tells me. She's employed by Pierre Lourat, but she assured him that she was still respectable—I mean, she'd never had a man before. And Mark swears it's true." Henry Bouchard's face reddened under his father's questioning look.

"I see," the old man's voice was dry and noncom-

234

mittal. "Well, at least, you're displaying a surprisingly honorable attitude toward your son's impulsive fling. But I think I can save you the trouble of making that trip to New Orleans, Henry."

"What do you mean, Father?"

"Try to draw upon your memory. About nineteen years ago, when I took you to New Orleans, you saw an elegant young woman in Rigalle's counting house. I see you're trying to recollect—I'll go a little further. Do you recall that you told me that there was a woman you would like to marry, and I told you that she was exactly one you would never marry because there was black blood in her veins?"

"I seem to, Father—" Henry Bouchard frowned and reflectively rubbed his chin.

"But I'll make it even clearer for you. Her father was Philippe Entrevois, a Creole banker of some repute, now dead and with his good name besmirched by bankruptcy and heavy indebtedness. His grandmother was black, and so it follows that his daughter would be an octoroon. And the slave that you say young Mark described as belonging to this woman happens to be her half sister, Entrevois' child by a quadroon with whose mother he made the usual financial settlement."

"My God—do you mean Mark got that nigger bitch with child and wants to marry her?"

"I should not put it quite so crudely as that, my son. As an octoroon, a woman of quality may still demand respect in New Orleans. That is, if she is not impoverished or her father's debts levied against her, in which instance she can very readily find herself on the auction block to be sold by this same Pierre Lourat, or perhaps to end up in one of his elegant houses of pleasure. I say simply that this woman who calls herself Louisa Voisin is actually that disgraced banker's daughter and the very same woman against whom I warned you in New Orleans so long ago. And if you're about to ask me how I know this, it was through a chance letter from Rigalle, when he sent me a statement of my account in his bank. I suggest, Henry, that you take im-

235

mediate steps to break off any thought of Mark's marriage with that woman."

"By God, you don't have to tell me that, Father!" Henry Bouchard slammed his fist down on his father's writing desk. "That young whelp has been very neatly taken in. And I wrote Rigalle myself to give that woman a draft for five hundred dollars as expense money until such time as Mark becomes sixteen and the marriage could be arranged."

"Consider that a better investment than what I am sure it would cost your pride if he married her, Henry. You would never let her forget that taint in her blood, I'm afraid, even if this were a case of true love—which I'm sure it's not."

"You know, Father"—Henry Bouchard's eyes narrowed with a sudden suspicion—"there's something more to this than Mark must have told me, I'm sure of it now. Why would a mere boy be so insistent on marrying a woman old enough to be his mother? I wanted him to go after Maybelle Williamson—"

"For what reason I've already guessed, Henry," his father cut in. "You'd like to acquire Williamson's land and slaves, wouldn't you? Only it appears that, to use a rather vulgar expression, Luke has beaten you to it."

"Don't rub it in, Father!" Henry Bouchard's voice trembled with scarcely controlled anger. "If you've no objection, I'll have Mark in here now, and I'll find out exactly why he's so stuck on that nigger bitch. Wasn't bedding her enough for him, that he'd try to disgrace me by bringing her here to this house?" Then, stepping over to his father's writing desk and seizing the little silver bell, he strode to the door of the study and shook the bell vehemently as he bellowed, "Matthew, Matthew, you lazy black bastard, get in here!"

The footman hurried down the corridor in answer to his master's summons, but before he had time to speak, Henry Bouchard thundered, "Go get my son, if you have to ride over to the fields yourself—just get him here as fast as you know how!"

The footman bobbed his head, turned and hurried out to the stable, where the Kru boy Jimmy was

236

feeding the horses, and bade him ride in search of Mark Bouchard without delay. As he saw Jimmy saddle and mount one of the pack ponies, Matthew dolorously shook his head and mumbled. "Mighty bad things gonna happen, Ah feel it in mah bones!"

As it chanced, Mark had been riding back to Windhaven from his father's fields when Jimmy came along the path and waved frantically to him. Spurring his horse, the youth galloped on to Windhaven, Jimmy following behind him. Dismounting and tossing the reins to the young Kru, the youth hurried to the study, where his father, in a cold rage, confronted him. "Get in here, boy!" he growled, stepping aside and glaring at the startled youth.

"What's it all about, Pa? All right, I'm going, you'd better not try to hit me again—you know what happened before," he sullenly added as he saw his father's fists clench.

"Come in, Mark," old Lucien Bouchard mildly urged, his weatherbeaten face expressionless.

"Why is Pa so angry? What's he told you, Grandfather?" Mark demanded.

"I want the truth out of you, you young devil! This Louisa you want to marry—you're sure you went to bed with her and planted your seed in her, are you?"

"I—I told you she wrote me that she's going to have a baby, Pa. You said it would be all right if I married her in September," Mark replied.

"Yes, I did, and I sent some money to Rigalle for him to give her to tide her over until the two of you got married. But now I'm not so sure you told me everything about her, Mark. By God, I want the truth if I have to beat it out of you!"

"You'd better not try, Pa!" the surly youth warned, clenching his fists and stepping to one side in a defensive reaction.

"Your grandfather has just told me who this woman really is, and you're never going to marry her, do you understand me?" Henry Bouchard burst out, his face florid with anger. "The name she goes by isn't her real one, boy; it's Louisette Entrevois. She happens to be

237

the daughter of a man whose grandmother was a nigger slave, do you understand that? She works for that gambler and slave dealer Lourat. That alone was bad enough, but to find out what sort of blood she's got, I'd see you in hell before I'd let you marry her."

"Oh Christ!" Mark muttered to himself, sweat beading his forehead as he bit his lips.

"Well, is that all you've got to say?" his father relentlessly pursued.

"I—I have to marry her, Pa."

"Because she's going to have a child? The hell you are, boy! Nigger wenches drop suckers all the time, but their white masters don't marry them!" his father snarled. "There's something else behind all this—now I'm telling you, Mark, you're going to tell me, or I'll take a cowhide to you, and this time I'll get the slaves to trice you up so you can't hit back at your own father!"

"Gently, Henry, no need to talk to the boy like that," old Lucien remonstrated.

"This is my affair, Father!"

"Not entirely, my son. It began a long, long time ago, when a girl I thought I loved married my older brother and then came to Mobile after he'd been killed in Haiti. She was a bondslave. She'd sold herself to pay passage on the ship that brought her to Mobile, and I bought the indenture and freed her, gave her money to set herself up as a seamstress to begin a new life, just as I'd begun mine. I thought then I had finished with her forever. But she married this banker whose grandmother was black, and thus her daughter is a woman of color." Lucien Bouchard sighed and closed his eyes for a moment. "Even beyond the grave, that faithless girl's spell of beauty has reached out to touch both my son and my grandson now in his turn. It's true, Mark. But don't judge that unfortunate woman too harshly, boy. When her father died in bankruptcy, she had no choice but to go to work for Lourat, and she could be sold as a slave to satisfy the creditors. I can see now the plan behind all this. He's a wily young schemer, and he doubtless thought that if he could marry her off to a Bouchard, he'd have a hold one day on our rich land."

"Are you convinced now, Mark, are you going to finish with this bitch once and for all?" Henry turned on the sweating, fearful youth.

"Sure—I guess—oh hell, Pa, you'll find out now anyway from Lourat, I guess I'd better tell you—"

"Tell me what?"

"I—I didn't bed her. She gave me her slave girl, Rosa. She said that when we were married, I'd have her and Rosa too."

"I'll be bound that tempting offer hooked you, boy," his father sneered.

"No, no, Pa, it wasn't only that—she told me how she was in debt to Lourat, see, and that if I could pay him off, then she'd be free and she'd marry me and bring Rosa along too—"

"Pay Lourat off? And how were you going to do that, may I ask?" His father took a step toward him, his face twisted with smoldering anger.

"I—I tried to do it at the roulette wheel, Pa—you remember that night when we were there, I put a few chips on numbers and they won. So I went back one afternoon and—and—"

"Go on, let me hear all of it!" Henry Bouchard furiously insisted.

"He said I could have credit on your name—I thought sure I'd win—I did at first—really I did, Pa—"

"You conniving little bastard you! And you lost, of course—how much?"

"About six—six thousand, Pa," Mark Bouchard faltered, turning to Lucien Bouchard, his eyes desperate.

"Sweet mother of Jesus, deliver me of such a stupid, loutish son!" Henry Bouchard's fury burst out. "And you used my name? How dared you do a thing like that? Did you think I'd honor such a debt?"

"He—Lourat—he said you were good for it—and I wanted Louisa so—and she was there with me—"

"Oh, it's very plain you've been taken! You, not yet sixteen, priding yourself on being such a man! I don't say the wheel was crooked, Lourat has a better reputa-

239

tion than that, but he knew exactly that you'd plunge and plunge again because you were besotted over that nigger bitch!"

"He said—he said that if I married Louisa, he—he might forget the money as a—as a wedding present," Mark faltered.

"Well, there's to be no wedding, so he won't forget. And if you think I'll pay that amount of money because you let that nigger whore trick you by letting you go to bed with her half sister—yes, that's what I said, that girl Rosa had the same father, out of a quadroon! You could have married Maybelle Williamson, helped me get a foothold on that land of his, but instead you had to go behind my back and get into a mess like this! I've a good mind to disown you, you stupid little bastard!"

"No, Henry, you won't pay off that debt. I shall." Lucien Bouchard rose to his feet. "It's a debt of honor, but more than that, it's truly my own debt for the reason you know. But this time, let there be an end forever after to Edmée and to her daughter Louisette. The first one would have trapped me into a dishonorable liaison, the second has very nearly endangered my grandson's future."

"But this young whelp has to be punished, in a way he won't ever forget!" Henry Bouchard insisted.

Lucien Bouchard shook his head. "No, Henry, you'd only turn him the more against you. There's been enough bad blood between you already. If there's a lesson here, Henry, it's that a man can make grievous mistakes in readily yielding to his emotions, and not listening to the voice of conscience and sensible reason. It's a lesson, as you will recall, that I myself tried to teach you. Now it's your turn to teach your own son."

Henry stared at his father, as his face turned a mottled red, and he finally lowered his eyes and cleared his throat, clenching and unclenching his fists, unable to answer. Mark, glancing covertly at his father, met his grandfather's gaze and in his turn bowed his head and compressed his lips.

"After all," the white-haired founder of Windhaven

said in an almost bantering tone, "it would be unfair of me to show partiality to one of my grandsons. I've already left a special legacy for Luke. Let's say, then, that in clearing Mark's name of this debt of honor, I've tried to balance the scales. And now, shake hands, both of you, and promise me, Henry, there'll be no retaliation on your part."

"Very well, but you're being damned generous to the young pup," Henry grumbled as he grudgingly extended his hand to his sullen-faced son.

"Perhaps because I've found that throughout my life I got more by giving than by taking, Henry. And now, I'm really very tired, and I'd like to take a little nap before supper, if you don't mind."

CHAPTER SEVENTEEN

Luke Bouchard and Lucy Williamson boarded the *Tensaw* on the second Thursday following Luke's call upon her father to request her hand in marriage. Both Henry and Sybella Bouchard accompanied them, as did Edward Williamson himself, each for different reasons beyond wishing to attend this union between their two houses. For Henry Bouchard carried with him old Lucien's draft for the sum which Mark had lost at roulette, and Sybella had insisted that this time she had earned a kind of second honeymoon and, since the young couple intended to go on to New Orleans to spend their honeymoon there, she saw no reason why she and Henry could not emulate their good example. Moreover, her wardrobe needed replenishing, and she needed a new riding skirt, among other things. And for Edward Williamson, apart from his joy in seeing that his favorite daughter would be cared for and protected by a young man of whom he thoroughly approved, there was once again the obsessive desire to go back to Pierre Lourat's gambling salon and try once more to recoup what he had lost.

He hadn't wanted to worry Lucy, and so didn't tell her that he was going on from Mobile, where she and Luke were married in a little chapel by an elderly, kindly priest, that he intended to go along with them to New Orleans. This time, he fiercely told himself, he wasn't going to lose. It was a happy omen to see Lucy stand beside that tall blond young man who kept his eyes on her all through the ceremony and who very obviously adored her. Now Lucy would have a real family to look after her, marrying a Bouchard the way she had. And Mrs. Bouchard, a fine, gracious and still very handsome woman, would help make up to Lucy for the mother she'd lost back in Georgia. No, he wasn't going to lose this time. He could play with a happy heart now. And he'd given the captain of the *Tensaw* a letter which was to be delivered to Grover Mason, the lawyer, as soon as the steamboat went back upriver from Mobile to Montgomery. It was his will, and it left just about everything to Lucy, the house, the land and the slaves. He'd stipulated that a third should go to Maybelle, and that Lucy's new husband should be the administrator. That was because a girl couldn't handle things by herself, if her parents were both gone. The law would set up a bank or some lawyer or legislator to make the decisions. But this way, no matter what happened to him, Lucy wouldn't be cheated out of what was due her.

The five of them spent the night in a new little inn not far from the wharf in Mobile. Williamson could not sleep, lying on his narrow bed and staring into the darkness as he thought of his growing loneliness since his wife's death, of the compulsive gambling passion which was all that seemed to consume him now, of his helpless awareness that Amos Greer was beginning to act as if he owned the land and the slaves and the house instead of being just a paid servant. Of how Zora, for all her being a tasty widow of color, had lately been acting bolder than ever before—and how he suspected that Amos Greer was putting her up to it. Well, by God, he'd made many mistakes, but not that one, not bedding a woman of color in the slave cabins. He'd freed Zora back in Georgia right after his wife's death, because she'd pitched in and been so good with the girls. But now, he wouldn't be a bit surprised to find out that she was sneaking out to Amos Greer's cabin at night and bedding with the overseer, then trying to fuss around him and give him little signs to tell him that she wouldn't mind at all if he ordered her to come to his bedchamber the way a master did with a slave wench.

In their room, Sybella and Henry made ardent love. Perturbed by not having found herself pregnant again as she had secretly hoped, she understood only too well her husband's brooding irritation with young Mark over the episode with Louisette Entrevois and the boy's disastrous gambling. Besides, convincing him that they both needed a second honeymoon and that her clothes were dowdy and out of style was the best way of making sure that he wouldn't spend his time in New Orleans sleeping with fancy girls.

But for Luke and Lucy, this wedding night was to be a gentle prelude to their conjugal joy, the kind of prelude that would have delighted the romantic soul of old Lucien Bouchard. He had remained at Windhaven, but this very night of his grandson's wedding, he was standing in the tower that faced the red bluff beyond. "Beloved woman, do you remember how you made the owl sound the name of Luke when I asked you if Windhaven could survive the conflict between father and son? Let your sweet spirit attend my grandson now, and bless and keep him and his young wife, throughout their years together, as it has blessed and strengthened me all these long years, my Dimarte."

After the hearty evening meal at the inn, Luke and Lucy had gone for a stroll along the wharf, hand in hand, each aware of the solemnity of this magical moment which heralded the beginning of their new life together. The lapping of the waters in the bay, the melodious call of the nightbirds, the pleasant warmth of the air and the bright full moon set like a shining globe in the cloudless sky, became an enchantingly evocative setting for their vows of communion.

Without a word, they had gone beyond the outskirts of the thriving little city, following the riverbank and beyond the wharf. Luke turned to stare across the placid water, as he gently put his arm around Lucy's slim shoulders and drew her close. "Do you see over there, darling?" he gestured with his other hand. "Almost fifty years ago, Grandfather crossed the bay in a flatboat after he had met Alexander McGillivray, the leader of the Creek Nation, with a pack pony and supplies. Then he followed that trail on the other side and upriver to what we now call Montgomery, which was Econchate, the Red Ground where the Creek village was. There weren't any steamboats in those days, and almost no settlers at all."

"How brave he must have been," Lucy mused, "knowing nothing about this country and going on through that wilderness trusting that he'd find a new home. How hard it must have been for him to have no friends, no sweetheart, to have given up everything—his family and his beautiful château and the girl he must have been in love with."

"And he found a sweetheart who was truer to him than the girl he'd left behind. But I'm luckier than Grandfather in so many ways, Lucy dear." He turned to face her, his hands caressing her shoulders, his eyes feasting on the sweet, heart-shaped face with its sensitive mouth, dainty nose, large dark-blue eyes which met his gaze so trustingly and eagerly. "I didn't have to go through a wilderness to find you, darling, or build my own house and go hunting to prove that I could provide for my wife. But I do swear this to you, Lucy, I'll provide for you and protect you and give my life for you, because I know that even if I'd had to battle a wilderness and wild animals and savage Indians, I couldn't have found anyone I'd ever love more than I do you."

"Oh, Luke, my sweet husband, my dear one!" she murmured, tears shimmering in her eyes as she arched to him to receive his kiss.

Then, as if ashamed of his own sentimentality, Luke gently disengaged himself, took her hand and continued their walk along the riverbank. After a moment, Lucy shyly murmured, "We'll have to be up early in the morning, darling, to catch the steamboat to New Orleans. Do you think we ought to go back to our room now?"

Now it was Luke's turn to blush and, squeezing her

hand, to whisper, "If you like, my darling, but you know, with my parents and your father here with us, I don't feel we've really started our honeymoon yet. I want you all to myself, my very dearest, and tomorrow night, when we're in New Orleans, we'll be by ourselves."

She caught her breath, understanding his tactful, considerate meaning. Then, lowering her eyes but unable to halt the furious crimson which suffused her satiny cheeks, she whispered, "I—I want to be your wife in every way, my darling Luke, my sweet husband. Mama talked to me about—well, about how a man and woman belong to each other. You—you mustn't be afraid to love me, Luke darling, because I want you so very much. I only hope—I only want to be everything you want of me."

"Sweet Lucy, dearest wife," he murmured, gently kissing her eyelids, her cheeks and then finding her soft quivering lips in a long ardent kiss which was his devout pledge of constancy . . . and it was not unlike the first kiss old Lucien Bouchard had given his beloved woman long ago.

Antoine Rigalle met the wedding party at the *Orion* late the next afternoon, awaiting them with an elegant carriage drawn by two bay mares and a liveried black coachman with top hat, a long-handled silk-tipped whip thrust into a tubular socket beside him. With typical Creole effusiveness, Rigalle greeted the young couple, praising Lucy's delicate beauty so extravagantly that Lucy turned away, blushing. "I've taken the liberty of getting you two lovebirds a very private and quiet little apartment on the Rue Saint-Honoré where no one will disturb you except the concierge to bring up a real New Orleans breakfast with the very best *café au lait* and freshly baked brioches and wild honey," he declared. "For you, *M'sieu* and *Madame* Bouchard," turning to Henry and Sybella, and graciously inclining his head toward the gray-haired widower, "and for you, *M'sieu* Williamson, I've reserved the best rooms at the Orleans Hotel. My coachman André will take you there first, and then dispatch the bride and groom to their quarters for the *lune de miel*. You have time to freshen up after your journey, and then I should like all of you to be my guests at Duchamps. In fact, I've already taken the liberty of telling the chef to prepare a special feast to celebrate this glorious occasion."

"You're very kind, *M'sieu* Rigalle," Sybella smiled warmly at the gray-haired Creole banker.

Rigalle took her hand and brought it to his lips. "And you, Madame, are still so beautiful that when I first caught sight of you coming down the gangplank, I said to myself that this surely must be the bride."

"Oh come now, *M'sieu* Rigalle," Sybella laughed, "you say exactly the things a woman loves to hear. You see, Henry"—turning to her husband—"didn't I tell you that New Orleans is the only place to come for a honeymoon, whether it's one's first or second?"

"Trust a Frenchman to be able to flirt with another man's wife and get away with it, my dear," Henry jokingly replied. "But I'll say this, Syb, if kissing your hand brings such a charming rosy color to your cheeks, I'll have to try the practice myself."

"That, Henry," his wife tartly though smilingly observed, "is what I've been trying to convince you of all these years."

Lucy, having discovered that her father was accompanying her on the journey from Mobile, uneasily watched him as he moved forward to murmur something to the banker, and turned to Luke, her face shadowed with distress: "Oh, Luke, I'm so worried about Papa. I just know he came here so that he could gamble again, and he just shouldn't, he shouldn't!"

"Hush, darling," Luke murmured back, his arm around his wife's slim waist, "if you'd like, I could go along with him this evening and see if I can't keep him from plunging too heavily."

"I'd be so grateful if you would, my darling!"

"Very well, it's settled. After dinner, I'll take you

248

back to the apartment *M'sieu* Rigalle has been so nice to arrange for us, and then I'll go back to join your father." He kissed her quickly, then teasingly whispered, "Of course, it means I might be coming back rather late."

"You know I'll wait for you," Lucy whispered.

The apartment which Antoine Rigalle had commandeered for Luke and his bride was within a stone's throw of the Vieux Carré, and was actually a small U-shaped house with its own porte-cochère and gardened patio. The iron-lacework balustrade of the balcony ran along all sides of the second floor, the first being the dwelling of the concierge he had mentioned, a middle-aged widow whose husband's account had been handled by the banker through whose efforts and recommendations Madame Cecile Turvalier was able to derive an excellent annual income by renting the beautifully furnished house to honeymooners, visiting business associates and touring celebrities. At the far back of the house, and alongside the railed-off garden of the patio, there was a red-brick carriage house and stable, with a *garconnière* built on the second floor, where André, Rigalle's coachman, had his quarters.

André drove Luke and Lucy to the restaurant after they had unpacked the things they had brought with them from Windhaven and washed their hands and faces in the basins of heated water which the pleasant widow brought to their apartment. Sybella, Henry, and Edward Williamson had taken a carriage from the Orleans Hotel to the restaurant, where Rigalle was already conferring with the proprietor and his chef, grandiloquently gesturing to illustrate the feats of culinary magic he wished performed for his guests and particularly for the bride and groom.

It was a banquet indeed—rice and tomato soup, boiled pompano in port wine sauce, a Westphalian ham cooked in champagne, with many ornamental dishes which included boned turkey, salmon in oyster sauce, cold French pies and chicken salads. A final entree was

249

a compote of pigeons as well as a duckling with green peas, served with turnips in butter sauce, carrots in stewed sauce, and cauliflower baked with cheese. Finally, after the French pastries, fruits and nuts, and strong Creole coffee, the beaming little chef and two waiters emerged from the kitchen carrying a huge many-tiered wedding cake exquisitely decorated, and set it before Luke and Lucy. As Lucy, her cheeks flushed from Antoine Rigalle's flowery toast in her honor as he stood lifting his champagne glass, almost fearfully cut the cake—shyly stammering that it was such a work of art that it seemed almost criminal to destroy it—her father lifted his glass and sipped it in response to the toast, his eyes filling with tears as he observed her radiant happiness.

Lucy served her father first, and the banker exclaimed, "Ah, *M'sieu* Williamson, you've drawn the black bean of good luck in your slice!" The gray-haired planter stared at it, then drew the bean out of the richly textured cake with his right thumb and forefinger and dropped it into the pocket of his waistcoat, his face brightening.

Lucy caught her breath and glanced toward her young husband, who had seen this gesture. He put a finger to his lips and then, in a bantering tone, chided her, "A dutiful wife would have seen to it that her husband got the black bean, my dear. Your father's already had his luck in getting an unmarried daughter off his hands."

"Oh Luke, how can you say such a thing to that sweet girl!" Sybella gasped. But Lucy understood: her father had looked upon that omen of good luck as a sign that fortune would favor him this time at the gambling wheel. So, in the same light-hearted tone, she retorted, "But you've already had more than your share of luck in getting me, don't you think?" and Henry and Sybella and the banker joined in the laughter.

It was nine o'clock by the time the last toasts to the bride and groom had been drunk and the wedding party prepared to leave the restaurant. Antoine Rigalle insisted that he be allowed the privilege of hosting this happy affair, and when Henry Bouchard tried to pay, drew himself up proudly and declared, "Sir, if you persist, you will impugn my Creole honor and I shall regrettably be forced to demand satisfaction. No, *jamais de la vie*, it is little enough to do to express my great privilege and joy to witness this union which continues the reputable Bouchard line!" And again, with a great flourish, he drew out a sheaf of banknotes and pressed them into the proprietor's hand, designating the *pourboire* to be given the waiters and a special bonus for the chef.

The coachman was then instructed to drive Sybella back to the Orleans Hotel and Lucy to the bridal apartment, the banker assuring Luke that he would see the young wife safely returned. After Sybella had entered the hotel, the carriage headed for the establishment of Pierre Lourat on Chartres Street, where Luke and Henry Bouchard and Edward Williamson bade their host a cordial and grateful *au revoir*. Lucy turned toward Luke and murmured, "Oh my darling, do watch out for Papa, don't let him play too long, I beg of you!"

"I promise, my darling. And I'll come back as soon as I can," he reassured her, giving her a quick little kiss and adding for only her to hear, "That will do until I can give you a proper kiss when I come back, my dearest one."

The auction room was crowded with wealthy planters and merchants, eagerly vying with one another for the human merchandise which Pierre Lourat's attendants led onto the raised platform. As the three men entered, a handsome mulatto in her late twenties, holding the hand of her frightened three-year-old boy, stood on the platform while a stocky, bearded assistant extolled her virtues and accepted an opening bid of $1600 for the mother and son. As a younger, beardless and dapper assistant approached the trio, Henry Bouchard whispered, "Is *M'sieu* Lourat here this evening?"

"*Oui, m'sieu*, you will find him upstairs in the *salon de jeux*."

A handsomely liveried young mulatto bowed to them and opened the door of the gambling room. Pierre Lourat stood just inside, talking to a fat, nearly bald merchant who was mopping his sweating forehead with a monogrammed silk kerchief and who, as the Creole turned to greet the three newcomers, importunately tugged at Lourat's wrist. With a disdainful expression, the slim black-haired Creole, without raising his voice, declared, "Really, *M'sieu* Danvers, you forget yourself. We'll discuss your business later after I've welcomed my friends, if you please." Then, coming forward, smiling and offering his hand, he exclaimed, "*Enchanté de vous revoir, messieurs*! But this handsome young gentleman I haven't had the pleasure of meeting yet, have I?"

"No, Pierre, this is my older son Luke. He's just married Mr. Williamson's daughter Lucy and has come to New Orleans to enjoy his honeymoon here."

"You could not have chosen a better place for a honeymoon, *M'sieu* Luke," Pierre Lourat said as he shook hands with the young man. "I bid you welcome to New Orleans and I wish you and your lovely wife long years and good fortune. But surely, so young and romantic a gentleman as you has no need to seek his fortune over my paltry games of chance?"

"Why, no, *M'sieu* Lourat, I've come to watch my father and my father-in-law for a bit, if you've no objection," Luke blandly replied.

"But of course not! I'll have Charmaine bring you refreshments, gentlemen. And now you, *M'sieu* Henry, and you, *M'sieu* Williamson, what's your pleasure?"

"First"—Henry Bouchard drew out his father's draft and, folding it, pressed it into the Creole's hand—"the little matter of my son's gambling debt to you. I think you will find the draft payable for the full amount."

"Oh?" Pierre Lourat frowned momentarily. "But I assure you, there was no need of such prompt payment. The credit of a Bouchard is beyond question in my establishment."

"That may be," Henry testily answered, "but I wish

252

to settle the matter once and for all. I have also come to tell you that my son apologizes to your *Mademoiselle* Voisin and regrets that he will not be able to keep his promise of marrying her."

He gave Pierre Lourat a hard look, and the Creole shrugged, then pocketed the draft with a polite smile.

"As you wish, then, *mon ami.* Now, what is it to be, the cards or the wheel?"

"This time I'll try my luck at *vingt-et-un*," Edward Williamson declared.

"*Mais certainement.* This way, if you please." The Creole led the way to a rectangular table covered with green velvet in the rear of the salon, where a dealer and three players already sat. With a polite flourish, he drew out a chair for Williamson, who quickly sat down, put his hand into his pocket to touch the lucky bean from the wedding cake, and then leaned back with an impatient exhalation as he waited for the hand to finish and the next one to be dealt.

Pierre Lourat drew Henry Bouchard toward the corner and murmured, "What you have told me will distress *Mademoiselle* Voisin. But that is the luck of the game, *n'est-ce pas?*"

"It was your game, I'm afraid, Pierre. You see, my father knows who this Louisa Voisin really is. She's the daughter of the woman whom he once fancied himself in love with. And he knows also that there's nigger blood in her. You could hardly expect my son to marry her, now could you?"

"The term distresses me, *mon ami.* But we'll let that pass. You must understand that in New Orleans the elite Creoles do not look down upon a touch of *sang nègre* as perhaps you do. However, I think I shall be able to find this charming and unfortunate lady some consolation by way of employment or another arrangement which will not concern you. I do hope that I have not incurred your enmity. I was thinking only of her welfare."

"I've no doubt of that, but I suspect you hoped you might get a hold on some of my land as well, Pierre. No, don't frown again, you know as well as I do it's

253

the truth. I admire a man who can be devious when it suits his purpose. Let's just say that this is one game of chance that didn't turn out successfully for you, and we're still friends. Agreed?"

Pierre Lourat shrugged again. "I can be as good a loser as I am a winner, *mon ami*, and may I congratulate you on your son's marriage. Now let us see if your friend has better luck at the cards than he had at the wheel."

The lucky bean appeared to have turned the tide for Edward Williamson, at least for this night. After an hour of play, he had won nearly $2000, and arose from the table. "This time I'll quit while I'm ahead," he announced. "Tomorrow night, I'll be back to play with the stakes I've won, and maybe, Mr. Lourat, I'll take back from you everything I've lost so far."

"I wish it sincerely for your sake, *M'sieu* Williamson." The Creole bowed, his face expressionless.

Luke Bouchard quietly entered the apartment. A candle had been left burning in the little foyer, and he took it with him to light his way through the darkened rooms. For a moment, he stepped outside onto the gallery and stared down into the flowered patio, breathing in the scent of oleander, magnolia, jasmine and roses, savoring the stillness of the night. Then he moved on toward the bedroom and stopped on the threshold to find the door open and a smaller candle flickering in its holder atop the little night table beside an enormous four-poster bed. The posts rose high enough almost to brush the ceiling, and Lucy awaited him, two large pillows behind her head, the shimmering honey-gold of her unbound hair cascading over the pillows. She wore a white silk shift, the covers drawn up over her bosom, as she awaited him.

"Luke darling? Is—is Papa all right?"

"He's fine, Lucy. He won tonight and he stopped playing."

"Thank God! You don't know how I've worried. Oh Luke, come to me, hurry. I've been so lonely here without you," she entreated.

254

He blew out the candle and then came to her bedside to blow out the other one, then swiftly undressed. With a happy little sigh she turned to face him as he lay down beside her, linking her soft arms around his neck and eagerly surrendering her warm moist lips.

"Don't be afraid, my darling, I want to be all yours tonight, I want it so very much, Luke, my husband, my lover," she breathed.

He felt a sudden almost anguished reverence for her in this communion of darkness, their first of the flesh. Himself unfledged as a lover despite his awareness of the manifestations of physical love from the romances, plays and stories he had read as a boy, Luke had pedestalled Lucy as an esthete might have done. He trembled at her kiss, urging the utmost restraint upon himself: he would not mar this moment by the least untoward gesture. Yet the sweet candor of her welcome and knowing that she too was virgin yet completely trusting in his powers of initiation, intensified his desire for her. Already, he had sensed, they were perfectly mated in spirit, in outlook, in their sharing of the arts and love of beauty; all the more important that this consummation draw them at last into the perfect union of mind and flesh.

Gently he cupped her swelling breast as he kissed her again, murmuring her name like a benediction in the still night, and Lucy sighed raptly, whispering, "Oh, my dearest husband, oh Luke, my love!"

He could smell the fragrance of her hair, feel its silken caress, and through the fragile stuff of the shift the palpitating young body moved against his adoring hand. Now, to his wonder and delight, she sighed again, released him from the exquisite enclaspment of her soft hands, and drew the covers off. It was so perfect a gesture of accord—not surrender or submission—that he felt tears burn his eyes, tears of longing, of rich passion, of truest, deepest love.

He bent his head to kiss her breast where his hand had so worshippingly touched, and again there came from her that deliciously plaintive little sigh which

255

wordlessly voiced her pleasure at such gentleness, while the tips of her slim fingers which pressed against the back of his neck imparted by the feverish augmentation of that pressure her growing delight, her eagerness to take part in their communal fusion rather than to be mere passive participant in the rites of love.

And as his hand left her breast to trace the warm quivering suppleness of her body, lingeringly, as if to seek permission for each new emboldened quest, Lucy uttered a stifled sob of ecstasy as, fitfully trembling, unconsciously, unbidden, her loins arched to him to bid him manifest the longing which she now almost impatiently shared.

And thus it was that here in New Orleans, like his grandfather before him, Luke Bouchard experienced the candid, tenderly cherished rapture of the gift of love.

CHAPTER EIGHTEEN

Sybella thoroughly enjoyed the week in New Orleans, because it seemed to fulfill her expectations of a longed-for second honeymoon. For one thing, it was her opportunity to be alone with Henry in a colorful and exciting locale where he was not confronted with his dogged quest for additional land and constantly increased cotton production. And since their shared activities of this halcyon week brought him into contact with members of New Orleans' elegant society, he was on his best behavior. They spent their evenings at fine restaurants, the theater or the opera, and one evening at a party given by Antoine Rigalle in his beautiful up-river summer home. For Sybella, it was a welcome chance to engage in intellectual conversation, to learn new viewpoints and to observe the latest fashions exemplified by the beautifully gowned women who attended these social and cultural functions. And since Henry Bouchard this time found himself pitted against well-educated, sophisticated people of a world whose scope went far beyond the boundaries of a cotton plantation, instead of lording it over black slaves as was true on his own holdings, he was compelled to display the more tolerant side of his usually brusque nature.

For Luke and Lucy, it was a time span of indescribable rapture, of felicitous discovery of each other. Despite her rather cloistered education, Luke's young wife was extraordinarily sensitive and perceptive, and

Luke quickly found that her idealism—which he had perceived at their very first meeting—had a strong spiritual kinship with his own. The young couple joined Sybella and Henry on two evenings to dine and enjoy a Shakespearean play one time and a Mozart opera the other, but on at least three evenings of their blissful week, they prevailed upon the widowed concierge to prepare dinner for them in their apartment, and then spent most of the evening in conversation on history, books, and music and painting, besides politics. And the gently bred demureness which Lucy displayed to the outside world was, to Luke's ecstatic delight, put aside when they shared the huge four-poster bed. Though innately chaste, the young woman responded to her considerate husband's tender wooing with an intuitively ardent and unselfish surrender.

Like all young lovers before them who had just discovered their great importance to each other and their expectancy of finding ever new delightful secrets unveiled, Luke and Lucy discussed their future. It was Lucy's hope that Luke would ultimately take over the management of her father's land, and inculcate on it the ideas which his grandfather had so wisely put into practice on Windhaven. Then, Lucy believed, Luke could discharge the hateful Amos Greer and, by kindlier treatment of the slaves, inaugurate among them a kind of incentive system whereby a certain amount of money would be credited to them so that after a given number of years they could buy their freedom. This practice, Lucy knew, had been used on several Georgia plantations, for her father had once disparagingly mentioned the plan to Amos Greer in her presence.

"You can already see that Mobile thinks, talks and dreams about nothing except cotton," Luke heartily agreed with her. "Now it's all very well so long as the English textile mills need our crops. But with everyone trying to outdo his neighbor in producing more and more bales, and the quality going down because of the weakened condition of the soil and the overly tight compression of the bales when they're shipped to market, the day isn't far off when it will hardly be worth the time and cost of producing that crop. I for one would much rather grow food for which there'll always be a need, good vegetables and fruits, and fodder for cattle and horses too. Come to think of it, raising cattle could be a very profitable operation. People are eating more and more meat and children will always be needing plenty of milk from the cows, especially when there are more and more large towns and cities in this part of the country."

"Oh, Luke, if only you could talk Papa into those things!" his wife exclaimed, rising from her chair and walking over to the balcony which looked down on the charming little patio. "It would give him a new lease on life, I know it would. Before Mama died, he had slaves, yes, but he never used to allow such cruelty to them as he's let that horrid Amos Greer carry out. Always the whip, and the worst of it is that Papa goes out and watches those poor men and women being lashed, just as if he enjoyed it like the overseer."

"Hush, my darling." Luke moved toward her, took her in his arms and turned her to him. "You know I can't do things like this overnight. Grandfather spent most of his life fighting for the freedom of the people who worked his land, but the laws governing slaves have been made by ambitious, profit-minded men who want to take all the advantage they can of this free labor and care nothing about the moral issues involved, of man's decency to his brothers. . . . Do you realize it's nearly midnight and we've been talking a blue streak ever since Madame Turvalier brought us our supper?" And Lucy had put her hand in his and led him toward their bedroom.

On the very night when Luke and Lucy had so earnestly discussed their new responsibilities, Pierre Lourat and Louisette Entrevois were closeted together in the Creole's private office just back of the auction room. She sat there sullenly, her eyes swollen with tears, nervously twisting her silken kerchief in her slim fingers as he unfolded Lucien Bouchard's bank draft and laid it face up on the table.

"I regret, *chérie*, that our little project wasn't a success. The old gentleman, you see, learned who you really were and I'm afraid he put his foot down. This draft pays Mark's losses at the wheel. Of course I shall be generous and give you a commission out of it, then apply the rest against your late father's still considerable debt. Henry Bouchard made it quite plain to me that there can never be a marriage between you and his son, and of course we both know the reasons, don't we?"

"How damnably cruel and vengeful that accursed Lucien Bouchard is!" Louisette Entrevois exclaimed, her eyes sparkling with hatred.

"You misjudge him entirely, my dear. Of course I understand your pique. And I can't blame you for it. It surely wasn't your fault that your mother chose as a husband an elegant gentleman whose grandfather had rather childishly become infatuated with a black woman to the extent of manumitting her and wanting to wed her. If he'd only taken the precaution of marrying a white woman and kept her as his *maîtresse*, you and Rosa and Diana wouldn't be in this deplorable situation, I agree. But that's life, *ma belle*."

"So what do you propose to do with me, Pierre? Sell me on the auction block?"

"I could, of course, and be within my legal right." He took a pinch of snuff, then a sip of Madeira from a glass before him. Then he frowned. "But you really would not bring too high a price on the block, to be brutally honest with you, Louisette. You're approaching forty, and though I'll be the first to admit that you have a still desirable allure, my clients want younger flesh to share their beds. No, I'm a good businessman, and also somewhat of a sentimentalist. I'm going to open a new *maison de luxe* in the fall, after the summer heat and the dangers of yellow fever leave our Queen City and visitors again begin to throng to it. I'm going to call it *Les Amours*; a pretty conceit, don't you think? And I shall put you in charge of it. In a word, my charming Louisette, you will be the

260

madame of the establishment, but you will not have to service the clients—unless of course you choose to."

The woman turned crimson with shame and indignation, bit her lips and in a dull voice replied, "Since I am still your employee, *M'sieu* Lourat, and I'd rather be dead than be a slave, it seems I have no choice."

"A very sensible decision. It would grieve me if you refused, because then I should be forced to sell you." He smiled maliciously and raised the glass to his lips. "And, you see, since I know something of your particular foibles in *l'amour*, I know that's not very likely."

"You devil!"

"Well, now, that's better. It's surely easier for you to hate me and more justly than old Lucien Bouchard, admit it, *ma belle*. This way, knowing that you hate me so will make you all the more attentive to business so that you won't compel me to the disagreeable alternative. We understand each other."

"What about Rosa and Diana?"

"We shall find a post for Diana as an attendant at *Les Amours*, I have no doubt. Now, since you've told me that you were ingenious enough to let young Mark Bouchard bed your half sister, is it possible that she may find the life in such a house pleasantly acceptable?"

"No, no! She sacrificed herself for me, so that I could marry that young idiot and be free of you forever!"

"Then what a pity it was all in vain. You will have that on your conscience too, I think. You see, I know that she shares your tender passion. But do not let me embarrass you, my dear Louisette. However, if she could submit herself to but a single protector, it's conceivable she and Diana might appear at one of the quadroon balls. You know how such arrangements are made. Often a very handsome and wealthy Creole gentleman visits these affairs, loses his heart, and makes a financial settlement on the mother of the charming girl he lusts after. Such arrangements, I'm told, often last many years. Well, there's your father's

261

example—only death unfortunately interrupted that situation."

"I—I'll speak to her about it," Louisette Entrevois said dully as she rose, her eyes bleak and unseeing.

But for Edward Williamson, the black bean of good luck proved to be a dark omen, not a fortunate augury. So, too, was the encouraging illusion of his winning at *vingt-et-un*. For he returned the very next night, by himself, and by midnight, playing the same card game, lost over $10,000; and on the next night, shaken and pale, in a final desperate attempt to recoup, saw his entire savings wiped out. In Pierre Lourat's office, his hand trembling so violently that he could scarcely write, he finally inscribed a note ordering the Mobile counting house to pay out all of his $20,000 to Pierre Lourat. And then, ignoring the Creole's offer of champagne and a graciously complaisant girl from one of his houses to provide distraction and consolation, the widower went back to his hotel room, jostled by passers-by on the brick sidewalk, cursed at by drunken rivermen and adventurers on their way to the same ephemeral pleasures he had just disdained.

He flung himself down on his bed and wept for a long time. And when the agonizing crisis was over, he sat up and said in a hoarse, trembling voice, "It was the father who led me into temptation, which I was too weak to withstand. But thank God it'll be the son who saves my girls from the disgrace I've brought upon them with my folly."

CHAPTER NINETEEN

The *River Queen* left Mobile a little after nine o'clock on the Sunday evening which concluded the honeymoon of Luke and Lucy Bouchard. Williamson, together with Sybella and Henry and the young couple, had boarded the *Orion* early that same morning at the New Orleans wharf for the journey back home, and had seemingly been in good spirits. When Lucy had anxiously asked him earlier that week whether his luck of the first night had continued, he had calmly replied, "Yes, my dear, I think I may have found the solution to my problem at last. Now you're not to worry, you've got a wonderful husband to care for you, with a level head on his shoulders and much wiser than his years. And I'm going to be fine, my darling."

He had kissed her good night and gone to his cabin, after a large glass of whiskey at the convivial bar aboard the *River Queen*. A few hours out of Mobile, there was a heavy thunderstorm, which soon cleared. But when the steamboat docked at the Windhaven levee, Williamson was nowhere to be found. Lucy, who had gone to her father's cabin, found it empty and, with a sudden terrified presentiment, had hurried up on deck in search of the captain. He and two roustabouts made a thorough search, including the hold, but there was no sign of her father.

Luke went back to the cabin while Lucy, fighting to control her tears, accompanied the captain and his men

263

in the futile search. The bunk had been untouched, Luke noticed, and as he stepped closer, he saw the edge of a folded sheet peeping out from under a cushion. Drawing it out and opening it, he uttered a stifled cry. It read:

My beloved Daughter:

I have taken the only honorable way I know to end this madness which has come over me ever since your mother's death. Now that I know you have a strong, decent and kindly husband to look after you, Lucy, I can take my leave in peace. I have lost all the money I've made on the land, but the land and the house and the slaves are yours. By law, your husband now owns them, except that I have willed a share to Maybelle to provide for her till she can be married to, I hope, as good a man as your Luke.

Forgive me, Lucy, but if I had gone on, I could not have resisted gambling again and again till perhaps I would have had to mortgage us into total bankruptcy. This way, you will at least remember that there was something redeeming to your father. May God bless you and Luke and give you long years of happiness.

Your Father

Slowly pocketing the note, he made his way to the deck and beckoned to the bearded captain. Lucy and the two roustabouts had gone to the stern of the steamboat, and Sybella and Henry Bouchard had accompanied her in that heartbreaking search.

"I'm afraid he jumped overboard during the storm last night, Captain," Luke murmured. "I just found this letter he left. We'll go ashore now, and I'm obliged to you for waiting for us."

"That's terrible, sir, just terrible! I wish there were something I could do—"

264

"Thank you for your thoughtfulness. Now I'll go fetch my wife and try somehow to make her understand the dreadful news," Luke said.

His arm round her shoulders, Luke protectively led the weeping young woman into the red-brick château, Sybella and Henry, exchanging compassionate glances, following silently behind.

"Have Matthew put her in the guest room at the left wing, Luke dear," Sybella gently murmured, and he nodded as the old majordomo hurried into the foyer.

"There now, Lucy, lie down and cry it out. He didn't suffer, darling. He thought he was doing it to ease your pain about him, truly he was," Luke tried to comfort his sobbing young wife.

"It was so selfish of us, in a way, Luke." She turned to look at him, blinking her eyes to clear them of the tears that streamed down her cheeks. "If only we'd thought to be with him every night, this wouldn't have happened."

"You mustn't blame yourself, darling. It was a kind of sickness, and he knew it, and he took what he thought to be the only cure. He wanted you to remember him as a devoted father, not as a dishonored, bankrupt gambler who couldn't hold on to anything. That's what he said in the letter, darling. Remember him as he was, all the good times and the kindness he showed. When he lost your mother, it must have destroyed him inside. And you see, he was true to her, he didn't turn to other women as many men would have done. He tried to fight this fever of his, and he had courage to the very end."

"Yes—yes, Luke, that's the way it must have been. Oh, my darling, hold me—you and Maybelle are all I've got now, Luke!"

"I'll ride over this afternoon and bring Maybelle back. I think it would be best if she stayed here with us for a while."

"Yes, of course."

"Your father was a good man, Lucy. What he thought about most was your happiness and Maybelle's. Now I'll leave you to get some rest,

265

dearest. I'll have Mammy Clorinda make some good strong tea for you, and maybe some biscuits with honey—you know how you like them."

"I don't know—oh Luke, don't leave me too long. Come back to me soon. I—I'll be all right in a little bit, my dearest."

He bent to kiss her cheek, and then left the room. Lucy covered her face with her hands and gave vent to her grief.

About an hour later, Sybella gently knocked at the door, and Lucy called out, in a voice still muffled with her weeping, "C—come in, please."

"I didn't mean to intrude, Lucy dear, but Arabella and Fleurette wanted to meet their new sister-in-law."

"We brought you our pets to cheer you up, Lucy," Arabella ventured, squatting down and patting the head of the little raccoon. Thomas had made a leash and collar out of soft, oil-rubbed buckskin, and after a few dubious and token resistances, Timmy had grudgingly permitted his young mistress to attach it to him whenever she wished to show him off or, as she proudly boasted, took him for a good long walk. Beside her, Fleurette cradled the white rabbit, whose leg had been properly set by the improvised splint and bindings so that it could now hop and run as well as ever. Completely tamed, it wiggled its long ears and soulfully looked up at the animated face of its little mistress.

"Oh, how nice of you dear girls." Lucy sat up on the edge of the bed, then gently put out her hand to stroke the raccoon's head. "That was very thoughtful of you. What's this one's name?"

"It's Timmy, and I'm Arabella," the older girl announced. "And this is my baby sister Fleurette and her bunny is called Sassy. You got married to Luke, didn't you?"

"That's right, darling. Now come give me a big sisterly kiss and hug, and you too, Fleurette," Lucy smilingly ordered. Her eyes rose to Sybella, who stood at the open door, and the latter gave her a sympathetic nod. Then Sybella added, "Luke has ridden over to the house to bring Maybelle back. She'll have the last room down this side of the hall, dear. If there's anything that you need or want us to do, please don't hesitate to tell me."

"You're so kind, all of you. I shan't ever forget it, Mrs. Bouchard—"

"Oh my, now, it's Sybella. And you're family, Lucy. I don't have to have anyone tell me how happy you've made my son, because that's the way I think of him, not as a stepson—and that's made us love you already. I think I knew at the housewarming that you and Luke were meant for each other, Lucy darling. Come along now, girls, don't wear out your welcome. Besides, Bella dear, you told me you were going to give Timmy a nice long walk, and it's such a beautiful day. We'll be seeing you later, Lucy, at supper. Just you rest and take care of yourself now."

At sixty-two, Grover Mason was still the same, fussy little man he had been when Henry Bouchard had first met his daughter, save that his hair and beard were now completely white. He was still as spry of mind and body, and there was still the same calculating shrewdness in his squinty, pale-blue eyes as he nodded to Luke Bouchard and beckoned him to a seat. "Sit yourself down, Luke, this won't take long, boy. Well now, it was smart of you to spark Miss Lucy and make her poor old father certain of your intentions. As it stands now, you're a fairly well-to-do citizen. You see, some weeks before he came to his untimely end, Lucy's father sent me a letter from aboard the *Tensaw*, leaving two-thirds of his estate—and that counts the house and the land and the slaves, you understand—to Lucy and a third for Miss Maybelle. Also, he asked me to appoint you administrator. I've had this will—for that's what it really is, and there's no disputing it, neither as to his sanity nor his signature—filed in our court, and everything's according to Blackstone."

"It's a very grave responsibility, Mr. Mason. I presume it means I can make decisions about the land

and the slaves?" Luke stared questioningly at Sybella's father.

"Of course, boy," the lawyer nodded. "But whoa, hold on there a second. I get your drift. You've got the same ideas as your old granddaddy, haven't you? You'd like to free all the slaves at a blow, just the way Jack killed the giant. Well, I'm sure your grandfather must have told you by now that the best you can do is free them if they leave the state. And with the market there is for prime hands these days, and the law forbidding any slaves to be brought in from Africa or anywheres else, the minute they set foot outside of Alabama, somebody else would grab them."

"I know that. What I had in mind was allowing them to buy their freedom, by crediting them with so much every year according to the nature of the work they did. Then, after a certain time, they could buy manumission."

"Well, well." Grover Mason scowled as he plucked at his straggly beard. "I daresay the law doesn't stop that, not exactly. But then suppose you do free them after a certain time, and you still got the law in the book that they have to leave Alabama? You won't be any better off than if you tried to do it right now. No, take my advice, you could be humane to them, the way your granddaddy is, but that's just about all. Unless, of course, you send them all off to Africa the way that fellow Birney is trying to get planters to do. And then you'd have no help at all for the fields, would you? You can't get any white furriners, or Americans either, to come down here and work like nigras picking and hoeing cotton, and you couldn't begin to afford the wages they'd want even if they were willing to do it. I'm afraid it's the system, Luke."

"I'm afraid you're right, Mr. Mason." Luke rose from his chair with a frustrated sigh. "At any rate, one of the first things I'm going to do is tell Amos Greer that if he expects to continue as overseer on the Williamson land he's going to have to throw his cowhide into the river."

"Well, since legally you're the new owner—you and

Miss Lucy, that is—you're also his employer. Only, I don't think Amos Greer is going to take to the change-over too kindly. And he's a mean one, Luke."

"If it comes to that, I'll discharge him. Well then, Mr. Mason, I'm grateful to you. And I want to pay out of my own pocket the bill for your services on this matter of the will. Believe me, sir, when I asked Lucy to marry me, I wasn't thinking of inheriting anything from her father."

"You don't have to tell me that, Luke." Grover Mason smiled, rose from his desk and offered a hearty handshake. "I'll tell you one thing, though, if there were more people like you and your granddaddy around these parts, I'd be out of business. Folks wouldn't need a lawyer 'cause they wouldn't be thinking up any tricks and shenanigans to diddle their neighbors. Give my best to that sweet wife of yours, and to Miss Maybelle too. And tell my daughter it's high time she invited me over for dinner, what with that Mammy Clorinda being the best cook between here and Mobile, from all I've heard!"

"I'll make sure she does it soon, Mr. Mason. Thanks again."

Amos Greer sprawled on his bed, naked except for his dusty boots, his head pillowed on his arms, a crooked grin on his thin lips as he watched the tall, svelte housekeeper tug off her long-skirted, black cotton dress. She stood at the table near the door clad only in a white cotton tunic, which descended to the tops of her long, sleek, ivory-skinned thighs, and black lisle stockings held up at mid-thigh with garish yellow satin-elastic rosette garters. A month away from her forty-first birthday, Zora Devlin was still a stunningly exotic woman, with slantingly set cheekbones, small but overripe mouth, an aquiline nose with very thin, widely flaring nostrils, and closely spaced, large dark-brown eyes. Against the thin fabric of the tunic, her sumptuous pear-shaped breasts boldly thrust out, the nipples hard. She wore a red bandanna bound around

269

the top of her forehead and knotted at the back over the thick oval bun of glossy black hair which was drawn up to leave her neck bare. Her dainty earlobes were pierced for tiny gold earrings, and there was a silver bracelet on her left wrist.

"Pour us out some of that *taffai*, Zora girl, and strut a little for me before you come to bed. You know how it gets me horny for you, you slinky witch," he lewdly chuckled.

"You're a fine one to call me names!" Her voice had the soft slur of the native Jamaican. With a brooding look at him, she turned to the clay jug and poured the rum into two mugs, moved toward the bed to hand him one, then stepped back with a teasing little laugh as he reached for her. "Not yet, Amos mon. We've talking to do, you know that. Now that the master's dead, that stuck-up Miss Lucy's going to take this place over. And you know she hates you, mon. Not that I blame her much for that."

Amos Greer put the mug to his lips and downed its liquor in almost a single gulp, then belched and patted his lean belly. The candle beside the bed flickered, shadowing the matted dark-blond hair on his sturdy chest. He glanced down at his already swollen manhood and slyly muttered, "I'll bet if I ever got that uppity little bitch here in bed with me, I'd teach her to sing a different tune about Amos Greer, I would."

"She's got a mon of her own now, aren't you forgetting, Amos?" Daintily, Zora Devlin sipped her rum, her eyes fixed on his upright, swollen virility, and slyly, her soft pink tongue furled a corner of her sensual mouth.

"That one!" Amos Greer uttered a derisive laugh. "They're perfectly suited for each other, I'm thinking, with all that book learning and holding hands and gazing at the stars. Besides, his pappy made him overseer over at Windhaven. That'll keep him busy this planting season, if I'm any judge."

"But she'll not be able to run this place, you know that, Amos mon."

"Most likely, the law being what it is, Zora, they'll

have a bank or some highfalutin' lawyer step in and handle Miss Lucy's affairs. Well, I'm not worried about that. They won't find a better overseer, not anywhere in Alabama. I'll get cotton out of those niggers if I have to flay them alive, you'll see, Zora. No, girl, what I'm worried about is you."

"What makes you say that, mon?" She put down her mug and turned to look at him, hands on her hips, smiling knowingly as she arched herself so that his narrowed, glinting eyes could admire the proud jut of her breasts, the lithe flare of her springy hips. With both hands, she pressed the tunic against her sides, so that the front of it intimately pressed over the plump, thickly fleeced mound of her sex, tantalizing him with the promise of her lasciviously graceful body.

"Because, Zora, all your fine little schemes to make that stupid old fool marry you went for nothing. I thought for sure after his wife came down with lung fever and you helped her along with some of that poppy juice you've been using on the old man the last few months, you'd get him to make an honest woman of you."

"You keep your mouth shut about that, mon!" Zora Devlin said fiercely, her lips compressed. "She was real bad, his missis was, and I gave her some to help her sleep."

"The long sleep, eh, Zora? Never mind, girl, I don't hold it against you. But I thought for sure you'd get him into bed with you."

"How was I to know the old fool would act like a preacher-mon and not think of any other wench except that saintly wife of his?" Zora burst out. "I tried, Amos mon, you know I tried. And when I gave him some of that juice so he wouldn't fret so much over her, instead of seeing how nice I could be to him if he'd only let me, what did he do but go off to New Orleans and lose all his money? The juice addled his mind, but not about me, more's the bad luck of it!"

"Never mind, Zora. We've still made a little money for our own out of this place, and if our luck holds out we can keep on doing it. Who's to know that I sold a

271

couple of young wenches to the Bufferys, and a young Angola buck who'll stud all the girls they give him to cover and give them plenty of suckers to sell at good prices when they grow up a bit? Poor old Williamson's past caring now, and I've doctored up the books to show that we've had some runaways that we never could bring back. And we can go on doing it if we watch our step."

Zora Devlin moved toward the bed, an enigmatic smile on her moist lips, her eyes heavy-lidded, shifting the hem of the tunic this way and that to tantalize him for the sight of her soft womancore. "Maybe you'd marry me, Amos mon, so we could be partners all the time?" she hazarded.

"Now you're dreaming for fair, Zora!" Again he uttered his braying, sneering laugh. "Marry you, the bastard daughter of a Jamaican house slave and a renegade Irishman? Think I'd take the leavings of a nigger buck who was your husband, that groom Jonas?"

Her eyes narrowed angrily and color blazed in her cheeks. "Mon, I had to marry him, you know that. He pestered me so much, he got my belly big and the old fool of a master said we had to get hitched, it would be sinful if we didn't. I ought to have known then I'd never have a chance to get him into my bed, the Bible-reading old fool! But the worst of it is, he gambled away all his money, and there's no way we can get any of it back now."

"Except by sneaking slaves off to the Bufferys if we're careful about it," Amos Greer corrected. "Now stop your fussing and get to bed with me. You know you want it just as much as I do." He pointed toward the yellow rosette garters on her shapely thighs. "Now that the girls are over at Windhaven, you've been sneaking through that trunk old Williamson kept of his wife's things to remember her by, haven't you? Take that damn thing off, just leave your stockings and garters on, you Jamaican slut, and start pleasuring me. If you're not nice, Zora, I can always trice you up and let you have a taste of the cowhide—you're no better than

272

a slave and I'd be the first to tell the lawyer or the bank people when they come to look over the accounts. Be nice to me and we'll make a go of it. And that's enough talk!"

"You're an evil, terrible, low mon, Amos Greer, and I ought to put poppy juice in your *taffai* some night so's you'd never wake up," she whispered as she clambered onto the bed on all fours, her long slim fingers stroking the insides of his thighs.

"You'd like to, wouldn't you? But you won't ever get the chance. And if you even think of lifting a hand against a white overseer, Zora girl, I'm afraid I'd have to hang you for the other niggers to see as an example of what happens when a slave turns against a master. That's it, look at me with those big eyes of yours, and take that thing off now and pleasure me!" He sat up with a bound, his wiry fingers twisting the thick bun of her hair till, with a cry of submission, Zora Devlin ripped off the tunic and, naked but for hose and garters, submissively bowed her head and fitted her quivering ripe mouth to the violent projectile of his savagely aroused manhood. . . .

Within a week, thanks to the kindness shown to her by Sybella and old Lucien Bouchard himself, Lucy was able to surmount her grief over her father's tragic death. She made fast friends by taking walks with Arabella and the inquisitive little raccoon, and by often accompanying Fleurette out to the stable to visit the rabbit in its hutch. And, swiftly falling into the role of planter's wife, she made it a point of going to the kitchen just before noon to help Mammy Clorinda pack a lunch into a basket which she carried out to the fields to her husband.

Lucien himself accompanied her on two of these noontime excursions, for in many ways the young woman reminded him of gentle Priscilla: in Lucy, he observed the same quick mind, the same innate kindness toward people and animals and the elements. And as the three of them took their ease, sitting propped up against the hayrack with a cotton cloth spread on the ground and the contents of the luncheon basket divided among them, Lucien regaled Luke's raptly absorbed young wife with stories of his life in the village of Econchate.

"Life was much simpler then, my dear," he reminisced. "Today people call them cruel, heartless savages, but their way of life had much to recommend it. They weren't concerned with material possessions, they didn't hate and envy their neighbors for having more land or more slaves. They got their living from the land, but they respected it. They hunted and fished and grew crops for their needs, and they shared their food with the poor and the sick and the disinherited. They couldn't read or write, but they had a rich culture all their own, and they taught their children to be self-reliant, courageous, and that their word was their bond. Soon all of them will be gone from this part of the country, for I've heard that the Cherokees of Georgia are about to give up all their lands east of the Mississippi in return for gold and land in Indian territory out West. Let us hope that those who come after us, like yourselves, Luke and Lucy, and your children and their children after them, will remember something of the simple, elemental world which they created out of a barren wilderness."

"Grandfather, you plan to bring Thomas's niece and nephew here to Windhaven, don't you?" Luke asked.

"Yes, my grandson. But they've already told Thomas that they want to stay with their people to the very end, and that is good. As soon as there's word that they're to be moved West, Thomas will bring them here, I'm sure of that. Ah, this warm sun is good for my old bones. I've been blessed with good health all my life, a priceless commodity, Luke. But most of all, I've been blessed with love, and now that I see the two of you together here with me, sharing our noonday meal, I've no fear about the future of Windhaven. One day, Luke, you and Lucy and the children God intends you to have will find your own frontier, just as I did."

"But your house will stand for many years, Grandfather," Luke responded.

"If God so wills, yes. Yet this new world in which it now stands is already beginning to change." Lucien sighed and turned his head to stare in the direction of the towering red bluff. "It will not come to pass within my lifetime, but it may well in yours, Luke, that even those who stand firmly against slavery will be condemned, with all their Southern brothers, because they are a divided part of this young nation. The North has factories which manufacture tools for farming and textile mills where much of our cotton is processed. Oh yes, there are abuses in those factories, where young children are employed from sunup to sundown—much like the slaves in the fields of the South—at pitifully meager wages. And yet the North has already learned the fundamental truth of diversifying crops and relying on many sources for its profits."

"I wish," Lucy declared, "Luke could turn Papa's land into such other crops as you've done here at Windhaven."

"He can if he wishes, my dear child. Grover Mason has read your father's will to him, by which you inherit most sizably, and it was your father's wish that Luke be administrator. And your sister Maybelle is to have a third."

"If that's so, Luke, please promise me you'll take charge at once and discharge that cruel Mr. Greer," Lucy urged.

"I plan to visit there next week, Lucy darling. That is, if Father can spare me here for a time."

"No need to worry about that, Luke," Lucien interposed. "I'll tell Henry myself to let Thomas look after Windhaven. After all, he's been doing it for years, and he understands why your father made you overseer. A title means as little to Thomas as the possibility of one did to me when I was your age, my grandson. Well now, let's go back, Lucy dear. I've a copy of that Channing pamphlet in my library you might like to read."

Luke Bouchard dismounted from his chestnut gelding and, seeing no stableboy around, led Jemmy himself toward the low, wide log-built stable. As he approached, the same young Hausa, seeing him, dropped the water bucket with which he had been filling the trough of a roan mare, and hastened up to him. "Ah'll do it, massa, suh! Ah didn't see you ride up, Ah's sorry, suh!"

"That's quite all right. If you've an extra stall, keep Jemmy there for me. I may be here a little while."

"Yassuh! Ah'll take right good care of dis yeah hoss, massa!" The boy grasped the reins and bobbed his head, glancing anxiously around.

"What's your name, boy?" Luke asked.

"It's George, massa suh!"

"You took good care of him before, George, and I'd like you to have this for this time," Luke explained as he drew out a coin from his pocket.

"Oh, no, massa suh, Ah cain't take nuttin', dat mah wohk, suh!" the young Hausa hastily replied.

"No, I want you to have it, George. I'm not your master—well, in a way, maybe I am. But when someone does me a service, I expect to reward him."

"Oh, no." The Hausa backed away as he led the gelding toward the stall adjacent to the mare's. "Mistah Greer, he'd whup me again effen Ah took money from you, massa!"

"Whip you again?" Luke wonderingly echoed.

"Dat right, massa suh!" Again the stableboy bobbed his head and looked anxiously around. "He done foun' out you gimme money when you wuz heah de las' time, he took his cowhide to me, suh!"

Luke's face clouded with anger. "Is he out in the fields now, George?"

"Dat right, massa!"

"Thank you, George. Don't give Jemmy too much water, now. And I promise you, nobody's going to take the whip to you again, if I have anything to say about it."

The Hausa looked wonderingly after Luke Bouchard as he strode out of the stable and out toward the fields beyond the opposite row of slave cabins. The cotton was coming up, and the male and female field hands were industriously weeding the rows. He saw the overseer, in a wide-brimmed hat as protection against the hot sun at the distant end of the fields, and quickened his steps.

Amos Greer bent over a comely young Fulani girl of about nineteen, and, reaching out his left hand, dug his fingers cruelly into her bare shoulder. "Are you still going to be ornery, Betty?" he growled. "If you behave yourself and treat me nice, you won't have to work out here in the fields. I'll let you stay in the house and maybe wear a nice dress instead of this rag."

"Please, suh, you knows Ah's Harry's wife, Ah cain't do wut you wants, please, massa, doan make me!" the girl sobbed.

Amos Greer's thin lips curled in a sadistic, gloating smile as he lifted the cowhide in his right hand so that she could not fail to see it. "Now listen, you black bitch, nigger marriages don't mean a thing and you know it. The master's dead and you've got to do what I tell you to, or I'll take you into the shed and let you have a real smart touch of this—you know I can do it, don't you, Betty?"

The Fulani girl's eyes filled with tears as she nodded. "Ah knows you cain, massa suh," she groaned, "only Ah begs you, Ah's got Harry's sucker in me already, suh, Ah wouldn't be no good foah you nohow, please, suh!"

Amos Greer grinned viciously. "Well now, Betty, if he's already busted you, no need for you to play innocent with me, is there? You know, girl, I've been watching you work all day, and you haven't chopped out all the weeds along your row. I think it's time for a little visit to the shed. Come along now, and we'll see if you'll want to be so set against coming to my cabin tonight, you hear? Get up now, leave that hoe right there and start walking, or I'll lace you good before you even get to the shed, you stubborn bitch!"

Betty burst into tears as she slowly, hopelessly rose to her feet. Two rows beyond, a stocky young Kru in his mid-twenties clenched his fists as he squatted beside a patch of weeds, a tall angular-faced Ashanti next to him shaking his head and whispering a warning.

"Get along with you there, or I'll warm you up before you have your thrashing," Amos Greer tauntingly directed as, uncoiling the cowhide, he expertly flicked it to make it wrap around the Fulani girl's hips. She uttered a shriek of pain and terror, glancing frantically back, then stumbled forward, covering her tear-stained face with her hands.

The stocky young Kru had risen to his feet, but the Ashanti beside him gripped his elbow. "No, won't do you no good, Harry, he could whup you to death and then take it out on Betty anyhow—Ah knows how you feels, boy, but dat Mistah Greer, he a mean debbil. And now we ain't got no massa, it's gonna be him lordin' it obah us all."

As the weeping Fulani girl reached the edge of the fields, stumbling blindly toward the whipping shed, Luke Bouchard stepped forward to confront Amos Greer. "Just a minute, Mr. Greer. What are you going to do to that girl?"

"Why, Mr. Bouchard, sir," again the overseer sarcastically underlined the title of respect, "just touch her up so she'll chop out the weeds in her row the way she was told."

"You're not going to whip her, Mr. Greer. Nor anybody else, for that matter. The lawyer Grover Mason just read me Mr. Williamson's will, and it leaves most of what he owns to Lucy, my wife. Mr. Williamson asked that I look after his holdings for his daughter's sake, which makes me master here."

"Well, now, Mr. Bouchard, 'pears to me you're starting to bite off more than you can chew, don't you think? Didn't I hear tell that your daddy made you overseer over at Windhaven? How do you think you're going to take care of all that land and this place too, if you don't mind my asking?"

"I do, but I'll tell you anyway. My father's put Thomas back in charge to look after Windhaven. Since this is my wife's property, and both she and her father

278

want me to look after it, I'm going to take over. In fact, my wife and I plan to move back into this house just as soon as Lucy gets over her grief. And the first order I'm giving you, Mr. Greer, is to throw that whip away and don't ever let me see you using it again on anyone, least of all a helpless woman."

"A helpless woman!" Amos Greer sniggered, glancing round and observing with satisfaction that several of the field hands had risen to their feet and were expectantly watching this confrontation. "That lazy nigger bitch, you mean, don't you, Mr. Bouchard? You talk a mite fancy, but then I 'spect it's because of all the books you read. Now me, I never had much schooling, but I know how to work niggers and get top quality cotton out of the land. 'Course, Mr. Bouchard, I don't say as how your book-learning way won't grow a little cotton, but Mr. Williamson said he didn't know a better overseer anywhere when it came to getting results. I'd just remind you of that, Mr. Bouchard."

"The fact is, Mr. Greer"—Luke Bouchard's voice was calm and unhurried—"I'd just remind you that by the terms of your late employer's will I now am in his place and you're accountable to me. And my order is that you get rid of your whip and don't ever use it again."

"What the hell do you want me to do when a nigger won't do his work, then?" Amos Greer put his hands on his hips, the coiled cowhide still circling his right wrist. His eyes contemptuously swept Luke Bouchard up and down, and his thin lips curled in a sneering grin.

"I expect you to show them what you want and then let them do an honest day's work without treating them like animals."

"You're going to spoil them rotten, Mr. Bouchard. I've worked in Georgia and here, and there's not a nigger anywhere who's got brains enough to do it on his own without a little persuasion from the cowhide. Leastways, I never met any."

"You never tried. I don't propose to argue with you.

You'll either do what I wish, or you can consider your employment at an end."

"Well, now, you young whippersnapper, you're mighty big all of a sudden. Come here to the fields and let these niggers of mine think you're so high-and-mighty important. Besides, you can't discharge me. I have a contract with Mr. Williamson and there's the matter of my money for the year."

"I'll see that the lawyer pays you off. And since you've brought up the subject of a contract, I'd like to see the records you've kept on the land and the slaves. I assume you do keep the accounts—that's the duty of an overseer."

"And now you're trying to teach me my business! I'll be damned if I'll take sass from a snot-nosed young upstart who thinks because he's married my boss's uppity daughter, he knows everything there is to running a plantation."

"You'll apologize for that remark about my wife, Mr. Greer," Luke said quietly.

"The hell I will! Oh, don't get me wrong, Mr. Bouchard, she's a purty, well-turned-out little lady, I'm not denying that, but with all the book-learning and la-de-da airs the two of you give yourselves, I wonder if you can raise an honest sweat in bed at night!"

Luke's face turned crimson at this obscene jibe, but he mastered himself with an effort. "You'll keep your filthy remarks to yourself, if you please, Mr. Greer. I've an idea that your way of courting a woman is with that whip, and you wouldn't know a decent lady if you saw one."

"That about does it, you damned snot-nose pup! If you'll forget just once that you're the new owner—which I'm not sure of yet, just on your say-so—I'll teach you a little lesson, sonny!" Amos Greer stepped back, uncoiled the whip and deftly swept it back in his right hand, then slashed it out at the young man before him. But Luke had anticipated the overseer's maneuver, and turning swiftly away from the whip, rushed headlong at the overseer and smashed his fist against Greer's jaw. With a grunt of pained surprise, the older man staggered, stumbled back over one of the rows of cotton plants, and sprawled ignominiously on his posterior. Beyond him, a burst of laughter rose from the watching slaves, all of whom had stopped their work to witness this duel.

"You bastard, I'll beat you to a pulp!" Greer snarled as he righted himself, swinging the whip again. It slashed out, this time cutting around Luke's right side. With a grimace of pain, Luke seized the thong with both hands and gave it an energetic jerk, at the same time lifting his right foot and thrusting his heel into Greer's belly. The overseer uttered a grunt as the wind was knocked out of him, dropped the whip, then stumbled back with hands clutched against his middle and sat down heavily. Now the laughter from the field hands was even louder.

Slowly getting to all fours, malevolently eying his young adversary, Greer now rushed forward like a maddened bull. Luke met the charge unwaveringly, his hands grabbing for and gripping the overseer's forearms and then pivoting as he released his hold. The overseer's momentum carried him forward, and he sprawled again, this time flat on his belly.

"Git him, massa! Dat de way!" Betty's husband shouted encouragement, excitedly waving his fists.

Amos Greer's right hand dug into the freshly hoed soil, clutched a handful, and as he straightened, he flung it into Luke's face. Momentarily taken by surprise, Luke threw up a fending arm but too late to ward it off, momentarily blinded by the dirt. Pressing his advantage, the overseer advanced and shot a right to Luke's jaw, and this time it was the younger man who sprawled on the ground, shaking his head, blinking his eyes and carefully brushing his fingertips against them to clear them of the blinding particles. "Get up and get your lesson, sonny!" Amos Greer exulted, fists clenched, his shirt half-open and drenched with sweat.

Luke managed to clear his eyes, and then flung himself forward with both arms gripping Amos Greer's calves. Toppling the older man onto his back, Luke profited from this advantage by crawling forward, clamping his legs around the overseer's, and then began to pummel him with both fists, smashing the sneering, hateful face in unreasoning fury.

Greer snarled and shook his head, his nose bloodied from Luke's blows, but doggedly fought back, striking out with his left fist and bruising Luke's cheekbone enough to unseat his young adversary. Rolling over on his side, he got to his feet and came forward with fists flailing. Luke stepped aside, and with all his strength drove a furious blow to the side of Amos Greer's jaw. With a choking gasp, the overseer went sprawling on his back and lay panting, groggily shaking his head, blood streaming down his face.

Luke seized the cowhide, then pantingly exclaimed, "And now, Mr. Greer, you'll thank me by getting your possessions and leaving here. I don't want to see you around here tomorrow when I come out to the fields with these workers, is that understood?"

"My money—"

"I told you I'll see that the lawyer gets it to you. No one's going to cheat you. You'll be paid for the full year, even though this is only May. Now, one last thing, where are the records? In the house somewhere, in Mr. Williamson's study?"

"You're the boss now, you find them. To hell with you, you young bastard, you just about broke my nose!" Amos Greer stumbled to his feet, ripping off a piece of his shirt to mop the blood from his mashed nose. His pale-blue eyes glowed with hatred. "I'll pay you back for this, in front of all these niggers too! You wait and see."

Then, picking up his wide-brimmed hat and tugging it down on his head, with a last vengeful glance at Luke Bouchard, he made his way back to his cabin. From the spellbound field hands there was a chorus of loud cheers and the waving of fists to signify their delight at this long-overdue retribution for a tyrant.

CHAPTER TWENTY

Old Obadiah opened the front door, his wrinkled face aglow, as Luke Bouchard greeted him with a cordial "Good afternoon, Obadiah. I'd like to see Mr. Williamson's study, if you please."

"Yassuh, yassuh, you come right heah along with me, suh! My, my," the elderly black chuckled, "you sho nuff learned dat Mistah Greer some respec', you sho nuff did, suh. Heah it is. And how's dat sweet Miz Lucy?"

"Just fine, Obadiah, thank you. I'll tell her you asked about her. And Maybelle is getting used to her new home. But confidentially, Obadiah, I'm planning to move back here with Lucy and her sister in another few weeks, and I'd take it very kindly if you'd look after things till I can get over here."

"Oh, suh, dat's wonnerful news, dat sho nuff is!" Obadiah beamed. "All us niggahs wuz worried when poor old Mistah Williamson died, we wuz mighty certain dat Mistah Greer would be the massa. Now, Ah bettah tell Zora you is here, she gwine want to see you. You know she been de housekeeper all dis hyeah time, suh."

"Yes, so Lucy told me. You tell her, by all means, and send her into the study, please, Obadiah."

"Right away, massa suh."

"You needn't call me master, Obadiah. I'm going to come out to the fields tomorrow and talk to the hands,

283

but I'd like it better if you'd call me just Mr. Luke or Mr. Bouchard, whichever you like."

"Lawd's sakes alive, suh, dey's sho nuff gwine be some changes round here, Obadiah kin see dat!" the jubilant old black gleefully cackled.

Luke swiftly opened the drawers of Edward Williamson's desk, finding at last a ledger in the bottom drawer covered by old copies of the Montgomery *Journal*. Seating himself, he flipped through the pages quickly, and was deeply engrossed in the book as the Jamaican housekeeper entered. She had on her high-necked, long-skirted, puff-sleeved black dress, her hair was primly coiffed in the thick oval bun at the back of her head, and from her there came a scent of expensive perfume—perfume she had appropriated from the late Helen Williamson's effects which the planter had brought from Georgia.

"Can I help you any, Mr. Bouchard, mon?" she murmured in a seductively husky voice.

Luke turned and courteously rose, closing the ledger and setting it down on the top of the desk before him. "Perhaps you can answer a few questions, Zora—am I right about your name?"

"It's Zora Devlin, Mr. Bouchard mon. What would you like to know, sir?"

"I find an entry here in this record of Mr. Williamson's accounts that there were three runaway slaves back in February. Have they been found yet, Miss Devlin?"

"My, mon, you don't have to call me that. I'm just the housekeeper, and I'm not white like you, Mr. Bouchard sir. Zora's good enough."

"Please answer my question."

She shrugged, her face impassive. "That wasn't my business to know, Mr. Bouchard sir. Mr. Greer just told me they were runaways, he never said anything about getting them back. I just did the cooking and looking after that poor old man and his girls, that's all."

"I see. Well, for your information, I've just discharged Mr. Greer. I'll come here tomorrow to instruct the workers in the fields, and you're at liberty to remain

284

here if you like. I don't know what your wages are, but I'll see that you're paid for your services, you can be sure of that, Miss Devlin."

Zora Devlin giggled, then slowly approached, arching herself and swinging her hips to display her body to its best advantage. Her eyes downcast, she murmured huskily, "But I'm just like the other slaves, Mr. Bouchard mon. I told you, there's black blood in me way back. You say you let Amos Greer go, Mr. Bouchard sir?"

"Yes I did. I'm afraid we had a rather violent discussion about it, and he insisted on fighting me."

Her eyes widened at this news. "You mean you fought that mon and you beat him fair and square, Mr. Bouchard?"

"Well, I don't know about that, but at least he had enough and he agreed to leave the plantation."

"Mon, you sure are something!" She expressively rolled her eyes, stepped forward until she was only inches away from him. "And you so young and all, you sure must have lots of strength in those hands of yours. You know, Mr. Bouchard, I told you I was a slave, you could order me to do anything, and I'd have to do it, you know, mon." There was no mistaking the bold invitation in her eyes, and the sensual curve of her moist ripe mouth as she stared archly at him.

"I'd like you to know something right off, Miss Devlin. It's true that slavery is the custom in this state, but I personally am not in sympathy with it. There's no need for you to think of me as your master, and I certainly wouldn't order you to do anything. I'd just ask you to go on being housekeeper and cook as you've been before. And as I say, I intend to see to it that you get some wages."

"You're awful nice, mon, and you're sure some improvement over that Amos Greer," Zora Devlin purred. Her tongue flicked the corners of her lips as she moved even closer. "I'm real grateful you got rid of him, Mr. Bouchard. Why don't you let me fix you some supper and make up old Mr. Williamson's room for you nice and comfortable-like? Then I could come in and see if everything was to your liking. I know how to take good care of a fine gentleman like you, mon, and that's the truth."

Luke flushed uncomfortably, the strong perfume's reek making his nostrils dilate as he stepped back. "No, thank you, Miss Devlin. I'm going to ride back to Windhaven in a few minutes. But to go back, you say these slaves are still missing?"

"I told you that's all I know." Her voice was sharp and her manner irritable now, sensing herself rejected. Putting her hands behind her back, she arched her bosom lasciviously, and then, her eyes half-closed, murmured, "Maybe you'd like me to fix you a nice posset? It's a special drink the old man always asked for, mon. I use some strong *taffai* and some herbs and a little of that red stuff there—" She gestured toward an almost empty decanter which stood on a sideboard near the desk. "It'll make you feel real nice and easy."

Luke followed her gesture and walked over to the sideboard. Taking the stopple out of the decanter, he tilted it to his nose and sniffed. "What is it, Miss Devlin?"

"Oh, just some poppy juice and stuff, that's all, master sir." Her voice was soft, her eyes still half-closed and fixed on him with a speculative gaze.

"Poppy juice—that's used for medicine, to put someone to sleep or when he's in pain," Luke declared, regarding Zora Devlin with a puzzled frown. "You mean Mr. Williamson drank this?"

"Why yes he did, mon, when he had his likker. He liked it a lot."

"Well, I've no need of it, thank you. Is there anything else you can tell me about this plantation, Miss Devlin, anything that you think I ought to know now that I'm going to try to run it to the best of my ability?"

"Are you going to have a new overseer?"

"Perhaps, in time. Meanwhile, I'm going to stay here and work the land along with the hands, at least until the crop's harvested."

"You know, Mr. Bouchard"—now her tone was

286

wheedling as she again moved closer to him—"there's lots of money to be made here for a real smart good-looking young mon like you. I could help you lots, if you'd let me."

"What are you trying to tell me, Miss Devlin? Money made from cotton—next year, I'm going to change the crops on some of the land."

"Oh no, not just cotton, Mr. Bouchard mon. You can sell slaves. There's some people Mr. Greer knows, they'd buy a nigger buck or wench to breed suckers with, and they'd buy suckers too, once they was past their weaning. They'd pay good prices, too, I heard tell."

Luke's face clouded with anger. "I don't propose to sell any of the slaves for breeding. That's treating them like animals, Miss Devlin. My feeling is that you know more about what's been going on here than you're ready to tell me. One thing I'm going to insist on is loyalty, if only for my wife's sake and for her younger sister's."

Again Zora Devlin shrugged, but this time her smile was honeyed, her eyes warm with promise as she murmured, "I never in my life met such a fine young mon who can be so downright balky at taking what's his for the asking, Mr. Bouchard mon. Now why don't you change your mind and stay the night, and then maybe I can feel like we're friends enough so's I can tell you—well, things. Wouldn't you like that, Mr. Bouchard mon?" Now, unexpectedly, she put her arms around him, pressing her jutting breasts against his chest as she offered her mouth.

"Miss Devlin, please don't belittle yourself. I'm married, and even if I weren't, I shouldn't think of taking advantage of you in this way simply because you're the housekeeper and I'm taking charge here."

Zora Devlin's face twisted with spite as she stepped back, hands on her hips, and in a sneering voice declared, "My, just like Amos Greer said, you're high and mighty, aren't you, mon? Well, just you run this place then, and you don't need me to tell you nothin'!

I'll go find a place where they appreciate me more, you hear that, mon?"

"That's your choice to make, Miss Devlin. I'm sorry you feel that way, and I didn't mean to offend you or to be rude."

"You know what I think? I think Miss Lucy's got herself a prissy prig of a husband, that's what I think. At least Amos Greer is a man, for all his faults." And with this, Zora Devlin turned and stalked back to her room. In a few minutes, she had packed her belongings in a gunny sack and swept out of the house and to the cabin of the deposed overseer.

During the growing season, Henry Bouchard spent most of each day supervising the work on his original hundred acres and visiting the additional sections of fifty and seventy-five which he had been able to acquire through the financial misfortunes of their first owners. The rude log cabin which had been built near the river on his own land and to which he had brought the unhappy young Dora Trask as his unwilling bride had been rebuilt with bricks and heavy timber. Mary, the light-skinned Kru wife of Abe, now thirty-six years old and still comely, had been appointed housekeeper and cook on those occasions when old Lucien's son deigned to remain overnight. He no longer showed any carnal interest in her, much to her relief, since she well remembered how he had made her submit under the lash. She and Abe had had four children, the first of whom was assuredly Henry's, for Dan, now nearly eighteen, was even lighter-skinned than his handsome mother. Henry Bouchard had not bothered to acknowledge this mulatto son of his, except to appoint him as an assistant foreman on the hundred-acre spread which had been his very first holding of land arranged for by Lucien.

He had just breakfasted and was enjoying a second cup of coffee and a hand-rolled cigar when Mary hurried in and exclaimed, "Massa, dey's a man and a woman here lookin' for you, suh!"

Henry Bouchard drained his coffee cup, set it down

288

with a clatter, and then strode out of the cabin. Amos Greer and Zora Devlin stood waiting in the clearing near the little house. The overseer, his face bruised and badly discolored, held the reins of a gray gelding on which he and Zora had ridden from the Williamson plantation.

"Well now, Amos," Henry chuckled as he puffed at his cigar and flicked the ashes to the ground, "you're a sorry sight, I must say. And Zora with you—if I didn't know better, I'd say you've been dispossessed."

"Damn it, Mr. Bouchard, no need to joke about it, but you've nigh hit on the truth for fair," the overseer growled, with an uneasy look at the faintly smiling Jamaican housekeeper. "You said to me once, if I remember right, that if I ever wanted to work some-wheres else, I was to let you know. That's what I'm doing right now, if you're still of the same mind."

"Of course I am. You mean you've given up the job because my son Luke stepped in there? I thought you had more stamina than that, Amos."

Greer muttered something profane under his breath and uneasily shifted his feet, gingerly feeling his swollen nose. "I guess you might say that son of yours ran me off, Mr. Bouchard. And damn it all, don't you go laughing at me neither, not the way I feel this morning. He came in there all full of high and mighty notions about my throwing my whip into the Alabama River, and when I took offense, he took me by surprise and knocked me down. I tell you, I didn't want to hurt the boy, but he fought real dirty. So I figured, no use making any more bad blood between us or trying to change that schoolmarm mind of his, so I just told him I was finished. Now what I came here for, Mr. Bouchard, was to find out if you can use me. Zora here, she didn't take kindly to your son's notions either, so she asked me if I'd bring her along and speak to you for her."

Henry Bouchard's eyes narrowed as they contemplated the handsome Jamaican woman, who wore the same black dress and only her shift and hose and the stolen rosette garters under it. She met his gaze with a faint smile, then lowered her eyes and waited for his

289

answer. He felt his pulses quicken at the meaningful intimation of that look of hers, and hawked and spat while he strove to compose his thoughts before speaking.

"Well, Amos, you've come at a pretty good time, I'd say," he finally replied. "Now what happened was that Luke sort of inherited the Williamson spread by marrying Lucy, and I decided to let the boy have his own place, seeing how he's newly married and wanting to make a good start for himself to show his young wife he's up to it. So I've got old Thomas back where he used to be, but between you and me, I'm not partial to nigger overseers. However, my father and I don't see eye to eye on that matter, but he's old and set in his ways and I'm not going to shout him down about that. No matter. What I can use is someone who knows his business and who can take good care of what you see here as well as two smaller spreads not far from where we are now. I've had to use nigger foremen on them because I haven't had a capable overseer, and it would be a weight off my mind to know that someone like you could put his mind to working for my profits."

"Then I'm your man, Mr. Bouchard. I won't even ask your terms, I'm that eager to get back to my rightful duties again," Amos Greer grinned, holding his wide-brimmed hat between his fingers and twisting it just as a beggar might who was supplicating for alms. Then, in a confidentially disarming tone, he added, "You see, Mr. Bouchard, I'm not a greedy sort, and your son tells me I can be paid my full year's wages by the lawyer handling poor old Mr. Williamson's affairs. Well, sir, all I'd want is my keep and a few comforts, and then when the crop's in and marketed at Mobile, you and I could sit down man to man and work out what you think is fair for me next year."

"I couldn't ask for any more honest dealings than that, Amos. My hand on it. Don't worry, if the price keeps good at Mobile this winter, you'll get a little more than your keep and comforts." Henry grinned amiably as he held out his hand. "Now Zora here, I think she could fit in quite nicely and look after this little place

290

of mine. I live in the big red-brick house at Wind-haven, you understand, but I'm out here a good deal of the time and it might just be that if she cooks as well as I've heard tell, I'd be inclined to sample her vittles. That's not to say a word against Mammy Clorinda's cooking, but a man likes a little variety now and then—isn't that right, Amos?"

He had accompanied this last remark with a broad wink, and the overseer eyed Zora Devlin, saw her imperceptible nod, and then himself heartily nodded: "It does a man good to hear somebody like you talk about the way things ought to be, Mr. Bouchard. Mind you, I mean no offense to your son."

"And there's none taken, Amos. Now you know I've got another boy, Mark, the younger, and to my mind he's a real comer. He's like me in a good many ways, drives right to the point without hedging around, speaks his mind, knows what he wants. He'll be working along with the two of us, and I'm sure you can take him under your wing and teach him what you know about getting prime cotton out of good land when you've got lazy niggers to work it for you."

"Well, I'm not one to brag about myself, you understand, Mr. Bouchard, but I think you remember what poor Mr. Williamson said about me when you came calling that time." Amos Greer modestly lowered his eyes and twisted his hat round and round between his strong fingers.

"Then it's settled. Now I've got some slave cabins out beyond there as you can see, but I'll have Mary and Molly clean out the biggest one at the head of the row, and that'll be yours."

"No objection to that, Mr. Bouchard. Fact is, the closer I am to those shiftless niggers, the more I'll find out about what they're thinking, so they won't be able to play any tricks."

"Now let's see about Zora here," Henry Bouchard drawled, again eying the tall, strikingly handsome Jamaican woman. "You can see that little log shed near the house—used to have that when we first

291

started here for one of the slaves. It could be fixed up and fit for sleeping and such."

Zora Devlin raised her eyes to his, her enigmatic smile deepening. "It'll do just fine, Mr. Bouchard mon," she agreed. "I'll be around whenever you need me."

"Good! Why don't you ask Mary to show you the little shed and tell her what you need and get yourself moved in? Amos and I can have a little talk about the crops," Henry suggested with a nod of dismissal. Zora Devlin inclined her head, and walked toward the Kru woman who was drawing a bucket of water out of the stone well at the side of the little house.

"Come in and have a cigar, Amos. There's something I'd like you to do for me, if you will," Henry Bouchard said as he put his arm around the overseer's shoulders and led him into the house. "Sit down there, make yourself easy. This is prime Virginia tobacco and that Kru bitch you saw there by the well rolls them for me. Now then, my neighbor Benjamin Harnesty rode over to Tuscaloosa last week to pay his taxes on the land, and he heard a bit of news he thought I'd be interested in. You know that the government is moving out these damned Indians and most likely will get the Cherokees out of Georgia before much longer."

"I'd heard that, yes, Mr. Bouchard." Amos Greer warily watched his new employer, puffing at his cigar and smacking his lips to show his enjoyment of it.

"Harnesty told me that he'd talked to a state congressman while he was in Tuscaloosa and found out that in a couple of weeks they're going to send a couple of bands of Creeks out of Alabama, off to the West where they belong. Now one of those bands is still nesting near Tuskegee—you know where that is, Amos?"

"I've been out that way a couple of times, yes, Mr. Bouchard. It's about fifty miles, a day and a half on a good horse if you're not pressing."

"That's what I figured too, Amos. Well, they're getting ready to move what's left of that village in just about two weeks. There are two Creeks I'm mighty interested in. Can you keep your mouth shut and be trusted, Amos? If you can, you'll find me generous."

"I'm working for you now, Mr. Bouchard, it's like I never had no one else before you. You tell me what to do, I'll do it."

"We're going to get along, Amos, I can see that already," Henry grinned and took another puff at his cigar. "That nigger overseer Thomas had a sister who married one of those damned Creeks and gave him a son and a daughter. Last year, just once, I drove out there with my father to take some supplies to the village—all his life he's thought that because they let him stay on their land without scalping him, he's beholden to them. I'm not arguing that, either. But the point is, that niece of Thomas's is a real beauty, half nigger and half Creek. She'd make a sweet bed wench if I could figure out a way to get her out of that village when the rest of them start marching off, and put her down in my books as a slave."

"I get your drift, Mr. Bouchard." Amos Greer scowled and tugged at his stubbly beard. "The law says Injuns can't be slaves, but then if she's got nigger blood in her, that ought to make a difference. Now maybe if she was to get into some trouble, and she was told they'd jail or maybe even hang her for what she did, she just might choose signing one of those indenture papers. You could put down any name you wanted, and you said her mother was a nigger—well, there you are, Mr. Bouchard."

Henry Bouchard's eyes sparkled with concupiscent pleasure. "Work it out somehow, Amos. I think you're on the right track, I do indeed. Her mother was mighty uppity to me once, and I've never forgotten it. Having her daughter here as my slave will just about balance the account." He crushed out the glowing stub of his cigar with an emphatic gesture. "Tell you what, Amos. Go see Benjamin Harnesty this afternoon and see if he can give you any more particulars about when the soldiers plan to move that bunch of Creeks out of the state. Then see that you get yourself over there just before that happens, and do what you think you have to do. I might just give you what you were supposed to get from poor old Ed Williamson as your wages this year."

Amos Greer's pale-blue eyes flickered with a sudden greedy glow. "That's mighty handsome of you, Mr. Bouchard sir."

"The names of these two I want brought back to me here are Manoka and the girl Shonanoy. The one thing you've got to do is make them willing to come back with you before they set out on that march, you understand? How you'll get it done, I'll leave to you, Amos." He rose from the table with a satisfied smile. "I'm expecting you to show me why poor old Ed Williamson swore by you, Amos."

Luke Bouchard had ridden over from Windhaven early the next morning, almost before dawn, so that he could meet with Williamson's slaves at their cabins just before they went out into the fields. The sleepy young Hausa, George, hearing the sound of Jemmy's whinny as Luke drew him to a halt and dismounted, came scurrying out of the stable, a happy grin on his face. "Mohnin', massa suh, you sho is bright 'n early! Lemme take Jemmy. Does he want some oats this mohnin', massa?"

"Why, George, that would be fine, thank you. And this time you're going to take the dollar and Mr. Greer isn't going to whip you for keeping it," Luke said as he took the coin out of his pocket and handed it to the stableboy.

"Thank'ee kindly, massa suh, thank'ee. Disyeah's de only dollah ah ebber had in mah whole life, massa suh. Mistah Greer, he done made me give him dat fust dollah you gimme—den he whupped me good for takin' it."

"In that case, George, here's the other dollar back. And nobody's going to whip you ever again, you've got my word on it."

"Thank'ee again, massa! Ebbrybody is sayin' how you done whupped Mistah Greer 'n made him skedaddle. Sho wish Ah'd seen you do dat, Massa!"

the grinning boy delightedly shook his head and rolled his eyes as he led the gelding into the stable.

Luke walked out to the rows of cabins, from which the field hands were beginning to emerge. An excited chatter of voices rose as they saw him. The women, pushing their children ahead of them with both hands, crowded out to see the new young master, bent down to whisper and to point him out to the wide-eyed children.

"Good morning, all of you," Luke called in a clear voice. "My name is Luke Bouchard. I've married Miss Lucy, and we're going to come back here to live, along with Miss Maybelle. First off, I want to tell you that Mr. Greer isn't overseer anymore."

At this news, there was a joyous shout from the slaves, and an excited babble of voices. Luke smilingly waited a moment, then went on. "I give you my word that no one on this plantation will ever again be whipped or badly treated. I come from Windhaven, where my grandfather taught me to work on the land. I plan to work with all of you in the fields, and to help you as I know you're going to help me. All of the land has cotton now, but next year I want to raise vegetables and corn and perhaps have a few sheep and cows and a good bull, so that there'll be more food for all of us here."

Again there was an excited clamor from the slaves and again Luke waited till it stilled. "Did Mr. Greer make any of you foremen?" he asked.

"Yassuh, massa, he done have two he puts over us," the tall Ashanti, who had urged Betty's husband not to defy Amos Greer, stepped forward. "Dey is John and me, suh, but mainly Mistah Greer say ebbrybody gotta do so much wuhk no matter whether he a man or a woman, massa."

"It's too late to get it done now, but if I'm going to stay on this place, I mean to put a cotton gin here next year to make it easier. Up to now, I know that Williamson had the cotton packed and hauled over to my father's gin."

"Dat right suh," the Ashanti nodded.

"What's your name?"

"It Carl, massa."

"Well, Carl, you and your friend will go on being foremen. Now that girl Mr. Greer was going to whip yesterday—I understand she's married."

"Dat right, massa, her man Harry, Ah tol' him he dassn't try to stop that mean ole Mistah Greer or he get hisself killed."

"Harry, will you come forward, please," Luke called.

The Kru stepped out, looking somewhat sheepish at being the center of attention.

"Harry, I'm going to make you a foreman too. And your Betty won't have to work in the fields. In fact, I'd like all the women to try their hand at planting a garden. I know you have flowers around the house, but do you have any corn or vegetables, like yams and beans?"

"Nawsuh," the Ashanti spoke up again. "Mostly we eats corn pone 'n a little bacon 'n hominy cakes and such."

"Tomorrow, then, I'll bring some seeds and supplies from Windhaven," Luke Bouchard promised. "I want to look into some of your cabins and see if you have decent beds."

"Nawsuh, not hardly." The Ashanti permitted himself a wry grin. "Just sort of like scaffolds nailed up to the walls out of poles, massa, and raggedy bedding throwed on 'em. It sho is hard sleepin', but even dat feel good to our weary bones after de wuhk in de field."

"Dat sho de truth," Harry eagerly confirmed with a vigorous nod of his head.

"Then I'll see to it that all of you get some new bedding, and if any of you are handy with wood and tools, you can make yourselves some good comfortable beds," Luke suggested. "Now one thing more, Carl. I was looking over Mr. Williamson's books and I see there's a notice about some runaway slaves in February. Do you know anything about them?"

The Ashanti looked uneasy, glanced at his fellows,

then shook his head: "Doan know nuttin' 'bout dat, massa. Mistah Greer, he say dey up an' run. Dey was here one night, and de nex' mohnin' dey wuzn't. Dat's all we know."

"I see. Well, I do hope that when I've made your life a little easier, none of you will feel like running away. And one thing more—from now on, you don't have to call me master. Just Mr. Bouchard, or Mr. Luke if you'd rather. I'm going to try my best to see if I can't make this a kind of home for all of you, where you'll be rewarded for your work and have a chance to bring up your families without being afraid of being sold away or traded. I don't hold with that. If I could free you all, I promise you I'd do it. But in the meantime, while I'm here, if there's anything that troubles any of you, I want you all to feel free to tell me."

"If dat sweet Miss Lucy pick you for her man, dat already tell us you gonna be a good massa, suh," the Ashanti grinned. "Now after all you done said to us, we gonna try hard to make you real proud of dis yeah plantation, suh."

CHAPTER TWENTY-ONE

Amos Greer halted the phaeton behind a thick clump of loblolly pine trees and got down from the coachman's seat. He turned to the two black Gullahs who rode in the back, and growled, "Now then, you've got it straight what I want you to do, have you, Tom, Ezra?"

Tom, a barrel-chested, heavy-set black in his early forties, dressed like his companion in white cotton breeches, cambric shirt and work shoes, grunted assent. "You gonna get dem two Injuns, and de boy's gwine ride wid you up front, Mistah Greer. Den Ezra and me, we take de gal wid us heah, and we staht pesterin' her jist a liddle bit; dat right, suh?"

Amos Greer's lips drew back in a wolfish grin as he nodded. "They'll come along with me all right, once I tell them their uncle sent for them to come back to Windhaven with me. And if they ask you, you're old Mr. Bouchard's niggers. Don't you spill the beans and let on you work for Mr. Henry, understand?"

"Yassuh, boss," Ezra, in his late twenties, tall, lanky, with splayed nose and thick lips, sniggered and touched his forehead to signify his understanding. "We is ol' Mistah Bouchard's niggers an' he done send us to bring dese two Injuns back to Uncle Thomas, suh."

"Now you've got it straight. You'd better not make any mistakes or I'll skin you alive with my cowhide. Handle it the way I told you, and when we get back to

Mr. Henry's place, you'll each get a jug of *taffai* and a nice black wench to cover, and maybe a little money."

"We sho ain't gwine make no mistake, not foah all dat pay, Mistah Greer suh," Tom cackled, with a wink at his crony.

"All right then. Just you hide behind these trees here, while I drive on into the village and bring Manoka and Shonanoy out. Soon as I get past the trees, I'll be driving real slow so you can catch up. Then you'll grab the girl and start fooling with her—but you better not fool too much, niggers."

"We do jist lak you tell us, Mistah Greer," Ezra reassured him.

They leaped out of the phaeton and crouched behind the trees while Amos Greer got back into the coachman's seat, clucked at the two black mares and drove slowly toward the sparsely settled village of the Creeks, those once proud descendants of old Tunka-mara, now dwindled to perhaps some sixty men, women and children in all. Starvation, disease, grief had thinned their numbers. Tomorrow, a government agent had told the new *Mico*, they would be marched out of Alabama to the land promised them in the West.

Amos Greer again halted the mares, tied the reins to the stump of a lightning-blasted oak tree, and walked toward the crude little cabin made of logs and daubed with clay which stood at the head of this desolate village, knowing that it was the lodge of the *Mico*, Turintaka. He took off his wide-brimmed hat and forced a respectful smile to his thin lips as the tall, solemn-faced Creek chief emerged. Turintaka was in his early forties, his black hair drawn into a single thick short braid with a quail feather thrust through it, and on his high-set cheekbones were painted in blue dye the symbol of his totem, that of the Beaver Clan. A ragged blanket was wrapped round his chest and waist, and he wore buckskin leggings and breechclout and moccasins.

"I have come, great chief, because the old Mr. Bouchard who is your blood brother sent me."

Turintaka's bleak face brightened and he nodded. "It is good that he still thinks of us. But you have come at a sorry time for what is left of our nation. To-morrow, the soldiers tell us, we leave the good land for our new homes. They tell us it is far from here and that the sun is not so warm, and that the hunting can-not be as good as it was here. But we are resigned. It is our fate, as Ibofanaga wills it."

"He has sent me," Amos Greer said, with a feigned smile as he stared into the *Mico*'s eyes so the latter would believe him, "to bring back Manoka and Sho-nanoy to their uncle, who is Thomas. He wishes to give them a home at Windhaven so they need not leave the land they love."

"That is very kind. I will send for them. They were ready to go with us, for they are good of heart. Be-cause they are young, they have strength to endure the sickness and the hunger we have suffered here." He moved down toward the tepee which stood a few yards from his own rude cabin, and a warrior came out of the opening, stocky, middle-aged and, like the *Mico* himself, decorated with the signs of the Beaver Clan. The warrior nodded at the *Mico*'s words, then strode along the little rows of shabby huts and tepees till he came to the end of the village where a group of chil-dren were playing. Squinting, Greer could see that a tall handsome girl in doeskin jacket and petticoat was directing their game, and that beside her stood a tall young Creek, nearly bald but for a scalplock.

He watched the warrior approach those two and talk with them, then saw them turn and follow, and again composed his features into a smile.

"I am Manoka and this is my sister Shonanoy," the tall young brave proudly announced. "Tisquago says you come to take us to our beloved uncle. But my sis-ter asks if she may bring with her the man she is to wed, Nisquame, who is a Beloved Man of our village."

Amos Greer thought quickly, then nodded. "He may come too. And old Mr. Bouchard will send food and clothing to the rest of the village tomorrow for them to take to their new land. I am to tell you this also."

"I will call my betrothed, Nisquame," the lovely Creek girl gently said to her brother, while Amos

Greer's cold eyes momentarily flamed at the sight of her. She was superbly built, about five feet eight, and because she had both black and Indian blood would be known as an *os rouge*, the Creole term of "red bone," which designated the issue between red and black. High forehead, slanting cheekbones, sweet firm mouth, strong yet delicately rounded chin, and large dark-brown eyes—the overseer, mentally stripping her naked, estimated that if she were adorned in a silk or satin gown and displayed upon a New Orleans auction block, she'd bring at least two thousand dollars. It was only with an effort that he forced himself not to stare too greedily at her, lest she and her brother doubt the role he was playing. But, having seen her now, he told himself that if he was able to effect her capture, Henry Bouchard would surely pay him even more than had been offered. The risks, the long journey to and from Tuskegee, and what was now to be done because the girl wished to bring her man along—all that should count for considerably more than the original offer.

He stood patiently, the fixed smile still on his lips, watching Shonanoy go toward a small, rickety hut and emerge with a handsome brave in his early thirties, bedaubed with the signs that designated him a member of the Snake Clan. He was strong and powerfully made, his muscles rippling in his upper arms and calves as he strode forward, and Amos Greer observed that a buckskin belt was fixed round his waist, with a scabbard into which a hunting knife was hilted. Indeed, this would make it much more difficult, for he could not deny Nisquame the right to accompany Shonanoy without raising suspicion. Decidedly, Henry Bouchard would owe him a great deal more than promised once all this was over.

"This is Nisquame," Shonanoy said in a low sweet voice, "to whom I am promised. He says that he will go with me to the lodge of the beloved brother of the Bear, who is dear to all of us who remember the old days and the old ways. First we must say our farewells to the others in the village, and to the *Mico*. And we shall tell him who is my kind uncle's dearest friend that

302

the rest of our people go with the soldiers when the sun is early in the sky, so that he will bring the things my uncle spoke of on his last visit to us."

"Of course he'll keep his promise," Amos Greer said, curbing his growing impatience. "You see the carriage out there? I'll be waiting for you and your brother and your man. It's a good long journey back to Windhaven, so be as quick as you can."

Shonanoy stared at him reproachfully. "It is not easy to say farewell to those with whom one has lived all one's life," she softly reproved him. "We shall make our farewells and then we shall go with you."

The overseer was about to speak, then curtly nodded and strode back to the phaeton. Climbing into it, he opened a box in which two loaded percussion cap pistols lay, and covertly checked the priming. He'd counted only on the brother coming with Shonanoy; but with two of those damned Injuns, he couldn't rely on Tom and Ezra, they might get squeamish at the last minute. He'd have to take care of it himself. Stealthily nudging the box to the back and behind his right boot, he waited, while the black mares tossed their heads and nickered softly, waiting to resume the return journey. He saw the trio going from tepee to hut to tepee, grasping the hands of the men and women who came out of those humble dwellings, saying their farewells, till finally they came to the hut of Turintaka. The impassive *Mico* stood awaiting them, his medicine man beside him. Gravely both raised their arms and began an incantation, while Greer stared angrily, his jaw muscles tightening over the delay.

At last it was done, and the three turned toward the phaeton. Manoka clambered up beside the overseer, while Nisquame was first to take his place in the back, Shonanoy following and sitting beside him, hands folded in her lap, head bowed and her eyes wet with tears.

"We are ready now," Nisquame said in a solemn voice as he raised his hand in farewell to the *Mico* and the medicine man. Amos Greer nodded, clucked his tongue, jerked at the reins, and turned the heads of the black mares back westward. The phaeton passed the boundaries of the village and then the clump of loblolly pine trees, and Greer swiftly turned his head to see Tom and Ezra crouching in readiness, made a covert sign to them to follow slowly as he slackened the gait of the black mares.

Shonanoy had turned and seen the two Gullahs, then asked, "Are those your slaves who come with you?"

"They'll run behind us for a spell, Missy." The overseer favored her with drawlingly respectful tone. "Till we get into the woods where I've got their horses tied up. There's not room for them here, you can see that."

"My betrothed has decided that we will stay only a little time with my uncle," the lovely Creek girl said, turning to Nisquame for confirmation and receiving his slight nod. "He says that it is his duty as the Beloved Man of the tribe to accompany his people, and I am to be his wife and must go with him when it is time."

"Well, suit yourself. You can tell all that to your uncle when we get back," Amos Greer impatiently declared. He turned the phaeton now to the northwest, till he came to a bend in the narrow road. Glancing back, he could see nothing more of the ravaged little village which was all that remained of what had once been the proud rulers of Econchate. Behind him, Tom and Ezra trotted easily, glancing at each other wonderingly, not certain yet what they were to do; like their master, they had not foreseen that there would be two braves instead of only one.

"We're just about where the horses are, and we'll stop a spell," he announced. A swift glance at Manoka beside him had told him that the young brave bore no weapon as did Nisquame. That would make it easier, he told himself.

About a hundred yards ahead, the road began to be framed with forest on both sides, of pine and oak and cedar, and there was a wide grassy knoll into which he now turned the mares, then halted them. Tom and Ezra came up abreast of the phaeton, standing and warily watching the overseer. Amos Greer reached his right hand down to the box, opened it, seized one of the pistols and then whirled to face Nisquame. Leveling the weapon, he pulled the trigger. Shonanoy uttered a shriek, her hands clapped to her mouth, as she saw the Creek warrior half-rise, then slump back with a bullet through his heart.

With a cry of rage and horror, young Manoka lunged for the carriage whip, tore it out of its socket and lifted it to slash at the overseer.

"You'd hit a white man, you damned redskin?" Greer snarled, as he reversed the pistol and struck Manoka on the forehead with all his strength. The youth tottered, then fell to the road, rolled over, and soon lay still. Shonanoy remained petrified, her eyes enormous, her hands pressed against her gaping mouth.

"See if he's dead, you black bastards!" Greer commanded. Ezra knelt down and gingerly put his hand over Manoka's heart, then lifted an awe-stricken face: "Ah kin feel his haht beatin', Mistah Greer suh!"

"Then put your hands round his neck and squeeze till it stops. You've been no help at all, I've had to do everything myself—go on, do it!"

Shonanoy had turned her head to stare at her brother's inert body, and then suddenly twisted and crouched over Nisquame's lifeless body, her hand reaching for the hunting knife in his scabbard.

"Oh no you don't, you redskin bitch," Greer said viciously. "Tom, grab the bitch before she gets that knife, if you expect to earn your pay!"

The Gullah sprang round to the right side of the phaeton, and, seizing Shonanoy by her upper arms, flung her back into the seat. But she had had time to draw out the hunting knife and, springing to her feet, lunged with it at Amos Greer: "Murderer, liar! The blood brother of the Bear would never have sent a murderer to our people!" she cried. Once again, her eyes shining with tears, her bosom heaving, she struck at the overseer with the gleaming knife.

Swiftly transferring the pistol to his left hand, Amos Greer leaned to one side to avoid the thrust, and deftly gripped her wrist in his right hand, expertly twisted it, till, with a cry of pain, the girl dropped the weapon, her face contorted with pain.

"That's better now," he grinned. "I'll gentle you, see if I don't!" Then, angrily, he bellowed to the blacks, "Tom, Ezra, pull that dead Injun's body out. Get in there and tie her up, you worthless niggers!"

Galvanized by the savage anger in his voice, the two Gullahs quickly obeyed. Tom dragged Nisquame out of the phaeton to sprawl on the grass, then climbed in and clamped both arms round the girl's waist, pinning her arms to her sides. From the other side, Ezra, who had completed his grisly work of choking out the last spark of life from Manoka's body, reached in from the other side of the phaeton and pulled aside a blanket to reveal a pair of iron gyves linked with short chains. As Shonanoy struggled and writhed and tried to kick, Ezra squatted down and locked one of the gyves around her ankle, then swiftly fixed the other in place to hobble her.

Wild with rage and grief, the Creek girl uttered a piercing cry and in her Creek tongue, screamed, "Help, my brothers, we are betrayed!"

"Quick, get those spancels on her wrists, pull them behind the bitch's back," Greer ordered.

Tom now seized Shonanoy's wrists and forced them behind her back while his companion completed the pinioning. Once again she shrieked out her cry for help, and the overseer swore angrily. "Damnation, haven't you the brains God gave you, you stupid niggers? Gag her, before her dirty redskin friends hear all the commotion and come after our scalps!"

Once again Tom locked his arms around Shonanoy's waist, pulling her toward him and grinning at the sight of her writhing, supple young body straining to be free, while Ezra stuffed a dirty kerchief into Shonanoy's mouth, then stopped to rip off a piece of the blanket and to bind it around her mouth and knot it at the back of her neck.

"That's better," Amos Greer said. "Now then, Ezra, drag those dead Injuns back into the trees where they won't be seen from the road. Then let's get back home!"

He turned back now to the reins, for the black mares had been frightened by the pistol shot and the sound of the scuffling and Shonanoy's cries, and were pawing the ground and tossing their heads nervously. "Whoa now, you beauties, easy does it, easy now!" he soothed them.

Ezra got back into the phaeton on the other side of Shonanoy, and both Gullahs dragged her down to the floor, Ezra grasping her braided plait in his left hand while with a lecherous grin he put his other hand on one of her breasts. She moaned and writhed, her face contorted with agonized fury.

"That's good now," Amos Greer chuckled. "In case we run into any Nosey Parkers, you remember now that she's a runaway slave and we're taking her back to Windhaven. Now let's put some miles between us and that damned Injun camp, and we'll have ourselves some vittles when we get to that inn about an hour's ride from now. All right, you beauties, giddyap!" The reins in his left hand, he seized the carriage whip and laid it smartly across the mares' rumps. With a shrill whinny, they plunged forward and the phaeton clattered down the narrow road to the southwest.

A few miles away from Henry Bouchard's brick and log house, Amos Greer drew on the reins and halted the mares, dismounted and tied the reins to a branch of an old cedar. The two Gullahs stared uneasily at him. "Wut we stoppin' heah foah, Mistah Greer suh?" Ezra anxiously demanded.

"So we can find out if the coast is clear, boys," the overseer explained. "Just suppose now that maybe old Mr. Bouchard or that pious nigger Thomas of his happens to be paying Mr. Henry a social call. We wouldn't want them to see what we've brought back, would we?"

"Guess not, massa," Tom said, nodding to his crony.

"Tell you what, boys. You've done a right good job, and you'll get the reward that's coming to you, just as I said. Now why don't you two go on ahead and see if the coast is clear? I'll go down the river and give this little redskin bitch a drink of water. She's a mite exhausted from the long trip. Go on ahead, but be careful nobody sees you. Then come back here and tell me if Mr. Henry is there in his house."

"Yassuh, massa," Ezra agreed. The two Gullahs got out of the phaeton and began to walk through the woods, while Amos Greer stood watching them, his eyes narrowed and baleful. Then he glanced down at the floor of the back seat and smirked. Shonanoy lay on her stomach, a rope fixing to the chain which shackled her wrists and connected to the chain between her slim ankles. "We'll all get our reward, gal," he muttered. Then, opening the box on the floor beside him, having already reloaded the first pistol he had fired at Nisquame, he grasped each by the handle, leaped down out of the phaeton, and stalked after the two Gullahs.

"Man, it be purty nice to hab a sweet fat wench to covah tonight," Tom was saying to Ezra as the two made their way through the woods.

"Ah sho lak to hab dat redskin gal in mah bed, she de purtiest wench ah eber done seen." His companion smacked his lips. "But Ah 'specs Mistah Greer an' Mistah Henry, dey gwine bust dat gal by deyselves, ain't gonna be no chance foah us. Hey, wut dat?"

Hearing the crackling of brush behind them, the two Gullahs turned, and stared open-mouthed as they saw Amos Greer approach, his pistols leveled at them.

"Wut de mattah, suh?" Tom gasped. "We doin' jist lak you tol' us, massa!"

Amos Greer shook his head, a cruel smirk on his thin lips. "I'm sorry, boys. But you were both just a mite too slow back there by the village. I had to do all the work myself, and there's no sense paying a man for a job half-done, now is there? And anyhow, you just might get a notion to wag your nigger tongues and let somebody find out who you did this for. But I'll make it quick and painless; you both deserve that much."

"Now wait, massa—" Ezra put out a placating hand just as the overseer fired. The Gullah stiffened, his eyes

308

rolling, then toppled forward. Tom uttered a frenzied shriek of terror, turned and ran. Amos Greer took careful aim, squinting along the barrel, then squeezed the trigger. The Gullah seemed to jerk, kept running a few paces as his hands flung up, then suddenly pitched forward lifeless.

Amos Greer blew the smoke from the barrels, then returned to the phaeton. "Now then, you sweet redskin bitch, on your feet. I'm taking you to your new master."

Henry Bouchard, his face dark with lust and eyes gleaming, strode into the toolshed far to the left of his little house. Amos Greer had stripped Shonanoy naked, leaving the shackles on her ankles, but tying her wrists high above her head to a solid wooden peg hammered into the wall of the shed. He had left her gagged, and he stood beside her, his hands running over her sleek body, licking his lips and savoring the shudders of revulsion at his touch.

"Afternoon, Mr. Bouchard sir," he greeted his new employer. "Like I told you, when I'm picked to do a job, I take care of all the details. Even to digging graves for those two stupid niggers."

"And you say you told the girl that she'd be likely to hang if the law found out she'd raised a weapon against a white man?"

"I sure did, Mr. Bouchard," Greer sniggered as his hands lingering over the victim's buttocks. Shonanoy moaned against her gag, arching forward to escape his libidinous proddings. "I told her the only way out for her was to sign a paper saying she was guilty as sin, and that instead of hanging as was coming to the bitch, she was willing to be your slave. And I told her the paper would say she was that anyhow, seeing as how she's got nigger blood in her from her mother."

"And I've got the paper with me for her to sign. Now let's see if she'll listen to reason," Henry Bouchard said, his voice thick with anticipation.

Greer untied the strip of blanket and tugged the wadded kerchief out of Shonanoy's mouth. She twisted about and saw Henry Bouchard's gloating face. "Who is this man, another murderer?" she panted.

Henry Bouchard approached, put out his hand and gripped the thick plait of glossy black hair, pulling it up short to tilt back her head. "Just as uppity as your mother, Disjamilla, ever was, aren't you, you Injun spitfire?" he chuckled vindictively. "We used to be playmates back in the old days, Shonanoy girl, only she wouldn't be nice to me, thought herself too good for a white man. Let's see now if her daughter can't learn to be more reasonable. You know what Mr. Greer told you—I could string you up by your pretty neck and nobody'd say I didn't have the right, not after you pulled a knife and tried to kill my overseer."

"Oh, it cannot be—Ibofanaga would not be so cruel!" Shonanoy gasped as her eyes widened with recognition. "Has he then delivered me into the hands of that heartless son of him who my people call the beloved brother of the Bear?"

"The very same, you pretty bitch," Henry Bouchard leered, yanking her thick plait as his eyes swept her arching, squirming naked body. "Now if you promise to be a good slave, I won't have Mr. Greer thrash you too hard, Shonanoy. You're to sign the paper, just like he told you."

"No! It is a lie! It was you, then, who had my brother murdered and my promised husband slain— when my people learn of this thing, they will punish you. They will know it was not the good old man who came to live with them and shared all that he had with his brothers the Creeks!"

"She'll sign that paper, Mr. Bouchard, don't you worry none about that," Amos Greer promised. He stooped and picked up the coiled cowhide, stepped back and flicked it out toward her, and drew it back and made it crack in the air.

"All right then, but don't mark her too badly," Henry Bouchard agreed in a thick, trembling voice.

"You forget I know how to use this, Mr. Bouchard. I can skin her raw or I can just make her burn and wish she'd died back there with those two murdering red

310

devils. All right, Shonanoy, when you've had enough, just say so!"

His lips tight and pale with his cruel joy, the overseer drew back his arm and made the cowhide coil round the tops of Shonanoy's long sleek thighs. She stifled a gasp of pain, lifting her face toward the roof of the shed, her fingernails driving into her palms to sustain herself. A crimson weal sprang up on the smooth satiny skin, and Shonanoy's muscles stiffened in a violent defense against the searing pain. Her toes dug into the ground and then she bent her head and closed her eyes, her breathing audibly quickened, as she sought to endure her torment with the born stoicism of the Creeks.

"A mite stubborn, this one, Mr. Bouchard." Greer sent Henry Bouchard a lewd glance. "But don't you worry, I'll have her gentle as a lamb when I've finished with her. And she won't have any ugly scars either. Fact is, when you warm up a woman's bottom the way I know how, it sort of lights a fire in the front of her, if you get my meaning." With a lecherous snigger, the overseer sent the cowhide whistling out across the small of the girl's back.

As Henry Bouchard stared with glazed eyes, flushed face, his breath quickened by the convulsive movements of Shonanoy's naked body under the lash, Amos Greer applied the cowhide with cruel accuracy. His eyes narrowed and glittering, fixed on the shuddering, arching body of the girl, he purposely prolonged the interval between lashes in order to savor the intensity of her suffering. He dealt the strokes capriciously, so that there was no regularized pattern against which she might steel herself and summon her resistance to remain passive under the whistling, coiling thong; yet he took pains not to draw blood or mark her permanently. At times the tip of the lash whisked into her armpit or around to sting the panting curve of a firm jutting breast, or again to bite viciously into the navel or the groin.

Her face uptilted, grinding her teeth to suppress her cries, Shonanoy persisted in her courageous silence.

311

But she could not suppress the moans of agony when a stroke perniciously attacked the most subtle nerves of her femininity, as she could not control the involuntarily lewd gyrations of her hips and thighs and loins that plunged and twisted and weaved under the burning kisses of the whip.

Dripping with sweat, his face a twisted mask of rut, Amos Greer at last lowered the cowhide and glanced at his employer. "Stubborn bitch," he panted, "let her rest a little, Mr. Bouchard. Then I'll really work her over till she's begging you to sign that paper you want."

"No, no, that's enough, Greer!" Henry Bouchard hoarsely exclaimed. "Get out now. I'll make her a slave myself and be sure of it. When I've had her, you can do what you like to her—just don't mark her up too badly or kill her. Then have Zora come in and take care of her. We'll keep her in the shed here for a time till she's willing to listen to reason."

"As you say, Mr. Bouchard. I'll have the whip here just in case you want to use it again on her." He grinned cruelly as he moved toward the shuddering, nearly unconscious girl. He put out his hands and squeezed her heaving breasts, moved them down over her belly, then between her clenching thighs. Shonanoy stiffened, her eyes opening, wide and blurred with great tears, then turned to stare at him, all her shame and agonized hatred burning in those dark, torture-dilated eyes.

"That's right, now you know who I am, bitch, and I'll be back to make you remember," he gloatingly murmured. Then, applying a stinging slap on her welted buttocks, he strode out of the shed.

"Now then, Shonanoy, you're going to be my slave whether you like it or not," Henry Bouchard growled as he unfastened his breeches. "A week locked up here with just bread and water and a good thrashing every day, you'll come around, see if you don't!"

She did not speak, closing her eyes again and sagging against the wall of the shed, but when his left hand clutched her thickly braided plait and viciously jerked at it, she noisily sucked in her breath and began to

312

murmur words in the Creek tongue. His hands dug into her thighs, hugely straddling them, and then with a savage oath, moving around and in front of her, so that she was arched back with all her weight bearing from her tied wrists, he brutally penetrated her.

A shrill cry of torment announced the rending of her maidenhead, but she endured her martyrdom valiantly thereafter; her face pale and drawn, her eyes tightly shut and lips compressed, she let him do as he would.

Releasing her, stepping aside, his chest heaving, he said triumphantly: "Now you know who your master is, you Injun bitch. I'll let Amos have a go at you too, just to teach you what happens to a balky slave. After that, I'm sure you'd rather belong to me and take your chances—and if you're accommodating, I'll treat you the way a good bed wench deserves."

Adjusting his breeches, he sauntered out of the shed and gestured to the grinning overseer. "I've broken her in, Amos. You've earned a go at her, but as I said, don't spoil her too much. Worst comes to worst, I can get a good price for her from Pierre Lourat down in New Orleans."

"You're a man of your word, Mr. Bouchard sir." Amos Greer winked bawdily. "And just so there's no misunderstanding between us, I don't own that Jamaican bitch Zora. So if you have a fancy for her, feel free to use her, and you'll not be hurting my feelings any."

"I'll just take you up on that, Amos. See you in the morning, then. I'll want you to go over to old Murton's acres that I picked up some years back. I'm not too satisfied with the cotton yield out of them. I think you can show those lazy niggers over there how I want land worked."

"You're going to find that you've less worries than you ever had before, Mr. Bouchard, now that I'm your man," Amos Greer boasted as he stepped toward the shed.

As he entered, Shonanoy was weeping silently, her shoulders heaving, her head bowed. The cords around her wrists had dug into the flesh, leaving purplish weals.

Amos Greer licked his lips and moved around her, studying the darkening striations his whip had left on her skin. "I told you I'd pay you back for drawing a weapon against a white man, you bloodthirsty little Injun bitch," he sniggered, his fingers squeezing and pinching her buttocks and belly and breasts while she again jerked and squirmed fitfully, uttering inarticulate moans which her pain-racked body could no longer suppress. "Too bad you aren't my slave, honey, I'd teach you not to look at me the way you just did when I was whipping you. Oh yes, you'll find Mr. Bouchard a gentler master, I've no doubt. But I owe you something, and maybe it'll help teach you to keep your place."

With this, digging his fingers into the welted cheeks of her buttocks, he pitilessly sodomized her. This time, revolted by his use of her helpless nudity, Shonanoy uttered a despairing, wordless shriek, twisting and arching and struggling to escape the odious violation.

When it was done, the overseer took his clasp knife and cut the bonds from her wrists, letting her crumple to the ground. He stared down at her seemingly lifeless body, cleared his throat and spat into her face. "Now we're even, unless you rile your master, so you'd better work hard at pleasing him or you'll be back here and I'll be thrashing you at his orders, understand?"

He restored the wooden peg bolts to the lock of the shed door, and went back to the cabin which Henry Bouchard had given him. Molly, the Fulani wife of Rastus, now forty-two, plump and still comely, had cleaned it industriously and brought new bedding and a chair and table for the overseer's comforts. As he entered, she instinctively shrank back, lowering her eyes, mumbling a fearful, "Ah's just finishin', massa suh!"

"That's enough, bitch, get out of here. If I need anything, I'll tell you and you'd best look smart when I do."

Molly bobbed her head and scurried out of the cabin to the one she occupied with her husband. Twenty years before, Rastus had seen his young wife whipped and ravished by young Henry Bouchard, and knew that

314

the slightest sign of disapproval might well have meant his death warrant. But as he listened to her describe the overseer and what she had seen take place at the shed just now through a peephole in a plank on the other side, he shook his head and muttered, "Times is sho gonna be hahdah foah us poor black folks, Molly. Dey ain't nuttin' we kin do 'cept pray to de Lawd Gawd Almighty help us take wut de massa say we gotta take."

It was midnight. Inside the darkened shed, Shonanoy painfully dragged herself toward the back, having seen the jagged peephole when a ray of moonlight illumined its outline. Groaning softly as she rose on her knees, she inserted her thumb into the aperture and began to break off tiny splinters till she had enlarged the hole. After half an hour's toil, she was able to grip the widened edges with both hands and to tug at the partly rotted plank until it gave way. She crouched down then, holding her breath, waiting for the slightest sound. When only the chirping of the crickets and the croaking of the frogs near the distant riverbank came to her straining ears, she forced herself erect with a groan of agony, turned sideways, and, heedless of the torturing rasp of the rough wood against her breasts and buttocks and shoulders, at last freed herself.

Glancing back at the brick and log house of Henry Bouchard where no light showed, the naked girl made her way toward the river. Then she knelt down on the bank and raised her haggard eyes to the moon-silvered sky. "Oh Ibofanaga, who sits above, preserver of breath, take mine now. Let me be with Manoka and Nisquame, with my father and mother. Let my death erase my shame, let those who shamed me taste vengeance in thine own time. Receive my spirit and forgive."

There was a splash in the still river, and then bubbles on its surface—and then silence, but for the call of the nightbird, the croaking of the frogs, in the immensity of night. . . .

CHAPTER TWENTY-TWO

Thomas had heard the news of the removal of the Creeks at Tuskegee on the very day when their trek to the West was to begin, and he went directly to old Lucien Bouchard to receive his instructions.

"Take two of the larger wagons and have some of the hands load them with supplies, Thomas. Choose two of the fastest and strongest horses to pull each wagon, so that you can catch up with them. I understand the Alabama Emigrating Company has arranged for private contractors to convey those unfortunates through Arkansas and on to the West. You're sure to intercept them along their route, Thomas, since they're being made to march on foot and will surely cover no more than ten or twelve miles a day."

"I'll deliver the supplies to their chief, Turintaka, and bring back Manoka and Shonanoy, Mr. Lucien," the Ashanti declared.

"Tell Turintaka that I will learn where he and his people are to be settled and that if it is within my power I'll make certain that supplies are sent to them in their new home. Tell him, too, that my spirit goes with him and the deepest feelings of my heart to wish all the Creeks a new life of peace and hope for the future. And that I shall always be, to the very end, his blood brother."

Greatly moved, the tall Ashanti could not bring himself to speak, but only nodded.

317

"You'd best take along two of the hands to help on the journey, Thomas. And they can distribute the blankets and the food and the tools. Let them ride horses that we can spare. One of them can drive the other wagon, the other can ride along as a kind of scout. Tie two extra horses to the back of each wagon, so that when you finish your journey all five of you may ride back and leave the wagons with their teams of horses as my gift to the Creeks. They may wish to keep their supplies in them, but there will also be room for the sick and the aged who are too weak for that dreadfully long march."

"I'll see to it at once, Mr. Lucien. I'd best have one of the foremen take over your fields while I'm away."

Lucien smiled. "I've no fear that my workers will slacken if you're away for a time, Thomas, nor have you. They've been loyal, and they've rewarded my trust in them by working well even without supervision—I only wish my son Henry could understand that you don't win such loyalty with the whip. Go then, and my prayers go with you for a successful mission. Manoka can share one of the field hands' cabins, and Shonanoy one of the women's until we've time to build them proper cabins of their own."

Shortly before twilight of the next day, Zeke, a middle-aged Hausa whose diligence in the fields had earned him a supervisory post in Lucien's cotton ginning shed, and who had ridden ahead as scout, rode back to Thomas's wagon and exclaimed, "Dey is 'bout three miles up ahead, gittin' ready to camp foah de night, Mistah Thomas."

"They've gone as far as Corrville, then. We can let the horses rest a little; they've earned it making this good time for us," the Ashanti decided. Leaning out of the driver's seat, he called to Andrew in the wagon behind him, "Three more miles, Andrew. Keep following, and easy on the reins, boy."

Half an hour later, the two wagons drew up alongside an army lieutenant and four civilians dressed in frock coats and heavy breeches, who were directing a

318

platoon of soldiers to help the dispossessed villagers make camp for the night.

"I've brought these supplies and the wagons and horses for the Indians, sir," Thomas respectfully explained to the glum-faced bearded lieutenant as he dismounted from the wagon. "Have I your permission to talk to the chief and have him divide the supplies as he wishes?"

"Don't suppose it'll do any harm. The poor devils can use those wagons, too. They've got some mighty sick children and old women there. Damn it all, I'm a soldier, not a wet nurse to a lot of redskins. But orders are orders. Go ahead." The lieutenant eyed Thomas, then slyly added, "If you've got a jug of rum in there by any chance, my men and I would sure appreciate it."

"I'm afraid not, sir," Thomas said. "Food, blankets, some clothing, and some farm tools. You're welcome to inspect the wagons if you like."

"I'll take your word for it. Didn't know we had that many Injun lovers left," the lieutenant said sourly.

The Creeks had settled in the shelter of a clump of cedars, and Turintaka stood in the clearing, ordering the able men to help the aged and the sick first and to make them comfortable. He handed one of his own blankets to a warrior: "Give this to Nurinda, she is with child," he directed.

Then his face brightened at the sight of Thomas and he held out both hands. "It is good to see you. And you have brought supplies that we badly need, Thomas. I knew our blood brother would keep the promise his overseer made to us two suns ago."

"His overseer?" Thomas blankly echoed. "But I am now again the overseer of your blood brother, Turintaka, and only his grandson was named overseer before me. Who was this man, then, who called himself the overseer of Mr. Lucien Bouchard?"

Turintaka frowned, put his hand to his cheek, and then replied, "It is strange now that you ask me this. He did not give his name, this white-eyes. He said that he had come because the old Mr. Bouchard who was our blood brother sent him. And he said that he had come to bring back Manoka and Shonanoy to you, to give them a home at Windhaven so they need not leave the land they love."

"But I have not seen my niece and nephew, Turintaka. Can you tell me what this man was like?"

"His hair was the color of wheat under the sun, his eyes were blue and cold, he was well-made and strong, and he wore heavy black boots—alas, we must march many, many miles, the soldiers tell us, and I should not mind having a pair of such boots for myself and all of my warriors."

As he spoke, Thomas stared at him incredulously, and then the Ashanti's face twisted with a look of utter consternation when Turintaka had finished. "That man you have just described, Turintaka, was not sent by my good old master who is your blood brother. His name is Amos Greer, and he is a cruel and heartless man. Did he then take Manoka and Shonanoy with him?"

"Yes," the *Mico* nodded. "And because Shonanoy is, as you know, betrothed to the Beloved Man, Nisquame, she asked that he accompany her also, and this white-eyes agreed. They rode off in a carriage behind two black mares after they had said their goodbyes to all of us. However, I think that Nisquame will make Shonanoy join us in the land which we are told is to be our new home. He will stay at Windhaven, he told me, only until his intended squaw and her brother have had a long visit with you, their beloved uncle."

"I must go back then at once, Turintaka. That man who took Manoka and Shonanoy and Nisquame with him did not intend to bring them back to Windhaven, I am sure of it. I am leaving the two wagons and the horses as old Mr. Bouchard's gift to you and your people, Turintaka. He bids me tell you that he will learn of the place to which you are being sent, and if he can, he will provide you with food and clothing even there."

"It is good. We give thanks to him, and we pray that Ibofanaga will bless him always and his descendants, Thomas," the *Mico* gravely declared.

"I'll say good-bye then, Turintaka. God bless you

and your people. I'm going back to Windhaven, there's no time to lose. I must find my niece and nephew and Nisquame before——" He halted, bit his lips, and with terrible foreboding, shook the hand of the chief and hurried back to his wagon. Untying the reins of the gray mare which had been tethered to the back, he called to the two field hands. "Help these people make their camp and pass out the supplies as the chief tells you. Come back when you've finished, I'm going on ahead, back to Windhaven!" Then, wheeling the mare around, his face drawn with apprehension, the Ashanti freedman kicked his heels against the mare's belly and urged it on at a gallop.

It was mid-afternoon of the next day when the gray mare drew up before the stable, its flanks and mouth clotted with lather, as Thomas flung himself off the exhausted animal and stumbled toward the château. Jimmy and Djamba came out of the stable, and the powerful young Mandingo hurried to the mare, stroking its head and murmuring soothingly as he gently took the reins and led it back to its stall.

Lucien Bouchard was taking his nap in his room. He had been dreaming, not of the fields of Yves-sur-lac, but of the village of Econchate and of the young, beautiful, grave maiden whom he had first seen beside her father, the *Mico* Tunkamara. Her sweet face, her clear eyes, her warm eager mouth were so near, so vivid, that it seemed like yesterday that she had first tended his wounds while he lay in the little hut after his perilous journey from Mobile. Somehow, he had known even then that his journey across the ocean had been toward a destiny to which he would devote all his life in the fulfillment of his dreams and hopes. Even as he slept, his lips curved to form the name "Dimarte," and there was an ineffable smile of joy upon his wrinkled, weatherbeaten face.

Sybella was descending the stairs when Thomas was admitted by Matthew. "Thomas, what's the matter? You poor man, you look half-dead—what's happened to you?" she cried, hurrying toward him.

321

"I—I've ridden since last night, Miz Bouchard. I had to get back to Windhaven to see Mr. Lucien—I've got to talk to him, Miz Bouchard!" the Ashanti panted. He wiped the sweat from his face with his arm, fighting for breath.

"He's taking his nap, Thomas. But I think it should be just about over by now. Why don't I go see? Please sit down. Matthew, get him some cold water right away."

"Yassum!" the old majordomo answered. "Ah'll git it from de well, dat'll be de coldest."

Thomas sank down into a straight-backed chair in the foyer, bowing his head and covering his face with his hands, uttering a long tortured groan. Sybella, her face clouded with concern, stared at him a moment, and then in growing perplexity went down the hall toward old Lucien's room. Gently she opened the door and moved quietly inside, bent over the bed on which he lay, clad in his buckskins, the bearclaw necklace around his neck, that gentle smile still on his lips. "Father?" she whispered, bending down to kiss his wrinkled cheek. "Father, are you still asleep?"

"My beloved—Dimarte—oh—why—why, Sybella dear!" His eyes opened, and his smile deepened. "I was having the loveliest dream. Why, is anything wrong?"

"It—it's Thomas, Father. He's ridden all night long; the poor man's ready to drop in his tracks, and he wants to see you."

"He's brought back Manoka and Shonanoy, so of course he's excited. Oh, but all those other poor devils who will have to march hundreds of miles, with no one to give them shelter or even a kind word—"

"No, Father, they aren't with him," Sybella interrupted.

"Not with him, my dear?" Lucien Bouchard put both hands on the bed and painfully forced himself into a sitting position. "What are you saying, Sybella?"

"He came alone, Father. The men who rode with him aren't back at all. I don't know what it means, and he seems so unhappy—please, Father, I didn't mean to distress you—wait here, I'll go get him."

"Oh no, I'm all right. You mustn't treat me like a child, my dear Sybella. There, you see, I can still stand erect. Why, before you came in, I was dreaming that I was back in Econchate, that I had just ridden into the village after my long journey from Mobile. Yes, I feel young and strong. But he didn't bring them back? I can't understand that, I can't at all." He rose and walked slowly into the hall, Sybella following him, her eyes wide and dark with concern.

Matthew had come back with the dipperful of water from the little well just outside the kitchen, and Thomas grasped it with trembling hands and gulped it down with a grateful sigh. At the sight of his beloved master—for as such all his life Thomas had considered him—he rose, stammering, "Excuse my coming in like this, all dirty and sweated up, Mr. Lucien—"

"Never mind that, Thomas. What's the matter, man?"

"Are they here now?"

"Why, Thomas, I counted on you to bring your niece and nephew here. No, they're not—certainly no one's told me—Sybella, didn't you say they hadn't come?" Lucien Bouchard turned to his daughter-in-law.

Sybella shook her head, lowering her eyes as she answered, "No one's here, Father."

"Oh my God, Mr. Lucien, I'm mortal afraid, I'm mortal afraid, I tell you!" Thomas broke out, his voice hoarse and trembling. "We took the wagons to the village as you told us. When I talked to Turintaka, he told me that a white man had come the day before, saying that you had sent him to bring Manoka and Shonanoy back to Windhaven. And Shonanoy's man, Nisquame, went with them."

"My God, what does it mean? Then where are they, Thomas? Who was that man?"

"But the worst of it, Mr. Lucien," Thomas went on in an unsteady voice, "is that the chief described this man who took my niece and nephew and Nisquame with him—he said the man had hair the color of wheat in the sun and cold blue eyes and heavy black boots—

Mr. Lucien, that sounds mighty like that overseer of Williamson's, that Amos Greer. My God, if he's got them, Lord only knows what's happened to them—"

"Thomas, Thomas, don't worry, I'm sure there's an explanation for it. You mustn't upset yourself so— you're bone-tired, you poor man—" Sybella tried to comfort the agonized Ashanti.

"But Luke discharged Amos Greer," Lucien Bouchard intervened. Then, his face tightening with anger: "How dared that evil brute say that I sent him to the Creeks, that I would trust a man like that with your niece and nephew?"

"I don't know, Mr. Lucien, I'm fair worried to death," Thomas groaned.

Sybella uttered a stifled gasp, then put her hand to her mouth, as both men stared at her.

"What is it, Sybella?" Lucien demanded.

"I—I was just remembering something, Father. It's—well, I heard Henry say he wished he could get a man like Amos Greer to work for him, because he'd done so well with poor Mr. Williamson's cotton."

"It couldn't be possible! Henry wouldn't have hired a man like that without my knowledge, without consulting me, surely!" Lucien Bouchard exclaimed, his eyes bright with indignation. Then, clenching his fists, and as if speaking to himself alone, he muttered, "Would he have dared to send that vile man to bring back Manoka and Shonanoy as his slaves and not to Windhaven? My God—I don't want to think that, I mustn't—oh dear God in heaven, let it not be so! Hasn't Henry caused me enough affliction without defying all the laws of humanity?"

And then, dully, he turned to Thomas and said, "When you've rested, try to find my son. I suspect he's staying on his own land these days. Or he may be on the Murton piece or that other one he's so proud of. Find him and bring him to me. I'm going to wait in the tower. I'm going to pray, Thomas."

"Father, you mustn't overexert yourself, it's not good for you—please, Father! Why don't you just rest here, and Thomas is so exhausted, I'll send someone else——" Sybella began.

"No'm, Miz Bouchard, thank you kindly but no, this is for me, they're my kin. I've got to find out for myself, begging your pardon, Miz Bouchard! I'll just rest a spell, then I'll get a fresh horse and ride over to Mr. Henry's land," the Ashanti declared in a voice choked with anguish.

"You can expect at least a hundred bales of prime cotton out of these acres this August, Mr. Bouchard." Amos Greer, his feet solidly planted apart, hands on hips, stood staring out at the field slaves, his cowhide whip coiled round his left shoulder and armpit. "You couldn't ask for better weather than this, so I figure we can start picking toward the end of August."

Henry Bouchard scowled, kicked at the ground with his toe. "You ought to have been more careful, Amos," he grumbled. "You oughtn't to have cut that Creek bitch down last night when you finished with her. It would have done her good to hang there and think about behaving herself—now she's run away and there'll be all hell to pay if she turns up at Windhaven."

Amos Greer eyed his employer with a look bordering on contempt. "I don't think you're going to have to worry, Mr. Bouchard. I followed her tracks this morning, soon as I found that plank she'd broken off. They went down to the riverbank, and there they stopped. If you ask me, she just threw herself into the river."

"But she could have swum to the other shore and got away," Henry Bouchard uneasily retorted.

Greer hawked and spat, then shook his head. "Not likely. The Alabama's pretty deep at that point, and anyhow, I forded the river in one of those old pirogues I found tied up there. Searched all up and down the other bank. Not a sign. Besides, it's just what one of those damned redskins would do, just to spite you."

"All the same, Amos, maybe you shouldn't have been so hard on her. Old Thomas isn't going to take this lightly, and I've got to figure out some way to make him think it was an accident."

Amos Greer turned to confront his employer. "Now, no offense meant, sir, but you were the one ordered me to bring back those redskins, and you told me I could have a go at her. I didn't mess her up too much, not any more than I would have done some balky nigger bitch."

"All right, all right, I don't want to hear about it," Henry Bouchard testily replied. "All the same, we'd best figure out some story that'll satisfy Thomas. And my father too—he's always set such store by those damned Creeks of his."

"Seems to me like that's your problem mainly, Mr. Bouchard—no offense meant," the overseer rejoined. "Of course, it's too damned bad the bitch got away. I could have sold her for you at a nice price over to the Bufferys. They're the ones run that breeding farm I was telling you about."

"How does that place of theirs work?" Despite his uneasiness, Henry Bouchard looked questioningly at the overseer.

"They're downriver, the other side, about fifteen miles from here. Been at it about five years, I understand. Jim Buffery used to be a slave dealer in Natchez, till he figured out this scheme of caring for and breeding, as you might say."

"Tell me about it. I wouldn't mind selling off some of my old, lazy niggers and having a little cash on hand to buy young bucks and wenches."

"Well, Jim Buffery bought a right nice piece of land, about two hundred acres all told. He's got a little cotton and a tobacco patch or two and he raises vegetables. But he doesn't make his money on any of those. You might say, the niggers he's got there learn their chores by working the land. You see, some of the planters like the idea of training their niggers, so they'll take a boy or a girl away from their own plantation when they get to be about ten years old, then send them over to Jim Buffery till they're about sixteen. Jim charges them five dollars a month for board and keep, and then he trains them to do whatever the owner thinks they'll be best at when they grow up. Like a wench that's going to be a private maid to the planter's lady—well, Jim's wife shows the gal how to wait on table and help dress her and such, and those niggers there learn real fast."

"Well, that's one way of making a tidy profit and getting your own land worked, I'd say," Henry Bouchard remarked.

"That's right, Mr. Bouchard. Also, some of their own slaves they'll rent out as workers during the picking season mainly, or if there's any special chores like carpentering and making bricks the other planters want done. And Jim tells me he's got a few lively wenches he owns hisself and keeps for pleasuring his friends and customers." Amos Greer favored his employer with a lewd wink. "That's why it's too damn bad I didn't get a chance to sneak that Injun gal off to the Bufferys, seeing as how all of a sudden you're so worried about Thomas finding out."

"Well, it's too late for that now. Let me think; I've got to figure something out that'll sound reasonable— Christ, there comes that damned old nigger now!" Henry Bouchard swore at seeing the Ashanti ride up to the slave cabins, dismount and tie the reins to a post, and hurry toward him.

Warily, Amos Greer slid the coiled whip down to his wrist, reached over with his right hand to grip the handle and tug it free, then cracked it in the air a few times and swaggeringly awaited the Ashanti. "I'll handle this, if you like, Mr. Bouchard," he said. Then, as the Ashanti halted a few feet away, his fists clenched, his face convulsed, Amos Greer called out: "What the hell are you doing off the land you're supposed to work, nigger?"

Thomas sent him a searching look, but directed his words to Henry Bouchard: "I was told by the chief at Tuskegee that my niece and nephew were brought to Windhaven, Mr. Bouchard. But they're not there. Do you know where they are?"

Henry Bouchard gnawed his lower lip, hastily

327

glanced at Amos Greer, then stammered, "They're not here either, Thomas. You can see for yourself if you want."

"What have you done with them?" the Ashanti's voice was low and trembling with fury. "I know it was this man here who went for them and brought them back. That's what the chief told me. Now where are they, for God's sake! You know they're my kin. What's become of them, and of my niece's promised man, too, because the chief said he went with Shonanoy. You've got to tell me!"

"Seems to me," Greer drawled, "you're forgetting your place, nigger. You don't talk to white men that way. No, maybe you do to old Mr. Bouchard, but he's spoiled you rotten. Just keep a civil tongue in your head when you're over here, understand?"

Thomas turned to regard the smirking overseer. "You lied when you said Mr. Lucien sent you. That's what the chief told me, too. Now I want to see them, and then I want to know why you told that lie."

"I'll see you in hell first, nigger, and that's where you'll find them too," Amos Greer said.

"No—oh Lawd Jesus, what's he saying, Mr. Bouchard? Tell me, I've got a right to know—Mr. Bouchard. Why don't you answer me?" Thomas beat his clenched fists against his thighs, tears blinding him.

"It—it was an accident, Thomas—yes—that's what it was," Henry faltered, retreating before the Ashanti's outburst.

"That's true—that they're dead—and Nisquame too? You sent that man to get them, you had them killed, you had him lie and say that old Mr. Lucien wanted them back in Windhaven? If there's a just God, Mr. Bouchard, you'll answer to him for it—oh my sweet Jesus—if Lucien finds out what his son has done and used his name, it'll kill him. You're not fit to be his son, you never were, not since you beat your horse and tried to force my poor little sister—oh, Gawd forgive me—" Thomas stood, raising his fists to the sky, tears pouring down his cheeks. Then, goaded by an over-

328

powering rage, he seized Henry Bouchard by the throat and flung him down on the ground.

"Thomas, no, listen—I didn't mean—aah—let go, you black bastard—you're choking me—Amos, help me!" Henry Bouchard cried as he twisted and rolled, smashing his fists into the Ashanti's grief-stricken face. But Thomas doggedly hung on, both his hands clenched around the white man's throat, and the overseer, raising his whip, brought it down with all his strength across the Ashanti's back.

Thomas gasped under the brutal stroke but did not relinquish his hold. Henry Bouchard's fingers clawed at his, trying desperately to break that maddened hold. His eyes bulging and glassy, his face florid, his voice wheezing, he drew up one knee and feebly tried to dislodge the vengeful Ashanti.

Again the cowhide whistled down, again and again, leaving bloody weals on Thomas's back. "He's killing me—for God's—help—help—" Henry Bouchard spluttered.

A few feet from the overseer lay a broken hoe. Dropping his whip, Amos Greer seized it, lifted it with both hands and brought the blade down on the Ashanti's head. Thomas uttered a gurgling cry, stiffened, and then his fingers relaxed their strangling hold. Weakly, Henry Bouchard groped with his trembling hands to force the dead Ashanti's fingers from his throat, and rolled to one side, gasping for breath.

Lucien Bouchard stood at the open casement window, his hands clasped in prayer, his eyes fixed on the distant red bluff. It was dusk now, and the gathering shadows crept like huge fingers over the trees and shrubs which garnished the sides of the bluff to its very top. There was an eerie stillness, broken only by the faint call of a distant nightbird. Even the river was still and hushed, as if time itself had halted and was waiting.

"He hasn't come back yet," the white-haired man murmured to himself. "He went to fetch Manoka and Shonanoy, but he hasn't come back. It's nightfall now,

329

and there's no word. I feel there's something dreadfully wrong. Oh my Dimarte, what has my only son done, that Thomas hasn't come back with them yet? Beloved one, in your wisdom, give me a sign to ease my troubled heart."

He leaned out of the open window, staring at the top of the bluff, willing himself to see through the darkness. But all was shadow now, and all was stillness until at last there came the mournful hooting of an owl. Thrice, the sad ululation rose, and then was heard no more.

Lucien Bouchard stiffened, his head rose, his eyes filling with sudden, blinding tears. There was a searing, wrenching pain, and suddenly it was as if the darkness consumed him.

Then his vision cleared, and he saw before him the sweet, wistful face of Dimarte. She held out her arms to him, and her eyes were soft and gentle and her lips were curved in that sweet smile which had won his heart that first day at Econchate.

"Dimarte, Dimarte, my beloved!" he gasped. He saw himself as strong and young and vibrant once again, and he could feel the twinges left by the great scars of the bear's claws along his left side. And she was clad in doeskin, and the Spanish comb he had bought for her in Mobile adorned her glossy black hair.

"Come with me, my Lu-shee-ahn, we shall be together again for always," her voice murmured in that hushed darkness. "Give me your hands and I will lead you back to Econchate."

"You've come back to me, my beloved, my Dimarte!" he whispered.

"Yes, Lu-shee-ahn, and I shall be with you always now, as I prayed Ibofanaga might grant. Come."

He grasped her soft slim hands, and once again the hoot of the owl was heard from the distant bluff, but this time there was no sadness to it.

CHAPTER TWENTY-THREE

When Henry Bouchard entered the red-brick château some two hours later, it was to find his wife seated on a stone bench at the side of the foyer and near the imposing staircase which rose to the second floor. Her eyes were swollen, her head bowed, and Luke was beside her with an arm around her shoulders, trying his best to comfort her.

Old Matthew, who had admitted him, gave him a reproachful look, and then, his own eyes suspiciously misty, turned away and tactfully disappeared.

He stood there nonplused, gripping his leather riding crop, eyes wide and mouth agape at the scene before him. Then Luke turned and met his father's gaze. The young man rose and said in a hushed voice, "Grandfather's dead. He was in the tower, and it must have been his heart."

"My God!" Henry Bouchard exclaimed. "But he's hardly ever been sick a day——"

Slowly Sybella raised her head, dropping her hands into her lap, and regarded him. "Henry, where's Thomas, and what happened to his niece and nephew?" Her voice broke with emotion.

Before her searching, unwavering gaze, Henry Bouchard nervously shifted his feet, stared downward, cleared his throat and then faltered, "He—he's dead, Syb. He had a stroke—he'd been riding to Tuskegee and back without hardly any rest, and he was upset about them—"

"He's dead too?" she echoed. "But what about Manoka and Shonanoy?"

"That—that's probably what upset him so, Syb dear." He did not look at her, but twisted his riding crop between both hands and stared dully at it. "They'd already left the village, you see—"

"Henry Bouchard, you're not telling me the truth," his wife interrupted, and now tears ran down her cheeks and she came toward him. "He rode here this afternoon, came to see Grandfather, and told him that Manoka and Shonanoy and the man she was to marry had already been taken from the village. Taken by someone who said he'd been sent by Grandfather. I think you know who that someone was, Henry."

"Listen, Syb, you're all unstrung now, this has been a terrible afternoon. I want to see Father—"

"There's time enough for that when you've told me the truth," she said. "What happened to them?"

"They—you see—" Desperately, he plunged into the story he had been constructing on the way back to the château: "I knew father was worried about them and didn't want them to go on the march, so I sent Amos Greer to bring them back here. But—but they didn't trust him—I don't know why—they got out of the phaeton when he stopped to water the horses, and—and they ran away—"

"And that's all you have to tell me about them, Henry?" Her voice was composed now, but her tear-filled eyes did not leave his flushed, uneasy face.

"He had the niggers he brought with him look for them, but they'd gotten too good a start—God knows where they've gone or where they are by now—I swear it's the truth, Syb, believe me—"

Sybella stared at him a long silent moment. Then she said, "You've done many things I haven't approved of since we got married, Henry. I know you haven't been faithful to me, but I understand that and I can even ignore it—so long as it isn't another woman of my own kind. But I don't remember that you've ever

332

lied to me before, and if I find you have, I don't think I shall ever forgive you."

"Syb, I'm just as shaken by all this as you are—my God, Father dead and then Thomas—and the Indians—how do you think I feel?"

"I only hope for your sake, Henry, that you aren't lying to me about why you sent that man Amos Greer to bring Thomas's niece and nephew back. If you are, you'll have Father's death on your conscience too."

"Now that's enough of that kind of talk, Syb—for God's sake, woman, let's not quarrel over these dreadful coincidences. How was I to know they'd try to run away? How was I to know Thomas would get so riled up he'd keel over right in front of me?" Henry blustered.

Again she stared at him a long moment in silence, and then went slowly back to the stone bench and sat down, putting her trembling hands to her tear-swollen face. "I'm not the one to judge you, Henry. Go make your peace with Father. Tomorrow morning, Luke is going to bury him in the bluff beside that Indian girl he loved."

He stared at her, then at Luke, who again bent to his stepmother and murmured words of consolation. Then, flinging the riding crop across the foyer, he strode down the hall to his father's room.

As he looked down at old Lucien's wrinkled face and saw the smile which wreathed his father's lips, Henry's eyes clouded with tears and he bowed his head in contrition. "Forgive me, Father. Oh my God, it was my fault you had to die this way—all because of my greed and lust, because I was so damned selfish. How many times I used to tell you not to sermonize me—well, you knew what was driving me all those years, didn't you, Father? And now—now it's too late for me to change, and it wouldn't bring you back if I did."

He turned away, conscious of his own guilt. Then he said to himself, half-aloud, "And Sybella knows I've lied, too, and she said she'd never forgive me if she found out. I've got to leave Windhaven for a while, at

333

least till she gets over the way she feels about me right now. Yes, that's the best thing to do. Right now, she wouldn't even let me kiss her—" He turned to his father's body for a last look, and then, with a groan, went out of the room, left the château without a word, and, mounting his horse, rode off. . . .

At dawn the next morning, Luke Bouchard carried Lucien's body out through the fields and toward the bluff, ascending it by a path from its eastern slope which rose gradually and without the steep perpendicular stature of the front and the river side. Lucien's body was not heavy, and his grandson carried it tenderly in his arms as he walked slowly toward the path of ascent. The field hands stopped their labors to approach, to say their farewells to the white-haired old man who had never thought of them as slaves and who had forbidden them to call him master in his hearing. And one of them, white-haired like old Lucien, David, a West Indian black whom Lucien had bought in Mobile at the turn of the century and promptly freed, reverently picked up a spade and followed Luke to the top of the bluff. When Luke turned back for a moment to look down at the river and saw David, he was about to speak; but the old black entreated in a tearful voice, "Please, suh, ah wants to say good-bye to old Mistah Lucien. Ah wants to dig his grave nice and wide, so's he'll have plenty room to rest till the Lawd Gawd Jehovah come call him to de judgment, suh." And Luke, his eyes filling with tears, could only nod and turn back toward the top of the bluff.

He held his grandfather's body in his arms while Old David scooped out the rich red earth. "I'll bury him as he buried his Dimarte, David," Luke murmured. "The Creeks believed that the dead should be seated in their graves so that they might spring up promptly when Ibofanaga, their supreme god, called upon them." And, stepping down into the grave, he gently seated the buckskin-clad body of Lucien Bouchard; then, composing the wrinkled hands in an attitude of prayer, gently closed the lifeless eyes, and kissed them, then the forehead in benediction.

334

Kneeling at the side of the grave, he took the first handful of earth, kissed that too, and let it fall onto his grandfather's body. Swiftly rising, he turned to the river and stood there while David filled the grave. When it was done, he looked upon the grave of Lucien Bouchard's young Creek bride, and it was strange that there was not even a single fragment of the Spanish comb left upon the ground which covered her last resting place.

It was the last week of August, and now the time of harvest was at hand on the acres of Windhaven devoted to cotton; and here as well as on those of the Williamson plantation, the field hands worked arduously, but they sang at their labors. Soon after burying his grandfather, Luke had gone to Mobile at his stepmother's request, and the counting house with which old Lucien had dealt for so long had been instrumental in finding him a new overseer to replace the loyal Ashanti Thomas.

Matthew Forsden, a mild-mannered man in his early thirties, born in Surrey and having come to Georgia with his widowed father, had just sold his land and slaves after his father's recent death and had come to Mobile to seek a new situation.

Elderly John Rigden, the factor at the counting house, arranged a meeting between Luke Bouchard and the congenial Forsden. From the very first, a sympathetic bond was forged between them when Forsden explained, "You see, Mr. Bouchard, I love farming and working on the land, but I must confess I'm not fond of slavery. When my father died, I tried to free my slaves, but I couldn't because of the laws. So I sold them, but I took pains to find them honorable, kind masters. What I want most to do is to work in the fields with my hands and to teach the workers how to be resourceful and how to lighen their labors, yet to try new crops and keep the soil fertile."

"My grandfather always believed in that, Mr. Forsden," Luke said. "If you're interested, I'd like to hire you as overseer at Windhaven, since I've my own two hundred acres to supervise now that I've married the daughter of the man who owned them. And I too share your views about the treatment of workers, rather than looking upon them as slaves to be driven by the whip."

And so it was that Matthew Forsden went back with Luke and, after talking with him, Sybella enthusiastically approved her stepson's choice of a man to replace Thomas.

Henry Bouchard offered no opposition to his elder son's decision. For the past two months, he had spent most of his time on his own hundred acres, living in the brick and log house and driving himself from sunup to sundown as arduously as he and Amos Greer drove his slaves. The guilt of Thomas's death had begun to weigh heavily upon him, and he had found Sybella cool and distant to his attempts at reconciliation. A week after his father's burial, he had come to her room and tried to cajole and woo her, only to have her look calmly at him and say, "I'm your wife, Henry, not your convenience or scapegoat. I'll always be faithful to you, but I've too much sorrow in me now to think of love-making."

He glared at her, and because she was still desirable and her candid nature was always an erotic challenge to him, he had seized her and crushed his mouth on hers. She submitted passively, and then murmured, "Of course I won't deny myself to you, Henry, it's your right as my husband. But if you take me as you would one of your black slave girls, I don't think I shall ever forgive you."

He had flung her down on the bed, his face dark with anger, and then ridden back to his own land. When his stableboy took the reins of the horse to lead it to its stall, he growled, "Send Mary in to me and be damned quick about it!" and once the Kru woman entered, he ordered her to strip naked and get into bed. Then he used her pitilessly, closing his eyes and pretending that it was Sybella he had thus mastered.

The sun was warm and the fields had never been more beautiful than in this August of 1835, with their dark-green foliage contrasted by bunches of the purest white, downy cotton, resembling meadows in which a light shower of snow had just fallen. It was at night that the pods began to open, and the cotton sprang out to swell to four or five times the bulk of the pod in a breathtaking softness and delicate whiteness. Each pod formed three oval bunches of snowy down, about as large as a hen's egg. As soon as the morning sun had absorbed the night's dew, the pods were fit for picking. And at dusk the men, women and children carried their large deep baskets to the gin house, where a new cycle of harvesting began.

Matthew Forsden and Luke Bouchard followed the baskets to the Windhaven gin house, the latter explaining that by next summer he planned to have a cotton gin shed built on the Williamson property. "It will cut down labor of hauling over here, you see, Mr. Forsden. Besides, it will make a profit on its own by being available to small neighboring planters, though I do not intend to put an exorbitant price on such a service."

"That's wise, Mr. Bouchard. My father took only a penny or two per pound when he ginned his neighbor's cotton."

"And I'm sure that you and I can devise a better method of baling than the screw press, Mr. Forsden. I've seen a good deal of cotton spoiled when the force of the jack-screw is dug down into the bale. By the time it reaches Mobile, the buyers from Northern mills and the factors from the English ones generally mark it down several cents a pound."

"This is an excellent machine, Mr. Bouchard. One man can easily clear three hundred pounds a day. And of course I presume you throw the seeds into heaps to ferment, so you can then use them as manure?"

"That's right. My grandfather believed in replenishing the soil. What you take out of it, you should put back so that it won't be weakened in the years ahead. That's why, too, he always believed in rotating his crops. The South needs more than cotton to keep alive. I plan to devote many acres to produce, and I'm thinking next year of bringing in some cattle, for beef, milk and cheese."

"I'm glad I was in Mobile when you were there, Mr. Bouchard. This is what I always believed farming should be like." Forsden smiled and held out his hand. And yet, despite this concord between two enlightened young men of the new South, there were ominous signs that both the foes and champions of slavery were beginning to draw their first battle lines toward a terrible conflict that would, a generation hence, destroy the innocent along with the guilty, pit brother against brother in hostility. Antislavery literature had just a few weeks before been taken by a mob from the Charleston, South Carolina post office and burned in the public square. The citizens then wrote President Jackson to urge him to grant federal aid in closing the mails to all abolitionist literature. Only a week before, an academy in Canaan, New Hampshire, had been dragged from its foundation because fourteen of its pupils were black. And James G. Birney wrote to Gerrit Smith, "The antagonistic principles of liberty and slavery have been roused into action and one or the other must be victorious. There will be no cessation of strife until slavery shall be exterminated or liberty destroyed."

On the same day that Birney had written his prophetic letter, young Celia was delivered of a pretty young daughter, whom she named Prissy, after her former master's mother, Priscilla.

Sybella Bouchard had attended the young woman, even helped deliver the child, and a day later she sent one of the house servants to Henry's brick and log house asking him to come to see her as soon as possible.

He rode back at once and hurried into the château. It was high noon of a scorching end-of-August day, and he was bronzed from the sun. But his lips were tight and his eyes uneasy as old Matthew ushered him to his wife's bedchamber.

Sybella regarded her husband, and in a calm, poised voice, remarked, "You're looking well, Henry. Work agrees with you. Is the picking going well?"

"Oh yes. We'll have a fine crop, and I've heard that the price will still be high this fall down at Mobile,

Syb." Then, twisting his wide-brimmed hat in his hands, his face flushing, he muttered, "I've missed you a lot, Syb."

"I suppose you have, in your way, Henry. I still can't forget about poor Father and Thomas. And I don't suppose you've had any word at all about Thomas's niece and nephew?"

Henry shook his head, his eyes on the floor.

"Well, it's God's will, I dare say. But how dreadful it all was, and how needless." She waited a moment, then looked up at him and in a steadfast voice went on. "I asked you to come here, Henry, because Celia's just had a child—a little girl. And of course you know whose child it really is."

"I know. It's Mark's."

"I can't very well blame you for that, can I?" She uttered a bitter little laugh. "I don't know, it seems that ever since that day you brought her to this house, brought her in secret so that I wouldn't know about your wanting a bed wench, things have gone badly between us."

"I didn't mean to hurt you, Syb, I swear before God I never did!" he groaned.

"I'm sure you didn't mean to, Henry. You were simply thoughtless. And, I'm afraid, very selfish too. Well, I'm not anyone's judge, least of all yours. I've been selfish in my way, too, staying away from you like this. But I think you understand—"

"Can't we—I mean—I'm lonely, I need you, Syb."

"Not so fast, Henry. You still have a habit of making it sound as if I were really the one at fault. The reason I sent for you, you know I had promised Thomas that he could marry Celia. He wanted to look after the girl and her child. And now of course he's dead, and she's all alone and still a slave. For the sake of the child, Henry, won't you free both her and little Prissy?"

"Sybella, you know the law won't allow it. You know that as well as I do. Even Father couldn't free all the blacks he had here at Windhaven, much as he wanted to call them freedmen and such."

"That may be true enough about the law—I understand from my father that you have to take a slave outside the boundary of a state, and of course then the slavers will capture the poor soul and take him elsewhere and make their horrid profits on human misery. But you know that Father told the blacks they were free, and he treated them that way. You could at least do the same, and you could write out a paper of manumission for Celia and her baby so that in case anything happens to either of us, some provision could be made to take them away, perhaps North."

"Syb, all that's going to happen is another argument that won't get us anywhere," Henry exclaimed. "The law's the law, I can't change it, neither can you. And what good does it do to talk about making someone free when the law won't recognize it? Things are the way they are, and we have to live with them."

"Enough of your fine-sounding talk about not freeing a slave, Henry," Sybella burst out as she rose from the table, pushing aside the sweater she had been crocheting for Fleurette. "What it really amounts to is that you mean to punish that poor girl Celia, all because your fine young son Mark got to bed with her before you did!"

"Sybella, that's not true—" he began, his face mottled with anger.

His wife sent him a scathing look in which contempt and anguish were mingled. "And you're punishing Mark too, though I can't blame the boy for his profligacy, not when he has his own father's illustrious examples to follow."

"Stop it, damn you!" he growled.

"Don't you see, Henry, by refusing, you're turning an innocent baby into a slave who, one day, God forbid, may have to submit to some other plantation owner—just as you intended Celia to submit to you?"

"I'm warning you, Sybella!" He rose, glowering, his fists clenched.

She shrugged. "Go ahead, beat me, Henry, why don't you? That's your customary way of wooing a woman, I suppose. Only remember, I'm not your slave and never will be. And now I'm going for a ride on Dulcy. Maybe the fresh air will clear my thoughts about you, Henry. And you'd best do some self-searching while I'm gone."

She flung out of the drawing room, leaving her florid-faced husband standing with mouth agape. She went out through the kitchen, scarcely noticing Mammy Clorinda's curtsy and greeting, heading directly for the stable just ahead of the rows of slave cabins. The sky had turned an ominous gray and the wind was rising, tugging at her long flowing skirt, at the ruffles on her bodice, but she paid it no heed. As the Kru stableboy, Jimmy, emerged, she snapped at him, "Saddle Dulcy, boy, and quickly!"

"Yes, Missy. Only looks mighty lak a storm comin' up, Missy—maybe it better—" he uneasily began.

"You heard what I said, boy! Do it—or would you rather have a whipping?" her lips curled with anger. *My God*, she told herself, *Henry's cruelty's starting to affect even me. Before I married him I'd never have thought of saying such a thing to anyone, not even a slave.*

"I'll saddle her, yes'm!" The stableboy fearfully bobbed his head and disappeared into the stable. A few moments later, he came out leading the spirited chestnut mare, and helped his mistress mount side-saddle, tendering her the reins. At a distant rumble of thunder, Dulcy whinnied and pawed the ground.

"Easy, girl!" Sybella jerked on the reins, then patted the mare's neck to soothe her. "Better hand me my riding crop too, Jimmy!"

"Yes'm." He hesitantly held it up to Sybella.

Snatching it from him, her lips tight, her forehead creased with exasperation, she directed the mare toward the narrow, cleared path which led through a clump of thickets, emerging beyond it into a wide stretch of grassy field as yet uncultivated. Miles beyond, it would eventually connect with the old Federal Road, where she loved to ride. Her mind swirled with the rift that had grown between Henry and herself, with her awareness of how much Mark was emulating

341

his father, in a kind of fierce blood rivalry to prove himself a man despite his years. Could she and Henry ever go back to those joyous days and nights of comradeship and sharing at the outset of their marriage? Yes, she was thirty-three, still vital, still attractive, she knew. And men were not the only ones with deep, underlying needs, even if it was a man's world.

Back in the stable, Djamba scowled at the timid stableboy. "Which way she go, Jimmy?" he demanded.

"That way, to the ol' road," the boy gestured. As he spoke, there was another rumble of thunder. With an imprecation in his own tongue, Djamba hurried to one of the stalls where the black stallion Midnight pawed its straw, swiftly applied bridle and reins and, mounting bareback, urged it in the direction Sybella had taken.

Again, thunder growled in a darkening sky along with a sudden spatter of rain. Sybella flicked Dulcy's haunch with a crop, commanding, "Steady, girl!"

But the mare had sensed her mistress' inner raging discontent and suddenly, as a shaft of jagged lightning illumined the sullen sky, bolted. Sybella uttered a cry of fear and strove with all her strength to draw on the reins, but the mare had taken her head and would not stop.

Jostled, panting, in danger of losing her balance, Sybella called as soothingly as she could, but to no avail. As the thunder growled again, the mare gave a frightened whinny and galloped on.

"Oh my God!" Sybella groaned as, in her heedless gait, the mare brushed her helpless rider against the overhanging branch of a small oak tree which tore the crop from Sybella's hand.

Sybella's lips moved in prayer and she closed her eyes. *Please God, let it be quick.* And then suddenly there was a shout beside her, and Djamba, reaching out with both hands, seized her by the waist and lifted her free, setting her down in front of him as he called out a command she could not understand, and the great stallion obediently slackened its pace and came to a halt.

"Oh thank God—oh Djamba—you—you've saved

me," she gasped, her arms clinging round his dusky, sweating body.

"Missy safe now. Dulcy, she run herself out, she be quiet soon," he consoled her.

Now he gently disengaged her arms, slid from the stallion and helped her down. Sybella tottered, suddenly weak. A sudden flash of lightning drew a terrified cry from her and again she clung to him.

"We hide down here from de lightnin', Missy," he urged, guiding her down into a deep wide ravine whose overhanging sides gave shelter from the storm. She could not know that, long years ago, it was in just such a ravine that Henry's father Lucien had taken shelter from a violent thunderstorm on his way to Econchate and his rendezvous with the destiny that awaited him in the Creek village.

There, huddling against the young Mandingo slave, Sybella trembled now, but not from fear of the raging storm. Rather, from the sudden inexplicable yearning that had seized her. He was a slave, yet he had once been the chief of his tribe; most of all, he was a man of indomitable courage and strength.

She stared up at him and read in his dark eyes a devotion and steadfastness that quieted her fears. Gently he murmured, "Missy safe now. Storm soon over, then I find Dulcy and we ride back home to Massa Henry, Missy."

And Sybella knew with a flash of feminine intuition that in that instant Djamba had sensed her momentary yearning, acknowledged it with his own, and yet had resolution and wisdom enough to ignore it for them both. . . .

CHAPTER TWENTY-FOUR

It was October 21st, the very day on which a rioting mob had prevented the English abolitionist George Thompson from speaking before the Female Anti-Slavery Society in Boston, and that same mob had seized William Lloyd Garrison and dragged him through the streets. Henry and Mark Bouchard now shared the same brick and log house on the former's original holdings, much to Sybella's distress. She saw that the estrangement between Henry and herself had deepened. And now that his younger son had left Windhaven to work his father's land and share his father's little house, her own opportunity to influence the arrogant, self-centered youth toward more compassion and tolerance would be nonexistent. But worst of all, she foresaw that it was certain to create an even wider bridge between Mark and his wiser, more humane elder brother Luke. At least Luke had been able to force Mark to exercise some restraint; now, under his father's aegis, Mark would be confronted with constant carnal temptations which could only shape his already egotistical nature into that of a young renegade who scoffed at laws and ethics when these did not permit him the full indulgence of fleshly pleasures.

By contrast, the pleasant, considerate and dedicated behavior of Matthew Forsden, the new overseer at Windhaven, eased her own responsibilities, let her concentrate on the household chores and make sure that all the house servants were well fed and cared for. As for Celia, Sybella Bouchard told herself that in spite of Henry's decision not to free the lovely young mulatto, she would see somehow that Celia did not fall prey to either Henry or Mark. Mark, having learned of the birth of Prissy, had shown not the slightest concern, even though he must have guessed it was his own child, sired that stormy November night when he had crept across the hall from his own room into the chamber where Henry Bouchard had smuggled Celia with every intention of exacting the rights of a master.

Soon after the noon hour, Amos Greer hurried up to Henry Bouchard who was taking lunch with Mark in the little house, served by Mary and Molly, and exclaimed, "Mr. Bouchard, sir, I've just had some news that I think you ought to know. You're always looking for more good land to pick up. Well, sir, here's a right smart piece that can fall into your hands if you act quick on it."

"What land are you talking about, Amos? Draw up a chair there, have some ham and biscuits and rum with us. Mark, shove the jug over to Amos."

"Thank you kindly, Mr. Bouchard. To your good health." Amos Greer grasped the jug with both hands, put it to his lips and took a hearty swig, then set the jug down again and smacked his lips. "Nothing like good *taffai*, Mr. Bouchard. Well now, I was out there looking at those last two rows of cotton on the west side—they look a mite peaked, and I told Joe that he'd better do some more chopping and cultivating or he'd find himself under my cowhide by the end of the week. Some nigger rides up on a horse, looks as if he's racing ahead of the devil himself, he does. He sees me, jumps off his horse and comes running and flings himself down and starts bawling, 'Oh, massa, it jist awful— dey all dead, massa suh.' We niggahs all scared, doan know wut to do, suh! Benjy, he de nex' foahman, he say I go look foah help!"

"Who did the nigger belong to, Amos?" Henry asked.

"I was just getting to that." Amos Greer sniggered

346

lewdly, reached for the *taffai* jug and took another hearty swig. "Well now, seems like that nigger was working over at the Ellerbys. And what happened was, after I told the old fool I'd larrup some sense into him if he didn't stop bawling like that, was that Ellerby's wife must have taken up with the nigger foreman George, and Mr. Ellerby caught them both, and then he shot them dead and turned the gun on himself."

"Well, I'll be damned!"

"You know what the talk was, don't you, Mr. Bouchard? You don't mind if I say it right out in front of Mr. Mark here, do you?"

"I'm no baby any more, Mr. Greer," Mark said, glaring at him.

"No you ain't, boy, got to hand it to you. Well now, this nigger who rode over, even he knew about it. All the slaves seemed to know about it over there except Ellerby himself till just now. You see, the way I heard it, Ellerby and this nigger George took their bed fun pestering each other—if you get my meaning, Mr. Bouchard? And then, again from what this scared nigger told me, that handsome wife of Ellerby's didn't like being neglected, so she set her cap for that big buck nigger to see if she couldn't teach him to poke women instead of men."

"What a damned shame," Henry muttered. He was thinking of his meeting with Wilma Ellerby in the gazebo on the night of the housewarming at Windhaven. He'd had the notion to follow up that little meeting, seeing how eager she was for a real man—now, damn the luck, it would never happen. What a waste of such a tasty, beddable wench!

"I guess," Greer went on, "that buck nigger must have liked the new way, because Ellerby caught them both poking away for dear life. That's when all the shooting started. So now, since nobody's left to claim that land around here, I was just thinking, sir, you might want to talk to your father-in-law, that lawyer you've got in the family so handy, and see if he can't hornswoggle it and make it yours."

"Amos, you've earned yourself a little bonus for that

347

piece of news. I'll tell you what. It's a good stretch to Montgomery, but I'd be mighty obliged if you'd saddle up after you've had your lunch and ride over there and talk to him about it. The only problem would be if Frank Ellerby had any living relatives who might claim it. There weren't any children. I think I can guess why, now. I feel sorry for that woman, she was a real charmer."

"Well, don't you go fretting any over that kind, Mr. Bouchard. In my book, any white woman that would peel down and bed herself with a black buck ought to be cowhided and tarred and feathered, that's how I feel. I'll just have another swig of this *taffai* and then I'll go over and see Mr. Mason. Oh, I almost forgot— weren't you and I going over to the Buffery farm this afternoon?"

"Well, I can take Mark along. You've told me where it is, and I'll just say that you recommended me."

"You do that. Jim Buffery is an honest man, he'll give you full value for your money. You know, if you get hold of those Ellerby slaves, you might decide to sell off a parcel of them. He'd give you the best prices around here without having to go all the way to Mobile or New Orleans. Well, I'm off. I'll stay the night in Montgomery, and be back here tomorrow and tell you what Mr. Mason thinks can be done about the Ellerby land." Greer nodded toward Mark, who gave him back a sullen look, and then left the little house.

It was mid-afternoon by the time Henry Bouchard and his son Mark had ridden on horseback fifteen miles downriver, tied up at the sturdy oak tree, and forded the river on a small raft which they found drawn up on the bank, with two heavy oars beside it. Pulling the raft high on the opposite riverbank, they went on through a cluster of cedar and oak trees and saw, about two hundred yards beyond, in a wide clearing, the sprawling one-story wooden house of James and Bethany Buffery. Buffery himself stood in the doorway, shading his eyes from the sun with his hand and squinting at the visitors, then came up to greet them. He was in his mid-forties, of medium height and noticeably corpulent, with heavy jowls and a round, stolid face. His already graying hair fell below his shoulderblades, his sideburns were long and thick, and he had a straggly beard. Wearing cotton breeches and a dirty buckskin jacket, he carried a percussion cap rifle whose muzzle he lowered to the ground as the two Bouchards approached. "Wal now, I see you used my raft to pay me a visit. That's what it's for, but mostly those who use it come to do business. Or is this a social call, as you might say?" He shifted the rifle and fixed his rheumy pale-gray eyes on them.

"I'd meant to call on you with my overseer, Amos Greer," Henry Bouchard explained, "but a business matter came up and I had to send him to Montgomery. He's told me a good deal about you and your good wife and this little farm you've got here."

"Oh, Amos, sure, good friend of mine. Prime judge of niggers, too. We've done some business. Who might you be? At a guess, I'd say you were one of those Bouchard fellows who got hold of all that prime riverfront land between here and Lowndesboro."

"I can see you're just as shrewd as Amos said you were, Mr. Buffery," Henry chuckled. "Yes, you're right, I'm Henry Bouchard and this is my son Mark."

"Come in, come in, always glad to meet someone in the business. Maybe we can be sociable and do some business too before sundown, eh?" James Buffery went back to the door of the house, opened it and beckoned to them. "Come in and take a load off your feet, you two. I'll have Beth rassle up some coffee and corncakes she just baked. Then I suppose you'll want to see my spread here. Reckon Amos has told you how I work it?"

"Yes. You train the young niggers to their jobs, you rent out some of the grown blacks to the smaller planters who can't afford to buy slaves outright, and they tell me you've a few likely wenches for pleasuring," Henry said, winking knowledgeably.

"Here, we'll go right into the kitchen. Do most of

349

my business there anyhow, and Beth's cookin' allus seems to seal the bargain somehow."

He led the way into the kitchen, jabbed his thumb at the woman standing there: "This is my wife, Beth. Don't mind telling you gentlemen nobody can teach a nigger bitch what's what or how to move fast better than Beth here." He leaned the rifle in a corner of the plank-floored kitchen, sprawled into a chair at the head of the table, which had been made with puncheon like the rough, heavy-timbered floors themselves, and added, "Beth, let's have some coffee and those cakes you just baked, and draw up a chair and join us. This is Mr. Henry Bouchard and his son Mark. Amos Greer's the one who told them all about us."

Bethany Buffery was a rawboned, handsome woman, about five feet eight inches tall, her dull hair pulled back from the forehead and gathered into a plait which dangled midway down her back. Her features were sharp and alert—bright hazel eyes set closely together at the bridge of a thin, slightly turned-up nose, high-set cheekbones and firm jaw. Her white cotton dress with its high neck and short puffed sleeves, shaped out high-perched, firm breasts, at which Henry Bouchard stared with frank admiration. Mark glanced up and flushed hotly, as her amused gaze intercepted his.

"Be right glad to and good to know you. I'll have the coffee hot in a jiffy. Some hold that hot coffee's out of place in country like this, but Jim and me allus like our coffee strong and hot." She volunteered this as she set down four hard-glazed clay mugs, moved to the end of the kitchen to the stone oven where the coffee pot was perched atop a small nest of coals, then unabashedly squatted, wadding up the hem of her long skirt to use as a pot holder, and returned to the table to fill the mugs. In so doing, she revealed long, suntanned legs, with slim calves and the hint of supple thighs.

This done, she went back to the oven to take out a pan of corncakes, placed it on the table and, flouncing down on a chair opposite her husband, announced,

"Pile in. I think you'll find my johnnycakes good and tasty."

"You've been teaching Nancy and Liz how to make 'em, haven't you, Beth?"

The woman nodded, her lips curling in a reminiscent smile. "Sure did, Jim. Had to take the switch to Liz; she spoiled three batches. She won't spoil another or my name's not Bethany Buffery." Then, eying Henry Bouchard with frank, sensual appraisal, she added, "You might say, Mr. Bouchard sir, we run a kinda school for niggers. We figure they didn't have any brains to start with, so we aim to learn them all we can while they're here. Now five-six years might seem a long spell to some, but not with niggers. 'Course, gals, if you get 'em young, you can learn 'em faster than bucks. And when it comes to gals, there's a difference in how you use the switch on 'em, too, something not everybody knows. Now you take Liz, she belongs to old Mister Danvers downriver 'bout forty miles from here. She's in training to take over as cook when the old mammy he's had for nigh on to thirty years turns up her toes, which is likely to be right soon, from what we hear tell. She's not going to be a bed wench, so you can lay it on real good and not worry about spoiling her hide. But with Nancy, she's Mr. Wilkins' intended bed slave, she is, so just switch her a little till it stings and makes her cry and warn her how hard you could really give it to her if she doesn't perk up some, 'cause you don't want to mark her bad and get her too scared." She uttered a coarse laugh. "I figger Mr. Wilkins would rather do the switchin' hisself when it comes time for her to warm his bed—that'll be about six months from now, won't it, Jim?"

"Just about." Affably, the fat man turned to smile at Henry Bouchard. "We keep good records. I used to auction off niggers in Natchez, and that's where I met Beth. When we had a mite of trouble with another auctioneer who was too big for his breeches, me and Beth figgered it might not be such a bad idea to get some land of our own when the gittin' was good, and make our own way teachin' niggers what-for. Been mighty good at it so far, if I do say so myself."

When they had finished their coffee and corncakes, Henry and Mark Bouchard accompanied the Bufferys on a tour of the training and breeding farm, as Amos Greer had characterized it. About fifty of the acres were devoted to cotton, another fifty to tobacco, with upright rows of thin planks separating and fencing in the two major sections. In each of these, young boys and a few girls worked under the supervision of what James Buffery called "my trusties," these being freed blacks whom he had contracted to work at a small annual wage. "But when you throw in their board and keep— and these trusties nigh eat us out of house 'n home," he said, "plus which they get a bed wench now and again when I get hold of some black gals I can buy real cheap and use for my own breeding suckers, you got to figger they're doin' better than lots of overseers in these parts."

Of the remaining hundred acres, perhaps thirty were set off for the growing of corn, yams, snap beans, okra, apples, peaches, and even a few orange trees. Elsewhere, there were several ramshackle sheds where, as James Buffery pointed out, the older boys from the contingent boarded out with him by neighboring planters for the purpose of acquiring a trade, were instructed in carpentry, masonry, horseshoeing, while in another shed girls were trained in sewing and spinning. There were rectangular windowless houses, each set some distance apart, in which the young apprentices were quartered, and segregated as to sex.

"I got me two trusties who patrol all night long, y'see," the Mississippian explained, "so these young bucks feeling their sap don't get a chance to pester the wenches none. You see that last house way down at the end of the pasture? That's where I keep my pleasure wenches. Now mind you, some of these gals haven't been pestered yet; that is, not broke in proper in bed. I aim to sell them in Mobile or New Orleans for a fancy price when they're just a mite older. The others, well— when I get guests like you 'n customers—both of which

352

I hope you'll be—I kin talk business 'bout rentin' them out as whores, y'see. Now you kin poke 'em here or, if you pay a bit more, take them with you for a coupla nights. 'Course, you better not damage 'em up much when you bring 'em back, or you'll have to buy them, y'see."

"I'd like to see those wenches of yours," Henry Bouchard declared, glancing sharply at his son.

"Sure, sure, Mr. Bouchard, I was aiming to take you over there. Now, like I was saying, these gals that haven't been busted yet, Beth teaches 'em 'long with the gals I keep in service, what's expected of 'em when they get theyselves sold to a master who wants a lively bed wench, understand? I tell you, Mr. Bouchard, when some Creole dandy finds out he can buy hisself a virgin who knows what to do in bed the minute he gets her peeled down and in there, he'll pay a good deal over the market price." This last he accompanied with a broad wink and Bethany Buffery permitted herself a titter behind her hand. During this tour, she had stared several times at Henry Bouchard, who was not unaware of her interest in him. He, too, found her rawboned, lithe figure intensely desirable.

She went ahead to open the door of the cabin-like house of pleasure wenches, and her husband called out, "All right now, you wenches, stand up and look right smart! Some fine gen'lemen here to see you!"

In the long cabin there were about a dozen wooden bunks, timbered boards crudely pegged together, over which cotton quilts stuffed with batting were placed to serve as both mattress and cover. In the center of the cabin was a low table, with stools, and some empty dishes from the girls' midday meal. At the far right was a stone fireplace, and Buffery felt the need to explain: "These Alabama winters sometimes get a mite frosty, and when the gals aren't servicin', they like a little fire to warm them." He guffawed and nudged Henry Bouchard with his elbow. " 'Pears now you're here, they won't need that kind of fire, now will they? Take your time, look 'em over. As I said, I've got some prime virgins for sale—and I don't mind disposin' of

353

them for a fair price to a fine upstanding planter like yourself."

The girls were between fourteen and eighteen, six of them black, three mulattoes, and three extremely striking quadroons. All were dressed in scanty shifts, the thin fabric boldly outlining nubile young breasts, plump buttocks and temptingly rounded thighs. At his gesture, the girls aligned themselves in two rows, through which he passed, briefly informing his visitors of each girl's name, age and background. Henry Bouchard stopped to consider one of the quadroons, a girl of seventeen, with almost bluish-black hair that hung in a cascade down her shoulders, with proud, widely spaced, full round breasts, slim waist and opulent hips and thighs.

"I see you're a gen'leman of quality, Mr. Bouchard," the fat Mississippian cackled. "This here's Dorothy. A prime virgin, but she knows all the tricks, don't you, gal?"

"Yes, master," the quadroon replied in a low husky voice, her eyes downcast, arms at her sides.

"In case you've any doubts that she hasn't been plowed yet, Mr. Bouchard, I'd take it right kindly if you'd have her peel down and you can finger her all you want. I don't want you to go back to your neighbors and tell them that Jim Buffery ain't honest in his dealings."

Henry Bouchard's throat had gone dry and he felt an agonizing ache in his loins. He had begun to realize how much he missed Sybella, now denied him; the awareness of this rift between them and his fear that it might continue endlessly had made him particularly morose the last few weeks. Seeing him hesitate, Buffery urged: "Go ahead, sir, they expect it. Fact is, Dorothy here is a little stuck on herself, and if you don't go ahead and finger her some, she'll think you don't favor her at all."

Henry Bouchard needed no second invitation. "All right, Dorothy, shuck it off," he ordered. The quadroon stooped to grasp the hem of the thin shift, then slowly lifted it, halting it at her belly so that this potential buyer might study the full, long but delightfully plump thighs, the enticing, fleshy mound of her sex, and the sleek flat belly with its shallow navel nook. When she heard him suck in his breath, she lifted the garment over her breasts and stood with it about her neck, her elbows bent back in a way that thrust out the cantaloupe-like globes with their dusky-rosy, well-developed nipples and small, coral aureolae.

"That's prime merchandise, that is, Mr. Bouchard sir," James Buffery declared. "I figger she'll bring as high as twenty-five hundred in New Orleans. 'Course now, no need to take her that far if you've a fancy for her. Go ahead, finger her some, see if I'm not telling you the truth when I say she's never been busted."

As the quadroon continued to hold the shift around her neck and to present herself with the utmost submission, Henry Bouchard extended his right forefinger and introduced it between the soft pulpy lips of her vulva, pressing inward till the presence of the hymen proclaimed that her owner had indeed not lied.

"You see, Mr. Bouchard?"

"You're right about her."

"Like I said too, even if she hasn't ever been busted, she knows how to pleasure a gentleman. Go ahead, Dorothy, show him what Trish learned you how to do last week." Then, by way of explanation to the planter, James Buffery added, "Trish, you'll remember, is that high-yaller gal your son here seemed to like so well. She's one of my best pleasuring wenches; earns me a heap, I can tell you. Go ahead now, Dorothy; want Beth should take a switch to your big backside?"

The lovely young quadroon promptly knelt down, doffing the shift entirely, and then, to Henry Bouchard's consternation, reached out her hands to undo his breeches and to take out his organ. Bowing her head, she brushed the glans with her lips, and then nimbly began to ply the tip of her tongue around it.

"That's enough there, Dorothy," her owner interposed. "He knows what you can do now. Now then, Mr. Bouchard, I can't let you be pleasured by Dorothy, not if I'm going to sell her as a virgin. But any of these service wenches I've shown you will be glad to entertain you proper."

"Yes—is there a place—" Henry Bouchard stammered, glancing self-consciously around the room.

"Oh no, it don't work that way at all, Mr. Bouchard, begging your pardon," James Buffery cackled again, in high good humor. "You see now, when a gen'leman like you studs a wench, it's a good lesson for all the others. I make them watch. And anyhow, 'specially with the older gen'lemen—not that you are that, as anyone can see—having an audience like that sort of perks them up, you might say."

"What about this Trish, then?" Henry demanded.

"A very good choice, Mr. Bouchard. Cost you ten dollars hard money. You can have her for an hour or more if you like. But didn't you say you might buy yourself one of my gals?"

"Might be I'd take a fancy to this Trish," Henry answered, "depending on how much you'd want for her."

"Yes, h'm, let me see now"—James Buffery stroked his beard, squinting in deep thought—" 'course if I sell her outright, I'll be losing her profits of the future from pleasuring gen'lemen like yourself. Let's say nine hundred dollars?"

"We'll see. Here's your ten dollars, Buffery. Now—er—I—"

"Haw, haw, I get your drift, Mr. Bouchard sir. Tell you what, Beth and me and your son, we'll go look round the rest of the place and give you time with Trish there. Wait now. That reminds me, I've got to go over and see how Bert is gittin' along teachin' these young nigger boys to cut and put wood together. I've got me a planter in Huntsville wants two young carpenters fast as I can train them. Willing to pay me a thousand apiece for 'em, he is too. Beth gal, whyn't you take Mr. Mark back into the house and keep him company for a spell—it'll take me an hour or so to finish supervisin'."

As the door closed behind the departing trio, Henry Bouchard, his face congested with lust, glanced around the room. The attractive young mulatto had already

356

peeled off her shift and got into her bunk, pillowing her head in her arms and awaiting him, a coy smile on her pretty face. She had small, firm-pointed breasts, long supple thighs and a glossy, satiny skin. The other girls had seated themselves on their bunks, their eyes intent on their young companion.

"Well now, Trish, how'd you like to come live with me and have a place of your own where you wouldn't have all this company?" His voice had a false, unsteady geniality to it as he approached the bunk.

"I'd like it right fine, massa," Trish giggled. "Fust off, though, don't you think you better poke me and see if you like wut you're gittin'?"

Her giggle was echoed by the other girls, and Henry Bouchard squirmed uneasily. But the sight of her sleek young nakedness overcame his embarrassment at having such an audience, and he mounted the bunk, his hands kneading her breasts as he thrust himself savagely against the soft, pouting orifice of her womancore. Trish uttered a gasp of pleasure, nimbly locking her calves over his thighs, and her arms hugged him convulsively as, closing her eyes, a dreamy smile on her ripe mouth, she joined him in his frenetic coupling.

"Lands sakes, Mr. Mark, you take after your father, but you're sure better-looking." Bethany Buffery sent the youth a provocative glance from under lowered lashes. "Now maybe Jim could sell you a bed wench—not that you'd be needing to buy one, I'm thinking, not a fine buck like you. Why, I declare, just the sight of you would send all the purty gals round your place into a tizzy, fightin' to see who'd be first to pester you."

Mark grinned, not at all displeased by this obvious flattery. Nor had he overlooked the appraising glances which the woman had been casting his father. The thought that she found him even more desirable spiced his growing hunger for her; as with Celia, the thought of besting his father to prove who was the more adept and shrewd advantagetaker stimulated him

357

enormously. "I don't care for just pretty young girls, Mrs. Buffery," he ventured as she paused at the door of the bedroom. "They're silly and full of daydreams, and they'd shy away when a man got really interested."

"You talk like you've had plenty of experiences with wenches, Mr. Mark," Bethany laughed softly, preening herself and arching so that he could not fail to notice the thrust of her bosom against the thin cotton dress. "Now I'll tell you a little secret. Jim, bless his old heart, is a fine provider, couldn't ask for a better—no woman could. But the truth is, even with all those wenches around, he doesn't show much sign of life at nighttime, if you catch my meaning. Guess maybe he's got to that time of age, or maybe he's pestered so many before I met him that he plumb wore hisself out. 'Sides which, he respects my feelin's enough so's he don't much mind if I take a hankerin' to a respectable young gen'leman. And anyhow, not that you'd be mindin' none, nor I don't want you to think I'd be the sort of female would give you any botheration on it, but I don't drop suckers anymore, so there's no worry none when I take it into my mind to pleasure someone real nice."

She had stopped, her hands planted on her hips, boldly staring at him with unmistakable meaning. Mark laughed softly, put his hands on her buttocks and pulled her up against him till she could feel his already vigorous manhood questing its haven in her responding loins. "Well now," she purred, "nobody needs to light a fire under you, do they, Mr. Mark? Wait now, lemme call Jolene. She's my own bound girl, and she's near-white as we can figger out—Jim bought her for me in Natchez just before we came here, you see. We can have lots of fun with her." As he nodded, his face flushed and his eyes glinting with passion, Bethany Buffery turned her head and called out, "Jolene, honey, I need you!"

The door across the way opened, showing a tiny cubicle with only a small bunk and a quilt atop it and a stool. A pretty yellow-haired girl of about eighteen,

358

wearing a shapeless red calico dress, barefooted, uttered a soft giggle. "I'm here, m'am."

"Then come on in and be quick about it, honey," Bethany Buffery said, reaching a hand out to the girl, who squeezed it and raised it to her surprisingly ripe breast.

Jolene obeyed, closing the bedroom door behind her. "Whyn't you peel down, Mr. Mark," Bethany Buffery whispered, her eyes narrowed and glowing, her tongue wetting the corners of her sensual lips. "I've allus wanted to feel a quality gen'leman's hide right up against mine. Mostly, young bucks like you are so all-fired in a hurry they just undo their breeches a little for the necessary. But we got a good hour. You heard old Jim say he had work to do. Come on now, Jolene, help Mr. Mark shed his duds."

With this, calmly drawing off her own frock and standing naked, Bethany Buffery moved over to the wide wooden bed and patted the thick quilts as if testing their comfort against the unyielding wood below. Then provocatively, sitting on the edge of the bed and swinging her long legs up, she waited, her knees arched up, her slim work-roughened fingers covertly stroking her breasts and sides as she watched the yellow-haired girl undress Mark down to his boots. "My, my, sure is a well-made gen'leman, m'am," Jolene giggled again. Stepping back, she now removed the single garment which covered her lushly ripe young body and then seated herself on the opposite edge of the bed, demurely crossing her legs and putting a hand over her plump, thickly golden-fleeced mound.

Mark Bouchard stretched out between them, turning to Bethany Buffery and nuzzling her breasts lightly with his teeth.

"Oh, you're a wicked one, you are, Mr. Mark," the rawboned matron coyly reproached him. "Bet you know more tricks already than even Dorothy could dream up. Go ahead, Jolene, don't be so bashful. Start playing with him a little to get him real worked up for me, then there'll be time for you, gal."

Shuddering with orgiastic rut, young Mark Bouchard

359

mounted the slave trainer's wife, while Jolene, crouching beside the embattled couple, stroked the youth's sturdy back and buttocks with her soft fingers, bending her head to flick her tongue along his spine and sides. And when he had wrenched himself free from the matron, panting and gasping with fulfillment, it was Jolene who knelt between his straddled, quivering thighs to attune him to a new erotic fray.

"You've made a right smart pick in Trish, Mr. Bouchard." James Buffery energetically rubbed his hands together. "I gen'rally ask for cash on the barrelhead, but you're known in these parts and that draft on your Mobile house is as good as gold. Now I'll tell you a little secret about that high-yaller gal you just poked and bought yourself. Do you know a neighbor name of Silas Jordan, came from North Carolina a while back?"

"Of course. He and his wife and boys were at my housewarming in January," Henry replied.

"W'al now, this is just a secret between us, as you might say. Y'see, that Silas Jordan is a mighty righteous man, and his wife's even more of the same, if you get my meaning. Thing was of it, he had hisself a fling with a juicy black bitch just six months before he up and married his wife. Tried all this time to keep her from finding out that Trish was his own git. Finally, about a year ago, he heard tell of me and came to see me and brought Trish along. Said he'd sell her to me outright because he was scared to hell and back his wife and maybe his boys would find out, and he didn't know what to do with her. 'Sides which, he said she was getting horny as a she-goat in heat, and he was mighty feared she'd come want him to pester her—that would just about break up the nice respectable life he was leading. So, like I said, you know you've got some good white stock in that high-yaller girl, and if you ever want to sell her, you'll get a good price. I fancy you might like to git some suckers out of her, and you can sell those to me if you've a mind to."

"We'll see, we'll see, Buffery." Henry Bouchard

scowled with embarrassment. Trish stood docilely to one side, wearing a new blue shift and shoes which Henry had induced the slave trainer to throw in as part of the bargain. Mark had come out of the Buffery house by now, looking a little sheepish as his father sternly eyed him, and at last the two took their leave of their genial, pandering host. As they shook hands, Henry Bouchard said to the fat Mississippian, "I might just have some slaves to sell you in a couple of weeks, as soon as I latch onto some land I've heard is up for sale."

"A pleasure to do business with you at any time, Mr. Bouchard sir. Feel free to visit whenever you've a mind to. Hope you'll have an easy fording with my raft—the river's not too high right now and it's sort of sluggish. W'al, see you soon, I hope."

When Amos Greer returned from his errand in Montgomery the next afternoon, it was with the news that the Ellerby plantation could be purchased for about $600 in taxes and another $2000 to the assessor at the land office in Huntsville. Frank Ellerby's father had died a year before, and there were no living relatives to claim the land and the slaves which the ill-fated couple had acquired. Once again, Henry Bouchard's greed for land and slaves had been sated through human tragedy.

CHAPTER TWENTY-FIVE

This November of 1835 marked the first time that Luke Bouchard took the Windhaven baled cotton down to Mobile, accompanied by Matthew Forsden. The price of cotton was still high, for it brought 17.45 cents per pound on the New York and Liverpool markets, and the Windhaven cotton was adjudged at the Mobile warehouse as being of the very finest quality. Luke and Forsden went on to New Orleans, and Lucy and her sister Maybelle made the trip as well. It was Luke's desire to give his bride an extension of their happy honeymoon, and he also intended to let precocious and flirtatious young Maybelle profit from seeing the educational sights of so thriving a city as New Orleans. Matthew Forsden acted as Maybelle's escort to the symphony, theater and opera, and to the fine restaurants. Luke observed, to his great satisfaction, that the quiet Englishman treated the younger girl as if she were a grownup, yet without the slightest insincere flattery or attention.

On the same steamship which brought the Windhaven bales to Mobile, Luke shipped the cotton from the Williamson land. Thanks to his own supervision during the harvest season, he was able to improve on the method of baling to prevent the crushing of the delicate fibers, and so these bales too brought an excellent price. Luke visited Rigalle's private bank and deposited the money from the Williamson cotton into a separate account which was to be shared by both his wife and her sister.

Henry Bouchard had visited Windhaven several times since the break with Sybella over Celia's freedom, and each time she received him graciously, even hopefully, but he made no further overture toward a lasting reconciliation. Doggedly, he refused to discuss the subject of Celia and her little girl any further, and insisted that he and Mark were getting along quite comfortably in their own house. Nor did he mention that his carnal gratification was being amply served by both Zora and Trish. He had his slaves build a separate cabin for the girl he had acquired from James Buffery, and he pointedly warned Mark to keep away from her. However, he did not object when his arrogant son sought out Zora's companionship as a solace. He and Amos Greer had taken their cotton to Mobile but averaged only about 14½ cents per pound because of the spoilage caused by the excessive force of the jack-screw pressing down into the bales.

In order to divert Mark from the temptation of Trish, whose proximity Henry Bouchard realized would inevitably inflame the youth, he kept reminding Mark that it would be wise to court and marry Maybelle Williamson. "I've told you before, Mark, that she stands to get a third of whatever the Williamson land and slaves are worth. Now it's too late to cry over your brother's having got a head start on you by marrying Lucy, but if you've got any gumption, you won't let any outsider grab that third interest. Besides, she's a lively filly, certainly the opposite of that simpering sister of hers, and I daresay you'll have considerable fun getting her used to your bedtime cravings."

"There's something else you're forgetting, Pa," Mark said in a surly tone. "Now that Grandpa's dead, you own all of Windhaven, don't you?"

"That's the way the law of inheritance generally rules, yes," Henry Bouchard glumly replied. "Only, for the time being, I'm not stepping in and taking over, not with things the way they are back there."

"You mean Mother?" Mark shot his father a taunting glance.

"Just watch your tongue, and try to listen to somebody older than yourself for a change," his father said with a scowl. "If you hadn't sneaked into Celia's room last year and waited until I could get you a bed wench of your own, all this trouble wouldn't have come about. Now don't answer me back, I know what you're going to say! What's done's done, only your mother wants me to set Celia and her brat—your brat, you know—free, and I'm not about to do that. It's a matter of principle with me. But besides that, this Forsden your brother picked up in Mobile seems to be a decent overseer, and he's done pretty well with the land, even if he didn't turn it all into cotton and take advantage of the good price we got in Mobile. The factor told me how much your brother and Forsden took in this year, and it's nothing to sneeze at."

"But what's stopping you taking over Windhaven, Pa?" Mark persisted.

"Damn it all," Henry Bouchard exploded, "I can't give you a pat answer. First off, you're only a few months past sixteen and not dry behind the ears yet. Mostly, you're not a married man, or you'd soon understand that if you've got a wife you're fond of, you don't feel like breaking things off forever between the two of you over a silly quarrel. Why the hell Sybella sets such store by that Celia, I don't know, but there's no accounting for a woman's mind. And that's enough talk about that. You just mind what I tell you, and the first chance you get, when Maybelle gets back, treat her nice and make her want to marry you, you hear?"

"Maybe I will at that," Mark said. "Maybe if I had a wife, Luke wouldn't lord it over me the way he's always done. He'd find out I'm a man with brains as good as his any day."

"That's the way to talk! But don't just talk; do something about it. Now I'm going to see Trish, so you amuse yourself with Zora if you've a mind to."

As 1835 came to an end, the pact with the Cherokee

Indians of Georgia took effect, and all their lands east of the Mississippi became the property of the United States. But in Florida, the Second Seminole War began, a bloody war that was to last until August 14, 1843, and which began with the massacre of General Wiley Thompson and his entire force at Fort King and, on the same day, the annihilation of a hundred soldiers under Major Dade at Fort Brooke. In this same month of December, the anti-Masons met at Harrisburg in the Pennsylvania state convention and nominated William Henry Harrison to succeed Andrew Jackson as President. At the age of sixty-three the hero of the battle of Tippecanoe in 1811 had already served in the Ohio Senate, the United States House of Representatives and the Senate, and briefly as minister to Colombia. Some sentimental oldsters, feeling that his glory days were long since past, declared that "Old Tippecanoe ought to be put in charge against those damned Seminoles. He'd wipe them out in short order."

In January 1836, James G. Birney published the first issue of his *Philanthropist* in Cincinnati as the official organ of the Ohio Anti-Slavery Society, and a powerful lobby of abolitionists petitioned Congress to abolish slavery in the District of Columbia. Cantankerous John C. Calhoun at once moved that the petition be laid upon the table as a foul slander of the South. In this same month, too, Henry Bouchard received the official title to the land and slaves left intestate by the death of Frank and Wilma Ellerby, and once again it was Amos Greer who brought him news of the possibility of still another acquisition of prime land and field hands.

On a chilly afternoon, Amos Greer rode back from a visit to the Bufferys and made his way into the fields where Henry Bouchard was supervising a group of slaves in preparing the furrows for a new planting of cotton. Mark had gone over to the acreage formerly owned by Granville Murton, his father having promised him that, in return for his labors, he would receive half the profits of the crop on these acres.

"That way," Henry said, "you'll be able to open your own account in Mobile and have money to buy a bed wench of your own without trying to steal Trish or anyone else from me."

"Afternoon, Mr. Bouchard." The overseer gave his employer a respectful nod and turned to watch the slaves ply their hoes over the winter's growth of weeds. Then, raising his voice to a snarl, he called, "Josiah, Enos, you two niggers look sharp there and put more back into those hoes or I'll brace you up with a good dose of cowhide, see if I don't!" Then, his eyes glinting with malice, he said: "Jim and Beth send their regards, Mr. Bouchard. They are mighty pleased, your bringing four bucks and a wench over to them last week and being so reasonable on the price. Jim told me a piece of news I thought you'd like to know about. You still want to get more land and slaves, don't you?"

"You know me well enough by now, Amos, that you don't have to ask such a question. A man can hold on to land and slaves when everything else starts to slip. What's all this about?"

"You didn't hear about old Alan Northby, then?" Greer pursued, savoring his news and wanting to whet his employer's interest.

"All I know is that Northby has about one hundred and fifty acres of pretty good land not too far from the river and two daughters he's been trying to marry off the last couple of years." Henry replied.

"That's the bare facts of it, yes. Only, you see, Jim Buffery hisself went over to old Northby couple of weeks back and made him an offer for the place. Northby's a widower. Came here from Mississippi, where his wife died of river fever. His father left him a sugar cane plantation down there, but Northby didn't care much for the work, sold it at a tidy profit and came up here about four years ago."

"I've never met the man, so you know more than I do. Amos. What are you getting at?"

Greer grinned crookedly. "Well, Northby wasn't what you'd call a sociable man. 'Cept he liked his wenches and his likker better'n anything else. Hired him a shiftless overseer who didn't know snap beans from carrots, from what Jim Buffery told me; lost a couple of his best bucks as runaways because the overseer was a mollycoddle. So the upshot was, Northby started losing a pile, couldn't get prime cotton and what he did get wasn't worth much down in Mobile when it got there. Now Jim Buffery tells me that the last year or so Northby started forgetting to pay his taxes, and just about drank and wenched up all he had in the bank. By the end of December he took one drink too many and keeled right over."

"So that means his daughters inherited, you're trying to tell me?"

"Now you've got a lawyer for a father-in-law, Mr. Bouchard, you know better than I do how things stand when there aren't any sons to take over. That's why Jim Buffery went over there to talk to the girls— they're more near like grown-up women than that, though—to see if he couldn't buy the place from them. They turned him down flat, were real nasty from what he told me. Uppity bitches, and then something else besides." Purposely, Green halted his narrative to study Henry Bouchard's face, then turned his attention back to the field hands and bawled out an order to put some muscle into their hoeing.

"All right, Amos," Henry Bouchard impatiently urged, "you're spinning it out like a man telling about how he caught the biggest fish ever. So the bank will probably appoint someone to be executor and take care of the daughters. And if the place is as rundown as you say, I'm not so sure I'd want it."

"You might just like putting the fear of God into those uppity bitches, Mr. Bouchard." Amos Greer hinted. He moved closer, and in a confidential whisper continued: "Now you remember what I found out about the Ellerbys—how Wilma's husband took his nigger foreman George to bed instead of that good-looking wife of his, till she figgered she'd wean George into poking the natural way?"

"Yes. What are you getting at, Amos?"

"Well now"—Greer gave him a broad wink—"Jim

368

Buffery about sized up those Northby gals. The reason their poor old daddy couldn't marry them off was, the way I hear tell, they've got no use for men no way. Maybe that was one reason old Northby took to likkering hisself up so much when he found he couldn't get them husbands. Now you don't think unnatural bitches like that are fit to hold land and slaves, do you?"

"They'd be better off in a crazy house than mixing with decent folks."

"You know, Mr. Bouchard, the first day I met you, I sized you up as a gentleman who knew what was what. You and I think alike in lots of ways, sir." Now the overseer's tone was ingratiatingly honeyed. "I know what I'd do if I was in your place."

"Tell me."

"Why, I'd ride over there one day and size up the place and then have me a chat with those gals—I'd be right nice, polite and all—and see if they wouldn't go along with the idea of selling out and leaving before all their neighbors found out about their dirty little ways. Then, if that didn't work, maybe we could have some night riders pay them a visit and show them they're not wanted around here. Tie them up and give them a good whuppin' and maybe some tar and feathers, then see if they wouldn't sell out fast."

Henry Bouchard's face was flushed and his eyes narrowed as he stared at the overseer. "How many slaves would you say they had, Amos?"

"Buffery figgers they've got about fifteen hands or so left. Plus maybe a couple of handsome wenches, their house niggers—and maybe those Northby gals even take them into their beds for all we know."

"Filthy whores—it's an abomination, Amos!"

"That's why I thought I would tell you what Jim Buffery found out."

"I might just ride over that way tomorrow and see what sort of price I could offer, Amos. No need for you to come along, though."

"Just as you say. I meant to ask you, is Zora giving satisfaction?"

"My son seems to be pleased with her, yes. Now that I've got Trish, I don't much mind."

"Well, you know when I brought Zora over and told you I wanted to work for you, I had an open mind about that Jamaican wench. I still do—and so far as I'm concerned, she's a nigger slave that belongs to you and your son, for all I care. But a man's got his needs, Mr. Bouchard, so I figgered you wouldn't mind if maybe I took one of the younger wenches for myself. I figger my helping you get the Ellerby place was worth a little dividend, and maybe if you pick up the Northby land too, you wouldn't mind my owning a wench for myself."

"Of course, Amos. Pick any one you like. You've made me a little money and you've helped me get what I want, so you're certainly entitled to a bonus, as you say. Now let's take a look at the far end of these fields. The cotton we've been getting from there the last year or two has been pretty shoddy."

"I know who's working down there, and you can bet I'll soon smarten up those lazy black bastards."

The Northby house, partly of pegged logs and partly of brick, was in even more dilapidated condition than James Buffery's farmhouse. Thin horizontal planks shuttered the windows from the outside, leaving only a scant inch between them for air and light. The flue of the stone chimney was badly cracked, and the roof was in need of reinforcement at its left wing. The ramshackle stable and cotton shed were in equally disreputable condition. Beyond and toward the north side of the fields, there were a dozen slave cabins of hewn logs. As Henry Bouchard dismounted from his horse, there was no boy to take the reins, and he tied them to a post a few yards from the house, then strode to the door and knocked loudly.

After a few moments, it was warily opened by a tall, sullen-faced brown-haired young woman about twenty-five, in a faded blue cotton dress. Her hair fell in a thick sheaf almost to the middle of her back, and was tied with a pink ribbon in the middle. Her gray-green eyes fixed him suspiciously as she demanded, "What do you want? If you've come about the job as overseer, you might as well come back next week when Mr. Jerrold leaves."

"My name is Henry Bouchard, Miss Northby, and I'm one of your neighbors upriver. Maybe you've heard of Windhaven Plantation."

"I s'pose." She shrugged. "Papa used to talk of what a fine spread you had, but he's gone now. And Mr. Jerrold says he won't wait for his money till the harvest this fall, so he's aimin' to leave right quick."

"I heard of the death of your father, and I came to extend my sympathy. Maybe we could talk a little—"

"About what?" Her voice and eyes were plainly hostile. Suddenly, from behind her, he heard another woman's voice call, "What does he want, Daisy?"

"It's a Mr. Bouchard, Sally Mae. You go back and finish your sewing, hear?"

"All right, if you say so, Daisy. What's he want?"

"I'm sorry to inconvenience you, Miss Daisy," Henry Bouchard said with a smile, "but I thought that perhaps I might make a good offer for your land and slaves."

"Oh, you're another one, I see." Her voice was icy now, and her full ripe lips tightened disdainfully. "I s'pose you'll be just like all those others who want to buy us out, just like a flock of vultures swooping down 'cause Papa's gone now. Like that awful fat man from Natchez who came here snooping around and wanted to know everything about us and then made us the silliest offer I ever did hear."

"That was Mr. Buffery, I imagine." Henry Bouchard was nettled by the comparison. "He mainly trains and deals in slaves, Miss Daisy. I'm a landholder, and I'm always looking out for a good piece of property, and of course some good strong workers to help produce on it. And I wouldn't cheat you, I can promise."

"I wouldn't take any man's promise, unless it was Papa's," Daisy Northby repeated. "If that's all you've got to say, I'm going to close the door now and you'd best take yourself off. And you don't have to bother trying to find us an overseer, either. I'd sooner use one of my own niggers than the white trash who've come callin' ever since they heard about Papa. I'll say good day to you right now." With this, she slammed the door, and he heard the fall of the heavy wooden bolt from the inside. His face darkened with anger as he strode back to his horse. *Uppity bitches,* he thought to himself, *thinking themselves so high and mighty when they can't even pay their overseer. And the way that Sally Mae sounded, the way she takes orders from that Daisy, it's probably true what Jim Buffery says about their being queer for each other. By God, Amos's idea about a visit from the night riders isn't so bad after all!*

"Pat Jerrold's in on this, Mr. Bouchard," Greer whispered as the four men dismounted and tied the reins of their horses to the branches of loblolly pine trees which shrouded the little glade several hundred yards to the north of the Northby house. "He's got a score to settle with those bitches, besides not getting his full pay. Made up to that younger one, Sally Mae, and she was sweet as honey to him for a spell, till he found out it was just to make him forget his wages."

Henry Bouchard squatted down in the dark woods, carefully tying a bandanna over his nose and mouth and knotting it at the back of his neck, while Buffery, Greer and the Northby overseer, a tall, gaunt-faced sandy-haired man in his early forties, followed his example.

"You know them better than we do, Jerrold"— Henry's voice throbbed with sadistic anticipation as he turned to the man at his left. "Are their niggers likely to give us any trouble?"

"Hell no," Patrick Jerrold muttered. "There's only about six or seven really prime workers, and they're in their cabins and likely to stay there. I've heard them talk about running away now that old Northby's gone, and they know I've given notice and pulled out. There's a couple nigger wenches, Suzy and Tansie, and they'll for sure be in the house when we get in there. Sally Mae and Daisy like fooling around with black

372

poontang. Oh sure, whatever Buffery told Greer and you, Mr. Bouchard, there's even more to it and I've seen it with my own eyes when those uppity bitches didn't think I had. That's when I knew I'd better get the hell out of there. You see, I was sort of sweet on that Sally Mae, and you'll see why, once you get a good look at her. She led me on, that queer little bitch, when I actually thought I'd marry her and maybe take over this place. But one night I was working on the records and the sisters didn't know I was around, and when I went by their bedroom, there they were naked, lyin' on top of each other and kissin' and rubbin'— well, it fair made me throw up. Then I heard Suzy telling Tansie one night what Miss Daisy made her do, and I knew this was no place for a man with balls."

"We'll tan their hides for them a mite," Amos Greer proposed, licking his thin lips with relish. "Maybe ride them on a rail too. And it'd serve them right if we all poked them, just to show them what women are meant fer, don't you think, Mr. Bouchard?"

Henry, trembling with a feverish lust he could hardly control, could only nod. His loins ached with a dull yearning at the very thought of the violence he and his companions intended for the lesbian sisters. And the reiterated refrain of *they're not decent, they deserve everything that's coming to them* ran through his mind as he gathered courage for the clandestine break-in on the unsuspecting women.

"There's a section of fence down there by the stable," Amos Greer whispered as he pointed toward the clearing beyond them. "That'll do fine for their ride after they've been peeled down and switched. Now then, Mr. Bouchard, so long as you git these uppity gals to sign over their land to you, you aren't particular whether we have a little fun with 'em, are you?"

"Of course not. They're unnatural, lawless creatures, and if this were a good-sized community, I'm sure they'd be tarred and feathered and driven out of town for good," Henry Bouchard declared. The blood was pounding in his veins, and the ache in his loins was savage now as he saw the glint of lamplight through

373

the chinks in one of the windows at the farther end of the Northby house.

"Think their field niggers'll come help rescue the gals, Amos?" Jim Buffery wheezed as he eased the knot of his bandanna which had begun to cut into his fat, sweating neck.

"Hell no, Jim, but if you're so all-fired worried, whyn't you take yourself a stroll down to those cabins and show 'em your rifle and tell 'em to stay put if they know what's good for 'em?"

"Good idea," the slave trader grunted and began to move, crouched Indian-style, in the direction of the cabins.

"Is there a ladder in that stable, Pat?"

"Sure is, Amos."

"That'll do just fine to tie those gals up to for the switching." Greer bared his teeth in a vicious grin. "All right now, the three of us'll go right on up to the front door bold as you please and take over. Look, there's old Jim scarin' the daylights out of those niggers. I'll make a sign to him to stay around the back just in case anyone tries to slip out of the house and get away. Let's go now!"

Henry Bouchard and the two overseers left their place of ambush and walked confidently toward the house, and it was Greer who pounded on the door with his fist. "Open up in there! Open up, I say!" he bawled.

After a few moments, the frightened voice of a young slave girl tremulously demanded, "Who—who dat makin' all dat noise out dere?"

"It's the law, that's who! Now open this door if you don't want trouble," Amos Greer commanded. Thrusting his hands into the pockets of his breeches, he pulled out the two pistols he had used on that fateful journey to the Creek village near Tuskegee. Behind the door, there was a frightened gasp, and then the sound of the wooden bolt being drawn aside. Jerrold turned his shoulder against the door and shoved vigorously, and another cry rose as the cowering young Angola

374

house servant sprawled to the floor, her eyes huge with fright, a hand at her gaping mouth.

"That's Tansie," Jerrold muttered to Henry Bouchard. "She'll take us to Sally Mae and Daisy straight off." Stooping, he seized the wrists of the teen-aged black girl and dragged her to her feet. She wore a pink night shift, and nothing more, which covered her from neck to ankles. Her face was winsome though angular, her body precociously ripe, as was evidenced by the jut of surprisingly sumptuous breasts thrusting against the thin cotton bodice.

"Where's your mistresses, Tansie?" the Northby overseer whispered. "You take us right to them, or you'll wish you had, so help me!"

"Dey's in—dey's in Miss Daisy's room, honest—doan hurt me, please doan!" Tansie whimpered.

"Go show us," Henry Bouchard hoarsely interposed, surveying the ripe hips and bosom of the Angola house servant.

Too frightened to speak, Tansie could only nod. Rubbing her bruised wrists, she hastened down the heavy-planked hallway toward the largest room.

"That used to be where old Northby slept," Jerrold whispered to his two accomplices. Then, striding forward and shoving the trembling Angola girl to one side, he flung open the door.

There was a shriek of mingled indignation and shame as Sally Mae, a honey-haired, buxom young woman of twenty-two, lay on her side, her white night shift rolled above her hips, in the embrace of a provocatively attractive Kru girl who was naked as the day she was born. Beside the bed, her back against the wall, petrified with shock, stood Daisy Northby, dressed in a blue frock which seemed to add fullness to her tall body.

"Well now, that's a pretty sight, that is," Amos Greer spat as he leveled the pistols at the couple. "I suppose that black bitch is Suzy, isn't that right?"

"It's Suzy for sure," Jerrold chuckled. "Out of bed, both of you!"

"Who—who are you men, breaking in this way? I'll

375

have the law on you—" Daisy Northby said in a shaky voice

"You might say we're the night riders of these here parts, m'am," Amos Greer snickered, boldly staring her up and down. "How come you're all dressed up? Or did we interrupt you before you could get peeled down and join that nigger-loving sister of yours?"

"How dare you! And you're masked, and you dare to point pistols at us—you'll pay for this!" Daisy Northby panted, her face ashen pale.

"Oh no, sister, you're the one's going to pay, you and your sister and that black bitch there. We're going to show you what we decent folks think of the filthy goings-on in this house. All right now, all three of you, out to the stable!"

He moved over to the bed and jabbed one of the pistols at the naked Kru girl, who, with a squeal of fright, scrambled out of bed and huddled, her hands trying to cover her thickly fleeced pubis.

"Sort of late for modesty, and modesty don't become a nigger bitch anyhow," Amos Greer chuckled. "All right, you Northby gals, Suzy'll lead the way out to the stable. It's a mite chilly tonight, but we guarantee you won't catch cold nohow! Move now, you damn bitches!"

"What about Tansie?" Jerrold muttered to Amos Greer.

"Hell, she's probably bedded down with the gals just like that Suzy there, so she's got her share of punishment coming. Bring her along," the overseer directed.

Jim Buffery was waiting for them at the stable as the naked Angola girl and the two Northby sisters stumbled ahead of Amos Greer, who swaggered behind them, brandishing the pistols, followed by Jerrold and Henry Bouchard. "Nobody's going to let out a peep about anything, boys," Buffery grinned evilly. "I put the fear of Gawd into all them niggers, and they'll stay put in the cabins till the Day of Judgment, I'm mighty certain. Wal now, if that ain't a purty sight, I never saw one before!"

Amos Greer nudged the Northby overseer. "Get a

lantern going so we can see to work by, Pat," he muttered, and Jerrold nodded and moved on into the stable. A few moments later, he called, "Everything's ready, ladder and all."

"Just you march in there, ladies," Greer drawled with another flourish of the pistols. "We'll give it to the niggers first, so Miss Sally Mae and Miss Daisy can sort of guess what we've got planned for them. Inside now, and no tricks. You ought to be grateful we don't shoot you down. It wouldn't be any great loss, scum like you living next to us decent folks!"

Jerrold had angled the heavy ladder against the wall of the stable just inside the door, while the flickering rays of a lantern which hung from a wooden peg nearby sufficiently illumined the scene which was to follow. From the stalls beyond, the soft whinnies of half a dozen horses accompanied the sobs of both Tansie and the naked Suzy, while Sally Mae stood with her head bowed and her face in her hands, sobbing convulsively. The older sister, her fists clenched at her sides, stared scornfully at the four masked marauders.

"Take the young nigger bitch that let us in first off," Amos Greer directed.

"Oh nassuh, ah didn't do nuttin'! Oh please, suh, doan whup me, Tansie, she's a good girl!" the teenaged Angola house servant whimpered.

With an oath, Buffery reached out and ripped off her shift to leave her naked, then shoved her toward the ladder where Jerrold waited to seize her wrists and drag them high, then bind them with strips of burlap as tight as he could. This done, he squatted down and bound her ankles in the same way. Tansie looked back over her shoulder, uttering a despairing wail as she saw fat James Buffery approach, brandishing a hickory switch.

"Found me a couple of these round the side of the barn when I was reconnoiterin', boys," he drawled. "Thought they might come in handy."

"You go ahead and give it to Tansie, I'll whup the one I found in bed with Miss Sally Mae," Amos Greer said.

Henry Bouchard's face was flushed as with fever, and he was trembling violently as he watched the Mississippian slave trainer place himself at the left of the naked girl bound to the ladder, raise the switch slowly to prolong her anguish, hover it in the air an instant, then slash it brutally across her opulently rounded young hips. It left an angry red weal on her brown skin, drew a piercing scream of torment: "*Aiiiii*, doan whup poah Tansie so hard, massa suh, I nebbah did nuttin' bad, hones' ah didn'!"

"You lying nigger bitch," Amos Greer growled, "I'll bet you went to bed with your mistresses here just like that Suzy—make her say she did, give it to her!" he directed the leering Buffery.

With wicked slashes of the switch all over her plump buttocks, the slave trainer at last forced plaintive, hysterical admissions of the sufferer's unnatural concubinage with the Northby sisters. Twenty stripes had drawn a trickle of blood from intersecting welts on her writhing posterior. Amos Greer turned to stare at Sally Mae and Daisy Northby, his lips curled: "If you two uppity white bitches was in a court of law right now and the judge heard what that black fancy girl of yours just said, you'd swing for it! You can count yourself lucky we aren't the murderin' kind, just fair-minded men who want to see justice done. Give her a couple more good licks, Jim, and make them hurt!"

Nothing loath, the corpulent slave trainer resumed the switching, till Tansie, dragging at her chafed wrists and flinging herself violently this way and that against the ladder, begged for mercy in heartrending, screeching tones.

Amos Greer made an impatient sign, and Jerrold took his clasp knife and cut the victim's bonds, letting her crumple on the floor of the stable. Then he came toward the shrinking, whimpering Suzy, seized her by a wrist and dragged her toward the ladder. In her terror, she held back, kicking and twisting and struggling, even clawing at him with her free hand, till Amos Greer stepped forward and, reversing one of the pistols in his hand, mercilessly clubbed the side of her head with the butt of the gun.

Half-conscious, she was swiftly bound to the ladder and Amos Greer handed his pistols to Henry Bouchard, who stood like one petrified, his eyes glazed and wide. "Hold these a spell till I wake that bitch up," the overseer directed.

Stooping to pick up a fresh switch, he lowered it, then cut it up savagely between the Kru girl's straddled thighs. Her body jerked fitfully, her head slowly rose, then her face turned back, contorted with anguish as a moan escaped her.

"I thought she was still alive, that tricky bitch. Now I'll make sure of it," Amos Greer promised. Moving from side to side, laughing in his sadistic fury, the overseer flicked the tip of the switch against the Kru girl's armpits and the sides of her high-perched breasts in a quick, merciless cadence aimed at sensitizing the victim's nerves and drawing her back to a full awareness of the suffering in store for her. Groaning and sobbing in pain, twisting and arching, then flattening herself so that her breasts mashed against the barrier of the ladder rung, Suzy fought her bonds as full consciousness returned and the searing, licking heat of the whistling, smacking strokes of the switch wrested uncontrollable gyrations from her tethered, naked, sweat-glossed body.

"You inhuman brutes, you animals!" Daisy Northby hissed at them, then moved toward her sobbing, more passive younger sister and whispered, "I'll see they're punished for this, honey, I promise I will!"

Amos Greer paused in his cruel work to leer at the two women and to summon Henry Bouchard to greater vigilance: "You'll just have to wait your turn, ladies. Watch those gals now, Henry, keep those pistols leveled on them and don't let them get away!"

"Henry—you're Henry Bouchard—you're the man who tried to buy this place!" Daisy Northby turned to confront him.

"Shut your mouth and stay right where you are," he warned, cocking the pistols, his eyes flicking back to watch Suzy's frenzied writhings under the switch which Amos Greer had now begun to ply against her shuddering thighs and buttocks.

Not till blood oozed from the crisscrossing weals on the Kru girl's flesh did Amos Greer lower his arm and fling away the frayed switch. "Cut her down and put her and that other nigger bitch on the rail. Their backs to each other—I've got a reason," he sniggered. Then, retrieving his pistols from Henry Bouchard who nervelessly let them go, trembling in every limb from the orgiastic fever of cruelty and lust which swirled in him, the overseer directed, "Time for you to go to work, Henry boy. Take Miss Sally Mae first and trice her up to that ladder. Pat and Jim will perch those niggers out in the nice cool air, and I'll bet it'll feel right good after that switching they got."

"Don't touch my sister—you animal, you cowardly skulking weasel!" Daisy Northby panted, clasping the sobbing Sally Mae in her arms and defying them with her blazing eyes.

"Let go of her, Missy," Amos Greer growled, "or by the eternal, I'll shoot you both down. Go take her, Henry. I don't reckon Miss Daisy would want her dear little sister to die, she's so fond of her and all—oh, I thought she wouldn't't!" The older woman uttered a despairing, defeated groan and stepped away.

Henry Bouchard seized Sally Mae by the wrists and dragged her to the ladder, binding her wrists and her ankles with frantic zeal. Then, setting both hands to the neck of her shift, he ripped and tore until the garment fell in tatters about her slim ankles, baring the ripe contours of her nakedness.

"We'll let Pat touch the younger one up a mite," Amos Greer pronounced sentence. "You can work on Miss Daisy, she knows you already, from what I just heard tell." He uttered a brutal guffaw. "She'll appreciate it from a fine gentleman like you, Mr. Bouchard sir."

Buffery and Jerrold stepped back into the stable, exchanging a conspiratorial, salacious grin. "They're mighty uncomfortable on their perches, Amos," the fat slave trainer announced. "It's getting right chilly, so the heat of the switchin' is gonna wear off right soon!"

"They'll have company before long," Greer promised. "All right, Pat, here's Miss Sally Mae, all nice and ready for you."

The Northby overseer grinned, stooped to pick up one of the pliant switches, whistled it in the air and then, stepping up close to the ladder, the fingers of his left hand twining into Sally Mae's honey-gold curls, yanked back her tear-stained, agonized face as he growled, "Now you're gonna wish you'd had me in bed instead of those nigger bitches, you uppity white trash you! Your poor pa is turning over in his grave, and I'll bet he'd be the first to say you and Miss Daisy have had this coming a good long while!"

Viciously, he cut the switch over her calves and lower thighs, then over back and shoulders while he punctuated the stinging lashes by yanking on her tumbled hair. As her sobs and tears and supplications rose, he at last stepped back and began to slash at the plump rotundities of her squirming posterior, angry crimson stripes instantly leaping onto the pale satin of that smooth skin. Daisy Northby watched, dry-eyed, fists still clenched, staring intently at Henry Bouchard, her lips moving as in silent prayer.

Finally, under a vicious stroke which sent the tip of the switch leaping down the crevice between her shuddering buttocks, Sally Mae Northby tilted back her tear-drenched face and shrieked, "Oh God, you're killing me, I'll do anything you want—only stop, oh dear God in heaven, please do stop!"

"I'll just hold you to that, Miss Sally Mae, m'am," Jerrold drawled as he flung away the switch. "Now I'll just perch you facing Suzy, so you two gals can kiss and cuddle some and get warmed up a mite before I see if you really mean what you just promised!"

Releasing the half-fainting girl, he carried her out to a section of fence nearly five feet high, made of split rails, the upper edge of each pointed and atrociously sharp. Tansie and Suzy already bestrode the topmost rail, ropes being passed round their sides to lash their

381

arms against them, while Buffery had hammered short stakes into each side of the fence, then tied the ankles of the naked house slaves to these. Thus the full weight of their bodies was forced down upon the triangular ridge of the rail, and their sobs and groans and convulsive squirmings as they desperately tried to ease the horrid chafing testified to the ordeal they were enduring.

Jerrold and Buffery lifted the weeping, pleading, naked Sally Mae astride the topmost rail facing Suzy, then wound ropes round both girls' backs as well as Sally Mae's arms which were forced against her sides. Her ankles were similarly bound to the stakes in the ground. "There now," Patrick Jerrold said thickly, "now you can finish the dirty business you were starting in bed when we came in, you bitches!"

Sally Mae uttered a horrified cry: "Oh my Gawd, don't leave me like this, it tears, it cuts me—oh Gawd, have mercy!"

But the two men laughed heartlessly and went back to the stable. Amos Greer had handed the pistols to Henry Bouchard and was now seizing Daisy Northby's wrists to drag her to the ladder. For a moment it seemed as if she would resist, and then, almost meekly, bowing her head, she let herself be led there, silently enduring the ignominy of having her wrists triced up high above her head and then her ankles.

The overseer proceeded to loft Daisy Northby's skirt, petticoats and chemise high above her waist, tucking them under her body so that they could not fall back down. Then he started with surprise: "Damnation, if she hasn't got on white breeches!" he said. "First time I ever saw anything like that on a woman's private parts!"

Daisy Northby was wearing long white cotton pantalettes, buttoned up all around, fitting snugly along her legs and reaching down to her ankles, around which the dainty frills at the end of this modish garment were tucked in with narrow pink ribbons.

"Maybe she's a man after all. Let's find out," Amos Greer drawled with a wink at florid-faced Henry

Bouchard, in whose trembling hands the pistols wavered.

Standing at her left side, he slipped his left hand down beneath the waistband of the garment. Daisy Northby sucked in her breath, closed her eyes.

"She's a woman, right enough," he laughingly declared. "Now let's get these trousers off so Mr. Bouchard can give her the switching she's got coming—and make it a real good one too, Mr. Bouchard sir."

With this, he ripped the garment down, and the spacious, tightly spaced oval hemispheres of Daisy Northby's buttocks contracted as with all her might she sought to diminish her nakedness before the men. Her skin was smooth and tawny, rippling with uncontrollable tremors as she lifted her face toward the roof of the stable and, the muscles in her cheeks and jaw flexing, awaited her ordeal.

Amos Greer stepped toward Henry Bouchard and took back the pistols, thrust them into his breeches, and moved back to the ladder. Once again, with a gloating, leering smile, he slid his left hand between Daisy Northby's clenching thighs. She stiffened, moaned, and then turned her face toward him and whispered something hoarsely, meant for his ears alone.

"Well now, d'you know what Miss Daisy just said to me, boys?" Amos Greer drawled. "She said I could take her to bed if I just wouldn't set her on that rail after she's had her switching. You know, Missy, I think I'll take you up on that. But you'd better know right here and now that if you don't give me a real good hot poke, back on that rail you'll surely go! All right, Mr. Bouchard, pick up one of those switches and warm her up for me, that's a fine fellow!"

Hugely amused at his own ingenious cruelty, the overseer laughed and winked at the other two men as he stepped back to watch, while Henry Bouchard, moving as in a dream, his eyes glowing and narrowed, stooped to pick up one of the hickory switches and took his place at the victim's left.

Henry raised his trembling hand, his eyes devouring the flinching buttocks and thighs of the victim. Then, with a muttered imprecation, he swept the hickory switch diagonally from right to left, imprinting a bright crimson streak from the edge of Daisy Northby's right hip across the tightening nether ovals and biting keenly against the base of the left buttock. Under the impetus of the stinging pain, she involuntarily flattened herself against the ladder, but only the hiss of sucked-in breath attested to her suffering. Eyes tightly closed, face upraised, fingers digging into her palms to sustain herself, she seemed to defy her executioner.

"Hell, Mr. Bouchard sir, she hardly felt that one!" Amos Greer's eyes glistened with lubricity. "You'll have to warm her up harder than that if you expect her to give me a good hot poke the way she promised!"

Yet Henry did not seem to hear this cynical exhortation: he saw only the spectacle of Daisy Northby's half-nakedness, fixed to the ladder with her clothes upturned about her waist and the expanse of tawny-skinned flesh. It was not so much Daisy Northby whom he flogged as it was his own defiant wife Sybella and the enticing young mulatto Celia, both of whom he was now denied. His lips trembling, his eyes burning with all the frustration dammed up in him, he swept the flexible switch again, again and again over Daisy Northby's buttocks and thighs, often turning to one side to administer a vicious backhanded cut which sent the tip of it curling round to bite against her belly and loins.

She ground her teeth savagely to suppress any outcry or plea for mercy, but she could not suppress the hoarse gasps and choking groans which the fiery kisses of the switch tore from her; nor could she control the spasmodic lunges, archings, flattenings and twistings against the ladder to which she was bound. After some twenty-five strokes, she turned her face away, the eyes huge and blurred with tears that had begun to trickle down her cheeks, her lips violently trembling, the wings of her nostrils dilating.

"That'll do fine, Mr. Bouchard sir," Greer panted,

stepping to the ladder and reaching up to cut the bonds round her slim wrists. "Now then, Missy, we'll go back to your room and just mind you keep your bargain, or you'll spend all night riding the rail!"

He freed her, and she slumped down to her knees, her trembling hands at once rushing to her furiously welted flesh to soothe it as best she could. The overseer laughed brutally and reached down to twist the fingers of his left hand into her disheveled tresses and to drag her to her feet with a shrill cry of pain. "Time enough for that when I've finished with you, bitch," he growled. "Now get moving back to the house!"

Releasing her hair, he applied a ferocious slap with his open palm against her welted buttocks, and Daisy Northby, again uttering a raucous cry of agony, stumbled out of the stable, her eyes haggard and tear-blurred as he stalked behind her like a predatory beast.

He turned back at the door to call out to his three accomplices, "When I've done with this bitch, you can have your turns, boys. But if you're too horny to wait, go ahead and take those two nigger gals down from the rail—they ought to be willin' enough by now to take on men instead of gals for a change!" Then, with a jeering laugh, he put his right palm against Daisy Northby's neck and shoved her forward back into the house.

Once inside the bedroom, he unbuttoned his shirt and opened his breeches to liberate his savagely swollen organ as he coarsely directed, "Just peel off all those duds, Missy! Then get yourself sprawled on that bed and ready—if your bottom bothers you, you can put that pillow under it—I've got some feeling left for an uppity white bitch like you!"

Daisy Northby fumbled with her shaky hands at the upturned, tucked-in dress, stays, petticoats and chemise, till they tumbled onto the floor beside her. In her stumbling march back to the house, the tattered remnants of the pantalettes which had festooned her ankles on the ladder had been left on the ground. Painfully scuffing off her slippers with one foot against the other, and grimacing with the pain the effort cost her, she placed her palms against the bed and slowly knelt on its edge, then dragged herself along and sank down on her back with a stifled cry of agony, closing her eyes and wincing with pain.

"No pillow? Yes, that's better now, you'll feel your first good poke from a man a lot more that way," he mocked his victim. Moving to the side of the bed, he stared greedily down at her sprawled nakedness, his stubby fingers squeezing and pinching her calves and the insides of her thighs as she dug her fists down into the bed beside her and turned her face to one side, a long shudder of revulsion and suffering rippling through her. Then, with a hoarse grunt of anticipation, Amos Greer flung himself down upon her, his hands squeezing her breasts, as he probed against the thick dark-brown fleece. Daisy Northby stiffened, her eyes opening, feverish with pain and loathing, arching as she felt the ruthless penetration.

"There now," he exultantly gasped, "now you know what real pokin's like, don't you, Missy? Now show some life, or when I'm done with you, you'll sit on the rail and I'll take Sally Mae down and give her just as good as I'm going to give you, you hear?"

"Yes—aah—please—not so hard—you're hurting —oh my God—aaaah!" Daisy Northby moaned. Nonetheless, as if cowed by his merciless threat, she managed to crook her right arm over his muscular shoulders and to lock her calves over his.

"Now that's more like it, gal. Sure, all you ever needed was a man to show you how, isn't that it?" he hoarsely bragged, plunging back and forth and sparing her nothing.

Through her glazed eyes, Daisy Northby saw him leer, then bury his face against one of her breasts, his lips nuzzling the dusky-coral bud of her nipple. Stealthily she reached her left hand under the rumpled pillow, drew out a pair of long scissors and with all her strength stabbed the points into the side of his neck.

Amos Greer uttered a gurgling shriek, straightened and wrenched himself out of the shuddering naked woman, clapping his hands to the bleeding wound, trying to extract the weapon, his eyes bulging, staring in horrified surprise at Daisy Northby's contorted face. "You bitch you—what have you done—"

Sitting upright and tearing out the scissors, gripping them with both hands, she stabbed again, upward. The overseer uttered a groan as blood spurted from the arterial wound, clapped his trembling fingers to the gleaming blades, his eyes rolling to the whites, then toppled to one side and off the bed to sprawl lifeless on the floor.

Amos Greer's agonized shriek had brought Henry Bouchard back to the house: irresolute as to how to satisfy his lusts, he had turned away from the fence on which Sally Mae and Tansie and Suzy were fettered, while Jerrold and Buffery had begun to release the young black house slaves. As he entered the bedroom, Daisy Northby had dragged herself out of bed, retrieved her crumpled dress and was pulling it on over her head.

"Oh Jesus Christ, Amos—" he shouted and ran to the fallen overseer. He bent down, pressing his palm against Amos Greer's left chest, then slowly looked up and in a hoarse, accusing voice, exclaimed, "You've killed him! My God, you've killed him! You'll hang for this, you and your sister. I'll swear to it in court, Miss Daisy, see if I don't!"

"He—he forced me—I had to—". she whimpered. She stared down at Amos Greer's body, and covered her face with her hands and began to sob.

"It'll be your word against the three of us," Henry Bouchard said, glancing down first at Greer and then at the cowering woman. "And when the three of us tell the judge how we found you and your sister and those nigger girls in bed, and how we made you a decent offer so scum like you would leave these parts for good, and you took those scissors and killed the best overseer I ever had, the very least you can expect is to have your neck stretched and Sally Mae locked up for a long spell! That's the way it'll be, Miss Daisy!"

"Not—not S—Sally M—Mae—oh my God, you

couldn't be so cruel, Mr. Bouchard——" she pleaded. He had pulled off the bandanna before entering the house, and he confronted her now, smiling coldly, standing like an avenging advocate with his hands on his hips.

"I might just reconsider if you'd sell me the place, Miss Daisy," he said after a long moment.

"If—if I do, you—you promise you won't let those men hurt my sister?" she faltered.

"I'll say yes to that. But those nigger gals, I won't be able to stop Jim and Pat from having a little fun with them. All right, Miss Daisy, let's talk business. I'll give you my draft on my Mobile house for three thousand—that's for the land, the house and all the niggers you've got. You'll take it, and then you and Miss Sally Mae will start packing and be ready to leave by sundown tomorrow. If you're not gone when we come over here again, you know what's going to happen."

Daisy Northby groaned, and then, her face haggard and wet with tears, resignedly nodded. "All—all right, Mr. Bouchard. And now, for God's sake, won't you please go back to them and have them let Sally Mae go?"

"Why sure, Miss Daisy, I guess I can do that much for you. I'm going now. I'll be back tomorrow afternoon with the draft, and I hope to see you both packed and ready to leave by then, remember." He made her a mockingly courtly bow, then turned on his heel and strode out of the bedroom.

388

CHAPTER TWENTY-SIX

A week after Henry Bouchard's nocturnal call upon the Northby sisters, Grover Mason recorded the deed by which Daisy Northby had surrendered complete title to the plantation house, the land and the slaves. The two sisters left for New Orleans on the steamboat *Tensaw* by dusk on the day following their forced acceptance of the sale. At Henry Bouchard's suggestion, Jerrold agreed to stay on as overseer, and was paid his overdue wages to seal the bargain. The two slave girls, Tansie and Suzy, threatened with implication in Daisy Northby's murder of Amos Greer (whose body had been buried in an unmarked grave behind the stable), fearfully swore that they would obey the orders of the new master of the plantation, and young Mark Bouchard chose the younger Tansie as his personal bed wench, while his father compelled Suzy, on the very evening of the day on which Grover Mason had given him back the registered deed of ownership, to come to what had been the Northby sisters' bedchamber and submit herself carnally to him.

March was warmer than usual, and it was marked by memorable events taking place far beyond the acres which Henry Bouchard so obsessively coveted. On March 2, Texas declared its independence from Mexico, and four days later General Santa Anna massacred the garrison of the Alamo at San Antonio. On the fifteenth, the United States Senate confirmed the appointment of Roger B. Taney as Chief Justice of the Supreme Court. Two days later, the Republic of Texas adopted its constitution and legalized slavery.

On this sunny Friday afternoon of the last week of March, Arabella Bouchard walked out to the kitchen where Mammy Clorinda was busy mixing a batch of biscuits and making her special Creole red-eye gravy for the ham that was basting on a spit turned by Nancy. Timmy, the pet raccoon, followed its young mistress, a habit which the good-natured cook regarded with no little apprehension when the raccoon decided to inspect her tidily arranged kitchen. Eyes rolling, moving with alacrity, she kept out of Timmy's way till at last Arabella, having filched a cornmeal cake and divided it with her pet, announced that she and Timmy were going for a walk around the edge of the fields. When she returned, she expected at least two biscuits liberally smeared with honey.

"Dat fine foah you, Miss Bella," Mammy Clorinda retorted, scowling at the raccoon which had sat up on its hind legs to accept a piece of cake, "only Ah asks you as a special favor, Miss Bella, please doan bring dat 'coon back wid you nohow! You know how it plumb scares de libin' daylights outa me, honey!"

"My goodness, such a fuss over Timmy, I do declare!" the little girl sniffed. "Why, he's neater and cleaner than lots of people, and 'sides, you know perfectly well he never bothers anybody."

"Dat mebbe so, chile," Mammy Clorinda dubiously granted, "but dat 'coon he got claws 'n teeth ah doan nebba wanna feel, not no way, Miss Bella!"

"Oh, all right," Arabella condescendingly replied with a flounce of her pretty curls, "I'll let Timmy in the front door, and then I'll come back round for my biscuits and honey, and you'd better not forget them either, Mammy Clorinda!"

"Ah ain't likely to fergit nuttin', Miss Bella, not when you comes raidin' mah kitchen all day long. Ah swears Ah nebbah did see a l'll gal eat so much 'n not get fat in all mah life, an' dat's a fac'!"

But Arabella and the raccoon had already left the

kitchen on their way to the fields. The sun was warm, but the air sticky with the moisture of the rainy season. In the fields, the hands were working to clear the rows of weeds and to break up the rich soil to give the cotton plants room to flourish. Matthew Forsden, wearing a black hat with wide brim, an open-necked cotton shirt and breeches and boots, stood talking to old Zeb, a Hausa who had worked for Lucien Bouchard for more than twenty-five years, and who was in charge of the acres planted with corn. Arabella called out to him and waved, and both the overseer and Zeb halted their conversation and turned to wave back, both smiling at the pretty little girl in her pink cotton dress and new lawn petticoat.

"Let's go down by the creek, Timmy," Arabella called, pointing in the direction she meant to take. The raccoon turned at the sound of her voice, sniffed the air and made a characteristic squeal, which Arabella had already translated as raccoon language for assent. She no longer bothered with the leash and collar, for Timmy followed her as devotedly as any pet dog.

"Oh, there's some pretty blue flowers growing over there right by the bank of the creek, let's go pick some for Mama!" Arabella suddenly exclaimed, and hurried toward a patch of bluebells near a hollowed-out log a few feet from the edge of the bank of Pintilalla Creek, which marked one boundary line of Lucien Bouchard's original acreage.

As she stood by the nearest flowers, there was a hissing sound, and suddenly Timmy sprang, darting its head forward and seizing a slithering water moccasin which had just emerged from the shelter of the log into the bed of flowers.

Arabella screamed and stepped back. "Timmy, what is it? Oh, Timmy, be careful, honey—oh help, someone! Mr. Forsden, come quick!"

At her cry, the English overseer hurried toward the creek just as Sybella, who was pruning her garden and heard her daughter's call for help, started running in the direction of the little girl's voice.

Arabella backed away, a hand at her mouth, as the

raccoon emerged out of the clump of flowers, dragging a four-foot-long water moccasin whose neck it held clamped between its sharp teeth, then began to shake as a terrier might a rat. "Miss Arabella, that was a mighty brave thing for Timmy to have done!" Matthew Forsden gasped as he squatted down beside the little girl. "It's all right, I can see it's dead—Timmy broke its neck with one bit and he didn't get bitten at all. He'll be just fine!"

"Oh, I was so scared, I couldn't see right off what it was. Ugh—that nasty old snake—drop it, Timmy!" Arabella grimaced with repugnance, tears of relief in her eyes as she saw that the raccoon was apparently unhurt.

"Oh God, it might have bitten you, Arabella dear!" Sybella was pale and trembling.

"I—I wanted to pick you some flowers, Mama," Arabella sobbed, running to her mother and flinging her arms around her.

"That was so sweet of you, darling." Sybella stroked the little girl's head till her sobbing diminished. "Can you—can you get that awful snake away from Timmy, Mr. Forsden?"

"I'll try, Mrs. Bouchard. Come on, Timmy, here, I've got a nice piece of corn pone in my pocket, brought especially for you." Smiling, his voice gentle, he took out a broken bit of corn pone, offering it to the raccoon. Timmy stood his ground, warily regarding the relatively strange intruder into his finite world, but curiosity and appetite overcame his suspicions. Opening his jaws, he dropped the lifeless snake and trotted toward the overseer, sniffed at Matthew Forsden's fingers a moment, then accepted the tidbit and whisked his tail in appreciation. Forsden moved quickly toward the water moccasin, reached to one side for a broken branch and gingerly prodded it. "Thank God it's dead," he breathed. "That raccoon acted just like a mongoose, Mrs. Bouchard. It was a good thing for Miss Arabella Timmy's so fond of her and knew the danger."

"You see, darling," Sybella murmured as she stroked her daughter's head, "friendship is a wonderful

392

thing in this world. And sometimes the best friendship of all is between a person and an animal because, you see, the animal can't talk and think the way a person can, but Timmy understood what was going to happen and so he saved you. He was saying thank you for being so nice to him, dear."

Matthew Forsden picked up the dead reptile and remarked, "It's an old one and it was going to shed pretty soon. I'll just look around that log and see if it has a mate. Sometimes they come in pairs, you know." Armed with the broken branch, he carefully approached the log and crouched down to peer into it. "No, thank goodness, it's the only one around. I'll have some of the hands take their hoes and wear their boots and go looking around the bank all the way down to make sure there aren't any more lurking around here, Mrs. Bouchard."

"Thank you, Mr. Forsden," Sybella said gratefully.

He turned back to the patch of bluebells, and then, with an embarrassed smile, impulsively bent and picked a bouquet. "Your daughter meant to bring you these, Mrs. Bouchard, so I just did it for her," he explained.

Sybella's eyes widened, and her cheeks turned a becoming crimson as she accepted the bouquet. "How very thoughtful of you, Mr. Forsden! Thank you very much." Then, to Arabella, "Let's go back into the house, shall we, darling?"

"I told Mammy Clorinda I wanted at least two of her hot biscuits covered all over with honey. Maybe now I'll have three!" the little girl announced as she strode back toward the kitchen. Matthew Forsden and Sybella Bouchard exchanged a smiling look. Her gaze suddenly lowered as the color continued to burn in her tawny cheeks.

A violent thunderstorm raged on the night of April 21st, and a sharp crack of thunder punctuated with jagged bolts of lightning which streaked the leaden sky seemed to shake the roof of the brick and log house in which Henry Bouchard had been living these past few

months. Perhaps the storm was an omen, for by nightfall hundreds of miles away at San Jacinto, General
Samuel Houston had just won a decisive victory over
the Mexican troops commanded by Santa Anna. But in
the darkness of the rumpled bed, Zora Devlin, her lithe
naked body entwined atop Henry Bouchard's, saw the
storm rather as an affirmation of her new master's
ruthless strength.

"Your son's fine, Mr. Bouchard," she slyly underlined that humble word which is the ever-glib avowal
of the complaisant slave, "but I'd just as soon you
knew I'd much rather have you take me. I declare,
master, you've fair neglected me all these weeks, with
those nigger wenches you got from the Northbys and
that Trish you bought from fat old Jim Buffery. Now,
make your slave real happy, master, 'fess up, now that
we're all alone in bed by ourselves, aren't I better servicin' you than those young nigger gals? Aren't I, master?"

As if to encourage his answer, she laughed softly
and, digging her fingernails into his shoulderblades,
arched herself so that the tumescent points of her
dusky nipples rubbed tantalizingly against his chest.

His fingers dug into her resilient buttocks as he
pulled her back down to him. "What are you aiming
at, Zora? You're a Jamaican witch, and for all I know,
you might be trying your voodoo tricks to put a spell
on me."

"No spell, master," she whispered, nibbling his ear-
lobe with her strong teeth, then flicking the tip of her
tongue deep into his ear, till he groaned and writhed
with sensual torment. "Just my bare skin, which is all
yours, master, you know that. I am just as frisky
pleasurin' a real strong man like you as any of those
stupid nigger gals, now you know I am. You know you
like me to do this—and this too, don't you, master?"
she said, slipping her left hand down to his buttocks
and nudging a fingertip toward the crevice while her
other hand moved between their bodies to pinch the
hilt of his manhood between right thumb and forefinger.

"You're a randy bitch, and you want something—out with it, Zora! Yes, damn you, you know what I like and you're still frisky enough for my fancy. Want a new dress or maybe have me build you another room onto this house so you can preen yourself in it?"

"Oh no, master," she murmured, brushing his lips with hers, pressing herself down hard against his body till he stiffened and groaned with the nearness of tumultuous fulfillment. "That great big house upriver, what I wouldn't give to have just a tiny l'il room in it so's my master could come visit me nights like this—that's what I'd really like, master! If I pleasure you good, can't I have it?"

"You mean you'd like me to put you up at Windhaven, eh, Zora?" His hands squeezed her buttocks fiercely, and she gasped as she felt her own tides respond to his, then nodded and, fusing her lips to his, furled her tongue deep inside his mouth.

"Well, by God, why not?" he growled. "Even that young pup of a son of mine has been telling me I'm master of Windhaven now that Father's gone. And a wife's duty is to obey her husband, isn't it? Yes, I'll go back there. I'll give the orders there from now on. Soon I'll have more land and slaves than Father ever dreamed of having, my own land that I can do with as I please. Well, I'll do it, Zora. Now, does that satisfy you, you Jamaican bitch?"

"Oh yes, master, I knew the minute I set eyes on you when poor old Amos brought me over to see you that you'd do right by your Zora," she whispered. Then, upon a sudden clap of thunder, she clutched him fiercely, panting, "Take me, use me, I'm your slave, Mr. Bouchard master!"

CHAPTER TWENTY-SEVEN

"It's Daddy come back home again!" Fleurette cried as she came out of the stable toward the chestnut mare from which her father was just dismounting in the yard. Jimmy and Djamba followed her, and the young Kru stableboy, grinning a welcome, hastened to take the reins and lead the mare back to a stall.

"Fleurette, sweetheart, how you've grown—you're a big girl now!" Henry Bouchard beamed as he bent down to kiss the little auburn-haired girl, then straightened: "Where's your mother, darling?"

"In the kitchen, with Mammy Clorinda, Daddy. Bella's out walking with Timmy. I'll go call her if you want."

"In a little while, honey. First I want to see your mama." Henry Bouchard eyed the towering young Mandingo who stood nearby, smiling and attentive. "Well, Djamba, been behaving yourself?"

"Yes, master," Djamba dutifully inclined his head. "Everything fine at the house. The horses, they are fine too, master."

"Well, see that you look after mine. I suppose Mr. Forsden's out in the fields?"

"Yes, master, he work very hard. All the hands, they say he a good man, master."

Henry scowled, resenting the Mandingo's unasked-for comment on the overseer. But Djamba met his gaze without fear or insolence, his attitude one of respectful

397

attention. With a shrug, he declared, "Rub my mare down. Not too much water but plenty of oats, you hear, Djamba?" Then, without waiting for a reply, he strode off toward the kitchen at the back of the château.

Luke had gone to Mobile the week before and brought back not only supplies but also a dozen sows and four boars which had been shipped back in the hold of the *River Queen*. Several of the field hands, under Matthew Forsden's supervision, had constructed a sturdy hog pen just behind the stable, and Mammy Clorinda was ecstatic at the prospect of plenty of bacon, lard and sweet roast pork for the house, with chitterlings in prospect for the slaves. On his way to the kitchen, Henry heard the squealing, and grimaced with disgust: "What the devil—we Bouchards aren't like dirty Missouri or Ohio pig breeders. More of Luke's newfangled notions, I'll wager."

Sybella, in a strikingly attractive dress of sage-green brocade, with leg-of-mutton sleeves very full above the elbow and reinforced with pads of cotton which kept their puffiness from collapsing, stood talking earnestly with the portly cook as Henry Bouchard entered the kitchen. Sybella's skirt was wide, kept extended by underskirts of crinoline, and descended to within an inch of the floor. Her auburn hair was caught in a Grecian knot at the back, and in front she wore the false curls that had just become the latest style, held on by hairpins.

"Afternoon, Sybella," he said gruffly.

"Land's sakes, effen it ain't Massa Henry!" Mammy Clorinda exclaimed.

Sybella caught her breath, then came forward to her husband, who took her hands in his, pulled her to him and kissed her hard on the mouth. "I'm back if you'll have me, Syb," he muttered.

Her face colored hotly and, seeing that Mammy Clorinda was all ears and eyes, murmured, "Wait till I finish giving Mammy her instructions, Henry, and I'll join you in the sitting room. You're looking very well."

"You're looking damnably irresistible, Syb," he said, and gave her another kiss, but this on the cheek as he released her. "I'll see you in a few minutes, then. And you, Mammy, you're fatter than ever."

"Hee-hee-hee, Mistah Henry, suh, dat 'cause Ah thrives on mah own cookin', dat's why, suh!" she rejoined.

A few minutes later, as Henry Bouchard paced up and down in the sitting room, Sybella entered, her face grave. "Did you mean what you said, Henry, about coming back?"

"Of course. I'm still your husband, aren't I?"

"Of course you are." Her brows arched in a disapproving frown. "I never gave you reason to suppose otherwise, did I?"

Now it was Henry Bouchard's turn to frown. "Damn it all, Syb, I didn't come back to start an argument. I've picked up some other land and I've been busy getting it in order. But mainly, I missed you."

"Did you really, Henry?" Her voice was impersonally cool.

"What's got into you, Syb?" he said, glaring. "Of course I did. You're still the most attractive woman I know. Besides, I'm master of Windhaven now and I think it's time I come back here and made sure everything's in order."

"You can be sure it is, Henry. Mr. Forsden's the nicest, most capable man. And the girls just adore him. Poor little Arabella was so scared when Timmy found a cottonmouth near some flowers she was going to pick for me, and he killed it, and Mr. Forsden talked to her so nicely she got all over her fear."

"Bella wasn't hurt, was she?" he asked.

"No, thank God, Henry. And Luke's been to Mobile and brought back some hogs so that we can have plenty of fresh pork and good smoked bacon and lots of lard for Mammy's wonderful cakes and pies."

"I know, I heard the racket they were making when I came looking for you," he said glumly. "By the way, you won't have to worry about Amos Greer any more. He's dead and gone, and Pat Jerrold is going to work the Northby place I just picked up and look after some of my own land as well."

"Dead?" Sybella's eyes widened. "How did it happen?"

Henry Bouchard shrugged noncommittally. "He had a hunting accident. Thought he'd got himself a she-bear, but she was only shamming and clawed him."

Sybella shuddered. "That's dreadful! I detested him, it's true, but I wouldn't have wanted him to end up like that. And I'll say something else to you, Henry, though I know one shouldn't speak ill of the dead—frankly, I'm glad he isn't around you anymore. He was an evil, harmful man and I'm sure that being around him did you no good."

"Damn it, Syb, there you go again, lecturing me. Don't you think I'm capable of making my own decisions and acting the way I want without any advice from anybody like Amos Greer?"

"I do indeed, Henry, but when you were back by yourself in your own house and had only him to suggest things to you, I'm sure you felt free to indulge your decisions, as you call them."

His face was red and his lips compressed with anger, but he controlled himself with an effort. "Syb, honey, I didn't come back to start a fight with you, truly I didn't. Let's make it up to each other, let me come back here and run Windhaven. It's my birthright, anyway, you know."

"Of course it is. You're your father's only son, Henry, and I know it was his dream of seeing you care for Windhaven and make it strong and lasting in the years ahead. But that didn't mean just possessions and luxuries. It meant happiness, because that's what he was always seeking. It wasn't at all because he wanted soft comforts for himself that he had this big château built. No, if he'd been born in a hovel back in France, I think he'd have had the same kind of place built here just to remind him of his first home where he knew happiness and love."

"We can be happy together, Sybella. You know I still want you." Henry Bouchard moved closer to her, his voice husky with yearning. "Even one of those New Orleans fancy girls can't please a man the way you can, Syb, when you've a mind to."

Now her face flamed and her eyes lowered before his ardent gaze. "I'm your wife, Henry, and I'm flattered to know that my husband wants me. But maybe, like every woman, I'm just a little jealous, yes, jealous even of the wenches you might take to your bed for only a single night. If we're to be together again, Henry, I want to be yours, I don't want to share you with any slave girl."

Henry made an impatient gesture with his hand. "Damnation, Syb, you just had your thirty-fourth birthday—"

"Which, by the way, you happened to forget," she interposed with an ironic smile.

"I—well, yes I did, but I'll bring you something from New Orleans to make up for it, you'll see," he blustered. "What I'm getting at is, you're no child any longer, and you know that a man's got needs. And taking a nigger wench to bed has nothing to do with a man's loving his wife."

"But I suppose if I took a black lover, I'd never hear the last of it from you, Henry," she said, her lips curling in a mocking smile.

"Good Christ, how can you compare that—how can you even say such a thing, Syb?" he angrily exclaimed. "A man's wife's supposed to be beyond reproach, she doesn't think such things, let alone say them!"

"It seems, Henry, that the rules of the game are different for men and women. And your sex appears to have made them all. You thought I was brazen on our wedding night because I honestly loved you and I'd never had a man before and I was eager to learn what it would be like with my own husband, my very first lover. Now you're shocked because it's all right for you to talk about sleeping with a black girl and then coming to me and expecting me to love you as if nothing had happened, but when I say that I might just try one time with a black man, you're outraged. Really, sometimes I think there's no understanding a man," she de-

401

clared, her eyes sparkling with the pleasure of this verbal duel between them.

"You mean, there's no understanding a woman," Henry countered. Then, with another ineffectual wave of his hand, he earnestly pursued, "Come now, Syb, let's have a truce between us at least. What's done is done. I'm not denying I've made mistakes, but at least Amos Greer is gone for good."

"And you still have never heard a word about Manoka and Shonanoy?"

"I'm sorry, no, Syb." He looked quickly away to escape her searching look; it was far too troubling a reminder of the guilty secret he had kept from her all this time. "Look, let's be friends again, let me come back to stay. I'll even help with the land here, because Pat Jerrold and Mark and a few of the better niggers can handle the other land well enough."

"If you do come back to stay, Henry, you'll bring no black wenches with you, that I insist on."

"All right! You know I want you and I need you, Syb. I'll let them stay where they are." He permitted himself a cynical grin: "I rather imagine Mark will see that they aren't neglected."

"I'm not exactly happy about leaving Mark away from Windhaven like that, as young as he is, letting him think he can do anything he pleases, Henry."

"He's feeling his oats, that's all. Let the boy alone for a bit, he'll settle down. I've been after him to marry Maybelle Williamson."

"She isn't exactly the best choice for Mark, and you know it. You'd like him to get hold of her share of her father's property—admit it, Henry."

"All right, since we seem to be in a mood for confessing, I'll admit it gladly. The boy needs a stake of his own, he wants to earn his own money raising cotton. It's not a bad idea at that, Syb; he'll have responsibilities and they'll make him grow up faster."

"Well, we can discuss that at another time. But you know very well he's headstrong and practically lawless, especially if he'll be all to himself with all those slaves to lord it over."

402

"Oh Syb, be nice now. Admit you've missed me a little," he murmured as he came to her, took her in his arms. She stiffened a moment, and then passively let him kiss her on the mouth. Gradually, she began to respond, closing her eyes and putting her arms around his shoulders. When it was over, she murmured, "Of course I've missed you. What wife who ever loved her husband wouldn't, for all his faults? Windhaven needs you, Henry, and the girls need you too. And so do I."

Zora Devlin sat alone, tailor fashion, naked in the bed which she had often shared with Henry Bouchard in his little house. Around her slim neck was a wreath made of glossy green leaves, and in her lap was a clay bowl in which leaves, bits of corn and millet were strewn. In her hands was a shapeless mass of red clay which she now began to knead and then to form into the figure of a woman. As it took shape, she raised her dark eyes to the ceiling and began a wordless incantation, swaying to and fro as, with the nail of her right forefinger, she traced a woman's face upon the head of the clay figurine.

Then, in a vibrant, low voice she murmured, "Oh Damballa, aid me. Erzulie, goddess of love, grant me your power. To you, mighty Damballa, I offer this *ouanga* as sacrifice. Take this woman, and you, sweet Erzulie, let me replace her in that great house. Let me hold him with my body and my voodoo spells, and I will sacrifice to both of you forever."

She lifted the clay figurine in her left hand, her face twisted in hatred, and then she jabbed her right forefinger into the left breast. "Thus may she perish, oh Damballa, swiftly and without pain—for I do not know her and she has not harmed me, but she stands between me and the master who can free me and make me his woman. Let it be so, and in that great house I will build a shrine to both of you, god of death, goddess of love."

There was a sudden peal of thunder in the silent night, and Zora Devlin smiled as she flung the *ouanga*

403

into a corner of the room and lifted the bowl in both hands toward the sound of that thunder.

It was the evening of May 25th, that memorable day on which the venerable John Quincy Adams made his great speech in the House of Representatives opposing the annexation of Texas if that action meant war with Mexico. The weather was oppressively warm, and flashes of heat lightning capriciously streaked the dark sky, seeming to concentrate over the towering red bluff downriver of the majestic château of Windhaven.

Henry Bouchard had made a temporary peace with Sybella. Contrite, he had moved back into his old room and, for a week, contented himself with being solicitously affectionate toward Fleurette and Arabella, even making a show of playing with Timmy and Sassy. He had conferred with Matthew Forsden in the fields, though he could not suppress his distaste at the sight of the hogpen and the many sections allocated to vegetables instead of cotton. There had been more rain this spring than was usual, some of it so heavy that it had damaged many of the cotton pods. To his mind, this was proof that the policy of planting cotton sparsely was unsound, since the more one grew, the more one could be sure of harvesting for good prices in the fall regardless of the adverse elements which could not be controlled even by the most skillful labor.

He had also taken more pains with his appearance than was his wont, shaving and bathing much more frequently and changing his shirts and linen. His black hair had begun to be streaked here and there with gray, yet it seemed to add the distinction of maturity to his aggressive features and his stocky figure. About ten days after his return to Windhaven, he had come unexpectedly to Sybella's room and there, complimenting her on her loveliness, holding her hands and kissing her with remarkable restraint and exemplary tenderness, had effected their conjugal reconciliation. Sybella hoped that this time she might conceive; last year, in spite of her prayers that another child would at last solidify their union and bring Henry to a greater sense of responsibility for his family, that hope had been illusory.

In yielding to him that night, Sybella had experienced the nostalgic bittersweetness of the past, had recalled the early days of their marriage when each was new and surprising to the other and there had been a zestful, however challenging, unison to their lovemaking. She had ardently clung to him, an unspoken prayer on her lips that old Lucien might somehow know of the restoration of this stormy marriage. In the fierce primal ecstasy which Henry's virility brought her, she could not completely put aside the grieving sorrow for Thomas and his niece and nephew in whose lives her husband had been so inexplicably involved. And, because above all else she was a passionate, life-loving woman, there entered into her thoughts, even at the moment of supreme carnal rapture, the memory of Djamba's selfless heroism and the gracious kindness of Matthew Forsden toward her and little Arabella.

All this afternoon, indeed, Henry had worked in the fields of Windhaven, and when Sybella had gone out, just before twilight, to call Fleurette and Arabella back from their excursions with Sassy and Timmy, she had seen him squatting down beside the English overseer, inspecting the thriving rows of plants and earnestly conversing. A swell of happiness rose in her, seeing him so occupied. Perhaps at last his restless nature was becoming mellowed; after all, he was forty now, at a time when the fierce aggressive passions of youth and the driving ambitions of a man's mature years began to be eased. There were still good years ahead for both of them, and, when all was said and done, he was still the only man she had ever loved. They could be wonderful years in store if he would only learn to be content with what he had and what could be his without the selfish taking of it. As the girls came hurrying toward her, she again looked out at the fields and smiled, then put her arms around Fleurette and Arabella and walked back to the château. Perhaps he would come to her tonight. *Let it be without warning, as it was that wonderful time last week when he came unannounced like an un-*

405

certain lover afraid of being rejected and made me his,
she thought to herself.

Celia slept fitfully in her room in the right wing of
the second floor, the very room into which Mammy
Clorinda had smuggled her that November night when
Henry Bouchard had brought her back from New Orleans, a comely bed wench bought on Pierre Lourat's
auction block and destined to satisfy her virile new
master. Little Prissy slept beside her in a crib which
Thomas had fashioned just before his death. As Celia
turned restlessly on her pillow, the distant mellow
chimes of the old grandfather clock sounded midnight
in the foyer of the château.

The door stealthily opened, and was closed again as
silently. A shadowy figure moved near the wide bed,
paused to contemplate the outline of Celia's lithe young
body curled on its side, the thin cotton sheet nestling
the sweep of haunch and thigh.

On a chair near the bed, her red calico dress and
undershift lay draped. In the still darkness, the
shadowy figure moved toward it, extending a hand to
touch the draped garments.

Then he unfastened the robe which alone concealed
his nakedness, bent to the bed and swiftly tugged back
the sheet. He put his hand out to encounter Celia's
firm warm breast, reached with the other to press
against her mouth when the young mulatto girl woke.

"Oh—what—oh, nossuh, please—don't—"

"Keep quiet, you teasing little bitch!" he muttered.
"I bought you for myself to begin with, Celia. I didn't
mean for Mark to get to you first, damn his hide.
You're my slave, you've got to obey me—now keep
quiet and make room for me!"

"Oh no, Mistah Bouchard suh, please, please—"

He laughed triumphantly. "You don't want me to?
Since when does a slave, a high-yellar bitch I bought
for as much as I'd pay for a whole plantation, dare to
tell her master what he can or can't do, eh? I'll take a
whip to you, Celia, I'll have you strung up by the
thumbs and thrashed till the blood runs down your heels

406

if you aren't nice to me right now. Get onto your back. You know what it's like, that brat in the crib proves you do! And I'll show you what a real man is like for a change—"

"Aw, no, foah Gawd's sake, please! Stop—you're hurting—"

Twisting away from him with all her strength, she uttered a despairing shriek as he flung himself upon her, his hands cruelly squeezing her young breasts, forcing her thighs apart with his knee, crouching over her with his face frozen in ungovernable lust.

"Stop your screeching, you bitch. Do you want to wake everybody in the house? Do that again and I'll gag you and thrash you good right now, do you hear?" he growled at her. Once again he strove to force her thighs apart, and once again she shrieked, "No, no, massa, oh Gawd, help me, help me please!"

The door was suddenly flung open, and the flickering glow of a candle pierced the darkness. Henry Bouchard, stricken with consternation, turned to see Sybella standing with a taper in her left hand, Lucien Bouchard's old flintlock pistol in her right.

"So that's why you didn't come to me tonight, Henry," Sybella said, her bosom swelling against her thin night shift, her eyes wet with tears. "This is why you came back to Windhaven, isn't it? You cozened me with all your sweet talk about wanting to be my husband again, when all you really wanted was this poor girl you wouldn't free! Let her be, Henry."

"Damn you, Syb, I bought her for myself, you know that, I told you—"

"I told you that even though I'm your wife, I can be jealous, Henry," she interrupted. "At least, when you were away from here, I might suspect you were consoling yourself, but to think that you'd dishonor me under our own roof—no, Henry, that I won't tolerate. Have the decency to put your robe back on and go to your room."

"Go back to yours, Syb. I'm master here, now that Father's gone!" Henry shouted, beside himself. "Yes, you're my wife, but you don't own my slaves and you never will. I told you before, it's got nothing to do with our love—"

"It has everything to do with it. You—you shameless animal—if you've no respect for me, at least have some for yourself. Put your robe back on and get out of here!" Sybella's voice choked with sobs.

"If you don't like what you see, then go back to your own room. Go, I order you as your husband!" he cried.

Her right hand trembled as she cocked the pistol, aiming it levelly at his head. "I swear if you touch that girl, Henry, I—I'll pull the trigger!"

Henry Bouchard, on all fours, crouching like a satyr over the terrified, whimpering, naked young girl, opened his mouth to speak. Then he seemed to shudder, his eyes rolling, a stertorous gasp emerging from his gaping mouth, and fell forward, lifeless, over Celia's thighs.

CHAPTER TWENTY-EIGHT

Luke Bouchard stood beside his stepmother, an arm protectively round her shoulders, watching as Matthew Forsden and Mark Bouchard dug a grave at the base of the towering red bluff to make the last resting place of old Lucien's only son. It was the English overseer who spoke the simple words of the ritual, so gently and movingly that Sybella's eyes filled with tears. Suddenly, she raised her head and found that Djamba, standing at a distance from the family group, was watching her. Their eyes met for an instant—and she became calm.

When the service was done, the overseer and Mark shoveled the earth into the grave and then Forsden hammered a wooden cross, bearing Henry's name and birth and death dates, deep into the earth at the head of the gravesite. Lucy and her sister Maybelle stood behind Luke and Sybella, Luke's young wife consoling her sister. For this death of a man she scarcely knew other than as her uncle by marriage had made a profound impact on adolescent Maybelle: the simple ceremony itself recalled her own father's death and her awareness of how alone in the world she really was.

As Luke gently led his stepmother back to the château, he turned to look back at his half brother. He had never been close to his father; they were opposed in most things and they usually avoided each other's company. But Mark was Henry's favorite—and he would feel his loss more deeply. The boy stood alone beside his father's grave, his face somber, and he slowly raised his eyes and stared at Luke, then clenched his fists and turned his face toward the river. Twilight was falling, and the twittering of the night birds in the trees which lined the steep bluff all along its nearly perpendicular ascent was a kind of gentle requiem for the troubled soul of Henry Bouchard.

"Is there anything I can do, Mother?" Luke asked tenderly.

She turned to look at him, her lips wistfully smiling, touched as she always was by that term he never failed to use when he addressed her. How strange it was, she told herself, that he was so much more a son than Mark, who was her own flesh and blood. And when she glanced back a last time, seeing Mark facing the river, ignoring them all, alone with his brooding thoughts, that feeling deepened. He had become a stranger, so much like poor Henry, hostile and suspicious of the least conciliatory gesture for fear that it would evince a weakness in his defiant male armor. Then she said slowly, "What grief it must be for poor Father and his Dimarte, united now, to see this terrible day and to know that his only son died so very young before he could do all the things he planned for Windhaven."

"Mother, you mustn't—" Luke began.

"No, I'm all right, Luke dear. I loved him, Luke; knowing all his faults, I loved him to the very last. But he was afraid of love, and demanded it instead as his rightful due. I think Father knew the secret of love, that one must earn it and never seek it or master it."

"Yes, I'm sure he knew, Mother. And I've learned what it is too, because Lucy's with child."

Sybella stopped and stared into Luke's concerned, handsome face. "Oh, I'm so glad for both of you, my dear!" Now the tears fell unchecked down her quivering cheeks. "To think of birth after the sorrow of death is to have hope for the future, Luke. I pray you and Lucy will have as fine a son as you've been to me." She squeezed his hand, and neither of them could speak as they went back into the château.

Lucy had gone ahead of Maybelle to offer words of sympathy to Sybella, and Maybelle walked slowly by herself back to the house. Mark Bouchard caught up with her, took her by the hand and said quietly, "I saw you crying there, crying for Pa, Maybelle. I—I want you to know that I'm grateful you did that."

"I—I'm so sorry for you, Mark, really I am. And I guess—well, I guess I was thinking about Papa too. Sometimes I think it's worse for a girl to lose her father than for a boy—I mean a man."

"I guess maybe it is at that. Maybelle—" He hesitated a moment, clearing his throat, uncertain of himself at this moment.

"What is it, Mark?"

"Do you remember the housewarming last year, when I said that you were my girl?"

Maybelle suddenly blushed and lowered her eyes. "Sure I do. But you were just fooling—"

"No I wasn't, Maybelle. You know, I'm alone now too. I mean, Luke's my ma's favorite, not me, and now that Pa is gone . . ." He reached for her other hand as he gazed at her. A year had made her prettier than ever, filled her out, and he couldn't help remembering his father's oft-repeated advice.

"I—I ought to be going in now—Mark—" she faltered, a wave of crimson suffusing her cheeks as she saw the look in his eyes.

"Sure." He released her hands, then moved beside her as they approached the porticoed entrance of Windhaven. "Think about it, though, Maybelle. I'd still like you to be my girl. Maybe even my wife, if you think you could like me well enough for that."

"Oh my goodness—you shouldn't—you shouldn't say such things—not at a time like this!"

"All right, honey. But you won't mind if I come sparking you maybe in a couple of weeks?"

Color burned even more hotly in her cheeks as she swiftly shook her head, then hurried into the château.

A new star was added to the flag of the United States on June 15th of this momentous year, when

411

Arkansas entered the Union. A month later, President Andrew Jackson issued his Specie Circular to direct that payment for government lands be made only in gold or silver, a policy which was to lead to the panic of 1837. And in September, the Republic of Texas by popular vote declared itself in favor of annexation by the United States. And it was during this same month that Sybella Bouchard, occupying herself with more of the domestic tasks at Windhaven than ever before in order to dispel the sorrow of her bereavement, determined to carry out the plan which Henry had always opposed.

One mid-September evening, she called Celia into her room and, after inquiring about little Prissy's health, gently said, "I'm going to write a paper, Celia dear, that will make you and your little girl free."

Celia gasped, her eyes widening with incredulity. Then she suddenly burst into tears, fell on her knees and sobbingly exclaimed, "Oh, Miz Bouchard, Ah doan deserve dat, Ah's brought you only trouble in dis house, m'am! If Ah hadn't been heah, Mastah Henry'd still be alive—you oughta hate me and want to whup me good foh dat, Miz Bouchard!"

Sybella put out her hand to stroke the girl's head. "How could I hate you, dear?" she said. "You didn't ask to be a slave, or to stand on that auction block in New Orleans for my husband to buy you. No, it's for you to forgive me instead, and to forgive him because you were so lovely that you tempted him—I'm the one you must forgive, Celia, for what my husband and son did to you. But you see, dear, even though I free you, it would mean you'd have to leave Alabama forever. What I'm going to do, if you wish, is give you some money and send you wherever you'd like to go. Perhaps the counting house in Mobile would find employment for you, or my good friend Antoine Rigalle at the New Orleans bank."

"Oh no, Miz Bouchard, m'am, Ah doan want to leave you, Ah doan hab anyone who cares about me. Please let me stay and work for you, please!" Celia entreated.

"If you really wish that, I'd be proud and honored if you'd stay and be my maid, dear. But you will be free all the same. You can have this paper, and one day, if our state law allows it, you'll know that you're no longer a slave anywhere in this country."

Celia seized Sybella's hand and kissed it fervently, her face wet with tears.

"You know, dear," Sybella said after a moment, "before he died, Thomas asked me if he could marry you so that he could take care of you and little Prissy."

"He was such a good man, Miz Bouchard, Ah'd have said yes to him right off, truly!"

"But I think it would be good if you found a husband, dear. Is there anyone here at Windhaven that you like and who would love you and little Prissy the way Thomas did?"

Celia dried her eyes, rose to her feet, then nodded, color surging to her face. "Dat big strong Mandingo, he's talked to me lots of times 'n Ah knows he likes me some," she hesitantly admitted.

She hesitated for just an instant—the only hint of the very private emotions that surged through her at that moment. "But that's wonderful, Celia," Sybella said quietly. "Because, you see, I mean to free Djamba too. I owe him that, for having saved my life when my mare Dulcy ran away and he came after me on Midnight. You go look after little Prissy now, Celia, and I'll send for Djamba and give him a paper just like yours. And if he does marry you, I'll have the hands build you both a big new cabin with plenty of room for both of you and little Prissy, and you'll have pretty new clothes for a wedding dress."

"Oh, Miz Bouchard, you're so good, so kind! Gawd bless you and this house forever, m'am!" Again Celia seized her mistress' hand and covered it with kisses. Then, overwhelmed by her emotion, she left the room, sobbing softly.

Sybella rose and went to the window, drew aside the bright curtains and repeated softly, "God bless this house forever indeed; I pray that too for your dear sake, Father." Then, straightening her shoulders and turning away from the window, she went to summon Matthew, the old majordomo, asking him to bring Djamba from the stable to see her at once.

The Mandingo had hastily donned a shirt and waited outside Sybella's door.

"Djamba, please come in." She sat at her desk, quill in hand, completing the article of manumission. Luke had already been told of her intention and had himself signed both papers for Celia and the Mandingo; in that way, there could be no legal dispute over the intent of the slaves' owner.

"Djamba, I want to thank you again for what you did that afternoon," she gravely looked at him, a world of meaning in her eyes.

The handsome young black smiled. "It my duty, Miz Bouchard, no need to thank Djamba."

"But I do thank you, and I want to do it in a way that shows my gratitude. After all, you saved my life, and that's not just your duty. Take this paper and keep it, Djamba. It says that you are free now. As I told Celia, whom I've also freed along with her little girl, unfortunately the law won't let you be free until you go away from this place, and the slave traders would soon catch you and sell you back into slavery. But when the day comes that there isn't any such cruel law, you will be free to go wherever you wish, to work for whomever you choose and to do what work you're most skilled at."

He took the folded sheet of paper which she handed him, stared silently at her a moment, and then softly replied, "You very kind, Miz Bouchard. I do not want to go away from you. And I like it here. I like the horses, they are my friends; and those who work in the fields, they are my friends also."

Sybella nodded. "My stepson Luke has arranged that everyone who works at Windhaven will have money credited to him, so that whenever you wish anything, you have only to ask for it, Djamba. There's one thing more—do you like Celia?" She stood very still, very proud.

414

"She very beautiful, she remind me of my wife Itulde in many ways, mistress."

Sybella rose, feeling something like joy, something like pain. "Then why not speak to her and tell her how you feel? I would like to see her take a husband to protect her and little Prissy. You would make her a fine husband, Djamba. You would have a family and you could begin your life now in this new country as a freed man."

Djamba's smile was radiant. He spoke solemnly, with his hand on his heart: "In my country, when someone saves another's life, that man owes him a debt of life forever. I will serve you always. You are good and kind."

Mark Bouchard and Maybelle Williamson sat in the little gazebo on this warm September evening, his arm around her waist, and his mouth insistently seeking her petulantly ripe lips. The color high in her cheeks, Maybelle exclaimed, "My gracious, Mr. Bouchard, you don't give a girl time to think—don't kiss me anymore now, I can't think when you do that!"

"You're not supposed to, you red-haired little minx," the youth replied, his right hand rising to cup one of the girl's amply rounded breasts through her pretty green muslin frock.

"And don't do that either—I never did see a fellow who couldn't keep his hands still a minute when he was next to a girl!" she scolded.

"Are you going to marry me, then? Come on, Maybelle, you don't have any other fellow and you know it. Leastways, no one who can make you want to be kissed and squeezed the way I do—and when I'm your husband, honey, I'll keep you in bed all the time and you won't need to think at all!" he boasted.

"Are you sure you love me, Mark?" She turned to look at him with a wistful, hopeful expression, her large hazel eyes humid, her dainty nostrils flickering with the sensual arousal his aggressive lovemaking had stirred in her ripe young body.

415

"I wouldn't be asking you to marry me if I didn't, silly! Well, will you?"

"If you—if you really want me to. I feel so left out and lonely now that Lucy's gone and married your brother—"

"My half brother, you mean," Mark corrected her. "Anyhow, I'm glad he didn't pick you. You're lots prettier and you've got more spunk than Lucy, that's for certain."

"That's not very nice of you to say, and after all, Lucy's your sister-in-law," Maybelle reminded him.

He pulled her roughly to him, silencing her protests with a demanding kiss. Maybelle moaned, squirmed, tried to push him away with her hands, and then with a little acquiescent moan, closed her eyes and responded fiercely.

"There now, you see?" Mark whispered, his face dark with lust, his chest heaving. "You need a husband real bad, Maybelle honey, so you better say yes right now. Look, if you do, I'll have Luke give us back your pa's house and go back to live at Windhaven where he belongs. And you and I can run the place ourselves, and the nice fellow we picked up as the Northbys' overseer will take care of the fields. Come on, honey, I'll take you to New Orleans on our honeymoon the minute you say the word."

Maybelle tried to smooth her rumpled bodice and rearranged her mussed skirts, her pretty round face crimson with sensual excitement. "I might as well, or you won't ever let me be, Mark Bouchard," she complained. Then, linking her arms round his neck and looking prettily up at him through long thick fluttering lashes, she whispered, "But you'd just better be nice to me and buy me lots of new clothes and jewelry and things like that if you want me to lord it over Lucy!"

"That'll be easy," he said, then drew her into his arms again, and this time Maybelle did not hesitate to part her lips and to meet the voraciously questing tongue of her dominant young suitor with her own in passionate response.

416

Earlier that same morning, Luke had brought Lucy and Maybelle to Windhaven at Sybella's invitation, and after supper, Mark Bouchard sought his half brother out as they were rising from the supper table. "Luke, I've got to talk to you alone," the youth muttered.

"Of course, Mark. Excuse me a moment, Lucy, please. Mother, it was a wonderful supper—my compliments to Mammy Clorinda. But Lucy herself is a marvelous cook, and you can see that already I'm putting on a little weight as a result of it." At his praise, Lucy lowered her eyes and flushed deliciously, reaching for Luke's hand and giving it a quick loving squeeze, then went off to chat with Sybella.

Mark followed his half brother into one of the sitting rooms, and as soon as the door was closed, defiantly declared, "I'm going to marry Maybelle, if you've no objections."

"Well, you're both young, but there's no reason why you shouldn't think of mature responsibilities, Mark. And you certainly don't need my permission. I'd say it's up to Maybelle, isn't it?"

"Hell, she's hot to be married and you know it." Mark gave his half brother a cynical grin. "The thing is, now that Pa's gone, I'd like to know exactly where I stand as far as money's concerned. If I marry Maybelle, don't I get that third of Mr. Williamson's holdings according to his will? That's what Pa told me before he died, you know."

"That's correct, Mark. You propose to live here at Windhaven with Maybelle or at the Williamson house?"

"That all depends on what you're going to do, dear brother," Mark sneered. "You and I never did see eye to eye about anything, and I figure we'd get a little crowded all living together."

"I see." Luke's sensitive face was shadowed with concern. "Well, I'm perfectly content to stay with Lucy in her father's house, and I'm taking care of the land. It's doing very well."

"But there's the matter of Pa's land, those two

417

pieces he took over and then the Northby place. And then there's Windhaven—isn't it share and share alike here, Luke? I'm Pa's son as much as you are."

"Grover Mason says that Father's will divides equally between us at Windhaven, yes. But I'd say you're a little young to take over all Father's land and half of Windhaven at the moment. You don't care for working on the land to start with, Mark. All you want is the money that comes from it, so you can live like a gentleman."

"Damn your hide, why shouldn't I? You've always got your nose in the air, thinking you're better than I am. Well, maybe you've got more book learning, but half the slaves belong to me and I want to sell and trade them when I feel like it, you understand?"

"By the same token, Mark, I have a half interest in them too, and that includes the Northby place and those two other pieces of land. Here at Windhaven and at Lucy's home I've told the hands that, so far as I'm concerned, they're no longer slaves. Now don't give me that black look, you know exactly what I mean. I can't let them leave Alabama, and most of them now are quite happy to work if they're given decent treatment and not abused like helpless animals. You may, as you say, have the legal right to half those other slaves, and a third of the hands at the Williamson plantation, but I'll never let you take a whip to them or make your money dealing in human flesh, I swear I shan't!"

"Then how in hell do you expect me to have money of my own so I can marry Maybelle?" Mark angrily burst out.

"Why, I understand you've kept on Patrick Jerrold to be overseer on those three properties Father acquired. What he gets for you out of the land will be all yours—I want no part of it, since I haven't worked on it. I'm saying only that as far as it's in my power I'll never let you brutalize the slaves who work there. And as for the land here at Windhaven, I'll see that when the crops are sold in Mobile this winter, you'll get your

418

rightful half share deposited in an account bearing your own name—surely that should satisfy you."

"Well, I guess so. Only I'm my own man now that Pa's gone, and I've got a right to sell his niggers if I feel like it," Mark growled.

"That will depend on exactly whom you sell them to and how you treat them!"

Mark clenched his fists in baffled rage. "If you were man enough, I'd tell you to come out behind the stable and we'd settle things once and for all," he said, glowering.

"I won't fight you, Mark, and there's no need for you to talk like that. You've everything in the world to live for, you're only seventeen, you're proposing to marry a nice girl, and you've enough land and slaves to keep you in material comfort for many years if you use your inheritance wisely. And I think Mother would like to have you back here at Windhaven if you marry Maybelle."

"Then you'll stay at the Williamson place, is that it?"

"Yes. I'll never stand in your way—unless you do something to dishonor the name of Bouchard. It's a name that Grandfather left us with honor and pride and hard work all his long life, and I'm sure that Father felt that too. Now there are just the two of us left, and we mustn't let differences of opinion separate us, Mark. I've always wanted to be your friend, you know that."

"Save your fine speeches. I'll live my own life and be damned to you and yours. But thanks for settling things so clearly. I'm going to ask Maybelle to marry me right now, and when we get back from New Orleans, we'll move in here."

"I'll ask Grover Mason to set up an account for you at the counting house in Mobile, and to give you a letter of credit so you'll have money for your honeymoon."

Mark shrugged, gave his half brother a hostile look, and then strode out of the sitting room in search of Maybelle Williamson.

419

On the 15th of October, exactly a week before Samuel Houston took the oath of office as President of the new Republic of Texas, Mark Bouchard and Maybelle Williamson boarded the *River Queen*, returning to Mobile where they would be married by the same priest who had married Luke and Lucy. To Maybelle's surprise, her aggressive bridegroom did not seek his conjugal rights that very first night, but waited until they had arrived in New Orleans the next afternoon, where Antoine Rigalle had arranged the best room in the Orleans Hotel for the young couple. After having installed his bride in the room, Mark took a carriage directly to Rigalle's bank and there handed the banker the letter of credit which Luke had given him as a wedding present. Putting the sheaf of bills into a handsome alligator-skin wallet (the gift of Rigalle himself to the younger Bouchard heir), Mark returned to the waiting carriage and ordered the black coachman to drive him to the auction rooms of Pierre Lourat.

The suave Creole, in a black frock coat and top hat, was extolling the virtues of several female mulattoes and three prime field hands. He observed Mark enter and permitted himself a faint smile in anticipation of their meeting. The youth seated himself in one of the chairs near the front, and followed the auction with interest, particularly the unveiling and introduction of three young girls, who ranged between sixteen and twenty-two. When at last the auction had been completed, he rose and went directly to the Creole dandy who greeted him with outstretched hand: *"Enfin, mon jeune ami!* You come again, and perhaps you will have better luck this time."

"This time, *M'sieu* Lourat," Mark Bouchard coldly retorted, "I'll be much more careful. I've learned a lesson which you so neatly taught me. By the way, I'm married now, and in the event that you hadn't heard, my father died late this spring."

"Yes." The Creole's face sobered. "I heard that distressing news from my good friend Antoine Rigalle. My deepest condolences, *M'sieu* Mark. What can I do for you?"

"I was wondering what happened to Louisette and Rosa."

"Ah," the Creole nodded with a shrewd smile, "you haven't forgotten your charmingly romantic escapade. Well, *M'sieu* Mark, Louisette is running one of my houses of pleasure, the latest one, and it's a great success. Only the wealthiest and most discriminating patrons are accepted there, you see. Rosa, I fear, decided to become one of the *belles filles de joie* in that establishment, but she seems quite happy. After all"— he winked knowingly—"she and Louisette are in that way inseparable and may console each other."

"I'd like to see Rosa one evening while I'm here, or, better still, an afternoon."

"Decidedly, *mon ami*." The Creole's smile broadened. "I should recommend the afternoon, as your charming wife might otherwise wonder why you take your leave of her at so romantic a time. You've only to let me know when you wish Rosa's services, and for old time's sake, it will be my pleasure to dispense with any fee. Of course if you wish to leave Rosa a little *pourboire*, that would be most gentlemanly."

"I've thought of something else, too, *M'sieu* Lourat. It's not quite time for it yet, but I'm wondering if you and I couldn't go into partnership in some way."

The Creole's eyebrows arched with surprise. "*Vraiment?* Now that presents some interesting possibilities. At the moment, I don't quite see how you could be of service to me. But, as you say, at a later time it may well be to our mutual advantage to discuss such a project. *À votre service, M'sieu* Mark." He made a little bow. "Now, if you'll excuse me, I must see to the transfer of the slaves I've just sold to their new owners. *À bientôt!*"

As he entered their room, Maybelle turned, lowering a silver hand-mirror in which she had been coquettishly studying herself. "Oh Mark, wherever did you go? I was getting so worried—are we going out for dinner now?"

"In time, Maybelle honey." Mark stared greedily at his pretty young wife, who looked older than her nearly seventeen years in a wide-skirted blue marcelline gown with puffed sleeves and high neckline. Her coppery-red hair was done up in a large psyche knot at the back of her head to leave her nape bare, and Lucy had given her their mother's aquamarine earrings in keeping with the quaint old tradition that a bride should wear "something borrowed, something blue."

"But I'm starved, honey," Maybelle peevishly replied, "and besides, I want everybody at the fancy restaurant you're going to take me to to see my scrumptious new gown—don't you like me in it, honey?"

"I'd like you better out of it, Maybelle," he muttered as he came to her, his hands gripping her by the buttocks and pulling her up against him. "Take it off right now!"

"But honey—oh my goodness, whatever are you thinking of—it's not even bedtime yet—oh no—don't you dare tear it—all right, all right—I think you're mean—you're supposed to be nice to a girl on her honeymoon, Mark Bouchard!" Maybelle pushed his hands away and stepped back, her face crimsoning before his hot gaze. Hastily she began to tug off the gown, and then to unfasten the stays with fumbling fingers. When she was down to chemise and drawers, Mark seized her in his arms and carried her toward the bed, callously tossing her onto it, then tugged off his frock coat and opened his breeches.

"For Lord's sake, Mark, at least turn out the light—oh you're just awful to me!" Maybelle gasped, her eyes fixed on the savagely swollen emblem of his virile young manhood.

His answer was to rip off the chemise, then tug down her drawers despite her squeals and the helpless opposition of her soft hands. She began to sob as he ruthlessly stripped her naked, then flung himself upon her. "Please don't hurt me—oh no—please, Mark, be gentle—be nice—I never did before—ah—oh, you're hurting me—"

His left palm stifled her outcry as he penetrated her, his right hand buried in the psyche knot and tilting back her head to immobilize her and destroy all her defenses. It was in spiteful rut that Mark Bouchard consummated his union, and when he had finished and walked over to a little tabouret on which a washbasin stood to sponge himself and then to fasten up his breeches, he callously said over his shoulder, "Now get yourself dressed. Since you're so starved, we'll go out and have that dinner you want and you can show off your new gown all you like."

CHAPTER TWENTY-NINE

On the third day of their honeymoon in New Orleans, Mark left his wife in their room and took a carriage to the elegant *maison de luxe* over which the woman he had known as Louisa Voisin presided. The rendezvous with the lovely octoroon Rosa had already been made for him by Pierre Lourat. When he entered the ornately furnished establishment, he hardly recognized the woman with whom he imagined he had been so desperately in love a little more than a year ago: her hair, set in a pompadour, was touched with gray, her face saddened and grave, and she conducted herself with such an air of aloof dignity that it was difficult to believe she was now little more than the madam of a brothel.

When she received him in the spacious sitting room, he sprang to his feet, his face flushing at the sight of her; then he stared, not immediately recognizing her. Louisette Entrevois pursed her lips and said, "You are the gentleman for Rosa, *M'sieu* Lourat has told me. Marie will show you to her room. All has been taken care of, but of course if Rosa pleases you, it would delight her to receive a small token of your appreciation, *M'sieu.*"

"Louisa—I—" he hoarsely began.

"I know what you are about to say, *M'sieu* Bouchard. It is not necessary. What might have happened was not to be, that is all. It is best that we both forget the past."

"You should have told me who you really were!" he declared.

"I must forget all that if I am to stay free. And that's all I shall ever have to tell you. Now, I'm sure you don't want to keep Rosa waiting. Marie, this gentleman to *le salon rouge, s'il vous plaît*." Thus she dismissed him and turned now to receive another afternoon client, a pompous, gray-haired man in tall top hat, fur-trimmed frock coat and costly new boots: "*Soyez le bienvenu, M'sieu* Dartran, Aimée will be ready for you in a moment—if you would make yourself at your ease here and enjoy some of our finest champagne?"

The attractive octoroon maid led him to a bedchamber in which the rugs and tapestries and the covers on the huge four-poster bed were as red as the color of blood. Rosa awaited him in a red silk peignoir, her hair drawn to the front of her head in a large knot, with tiny little spit curls all along the top of her forehead. She smiled at him mechanically, asked if he wished her to help him undress, and showed him no sign of recognition. As soon as he came to bed with her, he began to possess her furiously, mouthing obscenities in her ear, saying that he would complain of her to Pierre Lourat if she did not show more animation in their lovemaking. And finally, sadistically, he taunted her, "I know why you're really no good in bed with a man, Rosa. You'd rather be with girls, with your own sister, wouldn't you? Well, Pa told me about two sisters back where we come from, how they had nigger girls to bed with them, and how he whipped them and made them sit on a rail, and then he and his friends all poked them good! That's what you need, you tricky bitch!"

And when he had finished with her, when he saw that she would not be goaded but submissively endured all his sadistic whims, he flung her a dixie, a New Orleans ten-cent note, as the supreme insult. Then, dressing and leaving her at last sobbing softly in shame, he

426

strode back into the parlor and, interrupting Louisette Entrevois' conversation with a newly arrived client, exclaimed, "It's a good thing I didn't have to pay! That Rosa is stupid and lifeless in bed. You'd better tell *M'sieu* Lourat to replace her with someone who knows her business."

He slammed the door and walked out onto the sidewalk to hail a carriage back to the Orleans Hotel.

"What an unpleasant young man!" The client shook his head. "And I'm sure it's not true, what he's just said. Why, Pierre Lourat is known all through the South for the fine pleasure wenches he has in these comfortable little love nests! Can you recommend someone to me, someone mature, who is experienced and yet capable of youthful passion?"

"I think so, *M'sieu* Valvert," the woman declared after a moment. "We've a new girl, Zora, who came to New Orleans about two months ago. She's Jamaican, but wonderfully gifted in the ways of *l'amour*. You need pay only the minimum fee, *M'sieu* Valvert, unless she lives up to your expectations."

It was as well that old Lucien Bouchard was not alive to see the last days of the Creeks at Alabama, that once proud nation that had ruled the land long before the white man came, tilled the soil and grown crops, established humane laws for the governing of their own people. Although the Treaty of Cusseta in 1832 had provided that all white settlers on the lands which the Creeks had ceded were to be removed until those lands had been surveyed and the Indians settled on territory of their choice, the refusal of the whites to leave the still unsurveyed land, the defiance against President Jackson's threat to send federal troops to remove them, and the deception of the land speculators forced the few tribes remaining of the once mighty Creek Nation to a final brief death struggle of war in eastern Alabama. When it was over, those who remained were sent off in chains from Fort Mitchell, the men handcuffed two together, and a long chain passed between the double file connected them all together—

very much like a coffle of black slaves. Weeping squaws carrying their starving children, all of them tattered and unprepared for transportation to a bitterly cold land—such was their passing forever from the beloved country.

As this year of 1836 ended, Alonzo Dwight Phillips patented the first friction match, and the Democrat, Martin Van Buren, was elected President of the United States by the electoral vote of 170, with Richard M. Johnson chosen as Vice President by the Senate after no candidate for that office had received an electoral majority....

Sybella Bouchard welcomed Mark and his young wife back to Windhaven, noticing with almost maternal concern that the girl seemed strangely subdued. Luke and Lucy had gone back to live at the Williamson house, and once again it was Luke and Matthew Forsden who went down to Mobile with the baled cotton from both the Windhaven and Williamson acres. The price had dropped to fifteen cents a pound, yet there was still a tidy profit for the work expended. True to his promise, Luke spent some of his money purchasing a dozen Hereford cows and a strong young bull and brought them back to the Williamson plantation, where the hands had already constructed a strong wooden pen for the spirited bull and the fencing for the land which would henceforth be devoted to grazing for the cattle. If the experiment worked, Luke told Sybella, he would bring cattle to Windhaven the following year.

As the new year of 1837 began, Michigan entered the Union on January 26th, and Luke and Lucy eagerly awaited the birth of their first child, due early in February. It was the young woman's prayer that she would give her gentle husband a son to carry on the Bouchard line. And Maybelle was pregnant, too, to Sybella's delight, for she believed that the birth of a child would mature her undisciplined son and induce him to treat Maybelle with greater kindness than he had shown her. At their meals, whenever she timidly ventured into the conversation, Mark would often silence her with a sullen look or some disparaging comment, which made Sybella wince for the pretty girl who was so obviously trying to please. Sympathetic with Maybelle's adjustment to this stormy start of married life, Sybella took the girl under her wing and spent many hours with her teaching her how to sew and to cook Mark's favorite dishes, extravagantly praising her first efforts in an attempt to restore to Maybelle the pert self-confidence she had shown when Sybella had first met her at the housewarming party.

But Maybelle's uncharacteristic listlessness was quickly forgotten in the excitement of helping her sister bear a little black-haired daughter on February 5th, after a night of protracted labor. Maybelle herself hurried out to one of the slave cabins to bring back Dorcas, a middle-aged West Indian woman, herself a grandmother five times over and expert as a midwife who, unlike many of her slave status who performed that function where there were no doctors to serve, believed in cleanliness above all else and meticulously washed her hands before going to Lucy's bedchamber. Throughout the night, Maybelle joyously and tirelessly brought back cloths and heated water and, at Dorcas's instructions, disposed of the afterbirth.

Luke knelt beside his wife's bedside, his face lined with anxiety, and Lucy touched his head and smiled wanly at him. "I wish it could have been a son, my darling," she whispered.

"I'm happy with our daughter, and because she's got black hair, she won't steal away any of the love I have for a very beautiful honey-haired girl I met at a housewarming party two years ago," Luke gently teased, then kissed her forehead. "What shall we name her, dearest?"

"After my grandmother, Mara."

"That's a beautiful name, Lucy. Yes, she'll be our little Mara. And now, my dearest, you must sleep and grow strong again." He looked at Maybelle, who was smiling, exhausted and yet for the first time seeming not at all to be the scatter-brained teenager he had thought her at first meeting. "You've been very kind and good, Maybelle. Lucy and I shan't ever forget what a wonderful sister you are to us," he said. Maybelle blushed and lowered her eyes, then bit her lips and left the room.

"Poor darling," Lucy faintly murmured, "I only hope her first child won't cause her any more discomfort than I had—I was very lucky and Dorcas was so gentle and so helpful to me."

"Maybelle's a strong girl, Lucy darling. She'll be fine. In a way, I think last night was a very good experience for her; she feels wanted and needed again. I don't know, maybe I shouldn't have let her marry Mark," Luke said with a worried frown.

"One can't tell, Luke dearest. She told me she did love him. Maybe she'll settle him down now."

"I sincerely pray it will be thus, Lucy. And now I want you to sleep, my darling. Dorcas will stay with you, and she'll find a nurse for Mara."

"Oh no!" Lucy looked up at him with a radiant smile. "I want to nurse her myself. She's a part of me and of you too, my dearest husband, and it's only right that her own mother should nurse her."

"All right, Lucy, now you just close your eyes and drift off to sleep and dream about how grateful I am you said yes to me, my darling," he whispered as he kissed her forehead again and left the room.

It was March 3rd, the day before Martin Van Buren's inaugural, the day on which outgoing President Jackson had formally recognized the Republic of Texas following approval by Congress. The *River Queen* had docked at the Windhaven landing this afternoon and Matthew Forsden, together with a crew of field hands, had seen to the transfer of supplies to the large storehouse and accepted a packet of letters addressed to Luke Bouchard. The field hands also transferred six cows and a bull from the paddleboat to a special pen which had already been built at Windhaven.

One letter was from Antoine Rigalle, congratulating Luke on the birth of his daughter and acknowledging Luke's request that there be an account opened for Mark Bouchard at his bank as well as at the counting

430

house in Mobile. But the banker had added an ominous piece of news: the renowned cotton house of Herman Briggs & Company in New Orleans was about to close its doors forever, its cash being wiped out and its credit and notes virtually worthless because of speculative transactions. It was the prelude to the panic of 1837, a panic which would plunge the nation into a depression of seven long years.

"Happily, my dear friend," Rigalle had written, "I can tell you that our own house is in good order, for we have been most careful with our accounts and have been reluctant to extend unlimited credit to the planters as so many of our competitors have done. Some banks here have made loans to the amount of eleven and a half million dollars, loans secured by mortgages on marshes, cypress swamps, flooded land, and worthless notes arranged for six- and eight-year terms. Moreover, European imports are greater now than what we send out of our country, and this is increasing the price of goods fivefold. Loans on good security are bringing from twenty-four to thirty per cent. I foresee that within a few months at least eight of our leading banks will suspend payment and that only our bank and the Citizens' Bank will be able to pay out in specie. Already the mayors of our three municipalities are talking of issuing certificates with a value from twenty-five cents to four dollars—and I need not tell you what this circulation of paper money will mean to business."

Arabella, now thirteen, was to regard this day as the blackest in all her young life. As was her wont, she had taken the little raccoon Timmy for a walk near the creek, this time avoiding any hollow logs—for Matthew Forsden had warned her that the cottonmouth liked to appropriate such logs as its shelter and hiding-place.

She squatted down near a level clearing on the bank of the creek and took from the pocket of her pinafore a piece of cornpone. Breaking it into bits, she fed it, laughing gleefully as the bright-eyed pet daintily nibbled without ever biting her. "Good boy, Timmy!"

431

she applauded as she rose. "Now let's go down this way."

But suddenly the raccoon sat up and made a curious chirping sound. Across the creek, on the opposite bank, there was another raccoon, plumper and bushier, and it too was sitting up and sending back chirping sounds. Without warning, Timmy scampered down the bank to the sluggish water of the creek and plunged in, swimming to the opposite bank.

"Come back, Timmy! What are you doing? Oh my, you'll surely drown—oh my goodness! Mr. Forsden, come quick, Timmy's going to drown!" she cried as she saw the English overseer approach the stable in the company of Djamba.

"What's this, Arabella?" Matthew Forsden hurried up and stared out at the creek.

"It's Timmy, Mr. Forsden, it's Timmy!" Arabella tugged at his wrist and pointed with her other hand to the opposite bank of the creek. "He ran away! He was swimming the creek and he went over to that other coon—just look—oh please, get him back for me, Mr. Forsden!"

Timmy had indeed reached the opposite bank and was sniffing at the other raccoon, who pawed at his snout, uttering a sharp-pitched chirping sound, then turned and scurried off. Timmy raced in hot pursuit, and again the other raccoon stopped to swipe its paw at Arabella's pet. Then, as if by some signal of consent, it turned and raced off, Timmy keeping pace, till both disappeared into a clump of azalea bushes.

"Oh now he's gone, Mr. Forsden, oh this is just awful! Please bring him back for me!" Arabella was in tears.

"I can't, dear. You know what happened?"

"No," she shook her head, the tears rolling down her cheeks, "I don't care, I want him back!"

"But you see, dear, that was Timmy's sweetheart. She called to him, and that's why he went to her. And now they're going off to get married and to raise their own family and to live their own lives, because he's grown now and has responsibilities. After all, he figured that he saved your life and that paid you back for all the love and kindness you showed him. And he hopes you'll understand why he has to leave you."

Arabella tried to control her sobs, staring anxiously up at the overseer's gently smiling face. "Do you—do you think I'll ever see him again, Mr. Forsden?" she asked.

"Maybe, Arabella, maybe after he and his sweetheart get married and have their family, they'll come back and show you their little babies. But I wouldn't count on it too much, honey. You see, when you took off the collar and leash, you as much as told Timmy that you weren't making a slave of him, and that he could be free. Well, he's just decided to claim his freedom now instead of later. Don't cry, honey. I'll see if I can find you another pet you'll like just as much as Timmy. Maybe Mammy Clorinda has a big cool glass of milk and some of those famous honeycakes of hers for a big brave girl. Shall we go see?"

CHAPTER THIRTY

Timmy did not return, but Matthew Forsden, true to his promise, found a baby owl one morning, its feathers so sodden from a thunderstorm that it could not fly to safety. He made a wide circular wooden cage for the abandoned fledgling, and within a month Arabella, having named her new pet "Hoot-to-Whoo" because his call suggested that sound, had almost forgotten her romantically inclined raccoon.

By mid-May, the economic disaster which Antoine Rigalle had foretold in his letter to Luke Bouchard burst upon the nation as the major New York banks suspended all specie payment and the New Orleans banks followed suit. There were flour riots in New York, poorhouses were being filled all over the country. Yet President Martin Van Buren stubbornly insisted on a hard-money program, refused to rescind Jackson's Specie Circular. In his message to a special session of Congress, he advocated an independent treasury system and the temporary issue of treasury notes, a move which alienated the nation's bankers and caused vitriolic denunciations and even threats of impeachment in many of the leading newspapers. And with this economic panic came the renewed cry of the abolitionists urging him to act against slavery. Although he was opposed to its spread, he refused to interfere with it in those states where it already existed. There was thus nothing in this regime of a President whom Jackson himself had chosen to restore faith in the power of the government of this struggling new nation to emerge from its plight.

On July 14, 1837, a day when the compatriots of the founder of Windhaven were celebrating the fall of the Bastille and the emergence of a new France, Maybelle gave birth to a daughter with hair as red as her own. Her labor was even easier than Lucy's had been, and Lucy was beside her, comforting her and aiding Dorcas in the delivery of the healthy, squalling infant.

"What will you call her, darling?" Lucy gently murmured as she applied a cool wet cloth to her sister's damp forehead.

"I—I'm glad it's a girl, Lucy, and not a boy. Because maybe he'd be like Mark when he grows up and make some poor girl who falls in love with him wish she'd never met him," Maybelle whispered back, and began to sob.

"Oh my poor darling, is it that bad?" Lucy anxiously asked.

"He—he treats me like I was one of his slaves. I think sometimes he wishes I was so he could even—so he could even take a whip to me. And ever since he knew I had—well, was going to have a child—he goes off to the cabins on the land he got when his father died, and—and I just know he goes to bed with those n—nigger girls. Oh, what am I going to do? I still do love him so much, only he doesn't care for me at all."

"Shh, honey, you mustn't carry on so. You've got to get your rest. You'll see, once he sees how pretty the little girl is, I'll just bet he'll be nicer to you. Have you thought of a name at all?"

"I—I read a poem once when I was going to that lady's seminary, Lucy—you know. It was about a girl called Laurette. She was so pretty and so brave—I'd like to call her Laurette too."

"Why, I think that's a lovely name, Maybelle dear. That's what we'll call her, then," Lucy decided as she leaned forward to kiss her sister. "And now you go to sleep. When you wake up, I'll have a nice bowl of good nourishing broth Mammy Clorinda will make just for you."

Van Buren's Independent Treasury Bill was passed by the Senate in October, but tabled by the House of Representatives ten days later, and there it would remain until July 4, 1840. Seeking to ease the desperate financial situation of the nation, Congress in this same month of October authorized the issue of treasury notes not exceeding ten million dollars. And once again the bloody augury of an ultimate, divisory conflict on the issue of slavery was seen when, on November 7th, Elijah P. Lovejoy was killed and his antislavery printing press destroyed by a pro-slavery mob at Alton, Illinois. The only cheering news of this black year of 1837 came on Christmas Day, when General Zachary Taylor defeated the Seminoles at Okeechobee Swamp in Florida.

On that same Christmas Day, Sybella Bouchard had Matthew Forsden summon all the field hands to the back of the château, where Mammy Clorinda and half a dozen house servants had prepared a Christmas feast. Presents were given, sides of bacon, flour, blankets, new trousers and shirts for the men, sturdy cotton dresses for the women, toys for the children. And Sybella read off a list which the English overseer had prepared, showing how much money as wages for the year's work had been credited to each worker in the Bouchard account at Mobile.

Djamba and Celia were the last to appear, and Sybella announced that they would be married this very day and that they would have a large new cabin comfortably furnished as their new home. There was a new crib for little Prissy and dolls which several of the field hands had made in their spare time for her to play with. Although the weather had hurt the quality of cotton produced on the Windhaven acres, and the price had dropped nearly a dime a pound, there was food enough and ample supplies in the storeroom. There was beef, and milk and cheese, and the workers themselves were provided with these new additions to their diet.

"To all of you," Sybella said to the assembled hands, "I wish a very happy holiday and I want you all to know how grateful I am, as well as my sons Luke and Mark and my daughters-in-law Lucy and Maybelle, for the loyalty you've shown to Windhaven this difficult year. You shall all have a week off as a kind of vacation, and there will be no work done in the fields until after the first day of the new year. God bless you all, and remember, if there is anything that troubles you, or food or clothing or working conditions that do not please you, you've only to come to Mr. Forsden or myself, and we'll try to better things for you."

On the Williamson plantation, Luke Bouchard smilingly faced the black workers, Lucy beside him holding little Mara in her arms. Now almost eleven months old, the child could lisp "Mama" and "Dada" to delight its fond parents. And, just as Sybella had done at Windhaven, Luke told his assembled workers, "So far as my wife and I are concerned, all of you are freed, and I have drawn up papers of manumission for each one of you who has spent at least three years in labor on these fields. By our law, I cannot send you away and tell you to start your own lives where you wish, but you are to receive wages credited to you in my account, and in spite of the stories you have heard of the terrible shortage of money everywhere, in the bank with which I do business in New Orleans, the money is as good as gold. Whenever you need things for your family or yourself, come to my wife or me, and it will be supplied to you out of the money you have earned working here. God bless you all, and thank you for your loyalty to me, who was a stranger to you till I married the daughter of your former owner." As at Windhaven, gifts were handed to each worker, and Luke showed each of them the manumission paper he had prepared to prove that he spoke the truth.

When the people had returned to their cabins, Lucy turned to her husband and murmured, "I've a Christmas gift for you too, Luke darling. And this time I hope it will be a boy."

Mark returned to Windhaven for the Christmas

week, bringing Maybelle a brooch set with tiny seed pearls which he had purchased in New Orleans, and a huge doll dressed in an exquisite silk gown for little Laurette. He was in high spirits, for he had sold the cotton from his dead father's three sections totaling two hundred and twenty-five acres in addition to the Northby land; Luke had had Grover Mason draw up an agreement by which Mark's older half-brother ceded all lifetime interest in those properties in favor of Mark. And even though the price of cotton had almost ruinously declined, Mark had netted about $12,000 from 140,000 pounds of cotton sold at the Mobile dock. What Luke did not know, however, was that Mark had sold Tansie and Suzy to James Buffery for $1800. He had kept Trish in the little brick and log house where his father had lived, and during those long weeks when he had stayed away from Windhaven for the purpose, as he had glibly told Maybelle, of supervising his newly inherited land, she continued to be his submissive concubine.

Indeed, just before returning to Windhaven for his reconciliation with Maybelle, Mark had closeted himself with Patrick Jerrold and declared, "Things are in a pretty mess in Mobile and New Orleans, Pat. The cotton market's going to drop even lower than it is already for the next few years, and the big thing is going to be trading in slaves. Breeding, selling and trading, that's the new money-making way for this part of the country. We'll go on raising cotton, all the acres will take next year, but I want you to pick out your best workers and see if you've got any mechanics or carpenters or niggers with special trades, because I can get good cash from Jim Buffery any time I've got a coffle for him. I only hope my saintly half brother Luke doesn't get wind of what I'm planning, because he'd try to put a stop to it. Hell, I wouldn't be surprised if he's planning to free all the niggers over at the Williamson place. You know that over at Windhaven, thanks to Grandfather's notions, those hands consider themselves free already. Well, I can't do anything about them, maybe, but I've got a legal paper that'll stand up in any court to prove I own Pa's land and that means all the niggers on it."

But Mark would have been far less ready to enter the holiday mood in which he returned to Windhaven to console his young wife if he could have read the contents of a letter from James G. Birney which arrived the day before Christmas from Cincinnati, addressed to Luke Bouchard. It read as follows:

Mr. Luke Bouchard, Esteemed Sir:

Your letter expressing interest in my *Philanthropist* was deeply appreciated. Your name is not unknown to me, since it was your grandfather Lucien Bouchard who first communicated with me on my efforts to abolish the inhuman institution of slavery. How tragic that a man of his vision and humanity was not spared to this coming fight which I foresee will be an enduring one until the principles of righteousness triumph over greed and evil.

I had hoped to reply to your letter long before this, but this summer, alas, an unthinking mob destroyed my press and I was forced to suspend publication until I could again effect different accommodations. But my work goes forward. What is of most interest to you, if as you tell me you cherish your grandfather's beliefs that no man should be a slave, is that I am in the process of organizing what I call the Underground Railroad. In essence, it will be a line of communication and transportation toward freedom for the oppressed blacks of the unhappy South. There will be anti-slavery sympathizers in your state and in others all along the way from here to Ohio and thence to Canada. Once a slave crosses the American border, he or she will have achieved the glorious freedom which Almighty God intended all mankind to enjoy. I will write you soon

440

when there are more details to give you, and tell you how you can help in this great and noble work.

Yours for the eternal cause,
James G. Birney

Matthew Forsden had shown Arabella how to care for and feed her new pet. "You see, Miss Arabella," he explained, "Hoot-to-Whoo was about two months old when I found him, and from what I know about screech owls, he hadn't been very long out of the nest. That means he'll tame easily. You saw how he was all covered with grayish-brown down to start with, and now that he's about seven months old or so, he's started to get feathers. You ask Mammy Clorinda to give you little cut-up bits of raw meat for him, and every so often I'll catch him a field mouse as a special treat."

"Ugh, I don't want to feed him that, not ever. I'm scared of mice," Arabella said.

"You won't have to, if you just give him bits of pork and beef, but be sure they're raw. Now, you can let him out of the cage and get him used to you so that he'll take the meat in his bill right from your fingers. Usually, he'll stay in a dark spot for a long time, but when he grows older, you can let him fly around the room and come back to you with a bit of meat to reward him. Maybe in a year or so, you'll be able to let him fly out of the house and he'll come back because he'll be perfectly tame and want to see his mistress again."

As the owl grew, Matthew Forsden's instructions proved accurate, to Arabella's delight. In the late afternoon, she would let the little screech owl out of the wooden cage and walk to the other side of the room, then produce a bit of raw meat, and Hoot-to-Whoo would come to perch on her shoulder and gently nibble at the tidbit. When she stroked its head, it uttered its soft cry, and it was not unlike the call of the owl which old Lucien Bouchard had so often heard through the stillness of the night from the distant red bluff.

Sybella Bouchard still grieved for her husband, but as

the new year of 1838 began, her sorrow was assuaged by the joy of seeing Arabella and Fleurette take pleasure in the everyday routine of plantation life. And by the sight of Djamba and Celia going to their new large cabin hand in hand and smiling at each other warmed Sybella's heart, as did the sounds of singing from the workers' cabins at the day's end. Nearly all of the cows had calved by now, and Luke had more calves from the cows at the Williamson plantation as well.

These were happier times, the rewarding times of working on the land and knowing that there would be food for all and that there would never be the sound of the whip to replace the folk songs and chants in the fields. Maybelle, too, had learned to cope with her lot as Mark's wife, devoting much of her time to Laurette, who like Mara, was thriving. Like Lucy, Maybelle had insisted on breast-feeding her own baby, and when, one afternoon, Sybella entered Maybelle's room to bring her daughter-in-law milk and a piece of Mammy Clorinda's spice cake, she stood transfixed at seeing the adoring smile on Maybelle's face as the girl stared fondly down at Laurette, clinging to her breast and voraciously sucking her nipple.

This poignant awareness of the eternal cycle of life stirred in Sybella the reminiscent yearnings she had known as a teenaged girl who had unabashedly confronted her dominant young husband and met his possessive passion with her own capacity for love. Yearnings which Djamba had kindled in her, even against her will, that afternoon when he had saved her from being thrown by Dulcy and held her in his arms to protect her from the raging storm. On March 14th, she would be thirty-six years old, and yet she did not feel her age nor look it. The sun had bronzed her freckled, tawny skin, and her figure had ripened from that of the slim girl who had become a wife nine months after her sixteenth birthday. Yet her body was still firm and shapely, her skin soft and smooth where the sun had not touched it, and the warmth of her dark-blue eyes and the engaging smile of her full lips—now even more provocative with that tiny quirk of mercurial sadness which made their corners droop—made her still a vibrant woman not yet willing to spell finis to her emotional life.

On the day before her birthday, Sybella and Matthew Forsden were going over the account book in old Lucien's study, and she was seated at his desk, when Matthew begged her pardon for disturbing her and informed her that Silas Jordan had ridden up and was eager to see her.

"Come in, Mr. Jordan. It's good to see you again. But you've been a stranger ever since that housewarming of ours—as one of our neighbors, you certainly should have come visiting long before this," she chided the planter.

He twisted his wide-brimmed hat between his pudgy fingers and haltingly replied, "The fact is, Mrs. Bouchard, I've been so busy trying to make a go of it on my place, taking care of Helen—who's been ailing all the last year, I'm sorry to say—and seeing that Bobby and Ashton are learning to work in the fields, I've not had much time for social calling."

"I'm dreadfully sorry to hear that about your wife, Mr. Jordan. I hope it's not serious."

Silas Jordan sighed heavily, shook his head. "I don't know what it is, maybe the climate, maybe she just doesn't take to plantation life in these parts. She's lost her strength, and she's wasting away to a shadow. I've had Doc Nedley out from Montgomery, and he's given her some tonic and bled her a little and told her to rest easy, but it doesn't seem to do much good. Well now, I didn't mean to come tell you about my troubles, only maybe they're sort of the reason I did come—well, you see, I'm up against it this year, Mrs. Bouchard."

"Tell me if I can help, Mr. Jordan."

"Well now"—he gave Matthew Forsden an uneasy look, his face flushing with embarrassment—"I rightly ought to have come to talk to Mr. Luke, but I guess he's busy over at the Williamson place—I just thought I might find him here. You see, m'am, I had a bad time with my cotton last year, and what with expenses

443

and all and my wife's sickness, I'm short of ready cash—I guess you might say everybody in the country is." He gave a nervous laugh.

"I'm sure Luke and I can arrange to lend you what you need, Mr. Jordan. We've been most fortunate, thank heavens."

"Well, I'll have to buy seed, and now that your husband's gone—I suppose it'll be all right if I have my cotton ginned over to your place here?"

"Of course it will. And I'm sure that neither Luke nor I will charge you for it."

"Oh no, m'am, that's too generous—I don't want charity—"

"You see, Mr. Jordan," Sybella interposed, "we're not going all out on cotton at Windhaven. We've put in vegetables, and we're trying some cattle and hogs, and they're doing very well. As I see it, and as Mr. Forsden has explained it to me, the cotton market is going to be down for the next several years, and food is the most important thing of all, especially for the workers and the people in charge of them. So my hands will keep in good practice by ginning your cotton whenever you're ready to have it hauled over, Mr. Jordan. Now, how much do you think you're going to need for this season?"

"Maybe three thousand, m'am?" he ventured, looking hopefully up at her.

"Of course. I'll have Luke draw a note that you can sign, and there'll be no interest, Mr. Jordan. Please don't protest, it's our way of helping our neighbors."

"God bless you, Mrs. Bouchard!" Silas Jordan burst out, then turned away, took out a red bandanna handkerchief from his breeches pocket and loudly blew his nose to conceal his emotion. "There's just one other thing—but no—I'd better not say it in the presence of a lady—"

"I shan't take offense, no matter what it is, I promise. Do tell me what's on your mind, I'm not a child, Mr. Jordan, and I know that men do things they don't tell their womenfolk about, but that's not to say we don't understand and sympathize."

"Well then—before I moved out here, there was a black wench—well, the long and short of it is, she gave me a baby, but I didn't ever want Helen to know, so I bided my time and then when I heard about this slave trainer Buffery, I—well, I went and sold Trish to him, you see."

"I understand. You were thoughtful in not letting your wife know, I'm sure. I know that you're a devoted husband and father, Mr. Jordan, I can tell that from the way Bobby and Ashton behaved themselves. Matter of fact," Sybella laughed, "I rather think that Arabella has been wondering why in the world Bobby never came calling on her after the impression he made when they danced."

"Well now, you sure know how to put a man at ease, Mrs. Bouchard, I'm mighty beholden to you. Then about Trish, I found out that Jim Buffery sold the girl back to your husband—meaning no offense, m'am."

"I see." Sybella frowned.

"Now that he's dead, I was thinking—well, I've heard about this Underground Railroad thing, how they get slaves out of the South and away to Canada where they won't be slaves any more. I wanted to keep a little of that money I was going to borrow from you, get it to Trish and maybe see if she couldn't start a life of her own where she wouldn't have to be a slave."

There could be no doubt, Sybella reasoned, that Mark had "inherited" Trish along with the land which Henry had so obsessively sought. And she knew also that Mark would angrily resent her interference, and perhaps take it out on poor Maybelle. After a moment's reflection, she finally said, "I'll talk to Luke about that, Mr. Jordan. Maybe he can work out a way to get Trish back and out of Alabama. He'll ride over to your place tomorrow, I'll get word to him at once and he'll bring the note and the draft on our Mobile house, and then you and he can talk about Trish."

"God bless you again, m'am. I'd take it mighty kindly if this could be just between us, as you might say—"

"I understand perfectly, Mr. Jordan. You needn't worry, and Mr. Forsden, my overseer, is the soul of discretion. It's good to see you again, and I do hope your wife gets better soon so that we can have you both over to one of Mammy Clorinda's nice suppers."

Silas Jordan vigorously shook hands with her, blew his nose again, thanked her and Matthew Forsden, and then left the study. Sybella turned to the English overseer: "The poor man, I feel so sorry for him. And I do hope that Luke can help about getting that girl of his away."

"I've heard some talk about the Underground Railroad myself, Mrs. Bouchard," Forsden guardedly replied. "I know there's very strong feelings against all abolitionists in these parts, but there are times when I sympathize with the slaves and wish that some of the cruelly treated ones could be spirited away to freedom."

"Freedom," Sybella mused; "it seems so strange, Mr. Forsden, that we who talk about it so much take it for granted, and those blacks out in the fields have never known what it really is and so many of them are beaten and abused because they even dare to dream about it."

"I think that's one reason why I didn't want to run my father's plantation any longer, Mrs. Bouchard. I didn't want to go to sleep nights thinking that I owned people and that their lives were dependent upon my orders and my whims. You don't know what it's meant to me personally to work here at Windhaven for you and your stepson. And I only wish that your enlightened views would be contagious throughout all of the South before it's too late."

She rose from the desk, put a hand on his arm and smiled at him. "Do you know, Mr. Forsden, you're very good for me. You make me feel useful and needed again, and I've wanted it perhaps more than ever now that Henry's gone."

He stared at her, began to speak, then thought better of it and quietly said, "I think I'd better go over some of those entries in the account book, Mrs.

446

Bouchard. It's getting a bit late, and I want to see some of the hands about clearing the corn stubble tomorrow."

"It's my birthday tomorrow, Mr. Forsden. I feel like giving them a day off, if you've no objection."

"Of course not, if you like. We've pretty well caught up on the hoeing and the plowing and the seeding, and everything's in very good order."

"Have you ever thought of marriage, Mr. Forsden?" she asked him.

"I—no, I suppose I've been so busy trying to find myself after deciding that I didn't want to inherit my father's place that I really hadn't thought about it—"

"This is going to sound shameless, and if it embarrasses you, forgive me. But I can't help noticing how good you've been to the children, how wise and kind you are, and how all the workers love you. It would be very good for me if I could rely on you not just as an overseer, but as a kind of partner."

He stared blankly at her for a moment, then gasped: "Mrs. Bouchard, you're much too flattering—"

"No, I don't think so. You're exactly the sort of man, Mr. Forsden, who does things without blowing his horn about them or seeking praise before the work's done. You've no idea how restful and enjoyable that is for a woman, because she can feel secure without feeling under a man's thumb. In a word, I'm asking whether you'd consider marrying me."

He gasped again, then his face crimsoned. He took a step toward her and said in an unsteady voice, "You're so above my station, I wouldn't have dreamed of asking—but the truth is, Mrs Bouchard—Sybella—I admire and respect you tremendously, and I—yes, I'd be proud to be your partner and to have you share my name."

Sybella made a saucy face and exhaled a sigh of relief. "Thank goodness!" she exclaimed. "I was afraid you were going to tell me that no man in his right mind would ever hear of a woman proposing. But I'm very glad, Matthew dear, and I think we can be happy with

447

each other." She lifted her face, and he gently cupped her cheeks and kissed her lightly on the mouth. Her arms rose up to enfold him, and she responded warmly.

CHAPTER THIRTY-ONE

Luke Bouchard was delighted when Sybella confided that she and Matthew Forsden were to be married the last week of April. Mark, however, received the news glumly, and later that night, when he was alone with Maybelle, sneeringly declared, "It's a fine thing at her age, Maybelle! And the worst of it is, she's picked an overseer, the kind of fellow you don't invite to be an equal with you. Now I suppose she'll expect me to call him Father—damned if I will!"

For her part, Maybelle was happy for Sybella, whom she had come to love because of the woman's unfailing kindness toward her. Unashamedly, too, Maybelle much preferred her new home at Windhaven because of its luxury and beauty to the drab, sparsely furnished house Edward Williamson had had built for himself and his daughters; even their former Georgia house had been much more comfortable. The presence of Arabella and Fleurette and their cordiality had made it easier for her to endure Mark's frequent absences, for he spent three or four days of every week visiting the land he had inherited from Henry Bouchard and conferring with Patrick Jerrold on its prospects for a favorable crop this year. And Mammy Clorinda's meals, in contrast with Zora Devlin's comparatively meager fare, were so appetizing that Maybelle had gained a most becoming weight after Laurette's birth.

The consequence was that Mark found her even

more desirable, and Maybelle for a few short weeks enjoyed the illusion that her moody husband was falling in love with her again and, finding herself pregnant, hoped that this time she could give him a son and heir to make him completely satisfied with their marriage.

But during the last week of April, when Sybella and Matthew Forsden took the *Tensaw* down to Mobile to be married and from there to spend a week in New Orleans on their honeymoon, Mark told his wife that he was going to spend the next week or two with Patrick Jerrold supervising the hoeing and cutting, since several days of steady rain had made the weeds and grass spring up along the rows of cotton plants.

On this humid Friday afternoon, he dismounted from his horse and tied the reins to the branch of a tree near the brick and log house. Jerrold was waiting for him, a worried look on his gaunt face. "Good thing you got back here, Mr. Mark." He tipped his hat respectfully. "Jim Buffery came over for a visit yesterday afternoon and made me an offer for Trish. Seems he wants to buy her back for some planter friend of his in Natchez. He's willing to pay thirteen hundred for her; that'll give you a fair four hundred profit. Says he thinks that's mighty decent, considering you've used her considerable." He accompanied this last with a lewd wink.

Mark scowled. "I'm not selling that high-yeller bitch. I've broken her in right, and she's learned a few tricks I'm partial to, Pat. Anyhow, he got Tansie and Suzy, so he's got no cause to whine. And that reminds me, did you pick out a few likely bucks and wenches we can dispose of?"

"I surely did. Just waiting on you to give me the go-ahead sign. There's two hands, Lance and George, good workers but spoiling for trouble—they'd be better off on a sugarcane plantation in Louisiana where they'd get their uppity nonsense whipped out of them for sure. Jim Buffery's always in the market for cane field niggers."

"Then sell them. What about the wenches?"

"Well, there's Dottie, the one that married up with Jeptha. She's carrying his sucker right now, and I think

450

he's come down with the yaws. Moping around, can't do a day's work——"

"Well, sell Dottie and the sucker and be sure you get a good price from that Mississippi skinflint," Mark grumbled. "Think we ought to send for old Doc Nedley to give Jeptha a good physic?"

"I don't think it'd do much good, Mr. Mark. No physic's going to cure the yaws, that I know of."

Mark shrugged. "Maybe it'd be simpler to put a bullet in him and get him out of the way so he doesn't linger, then. I'll leave that to you, Pat. Anything else?"

"Nothin' I can think of, no sir. I've got the niggers on your land working their black tails off hoeing up the weeds—this rain spell we've just had sure brought them up fast."

"Well, keep them at it, then. Guess you'll want a little advance on your wages?"

Jerrold grinned, revealing strong, yellowing teeth. "Never say no to money, Mr. Mark, not me. Thank you mighty kindly."

"I'll write you out a draft on Mobile directly I've had supper. Get Mary to fixing it, and yours too. Think maybe I'll stay here a night or so, then go on down look at the rest of the land with you tomorrow."

Jerrold nodded, then went to one of the slave cabins to order Mary to prepare supper for both men, while Mark Bouchard strode into the brick and log house, tossed his wide-brimmed hat on a chair, and strode into the bedroom where Trish awaited him. She sat nervously on the edge of a low chair, twisting her fingers restlessly, dressed in a white shift and a pair of fancy cloth slippers which Mark had bought in New Orleans and liked to have her wear when she paraded naked before him at night.

"What's this about your moping around while I've been away, you high-yeller bitch?" he glowered.

The slim mulatto lowered her eyes, shivering and huddling in anticipation of her master's vindictive cruelty. "Please, massa, don't be mad with Trish," she forlornly pleaded. "It ain't nothin', jist I thinks I'se gwine

451

to hab a sucker, that's all, massa. I sorta feel sick and such, I don't mean nuttin', honest, massa."

"Then get rid of it, do you hear?" he said. "I don't want a brat that's got nigger blood in it, no matter how good you are in bed, you hear me, Trish? Go see Mandy, she'll tell you how to lose it."

"But, Mistah Mark, suh, please, I—I want to keep it, please!" Trish fixed him with her expressive eyes, her tears glistening.

"You heard me! If you dare have it, I'll sell it right off to Jim Buffery. I mean it, you uppity little bitch. You've been needing a good lesson for the last few weeks, from the way you've been pining and moping around your chores, Pat Jerrold tells me."

Roughly he began to undress, stripping down to his boots, while the girl shrank back in the chair, crossing her arms over her small, hard-pointed breasts.

"Oh, please don't, please, massa!" she tearfully faltered.

"Stand up and take off that damn dress and be quick about it!" he snarled. Though paralyzed with fear, the girl knew better than to disobey and, sobbing now, she drew off the single garment and let it fall to the floor. He came toward her, thrust out his left hand to yank at the thick plait of glossy black hair, then, buffeting her head to and fro, he slapped first one cheek and then the other with his right palm till she was wailing for mercy and trying to slip down onto her knees in submission.

Tugging the leather belt out of his breeches, Mark lashed her savagely as she crouched, bowing her head and covering her breasts with her arms to keep them from the stinging swipes of the leather. Angry red streaks rose on her back and shoulders, her buttocks and thighs, and Trish twisted and writhed frenziedly but made no effort to escape.

"There now, that's just a start of what you'll get if you ain't rid of that brat the next time I come back here, understand, Trish?"

"Y—yes, massa!" she moaned.

Dragging her up by the hair and cuffing her swollen

face again, he flung her onto the bed and savagely penetrated her, while Trish sobbed, her face twisted to one side and an arm crooked over it, passively surrendering her shuddering, pain-wracked flesh.

Soon afterward, Mary entered with the supper tray, and stood transfixed, for the door to the bedroom was open and she could readily see what had taken place. Sensing her presence from Trish's convulsive gasp of shame, Mark snarled, "Put it down and get out, you black bitch, or I'll take my belt to you too!"

Then he seated himself at the rough-hewn table and fell to eating, without a thought for the weeping girl in the room beyond.

It was nearly four in the morning when Trish, her cotton dress torn by the twigs and branches through the forest-like terrain she had hurried through, sank down on her knees exhausted, on the edge of the clearing before the sprawling Williamson house. She burst into hysterical sobs, and then, recovering, looked tearfully over her shoulder to see if anyone was in pursuit. Stumbling to her feet, she made her way to the door of the house and began to beat on it with her clenched fist, sobbing loudly and continuing to look frantically back as she did so.

Luke Bouchard wakened with a start, propped himself up on his elbow and looked down on his sleeping wife. Blinking, he listened and heard the thump-thump-thump of Trish's pounding. Putting his robe on over his underdrawers, he made his way to the door and carefully opened it, and was surprised to see the tear-stained, swollen face of the young mulatto. "My God, girl, what's happened to you? Come in, come in. There, sit down on that hassock till I get a light and see what's the matter."

A few moments later, he returned with an oil lamp which he set down on the little table near the hassock. Trish moaned and shrank back, raising her tear-swollen eyes to his. "Please don't make me go back, massa!" she pleaded.

"Go back to whom, girl? Who beat you this way?

453

Your face is swollen, and you're suffering—you must have run a long way—"

"It's Mistah Mark, suh, he's the one that whupped me—I told him I'm going to have a s—sucker and he said I was to get rid of it, and then he hit me and took his belt before he took me in bed, massa!"

"My God—to treat a young girl this way, it's monstrous!" Luke gasped. "Where did you come from originally? Who was your first master before Mark bought you?"

Trish covered her face with her hands and burst into convulsive sobs for a moment. Then falteringly, she said, "I'm Mistah Jordan's git, right off, suh. He got me by my mammy back in Noath Carolina, 'fore he come here. He didn't want his wife to know I was his git, so he sold me to Mistah Buffery. Then Mistah Henry bought me from him, and when he died, Mistah Mark kept me as his bed wench. Dat's the truth, massa, I swear it is!"

"You're Trish, aren't you? You poor girl!" Luke murmured. "Then you wouldn't want to go back to Mr. Jordan?"

"Oh no, he don't want any part of me, he said so when he sold me, he said it wasn't ma fault, but he couldn't stand to have me around and know that he'd had ma mammy when he was married all the time, suh."

"I see." Luke thought a moment, his face drawn and angry. "I'll tell you what, I'll get you some food and find a place for you to sleep. Then in the morning we can talk about what's to be done with you."

"You're awful kind. I'd be plumb scared if Mistah Mark came after me, the way he acted so. I want to keep the suckah, I truly do, suh!"

"Of course, and you've a right to your child." Luke straightened. *My God*, he said to himself, *it's Mark's child and he wanted to destroy it. I have to get her away from him—I know how, I'll use that Underground Railway James Birney wrote me about.* Then, his voice gentle, he said, "Come along to the kitchen, Trish. I'll get you some milk and something to eat, and

454

put a cold compress on your face to take down the swelling. Then we'll find you a bed and we'll see what we can do to help you after you've had a good night's sleep."

"That poor girl!" Lucy indignantly declared, "we've got to free her—can't you buy her yourself, Luke, and then set her free?"

"It's not all that easy. If she left this state by herself, she'd be picked up on the border by half a dozen unscrupulous slave traders and sold into a far worse situation. But I've thought of something, because last week James Birney wrote me that in Cairo, Illinois, there's an underground station already operating. It's kind of a huge underground cellar, and from there the slaves are taken to Ohio or Canada. He also writes that there's a family in Cincinnati who lost their two girls to scarlet fever. They'll give anything to have a girl to bring up to help them ease their grief. If I could get Trish there, she'd be free forever."

"Why can't I take her, Luke?" Lucy quietly spoke up, her eyes shining with eagerness.

"It's out of the question, darling. I wouldn't allow it, seeing that your baby's due in August. It'd be much too dangerous and arduous for you. When Matthew Forsden gets back from his honeymoon, I'm going to ask him if he'd take her there. Once in Cairo, there'll be people in this underground system to take her on to the Zotlows in Cincinnati. And if Mark comes looking for her here, I'll give him back her purchase price and something into the bargain to satisfy his mercenary feelings about the poor girl."

A week later, when Matthew Forsden returned to Windhaven, Luke found him a sympathetic and willing aide. Two days later the English overseer and Trish, dressed in one of Sybella's most fashionable gowns and an elaborate bonnet, her face liberally coated with rice powder and a touch of rouge on her lips, boarded the *River Queen* to Mobile, thence to New Orleans and up the Mississippi to Cairo. It was a journey that would take Matthew Forsden a month in all before he could return to Windhaven and his devoted Sybella.

Mark Bouchard, furious over Trish's escape, had spent several days in futile search, first going to the Buffery farm and then to the Jordan plantation. There, Silas Jordan, his face haggard because of his wife's illness, swore that he had not seen Trish since he had sold her to the Bufferys, and begged Mark not to mention the girl's escape to any of his slaves lest Helen Jordan hear of it and guess at his long-kept guilty secret.

Two days after Matthew Forsden had taken Trish on the *River Queen*, Mark came back to Windhaven in a black rage. Added to his fury over Trish's disappearance was Patrick Jerrold's news that most of the cotton on old Granville Murton's acreage which Mark inherited from his father was infested with boll weevils and would have to be destroyed. In his anger over that news, Mark ordered the overseer to whip the two black foremen who were responsible for the cultivation of that cotton, and to take what measures he could to prevent the spread of that blight to his other acreage.

Luke had ridden over to Windhaven that same afternoon to visit Sybella and to thank her again for Matthew Forsden's kindness toward Trish as well as to offer his services during the overseer's absence in helping with the cultivation of Windhaven crops. As he left Sybella's room, he saw Mark coming up the stairs to Maybelle's room, and intercepted him: "Mark, I want to talk to you."

"I've no time for talk now," Mark said, about to knock on Maybelle's door.

"It's talk that concerns you, I think. I imagine you've been looking for Trish."

Mark's hand dropped to his side and he gaped in stupefaction at his half brother. "What the hell do you know about Trish?" he growled.

"Only that she came to our house a few days ago and begged for help. She's bearing your child, Mark."

"Why, you—damn your soul, what right have you to meddle in my business? Pa bought Trish, and I own her now. I know how you feel about slaves, but she's not your affair, remember that. What the hell did you

456

do with her? By God, you ought to have told me sooner——"

"I'll admit I didn't want to and for an excellent reason. Trish is where you'll never find her again. She's gone along the Underground Railroad and she'll be free when she reaches the end of it."

"You son of a bitch—you did that, you stole my slave?" Mark clenched his fists and took a step forward.

"I know that Father paid nine hundred dollars for her, Mark. I'll give you two thousand dollars, which certainly ought to buy you some other poor creatures you can vent your cruelty on."

"Don't you lecture me! You're so high and mighty, you and your book learning, your abolitionist ideas— by God, the day's going to come when people like you will be tarred and feathered and ridden out of the state on a rail, and it can't come any too soon for me! I ought to go to court about this."

"I'll face you in court, and Lucy and I will tell the judge how you told Trish to kill her unborn child."

"She's a nigger and——"

"She's a human being, and an unborn child, no matter what race, creed or color it is, has a right to protection under the law. I don't think you'll win that case, Mark."

"You goddamned lily-white abolitionist you! You think you're so pure you wouldn't sleep with a nigger bed wench, would you? I won't forget this, Luke, and I'll get back at you some way."

"Just make up your mind that when you go see Maybelle, you don't try to take it out on her," Luke quietly interposed. "She's not one of your niggers, you know. She's your wife, she's borne you a child and she deserves just a little affection from you."

"I've had a bellyful of your preaching to me! You're worse than Grandfather ever was, Goddamn your soul to hell!" Mark shouted. Then, opening Maybelle's door, he slammed it behind him as he strode toward his startled wife. "I ought to kill him," he muttered as

457

he seated himself beside Maybelle and, pulling her to him, kissed her fiercely, bruisingly on the mouth.

It was the next afternoon, just before sundown, and Luke was standing near the stable, as the stableboy Jimmy tendered him the reins. "He's sho fat 'n sassy, Mistah Luke suh, de way you treats him. Bet there ain't anudder hoss in dese heah pahts git treated so good, 'less'n it be Dulcy, Miz Bouchard's mare, and dat ol' debbil Midnight."

"I guess you're right, Jimmy. Where's Djamba? How are he and Celia and little Prissy getting along?"

The Kru's face beamed as he said, "Dey's all fine, Mistah Luke suh. Ah tol' Djamba dat high-yeller gal Celia, she done fall plum' smack in lub wid him so no other gal roun' heah ebbah gwine hab a chance to steal huh man from huh, yassuh! Right now, I think he in de kitchen wid Mammy Clorinda, gettin' some milk foah little Prissy, suh."

"Well, I'll wait to say hello to him. No, no, Jimmy, no need for you to go there, he'll be out and I'll wait."

A few moments later, Djamba emerged from the kitchen, and Luke raised his hand in friendly greeting. The Mandingo grinned and came forward, delightedly shook hands and declared that Celia and the little girl were thriving. "I feel free, Mr. Luke, almost as good as back in Africa now, thanks to you and Mrs. Bouchard."

"That's good. I know how good you are with horses, and this fall I'm going to bring some more cows and another bull here to Windhaven, and I'll put you in charge of them. We'll have lots of beef for all the workers, and good milk and cheese for little Prissy too."

"I want to serve, Mr. Luke, I want to do all I can to say thank you for my freedom—"

Djamba's earnest statement was suddenly interrupted by a shout as Mark Bouchard came forward, a box tucked under his arm. "Luke, don't run off, I've got business with you!" he called.

"I thought our business was concluded when I gave you that draft for two thousand dollars, Mark."

458

"Hell it is!" Mark sneered, opening the box. Inside lay the two pistols which Amos Greer had taken to the Creek village near Tuskegee. "You and I are going to settle this once and for all, d'you hear? I'm challenging you to a duel. By God, I'll kill you and then there'll be an end to all this abolitionist nonsense—otherwise, first thing you know, you'll be trying to liberate all the niggers here in Alabama!"

"Don't be ridiculous, Mark. You know that I won't fight you."

"Because you're a lily-livered coward, that's why!" He came forward and, drawing back his right hand, struck Luke across the jaw.

Djamba uttered a gasp as Luke winced, put a hand to his mouth and brought it away covered with blood from his cut lower lip. But very calmly he replied, "Perhaps I had that coming for interfering in your life, Mark, but some things go beyond just plain interference. Now put away that box of pistols before you do something you'll be sorry for."

"I didn't think you'd fight me, brother; you'd puke your guts out just holding a pistol. Well, by God, if you won't fight, there's nothing to stop me from killing you anyway—stealing Trish out from under me and being so mealy-mouthed about it—you think your two thousand dollars can buy me off?" Before Luke could anticipate his half brother's intention, Mark had seized one of the pistols and cocked it.

Before he could level it, Djamba rushed forward, seizing Mark's right wrist and forcing it upward. The pistol discharged harmlessly in the air.

"Take your nigger hands off me, you bastard! So this is what all your book learning's come to, is it? Letting this nigger lay his hands on a white man! Well, I've had my fill of Windhaven, of you, of Maybelle, of every goddamned nigger here! I'm leaving, and you can do what you please with your niggers, till some of these planters around here find out what fancy ideas you've got. They'll come gunning for you and they'll get you too, just you remember that!"

His face warped with hatred, Mark wrenched free of

Djamba's hold, strode into the stable, and emerged riding Midnight. He drew on the reins, halting the stallion and stared murderously down at Luke: "I'll be writing you from New Orleans," he said. "And I'll take half my inheritance, half of Windhaven. Just see that you raise enough cash to buy out my interest. Then you can run it into the ground, for all I care."

"And what about Maybelle and your daughter?" Luke asked, a pitying look on his face.

"To hell with them too—but thanks for reminding me—I've got a third of Maybelle's property coming, and don't you cheat me out of it. Better not come looking for me, or I swear I'll kill you the next time I see you!" Then, yanking viciously on the reins till Midnight reared at the bit, Mark kicked his heels against the stallion's belly and rode off.

CHAPTER THIRTY-TWO

Two weeks after Mark Bouchard's stormy leavetaking, the captain of the *River Queen* docked his paddle-wheeler at the landing, took on fuel from the wood yard which Luke had had built beside the dock, and delivered a packet of letters which included Mark's formal demand for a settlement of his rightful share of Windhaven. Luke at once conferred with his stepmother. "I've failed somewhere, Luke." Sybella sadly shook her head. "I thought I was a match for your father, but I wasn't. And I could never reach Mark at all, no matter how hard I tried."

"You can't reproach yourself, Mother. I'll keep my promise to him. He's to get the third of the Williamson holdings because he married Maybelle, even if he seems to have deserted her now. He's left her a child who bears the Bouchard name, and that's reason enough to honor his demand. But you, Mother, you're the one who must decide what's to be done with Windhaven. It doesn't matter about me. Grandfather left me that money in the Liverpool bank, and for certain it's all I shall ever need. The only thing is, with money so tight right now, it will be very difficult to give Mark his share of the cash."

"How can you put a money value on Windhaven, Luke? I know I couldn't begin to think of it. I don't mean just the land and its value now, or this house either, even though I know what it cost to build and to furnish. It's all the hard work and the love and the trust that went into building it, Grandfather's dreams—such things are priceless."

"I'd say that the Williamson place is worth about fifteen thousand and the workers there would bring about fifteen thousand more at Mobile or New Orleans if they were sold as slaves, which they'll never be. That means his share is about ten thousand, and when I sell the cotton and the produce from those acres this fall, I'll see that he gets that much. He can hardly hope to force any legal settlement so long as you and I are living. He'll just have to take what bounty you decide to give him, and it won't be enough to satisfy his greed."

"I know that, Luke. If only Grandfather were alive to settle this. What hurts me most is the thought of the bad blood between the two of you. I wish to God it had never happened, and all over an unfortunate girl who was in no way to blame. That's why I oppose slavery as much as Grandfather or you ever did, but there's little I can do as a woman. And even though I'm proud of the policies you've put to work here at Windhaven and over on Lucy's land, you know that many of our neighbors will condemn us, even hate us and call us abolitionists. Every time I read the *Journal*, I'm made aware of the growing hatred between the North and the South. Where will it all end, Luke?"

"I don't know, Mother. And I'll admit I acted rashly about that poor girl Trish, because I didn't have the right to take someone else's property away—even if every fiber in me cries out against the injustice that allows a girl to submit to any white man who lusts after her. But I know this, that I'm going to do all I can to help the Underground Railroad. If any of the workers here or on the Williamson land honestly want to be free and to leave Alabama, I'll do everything possible to get them to the North and pay them the wages they've earned for their faithful service here."

Sybella stared at her stepson, then took his hand and squeezed it and smiled, her eyes misty with tears of pride and love.

Mark had indicated that all correspondence was to

be sent to him at the auction rooms of Pierre Lourat in New Orleans. Accordingly, the next day, Luke wrote a long letter announcing his decision. He would, he told his half brother, pledge that a draft in the amount of $10,000 would be forwarded as soon as the Williamson crops had been sold in Mobile. Further, he was writing Antoine Rigalle to draw $25,000 in gold out of his personal trust fund deposited in the Bank of Liverpool and to remit that amount. It would represent his own settlement of what he believed Mark's share of Windhaven should be. Further, he added, because of the financial panic besetting the country, it would be impossible to arrive at any true commercial value of the entire estate, and he, as the elder son and heir, would naturally maintain a lifetime interest in all such property. He begged Mark to be content with this proof of good faith. Finally, he added a postscript reminding Mark that Maybelle was a loyal, devoted wife and had done nothing to deserve being cast aside; he sincerely hoped that Mark would reconsider and, if he did not care to remain at Windhaven, would at least make some arrangement to reunite her with him in New Orleans.

The summer was stiflingly humid and arduous, and Lucy's time was at hand. On August 7th, after a protracted labor, she bore a healthy black-haired boy. And when Luke asked her if she had thought of a name for the child, she murmured, "Let it be after your grandfather, Luke, and after that tiny baby who was your grandfather's first son by his beloved Dimarte, Edmond. Do you remember how your grandfather told you why he named that child after that brave stable boy who tried to recover his purse aboard the ship that brought him to this land?"

"I couldn't have thought of a better choice, Lucy. Lucien Edmond it shall be, names to be proud of, as I am proud of you and thank God for you every day of my life," Luke replied.

Maybelle, who had been despondent after Mark's abandonment, seemed to have been somewhat cheered by the advent of her sister's second child. Now in the fourth month of her own pregnancy, she had never been more lovely, though the shadowy look in her eyes told of her brooding over Mark's departure. Although Sybella felt sure that Mark would see the error of his ways and return, or at least send for his wife, Maybelle could not be persuaded to believe that. And, two days after the birth of Lucien Edmond, the *Tensaw* brought a letter from Mark addressed to Luke, with an enclosure for Maybelle. In the former, Mark grudgingly acknowledged the draft for $25,000 which Luke had had withdrawn from his own trust fund and conveyed by Antoine Rigalle, and urged his half brother to send him the share of the Williamson crop money as soon as it was paid out in Mobile. His note to Maybelle was brutally final:

Maybelle—

I don't plan to come back to Windhaven again. I'm working for Pierre Lourat, and I've bought into one of his pleasure houses. I'm helping him run that and the slave auction rooms too, and I'll be traveling through the South looking over likely niggers for good sales in New Orleans. You might as well forget all about me, find yourself another sweetheart, because I've all the girls I want. Maybe if you'd given me a son, I might have thought about having you here to bring him up for a spell. But daughters get married and they're only a botheration anyway. I'll see that you get some money every now and again for Laurette, but don't count on me for anything else.

He had not even bothered to sign his name to that callous rejection. Maybelle locked herself up in her room for most of the day, refusing even to take a tray of lunch which Mammy Clorinda sent up to her. But about twilight, she let herself out of her room and hurried down the stairway, pausing to see if anyone was nearby. Opening the front door, she hurried around the side of the château and beyond the stable in the direction of Pintilalla Creek. She clutched Mark's note in her hand, the paper stained with her tears, her eyes red from weeping.

Djamba had been rubbing down Sybella's mare Dulcy, promising her that her mistress would soon take her out for her daily ride. He glanced over at the empty stall that the black stallion Midnight had once occupied, and dolefully shook his head. "Too bad that big black horse gone out of your life, Dulcy girl," he said affectionately. "Maybe if he'd stayed, he'd have given you a colt faster and bigger and stronger than he ever was, girl. Don't you get too fat and lazy now, you keep in shape for Miz Bouchard."

Dulcy nickered and rubbed her muzzle against his palm, and Djamba laughed softly and stroked her ears, then walked out of the stable back toward the cabin where Celia and Prissy awaited him. In the dusk, he could just make out the shadowy outline of Maybelle as she walked determinedly toward the bank of the creek, and out of a sudden presentiment, he began to run toward her.

The water of the creek was high, though stagnant, and Maybelle sobbingly scrambled down the bank to the edge, losing her balance and nearly falling. Righting herself, she looked up at the gloomy sky and then leaped into the dark water. Djamba had reached the bank now and dived in after her, surfacing a few feet away from the young woman who had clenched her fists and closed her eyes, willing herself to drown.

When he seized her, she began to struggle, "No, no, don't. I want to die, please, let me be—oh no!"

"No, no, Missy, that no way to talk, Miss Maybelle. What poor little Laurette going to think when her mama go away without even saying good-bye? Now you stop fighting Djamba. Come on now, honey, it'll be all right," he told her as he swam toward shore, one arm around her waist. Djamba grasped her firmly and brought her safely to dry land.

465

"There," he panted, "you'll be all right, Miss Maybelle. Things aren't that bad, they can't be—"

His face suddenly contorted, and he looked down to see a water moccasin drawing back its ugly head. Its fangs had just pierced his left calf through the thin cotton breeches. With a growl, he stamped the heel of his heavy workshoe onto the reptile's head and twisted it until the writhing coil loosened. Then, bending down, he lifted Maybelle to her feet, picked her up in his arms and carried her back toward the château.

"Djamba—what happened to you—oh my God—it's my fault—oh, I want to die!" Maybelle sobbed as he hammered with his fist on the door.

Old Matthew came running to the door. Djamba panted, "Get Miss Maybelle to her room, I think she's hurt. Have Miz Bouchard come quick!"

Then he turned and hobbled back to the stable. "Jimmy, give me your knife, quick," he commanded the boy. Pulling up the leg of his breeches, he stared at the fang marks, then dug the blade of the knife around the wound, gouging out the discolored flesh. "Jimmy, suck the poison out, quick! I think I can catch it in time—the breeches helped a little, but it stings real bad," he gasped.

Jimmy flung himself down and obediently began to suck out the blood. "That's fine, Jimmy, that's fine," Djamba groaned. "Now get a rag and tie it round my leg there, tight as you can."

When it was done, he seated himself on the ground, leaning against the wall of the stable, his face contorted with pain. "If you've got any *taffai*, I can use some right now. . . . Ah, that's better. Thank you, Jimmy, you're more than my friend now, you saved Djamba's life."

"Who dat you pull outa de creek, Djamba?" Jimmy asked.

"Never you mind, Jimmy. We don't talk about it now. I feel better, yes, I don't think that old devil snake going to kill Djamba; Djamba too tough for him. Now I'm going back to Celia. You take good care of the horses."

466

The old majordomo had summoned Sybella after admitting the half-fainting Maybelle and her rescuer. When the woman came down from her room, she found her daughter-in-law lying unconscious, her soaked frock streaked with blood. "Matthew, go get Amy. Tell her Miss Maybelle's losing her baby," Sybella ordered.

Maybelle's suicidal attempt had resulted in a miscarriage. And when Amy, who served as midwife to the black families of Windhaven, examined the fetus, she muttered, "Poor Missy Maybelle, she done lost a little boy. She hurt so bad, Ah doan think she ebbah gwine hab a chil' again nohow."

CHAPTER THIRTY-THREE

Maybelle soon recovered after the loss of her baby, and it was Sybella who saw to it that every possible kind of worthwhile distraction was arranged for her daughter-in-law. By the end of August, she had arranged a soirée and hired an eight-man orchestra from New Orleans to play classical and operatic airs in the spacious drawing room while the guests were treated to a buffet collation of Mammy Clorinda's most tempting dishes. Silas Jordan's wife had died, but the middle-aged planter and his two sons, Bobby and Ashton, were invited to the party because Sybella had news for him. A week before the soirée, a letter had come from Cincinnati, addressed by the Zotlows, with Trish's scrawl informing Sybella that the kindly Germans were going to adopt her and her child and that she would never forget what Luke, Sybella and Matthew Forsden had done to bring her to freedom.

But Sybella had joyful news for Matthew Forsden's ears alone just before they went downstairs to greet the first of their guests. "Matthew, we're going to have a child in January, I think," she whispered as she took his arm. "I'm so glad, my dearest, and you've made me shamelessly young again, I confess it;" she added, giving him a quick kiss on the cheek. And when she saw him blush like a schoolboy, she laughed affectionately, a laugh that rang with the same zest for life which she had had as a girl and which, until now, had been a rarity.

The two bachelor planters, James Cavendish and Benjamin Harnesty, who had been guests at the great housewarming of Windhaven, were not present at this soirée. Both men had sold their land and slaves, and Cavendish had gone to Natchez to become a slave dealer, while Harnesty had left for New Orleans to run a faro table for a notorious gambler whose new establishment was said to be even more ornate than Pierre Lourat's.

By October, Luke had brought the promised cows and another pedigreed bull to Windhaven, and Matthew Forsden had had the workers fence off about a hundred acres of land for grazing. Beyond the cattle, the red bluff loomed as a boundary marker, not unlike that hill in the village of Yves-sur-lac up which Lucien Bouchard had once ridden on a fateful May afternoon to ask for the hand of Edmée de Courent in marriage. In this same month, Texas formally withdrew her request for annexation to the United States, and the administration of President Van Buren had lost control of both houses of Congress in the mid-term elections.

On January 12, 1839, Sybella Forsden gave birth to a healthy son who, at her husband's eager suggestion, was named Paul, after the overseer's father. Maybelle aided her mother-in-law during the brief labor, and was as overjoyed as Sybella at the birth of this little boy. She had by now completely reconciled herself to the rupture of her marriage; she spent a great deal of time with Arabella and Fleurette as well as with Laurette, often riding on horseback over to the Williamson plantation to visit her sister and the children and to have supper with them and Luke. It was a peaceful year, a restful year, and the Bouchards and their workers enjoyed the bounty of the rich earth.

It was a momentous year for the nation as well: the horse-drawn, double-row cornplanter and the power loom for weaving two-ply ingrain carpets were invented, and Charles Goodyear discovered the method for vulcanizing rubber. Samuel F. B. Morse brought from Paris the process of photography he had learned from the great Daguerre, and with Dr. John W. Draper

470

made the first daguerreotype portraits in the United States. Abner Doubleday laid down the first rules for baseball at Cooperstown, New York, and Joseph Smith established Nauvoo, Illinois, as a Mormon town. In September, a commercial treaty was signed between France and Texas, France being the first European nation to recognize the independence of this new republic. In November, the abolitionists met in their convention at Warsaw, New York, and formed the Liberty party which named James G. Birney—by then a resident of New York—for President. A month later, the Whig National Convention at Harrisburg, Pennsylvania, nominated William Henry Harrison for President and John Tyler of Virginia for Vice President. Once again the Presidential aspirations of the great Whig Henry Clay were dashed to disappointment.

In 1840, an exploring expedition commanded by Lieutenant Charles Wilkes discovered the Antarctic continent, and President Van Buren established a ten-hour day for federal employees on public works. He was renominated as President in May by the Democratic National Convention in Baltimore. Harrison and Tyler won a resounding victory over Van Buren on December 2nd by the electoral vote of 234 to 60, while James Birney garnered a popular vote of 7069. The Democratic newspapers had stirringly referred to Harrison as a man who would be better off spending the rest of his life in a log cabin, guzzling hard cider. Overnight, log-cabin political headquarters sprang up everywhere, log-cabin floats were paraded in the streets, cider was dispensed free at giant rallies, and even pious farmers went to church with canteens of cider slung round their necks. The popular cry of "Tippecanoe and Tyler, too," had galvanized the nation into ousting Jackson's man, who was blamed for the panic of 1837.

But even more significant to the struggling economy of the South was the lowering of the price paid for cotton down to a little less than nine cents a pound on the finest quality. In Alabama, where about one-fifth of all the cotton in the nation was produced, this depression

471

was felt most keenly. It was a time for profiting by the selling and trading of slaves rather than tilling the soil . . . the policy that was to lead to the inevitable crisis. But the Bouchards, offering their gins to their neighbors without charge for preparing cotton for the Mobile market, diversifying their crops and concentrating on food for all the workers and themselves, stood firm amid the economic tumult that beset so many planters and forced the small farmers to abandon their holdings in despair or to lose them in bankruptcy.

And on the very day of President Harrison's election, young Celia presented her husband with a son, whom Djamba named Lucas, as his way of paying tribute to the master of Windhaven who had been instrumental in granting him his freedom.

On April 4, 1841, a month after his inaugural, William Henry Harrison died of pneumonia and John Tyler succeeded to the Presidency, with Daniel Webster as Secretary of State. Six days later the New York *Tribune,* with Horace Greeley as its editor, began publication. In June, Senator Henry Clay introduced the Whig program into the Senate, calling for the repeal of the Independent Treasury Act, the incorporation of a new bank, the adoption of new tariff, and distribution among states of proceeds from the sales of public lands. The new President vetoed that Fiscal Bank Bill in August, for he was a lifelong Jeffersonian, a strict Constitutional constructionist, a states' rights man and a deadly opponent of protective tariffs and the national bank. A week after that veto, Clay pressed for the Second Fiscal Bank Bill, and again President Tyler vetoed it in September. All of his Cabinet resigned excepting Daniel Webster. The House of Representatives moved to impeach Tyler, the first such action in American history, charging him with the misuse of power, but that partisan move failed by a vote of 127 to 83.

The price of cotton tumbled a few cents lower than the previous year, and there were more bankruptcies in the smaller plantations of the harassed South.

Mark Bouchard did not write again to either Luke

or his estranged wife Maybelle. But, through aging and ailing Grover Mason, who still conducted his attorney's practice in Montgomery, it was learned that the younger Bouchard heir had arranged for the lawyer to sell his father's original hundred acres and the two additional pieces of fifty and seventy-five acres to James Buffery, who, much to Luke Bouchard's disgust, extended the scope of his breeding and training farm onto those lands. All that Grover Mason could tell Luke was that Mark had casually stated in the letter that he was prospering as a partner of Pierre Lourat and that he was traveling through Mississippi and Louisiana.

In March of 1842, Henry Clay resigned from the Senate after forty years of public service, but he would return seven years later, for once again he planned to campaign for the Presidency. In August, Secretary of State Daniel Webster concluded the famous Webster-Ashburton Treaty between the United States and Great Britain which defined the boundary between Maine and Canada and at last settled minor boundary disputes between the Atlantic Ocean and the Rocky Mountains. In that month also, the highly protective Tariff Act restored tax duties to the general level of 1832. And on the next to last day of the year, President Tyler, relying upon the advice of his gifted Secretary of State, declared in his message to Congress that the United States would look with disfavor upon any attempt of another power to take possession of the Hawaiian Islands.

On May 15, 1843, a week after Daniel Webster had retired from President Tyler's cabinet, Sybella's father died in his sleep, at the age of sixty-nine. The day after the funeral in Montgomery, the *River Queen* docked at the Windhaven landing to discharge an elegantly dressed, sleek young man in frock coat and high silk hat, carrying a valise, who had told the captain of the paddlewheeler that he would be happy to deliver in person the packet of letters addressed to Luke Bouchard.

It was William, a sturdy Angola in his early thirties, who admitted the suave visitor to the château, for old

473

Matthew, the former majordomo, had died at the beginning of this new year. William ushered him into the sitting room and went to fetch Matthew Forsden from the fields, who in turn had Sybella come downstairs to greet Edouard Villiers, the visitor from New Orleans.

"A pleasure to meet you, Mr. Villiers." Matthew Forsden came forward to offer his hand. "William tells me that you have some letters for Luke Bouchard. He's in his own house downriver, supervising the crops. If it's urgent, I can have one of our workers ride over and bring him back."

"Well, sir, the letters I have are from the Rigalle bank in New Orleans. You see, poor old Antoine was a dear friend of mine, but he has retired because the doctors tell him he has very little time left to live. He has appointed his young assistant—oh, a most capable administrator, I assure you, sir!—one John Brunton, who at one time was head clerk in a leading Mobile bank, but has been living in New Orleans and working for my friend Antoine the past decade."

"I see. I know that Luke will want to have the news about our accounts in New Orleans—as I understand, he was planning to visit there next month," Matthew Forsden replied. "My wife and I would be honored if you'd join us at supper tonight, stay the night as our guest, and tomorrow Luke will be here to receive these letters."

"You're most kind, sir. I'd hoped, to be very frank with you, to have the opportunity of seeing this magnificent château, of which Antoine has told me so much. Also, my other good friend in New Orleans, Pierre Lourat."

Sybella and Matthew Forsden exchanged a knowing glance, and Matthew casually remarked, "By any chance, do you know Mark Bouchard?"

"To be sure I do, sir," the Creole replied. "He's quite well known throughout New Orleans as Pierre Lourat's right-hand man. Why, I've heard it said there's no sharper trader when it comes to judging a prime field hand or a wench—begging your pardon, Mrs. Forsden. And he's a ladies' man too, I'm told—

several duels of honor have come about as a result of his *affaires du coeur*, in all of which he successfully acquitted himself. Why yes, I do believe, he must be Mr. Luke Bouchard's brother; isn't that so?"

"His half brother," Sybella amended with a look of distress. "I must ask you, Mr. Villiers, at supper tonight, do not discuss anything that you have just told us. It would be rather trying."

"But of course, Mrs. Forsden, I am always discreet, especially when I am warned by so beautiful a lady." The Creole executed an elegant bow. At this moment, Arabella Bouchard entered, and Villiers promptly rose again, his eyes wide with admiration.

At nineteen, Arabella was in the full bloom of her young beauty, tall and slim, but with a gracefully developed figure which the style of the period rather overemphasized, particularly in the tournure of her silken skirt with its horsehair muslin petticoat buttoning under the base and exaggerating the fullness of hips. Her black hair was done up in a pompadour, with a chignon at the back of her head, her creamy neck left bare. "How do you like my new frock, Mama?" she exclaimed before she saw the admiring visitor, then clapped her hand to her mouth and promptly blushed.

"If I may be so bold, *Mademoiselle*," Edouard Villiers smilingly said, "all eyes in New Orleans would be upon you when you entered the theater or the opera in such attire."

"La, sir, how very flattering!" Arabella had not broken herself of her childish habit of giggling when she was especially moved, and Sybella could hardly suppress an indulgent smile as she hastened to introduce her irrepressible daughter: "Arabella dear, this is Mr. Edouard Villiers from New Orleans. My daughter, Mr. Villiers. I'll have William show you to your room, Mr. Villiers," Sybella offered, "for I'm sure you'll want to rest before supper. We look forward to news from New Orleans. Is it still the same exciting place as ever?"

"More so, Mrs. Forsden. Now we claim that our city has more skilled chefs and fine orchestras than any other in these entire United States. And our port boasts more and larger steamboats than even New York. You must surely come visit soon, to see all the marvels, and the magnificent homes and their decor. And of course"—he drew himself up proudly—"we Creoles have the last word in good taste in tapestries, furniture, paintings, vases from the house of Sèvres itself, and our hospitality is, as ever, incomparable."

At this, he took out a little silver snuffbox and, eying Sybella and Arabella, politely asked, "May I, ladies?" and, receiving Sybella's silent and amused nod, promptly tapped a pinch into each nostril and inhaled deeply. "Most refreshing after so tedious a journey up-river," he declared. "And how good it is of you to receive me and to invite me into the wonders of this château."

Supper that evening was prepared by Nancy, for Mammy Clorinda was seriously ill with a condition which old Dr. Nedley diagnosed as dropsy and which would bring her to her grave two months later. Edouard Villiers monopolized the conversation at the table, his eyes resting first on Arabella and then the voluptuous Maybelle, now twenty-three. Tactfully, remembering Sybella's injunction throughout his anecdotes of life in New Orleans, he made no mention of either Pierre Lourat or Mark Bouchard. Yet Maybelle listened enthralled, her eyes mournfully fixed on his handsome face with its waxed moustache adorning his upper lip. Fleurette, now eleven and already giving promise of loveliness, was equally absorbed in his accounts of the magnificent balls and costly gowns and jewelry which adorned the New Orleans belles. Little Laurette, six years old and precocious for her years, sometimes broke into the conversation of her elders by asking Villiers to explain some of the words he used in his descriptions which were utterly unintelligible to her, and Maybelle's beautiful, sad features brightened at these interludes.

The next morning, Luke Bouchard, summoned by Jimmy, rode over to Windhaven to meet the Creole dandy and to receive the letters from Antoine Rigalle.

One contained a current statement of the Bouchard account in the Rigalle bank; the other bore out Villiers' comment that Rigalle had already appointed his successor in view of the illness which had caused him to retire from all affairs of the bank. In a short paragraph, he introduced the Creole visitor as a trustworthy friend, a wealthy and discriminating bachelor.

Luke carefully studied the statement of the family account, then handed it to Sybella, putting his finger on an entry which indicated that Mark Bouchard had received the transfer of $25,000 in gold from the Bank of Liverpool as well as the draft for $10,000 as his share of the crops sold in Mobile. Sybella nodded and showed the statement to her husband. Edouard Villiers, patiently standing to one side, now turned to Luke and politely asked, "Is there any service I may perform for you on my return to New Orleans, Mr. Bouchard?"

"I'll send a letter off to Antoine, of course, and one to the new manager of the bank. Everything seems quite in order, and all of us are much in your debt for having brought us these letters, Mr. Villiers."

"Not at all, it was my pleasure, and you've certainly made me feel welcome. Indeed, I find myself somewhat embarrassed now, for I should like to extend my visit, unless it is inconvenient to you."

"That would be for my stepmother and stepfather to decide, Mr. Villiers," Luke said.

"But of course you may stay as long as you wish, Mr. Villiers, you've greatly entertained us with your stories of New Orleans, and I know the children are dying to hear more about what grownups wear—you know how girls are," Sybella laughed.

"I am a Creole, Mrs. Forsden," Villiers said, putting his hand to his heart in a melodramatic gesture, "and if you know anything of the Gallic soul, you know that we are easily affected by beauty. When I met your daughter Arabella, I was smitten. I hasten to ask you—and I implore your pardon if I seem importunate—is she spoken for?"

"Why, no, Mr. Villiers. But really, romantic as she

477

may be and I myself once was, I can hardly believe that it could be love at first sight," Sybella remarked.

"*Les flèches du Cupidon sont inexplicables, madame*—that is a Creole proverb, and it means that Cupid's arrows are unpredictable. I felt one of them wound me grievously when, yesterday afternoon, *Mademoiselle* Bouchard entered the room where we were conversing."

Sybella exchanged a glance with her husband, then shrugged. "Well, at nineteen, I rather think that Arabella is capable of weighing such a matter for herself. I have no objection if you wish to court her in the conventional manner. But I must tell you that here at Windhaven, over the past few years, we've lived in a kind of world of our own, and our opportunities for socializing have consequently been limited. Many of our oldest neighbors have had severe financial reverses because of the panic; some have moved away. As a consequence, my daughter has not yet been formally courted, despite her age. I say that, Mr. Villiers, only to urge that you do not seek to trifle with her, to look upon her as a mere country girl who might offer you a temporary diversion—of which I am sure you will find abundance in New Orleans."

"*Touché*, Mrs. Forsden!" the Creole exclaimed and took her hand, bowed and kissed it in a courtly manner. "I assure you I should never trifle with so beautiful and intelligent a member of the female species who obviously has inherited those qualities from her very admirable mother."

Matthew Forsden arched his eyebrows at this, and struggled to hold back the smile which crept to his lips.

"Then, with your permission, I shall chat with your daughter, Mrs. Forsden, and I shall pray that she will respond to the *grande passion* which presently consumes me. I have the honor to wish you a very pleasant good day."

"And good day to you, Mr. Villiers. I think you'll find her watching her pet owl hunt field mice."

The screech owl, Hoot-to-Whoo, had grown to its full size, yet had become the tamest of pets. At night,

Arabella would let it out of its big wooden cage, and by morning it would return, pecking at its feathers and huddling its head under a wing and emitting its characteristic soft hoot. Often, during the late afternoon, it would soar above its mistress' head, perching at the top of the stable or the kitchen, surveying the terrain, till it saw a scurrying field mouse; and then it would swoop down with a great flapping of wings and make its meal. It took bits of raw beef and pork from Arabella's fingers, and enjoyed to have its head and throat scratched, emitting sounds almost like those of a cooing dove when Arabella caressed it.

As Edouard Villiers walked out to the back of the château, he saw the screech owl swoop down after its prey, and with a smile exclaimed, "You've a fierce protector there, *Mademoiselle* Arabella!"

"Oh, you—you startled me, Mr. Villiers—"

"Let it be Edouard, *s'il vous plaît*, and let me call you Arabella. It's a most appropriate name too, *ma belle,* since, you see, it already has the French word for 'beautiful' in it. I'm sure your mother named you that by design, knowing how you would grow up to surpass even her."

"My goodness, you've only just met me, Mr. Villiers!" Arabella snapped her fingers and Hoot-to-Whoo flew toward her and perched on her shoulder, its eyes fixed on the Creole who stood a few feet away from its beloved mistress. It ruffled its feathers as a kind of warning to him, and Edouard Villiers unconsciously took a backward step or two, cleared his throat, and then somewhat nervously resumed, "But have you never heard of love at first sight, *Mademoiselle* Arabella? That is what has afflicted me, and it is all your fault. If you had not come into that room yesterday afternoon, I should never have known what anguish it is to see so beautiful and desirable a creature and to know that she is not mine."

"Oh my gracious! Do you talk that way to every girl you meet, Mr. Villiers?" Arabella laughed, but her cheeks flamed.

"I assure you," he said, drawing himself up stiffly, "I

479

am not in the habit of addressing speeches of love to every girl I meet."

"Oh but surely, Mr. Villiers, you just can't be in love with me so soon!" she protested, furious with herself for blushing even more before his intent gaze. *What wicked dark eyes he has, almost black,* she told herself, then bit her lips at finding that even against her will she was responding to his magnetism.

"But I assure you it's true, and I'm a bachelor, *Mademoiselle* Arabella. Do please call me Edouard, for you see, I intend to stay here at Windhaven until you admit there is a chance for me."

"But that might be forever!" she blurted out, and then resorted to her girlish giggle.

"I can hardly pay you the serious court I mean to, *ma chère* Arabella, with that savage bird perched on your shoulder," he protested.

"You aren't afraid of Hoot-to-Whoo, surely?"

"Of course not!" He flushed with annoyance at her teasing sally. "But I have the feeling that if I should advance a step or two and try to kiss you, he might peck me as he did that poor field mouse a moment ago."

"And it would serve you right for trying to be so bold," she countered. Then, seeing his face fall, she giggled again, and snapped her fingers. The screech owl flapped its wings, hovering about her head a moment, and then flew off toward the roof of the stable where it perched, watching with its great round eyes.

"Ah, *ma foi,*" he sighed as he took out a silken kerchief and patted his forehead. "That's much better. For a moment, you reminded me of Diana the Huntress, the goddess of the chase. Please, if you communicate with that vigilant owl, entreat it not to interrupt me if I come closer to tell you how deeply I care for you—yes, even on such short acquaintance. I should be the happiest and most fortunate man in all New Orleans, *ma chérie,* if you would find it in your heart to look upon me with favor. Dare I hope that there are no others who seek your hand in marriage?"

"Not so far, Mr. Villiers. But I don't know anything about you."

"I'm wealthy, I live in New Orleans, and have a beautiful summer house up the river. I own slaves and I could give you every luxury. There now, what more do you wish to know?"

Arabella cast him a glance from beneath the lashes, then murmured, "I think I should be getting back into the house, Mr. Villiers. It isn't proper for a young lady to be alone with a gentleman. And I think you've told me enough for the time being."

"Then, *ma belle chérie*, perhaps tomorrow I shall tell you more," he promised. To Arabella's confusion, he came now to take her hand and bring it to his lips as he bowed low, acting as a courtier might to a queen. . . .

Edouard Villiers extended his stay at Windhaven for the entire week and spent most of the afternoons strolling with Arabella. On the fifth afternoon, bedazzled by his effusive compliments and his protestations of love, she hesitantly permitted him to kiss her. Her trembling reaction to that first kiss from a man who desired her led the suave Creole to further kisses and deft touches of her shoulders and bosom till Arabella felt herself nearly swooning with sensual awakening, and at that exact moment he halted his skilled lovemaking. "There, you see, my beautiful darling," he murmured as he kissed the lobe of her ear, "it proves that you share the passion I have for you. Wait a bit, lovely Arabella, and when I have the privilege of asking your parents for your hand in marriage, you'll be willing to come with me to New Orleans and be my adored wife and command my slaves as you'll command me, the humblest of them."

On the morning of the sixth day, declaring that he wished to visit Luke Bouchard at the Williamson plantation, Villiers borrowed a horse which Djamba promptly saddled for him, and rode off along the pathway which wound beside the gently flowing Alabama River.

Luke was out in the fields, directing the foreman in charge of his cattle to build a separate pen for one of the cows who was about to birth. Seeing Villiers

481

dismount and come toward him, he nodded to the brawny Hausa worker and turned to greet the Creole.

"I wished a word in private with you, Mr. Bouchard," Edouard Villiers said. "I see you've quite a few prime field hands here. And you're growing quite a few other crops besides cotton, it appears. This business of cattle is new to me."

"I believe it to be extremely important in this area. Since you're from New Orleans, you must know that cotton is expected to go down to six or seven cents a pound this fall. If one has a great many workers, it's hardly profitable to devote all the land to cotton these days."

"Workers? I call them slaves, Mr. Bouchard."

"That's your privilege, sir. Now how can I be of assistance to you?"

"The fact is, my good friend Pierre Lourat asked that I inquire as to whether you would be interested in disposing of some of your—shall we say 'workers'? He's prepared to pay top prices. We need hands for the sugarcane plantations along the Mississippi, as well as good carpenters, blacksmiths, footmen and the like."

"I have no one for sale either here or at Windhaven, Mr. Villiers."

"A pity. *M'sieu* Buffery is not of the same mind, and indeed, since he appears to have several other outlets for his *nègres*, he thought that you might be able to spare a few from your lands."

"What Mr. Buffery does is of small concern to me now or at any time. I told you, my men are workers and I have no slaves to sell."

"Can it be"—Edouard Villiers' eyes narrowed— "that what Mr. Buffery gave me to understand may be true, that you are an abolitionist and that you wish to send the *nègres* along this accursed Underground Railroad?"

Luke's face froze in anger. "That, sir, is none of your business. I will tell you only this: I detest slavery, but I'm also aware of the legality of property rights. I would not take another man's slave away from him— unless of course that slave were so viciously treated

that my pity might overcome my sober judgment. Thus
far, only three of my own people have asked to go
North and I've arranged it. If you wish to convey that
to Mr. Buffery, you are at liberty to do so. And that's
all I have to say on the subject."

Villiers shrugged. "Even that Christian attitude,
M'sieu Bouchard, may not be looked upon to your
credit in the times ahead. I say this as a friendly warning."

"Then I say to you, I should be pleased if you would
conclude your visit to Windhaven. Moreover, since I
understand that you have seen a good deal of Arabella,
I hope you entertain no foolish notions about seducing
her. You see, Mr. Villiers, I know more about you
than you think I do. As it happens, the *Tensaw* came
up river this morning and brought a letter to me from
John Brunton of the Rigalle bank. In it, he advised me
that a certain Edouard Villiers is a partner with Pierre
Lourat and Mark Bouchard in the detestable business
of human merchandise."

Villiers gasped, then gave Luke a look of undisguised hatred as he turned back to his horse, mounted
it and rode away. Next morning, taking a coldly formal
leave of Matthew and Sybella Forsden and without a
word to Arabella, he boarded the *Tensaw* on its return
journey downriver.

When Sybella told her daughter that evening that
their guest had left without the slightest reference to
his earlier declaration of courting Arabella, the girl
burst into tears.

Sybella waited till the emotional crisis had subsided,
then gently admonished the unhappy young woman:
"You thought you'd fallen in love with that polished
scoundrel because he flattered you, built you a little
world of fancy in which you believed you'd rule like a
queen. But that was an appeal to your selfishness, Arabella dear. True love is never like that. Think of your
father, dear, and how often the two of us were at
swords' points. Yet I was always faithful to him because I could remember how, at the beginning, there
was real love between us. You deserved this heart-

break—though it's not really that. Now take stock of yourself, learn how to use your mind, not just your lovely face and body, and you'll find what real love is one day. Think, too, of your stepfather, and how he and I discovered, when we were no longer young, a love that will last for the rest of our lives together—and that's the very best kind of all."

CHAPTER THIRTY-FOUR

The year of 1844 was fraught with unrest. The Baptist Church split on the issue of slavery, dividing into Northern and Southern conventions.

Although President Santa Anna had served notice upon the United States that the passage of an act to annex Texas would be considered equivalent to a declaration of war against the Mexican government, President Tyler himself submitted to the Senate the Texas Annexation Treaty on April 22nd. Five days later, Martin Van Buren and Henry Clay, both presidential aspirants, published letters opposing the annexation of Texas without Mexico's consent. Van Buren's letter was to cost him the Democratic nomination, while Clay's would lose him the support of the South in the coming Whig campaign.

On May 24th, Samuel F. B. Morse sent his telegraphic message, "What hath God wrought," from Washington to Baltimore. Three days later, the Democratic National Convention met at Baltimore and, after eight ballots, nominated the nation's first "dark horse," James K. Polk of Tennessee, and George M. Dallas of Pennsylvania for the two highest offices in the land. It was the first nominating convention to use the telegraph, and its platform included the vital planks of reannexation of Texas and reoccupation of Oregon.

Although the Tyler Democrats had their own meeting in Baltimore on the same date and nominated the incumbent President for re-election, Tyler withdrew from the campaign on August 20th, after being assured that Polk favored his own dearest wish to annex Texas.

In June, Joseph Smith, the head of the Mormon church, was killed in a bloody riot at Nauvoo, and Brigham Young succeeded him as spiritual leader of that sect. In the following month, Henry Clay published his two famous "Alabama Letters" in which he declared he had no objection to the annexation of Texas if it could be accomplished "without dishonor, without war."

On December 4th, Polk and Dallas were chosen by an electoral vote of 170 to 105 for Henry Clay and Theodore Frelinghuysen. James G. Birney of the Liberty party, who registered 62,300 popular votes, cost Henry Clay the election by besting him in the State of New York; in his overwhelming disappointment, Clay wept in his wife's arms when he learned that his presidential aspirations had been doomed for all time.

In 1845, the potato famine in Ireland led to an enormous increase of Irish migration, and the clipper ship era began with the *Rainbow,* built in the New York shipyard. The Methodist Episcopal Church became divided over the question of slavery, and the general Conference ordered Bishop James O. Andrew of Georgia to give up his slaves or his bishopric. On March 3rd, Florida entered the Union, for now the Seminoles had surrendered, that proud tribe which claimed never to have been defeated by the white man in pitched battle. President Tyler's last official act was to approve the joint resolution of Congress for the annexation of Texas, and on March 4th, James Knox Polk and George M. Dallas assumed the highest offices in the nation, with James Buchanan the new Secretary of State.

One of Buchanan's first acts, on June 15th, was to assure Texas of full federal protection if it consented to the annexation terms, and General Zachary Taylor was ordered to occupy a point on or near the Rio Grande to defend the new territory.

During this year, Alabama's cotton planters could earn only five and six-tenths cents per pound for their crops at Mobile. But again Matthew Forsden and Luke Bouchard weathered the economic storm that beset their neighbors, for their food crops and cattle and hogs amply fed their two plantations and provided a satisfactory if small profit. Maybelle, at Lucy's urging, had resumed her education by studying the books in old Lucien's library and acting as eight-year-old Laurette's teacher. There was no word from Mark Bouchard, except John Brunton's comment to Luke in a letter at the end of the year enclosing the statement of the Forsden and Bouchard accounts, to the effect that Mark and Pierre Lourat had become enormously wealthy in their operation of the elegant bordellos and the slave auction rooms.

Luke Bouchard remained discreetly active in the Underground Railroad, but made no attempt to aid other owners' slaves in their quest for freedom. Tacitly, however, about a year after he had arranged for Trish's journey to Cairo, he had summoned two of his foremen and, swearing them to secrecy, told them of the work of the Underground Railroad. These were the tall Ashanti, Carl, and the young Kru, Harry, who had become Luke's most devoted and enthusiastic workers. With Lucy's help as a teacher, they had learned to read and write. "Each of you will carry a pass from me," Luke had told them, "permitting you to leave this plantation on errands. If in your excursions you should meet any slaves who are the victims of brutal treatment, let them know that there are those who will help them get their freedom. Make sure that no overseer recognizes you, but tell them that if they decide to run away, to come hide in the little shed at the very northeast end of my cornfields."

Over the past year, half a dozen slaves—four men and two women, had sought Luke Bouchard's aid in escaping from the tyranny of James Buffery, leaving the latter's new holdings of the fifty- and seventy-five-acre farms which Mark Bouchard had sold to him.

Carl and Harry had led these fugitives in the dead of

night to the stables, given them horses and a note to a Mrs. Elmer Johnston, the Quaker widow of a pious farmer in Prattville. There, after giving them new clothes and disguising them with dyes and hairpieces, she had her two brothers take them by wagon to the next station at Sheffield, where another family of abolitionists brought them on to Memphis and thence up the Mississippi to Cairo.

Carl and Harry had done their work well, and although Buffery visited Luke early in January 1846 and blusteringly accused him of collusion in "stealing of my prime niggers," he could prove nothing and was forced to withdraw, threatening, "You high and mighty goddamn abolitionist nigger-lover will have the nightriders call you out sometime to account for your thievin' ways with other folks' property."

Polk, the obscure "dark horse" who had become at forty-nine the youngest man yet to be elected President, and who had twice been defeated in running for re-election as Governor of Tennessee, had been picked by Andrew Jackson in sympathy with the nation's expansionist mood that would acquire all Texas and Oregon. Through Polk's efforts, Great Britain agreed to the 49th Parallel as a dividing line of the Oregon territory, once the new President had threatened to abrogate the original treaty of joint occupation. But his main and secret objective was to acquire California; he had already offered to buy it, but the Mexicans, incensed by American attempts to acquire Texas, refused to consider the proposal. On January 13, 1846, he ordered General Zachary Taylor to advance from the Nueces River to the Rio Grande, and prepared a message to Congress asking for recognition of a state of war, and waited for a pretext. It came on April 25th, when Mexican troops under General Arista crossed the Rio Grande and engaged in a cavalry skirmish with a reconnoitering party, killing, wounding and capturing sixteen Americans. On May 13th, Congress declared that a state of war existed between Mexico and the United States because of that invasion. An enlistment of 50,000 soldiers was authorized and

Congress appropriated ten million dollars to prosecute the war. At the same time, President Polk ordered General Stephen Kearney to march to Santa Fe to protect American traders there, and then on to California, where Polk had already commanded naval forces to capture San Francisco and Monterey. On July 7th, Commodore John Drake Sloat took possession of Monterey, hoisted the American flag, and took possession of California for the United States.

As the war with Mexico continued, Captain John Frémont, with a hundred dragoons, trekked from Kansas to take the city of Los Angeles on August 13th. General Santa Anna, who had been exiled in Cuba with the fall of the Paredes government, returned to Mexico City to become commander-in-chief of the Mexican army. In the waning days of December, Iowa entered the Union.

Santa Anna was decisively defeated by General Zachary Taylor at the battle of Buena Vista on February 22 and 23, 1847, while General Winfield Scott took Vera Cruz from the Mexicans in the following month and, on September 14th, took Mexico City. Meanwhile, David Wilmot had added his famous Proviso to the McKay Appropriation Bill for the adjustment of the boundary with Mexico, which would exclude slavery in any territory acquired from Mexico. It was promptly defeated in the Senate, and once again the growing conflict between North and South over this insoluble issue of slavery had come into new and fearful outline.

On December 22, 1847, an obscure Congressman from Illinois, Abraham Lincoln, made his debut in the House and introduced his "spot resolution" as a "conscience Whig." He asked President Polk to describe the exact spot where American blood had first been shed and to say whether or not that spot was on soil rightfully claimed by Mexico. Senator "Black Tom" Corwin of Ohio compared Polk to Tamerlane sitting on a throne of 70,000 skulls, and condemned the war with Mexico as a "bloody Southern junket to find bigger frontiers in which to come catch slaves."

Although the price of cotton fared no better than during the past several years, Windhaven prospered. Alabama legislators had voted in 1846 to transfer the capital of the state from Tuscaloosa to Montgomery, and consequently land values along the winding Alabama River rose sharply, while Tuscaloosa speculators suffered great losses. In this new year of 1848, William L. Yancey introduced the Alabama Platform which emphasized the duty of Congress to protect all persons and all their property in the territories, a resolution adopted by the Alabama legislature. On January 24th, James W. Marshall discovered gold at Sutter's Mill in California. On February 2nd, the Treaty of Guadalupe Hidalgo was signed with Mexico, stipulating that Mexico accept the Rio Grande boundary and yield New Mexico and California to the United States upon payment of fifteen million dollars. On February 23rd, one of the greatest statesmen the young country had ever known, John Quincy Adams, died at the age of eighty-one.

In May of this year of 1848, the Democratic National Convention met at Baltimore to nominate Lewis Cass of Michigan for President and William O. Butler of Kentucky for Vice President. A week later, Wisconsin entered the Union.

As the end of the spring semester at Lowndesboro Academy neared, ten-year-old Lucien Edmond Bouchard, who was residing at the school much as a military academy student might, proudly wrote his father, "Your obedient son will have good marks to show you upon his return home in June." His sister Mara, a year older, was equally proud of her high marks at Miss Hardy's Seminary for Young Ladies, a new school about four miles away from Windhaven, which had been opened three years previously and in which Laurette, the same age as Mara, and sixteen-year-old Fleurette were already enrolled.

On the rainy night of June 7th, the first day of the Philadelphia-sited meeting of the Whig National Convention, which was to nominate General Zachary Taylor of Louisiana for President and Millard Fillmore of

New York as Vice President, Luke Bouchard was wakened from fitful sleep by the urgent whisper of Clarence, a young Fulani who had replaced old Obadiah as majordomo at the Williamson plantation. "Please get up, Mr. Luke," Clarence begged. Luke sat up with a start, glanced at his sleeping wife, then carefully got out of bed and went into the hall with the anxious Fulani. "What's the matter, Clarence?"

"Two slaves, Mr. Luke, they ran away from that old man Buffery's smallest farm—you know, the one that used to belong to old Mr. Murton—but they didn't come to the shed in the cornfields. I don't know how, but someone must have told them to go to Windhaven, and Jimmy just rode up here and told me they're hiding in the stable there."

"My God, we've got to get them over to the widow's place and start before dawn, or Buffery's slave catchers will be after them," Luke said. Hastily dressing and saddling Dandy, a dun-colored stallion, he rode back to Windhaven with Jimmy, who had been appointed head groom at Windhaven by Matthew Forsden.

Entering the stable, he found Djamba, now the foreman of all cattle and hogs at Windhaven, trying to calm the two runaways. One was a tall young Hausa in his late twenties, the other a pretty, petite mulatto hardly sixteen years of age, who clung to the Hausa and stared at him with tear-blurred eyes.

"Don't be frightened," Luke assured them, "I'll help you get to freedom. Who are you, and what happened to you to make you run away?"

"It dat cruel ol' Massa Buffery, dat wut," the Hausa exclaimed. "Ah bin wuhkin' two years in de fields 'n done mighty good, de overseer say, so Ah asks effen Ah kin marry up wid Jenny heah."

At this, the teenaged girl burst into sobs and buried her face against the Hausa's chest.

"And I suppose he told you you couldn't?" Luke pursued, his face taut.

"Nassuh, he say no, all right, 'n he whup me firs'," then he take poah l'il Jenny 'n peel her down 'n whup her even moah. He say Massa Buffery gwine break

491

Jenny in hisself, den sell her down to N'Orleans to be one ob dem fancy gals, to a man dat pays real good foah gals like mah l'il Jenny, suh."

"Do you think you can both ride horseback tonight? I'll go with you to Prattsville. There's a woman there who'll help you get to the Underground in Cairo and then you'll both be free."

"Ah kin go right now, massa, 'n so kin Jenny, though her backside's fair raw from de whuppin'," the Hausa said.

"I'll go with you, Mr. Luke," Djamba offered. "It's too dangerous for you to go alone. I want to help. You gave Celia and me our freedom; I want to earn it."

"Thank you, Djamba. I'll admit I can use someone with your strength on a journey like this. Jimmy, get four fresh horses and pack some beef jerky and some cornpone in case these two get hungry before they get to Prattsville."

"Ah kin come too, Mistah Luke," Jimmy volunteered.

"No, Jimmy, we don't want to attract attention on the roads with too many riders in one party. It'll be dangerous enough as it is. Djamba, better get a rifle from the storeroom and a pistol for me. I pray God I don't have to use weapons and shed blood to save lives, but with Buffery's slave catchers on the trail, it's just as well to be armed—maybe if we come upon them first we can take them by surprise, without the use of weapons."

Half an hour later, Djamba and Luke and Ned and Jenny forded the river near Montgomery and galloped northwest toward Prattville. As they halted their horses to rest and to let the runaways eat, Djamba scowled and quickly dismounted. "Seems like I hear riders coming behind us, Mr. Luke," he said. "Ned, Jenny, go hide behind that bush there. Keep out of sight and as quiet as you can!"

Then, making sure that his rifle was primed, he waited, crouching beside his horse, while Luke remained in the saddle, his hand on the butt of his pistol.

A few moments later, three horsemen rode up, cursing and tugging at the reins, their horses lathered with foam. At the head rode James Buffery, more corpulent than ever, his beard and hair a dirty gray, his piggish little eyes squinting and glittering with fury. "Might have known it was you, Mr. Bouchard," he snarled. "Now, where's my two niggers? Don't you lie 'n say you don't know. Me 'n Jeb 'n Hurley there behind me, we been following your tracks the last hour, even where you crossed the river. Now jist you hand 'em over, then me 'n the boys are gonna take you 'n your nigger back to Montgomery and have you jailed. If the court don't find you both guilty as hell, we're gonna come take you outa jail and string you both up, you hear?"

His two companions were burly Mississippi men who had come from Natchez to join his enterprise. In buckskin jackets and breeches, carrying percussion-cap rifles and pouches of powder and balls, they moved in an arc to flank Luke and Djamba.

Suddenly there was a frightened cry from Jenny, and Buffery wheeled in his saddle, cocked his pistol and fired into the clump of bushes. There was a shriek of pain. Luke reached for his pistol.

"I wouldn't, Mister," the younger rider, Hurley, warned, cocking his rifle.

Djamba, crouching beside his horse, suddenly reversed his grip on his rifle and swung it butt foremost, slamming the stock across Hurley's jaw. With a scream of pain, the Mississipian tumbled from the saddle, his rifle dropping in front of Djamba. His companion, with an oath, turned to level his rifle at the Mandingo, but Djamba had swiftly retrieved Hurley's weapon and, flinging himself down on his belly, lofted it and pulled the trigger. The older slave catcher stiffened, then slowly slid out of the saddle and toppled to the ground.

"By Gawd, you killed Jeb, you lousy goddamn nigger you—and look what you've done to pore Hurley—you black son of a bitch. Now you'll get wut's comin' to you!" Buffery bellowed. Wheeling his horse, with a wary glance at Luke who had sat motionless astride his horse, he turned toward Djamba. The horse,

493

its eyes rolling, fought the bit and reared, pawing the air with its hoofs as Buffery, cursing at the top of his voice, yanked at the reins. Steadying the pistol, he rode toward Djamba, who crouched on the ground. The Mandingo instantly leveled the rifle and fired point blank, but the weapon jammed.

"That's what I want, you murderin' nigger bastard!" Buffery gloated, aiming at Djamba's forehead.

But Luke, his face tortured, was suddenly galvanized. Cocking his pistol, he pulled the trigger. The fat slave trainer stiffened in his saddle; the pistol dropped from his nerveless hand. Slowly he turned his face toward Luke. "You—you yellow-livered ab—abolish'nist—never thought you—had—the—g—guts—" he gasped. Then, as a crimson circle spread on the back of his dirty shirt, he slid off the saddle and lay with eyes staring upward.

Numb, incredulous, Luke slid off his horse and stumbled toward Djamba. "Are—are you all right, Djamba?" he gasped.

The Mandingo rose, his face grave. He put his right hand on Luke's left shoulder, and he spoke words which Luke could not understand. Then he said softly, "I called you a great warrior, Mister Luke. A warrior who in my country would be worthy of the throne. You saved my life, as you did Celia's. I am your man for life, and you are my blood kinsman, Mister Luke."

Luke trembled. He put a hand on Djamba's shoulder. "I could ask nothing better, Djamba. I thank God He gave me strength against my own convictions of not taking a human life."

"We'd better rest before we go on, Mister Luke." Djamba's voice was level now. "And there's something more I've got to do before I see if that man's bullet hurt Jenny or Ned."

He walked over to the sprawled body of the younger slave catcher, Hurley. The latter's jaw was broken, and his eyes rolled fearfully up at Djamba, who squatted down beside him. Suddenly, with his waning strength, the Mississippian drew a knife and thrust it into Djamba's right shoulder.

With a roar of rage and pain, the Mandingo pulled the knife out of his shoulder and flung it to one side. Then his hands closed around Hurley's throat. A few moments later, he straightened, swaying from his wound, and muttered, "First off, maybe you can help me stop this bleeding, Mister Luke. It wasn't too deep a cut, just messy. Then, when I get a little rest, I'll dig three graves and we can go on to Prattville."

Djamba's need strengthened Luke, still emotionally drained from seeing a man die by his hand, and he swiftly improvised a tourniquet for the wound. Then both men went into the bushes where Ned and Jenny were hiding, to find that Buffery's bullet had only grazed Jenny's arm and left nothing more than a scratch.

It was Luke who dug the graves while Djamba rested, gulping down water from a leather flask. And when it was done, Luke and Djamba rode on to the first step toward freedom for the grateful slaves.

CHAPTER THIRTY-FIVE

Djamba's wound, though ugly, soon healed, though it took two weeks to regain the freedom of movement of his right arm. There was no legal repercussion over the death of the three slave catchers, although Luke was inclined to regard the fate of Bethany Buffery as a direct consequence of his own participation in the Underground Railroad. When the three riderless horses found their way back to the Buffery breeding farm, one of the male slaves spread the word that the hated Mississipian must have been killed by abolitionists. The rawboned wife of Buffery, infuriated because two of the girls in the special "pleasure house" had asked her if her husband was dead, took a cowhide and began to flog them, whereupon five of the other girls disarmed her and strangled her with the whip. Taking advantage of their temporary freedom, a number of boys and girls of the Buffery training and breeding farm escaped into the woods and tried to make their way downriver to Mobile. Some were caught by neighboring plantation owners and turned over to the county sheriff, but the rest made good their escape, or at least were never seen again.

About a month later, Mark Bouchard, learning about the death of James and Bethany Buffery and the escape of the young slave apprentices, sent capable white overseers to take over the Buffery farm as well as look after his three other properties. Three months after that, he acquired title to the Buffery holdings. After all these years, he finally broke the long silence between himself and his half brother by having an attorney in Montgomery relay a message declaring that he was now the new and rightful owner of the Buffery land. With that statement was a personal note signed by Mark; it read: "There's no proof you had anything to do with what happened to the Bufferys. But if I ever find out that you did, I'll kill you out of hand."

On November 7th, Zachary Taylor and Millard Fillmore swept to victory by 163 electoral votes. In the fall of the following year, the California convention met at Monterey to draft a constitution prohibiting slavery, and petitioned Congress for admission to the Union as a free state. Early in 1850, Henry Clay introduced in the Senate a series of eight resolutions "to settle and adjust amicably all existing questions of controversy . . . arising out of the institution of slavery." A week later, he gave his last great speech in support of his famous Compromise. It was answered on March 4th by John C. Calhoun's last effort for the South, denouncing the Compromise. Soon afterward, Daniel Webster's immortal "Seventh of March" speech, the last he was ever to make, upheld Clay's earnest Compromise intended to solve the issue of slavery expansion and to pacify both sides.

President Zachary Taylor, now sixty-four, though a Southerner and plantation owner with slaves, took a strong Union line, and proclaimed, "The people of the North need have no apprehension of the further extension of slavery." He actively urged California and New Mexico to apply for admission to the Union as free states, and swore that, if Southern states attempted to secede, he would personally lead the Army to put down the revolt. It was plain that he would veto the omnibus legislation of this 1850 Compromise which satisfied no one—but fate decided otherwise. On July 9th, after eating of fruit and quantities of milk and ice water, he was taken with severe cramps and died three days later. Millard Fillmore assumed the Presidency.

Arabella Bouchard, now twenty-six and still unwed,

was walking along the bank of Pintilalla Creek with Sybella, saying that she wanted to go to New Orleans in the fall to study painting. Three years earlier, she had begun to dabble with water colors, and Sybella had praised her sketch of Hoot-to-Whoo, the screech owl pet of her childhood, which had flown away one night and never returned.

Sybella opposed her daughter's wish and bluntly told her why: "I can see through you, Missy. You're feeling restless now because you haven't found a husband. Well, didn't I tell you that when you found out what love really is, you'd know right off when the right man came along? But this notion of gallivanting off to New Orleans, to be away from supervision—you think it's fashionable to take a lover. The next thing you know you'll attract a swarm of glib-talking Creoles as shallow as that Villiers fellow, and you'll disgrace yourself. No, Missy, your stepfather and I won't hear of it, so make up your mind that what social life you're after, you can find just as well in Montgomery. Besides, aren't you satisfied with your little ladies' group there, who meet once a month and talk about the arts and show off their drawings and samplers and such?"

"Oh heavens, Mama, it's not the same thing at all and you know it!" Arabella impatiently stamped her foot, her lovely, animated face vivid with color.

"Same thing or not, you just go on with your water colors, and be sure you show that sketch of yours at the meeting next week. I'm going to ask our carpenter, David, if he won't try to make a frame for it."

"Oh very well, Mama. There's no use arguing with you, I guess."

Sybella smiled and put her arms around her daughter's shoulders. "No, dear, because you and I are very much alike in so many ways. I was just as spunky as you when I was your age, heaven knows, and I don't ever want you to lose that spirit, even if I have to say no to you lots of times. Now go back and freshen up for supper, and then you take that framed sketch of yours off to Mrs. Gurley's next Monday sure."

Mrs. Abel Gurley, a gentle, self-effacing matron in

her late thirties, held open house in her Italian villa-
type house on the outskirts of Montgomery, where she
and her husband entertained young women of the area
who showed talent in painting and sketching, music,
fancy sewing and quilting, and ceramics. She had visited Windhaven about two years ago, learned of Arabella's talent, and eagerly invited the young woman to
membership in her circle.

And so, the following Monday after lunch, Arabella,
in a pretty blue riding skirt, rode her gentle mare
Emma side-saddle to the Gurley home, and was admitted by the genial Angola houseman, Fred, who ushered
her into the spacious sitting room which Mrs. Gurley
liked to call her "cultural salon."

Much to Arabella's surprise, a tall, dark-haired man
in his late twenties, who was seated beside her best
friend of the circle, the young widow Jean Demarest,
courteously rose and bowed to her.

"Oh, Bella dear, I want you to meet my second
cousin, James Hunter from Tuscaloosa," Jean exclaimed.

"A pleasure to make your acquaintance, Mr.
Hunter," Arabella said as she dropped him a polite
curtsey.

"Whatever have you got there, Bella?" Jean Demarest demanded, seeing the packet of cotton cloth
with which David had wrapped the newly framed
sketch of the screech owl.

"Oh, it's just one of my water colors," Arabella replied.

"May I see it, please, Miss Arabella?" James Hunter
asked.

Jean Demarest clapped a hand to her mouth. "Oh
my goodness, I was forgetting my manners! This is
Miss Arabella Bouchard, Jimmy. Isn't she just a darling? And you know something, she's not spoken for
yet—whatever can the young men of Montgomery be
thinking?"

"Jean, really!" Arabella's cheeks burned, but not before James Hunter had taken the cotton-wrapped
frame from her unresisting hand, unwrapped it, and ut-

tered a long "Mmmm!" of approbation. "Really, this is extremely good!"

"You—you think so, Mr. Hunter?"

He had no beard, which was a blessing, she instantly thought to herself, and his sideburns did look ever so distinguished. "Do you paint yourself perhaps?"

"If I painted, I certainly shouldn't paint myself, I'm much too homely," James Hunter chuckled, and again Arabella's face burned. But as he handed back the water color and their fingers brushed, Arabella shivered. Her eyes met his, and Jean Demarest, for once, had the tact to keep silent as she sensed what was happening between the two.

From that day forth, Sybella had no need to worry about her daughter's dream of going off to New Orleans by herself and establishing her own art studio. James Hunter was a frequent caller at Windhaven, and on October 5, 1850, an idyllically happy Arabella, her mother and stepfather, and Luke and Fleurette, rode to Selma in phaetons drawn by the finest Windhaven horses to the little church where the couple were married.

And this time it was a happily tearful Sybella who kissed her daughter and wished her the happiest of honeymoons in New Orleans, whispering, "I told you so, Missy darling!"

In September, about eleven weeks after President Fillmore had assumed office, five of the notorious Compromise bills were passed and signed into law. Congress organized the territories of New Mexico and Utah without provision regarding slavery, forbade the slave trade in the District of Columbia after January 1, 1851, settled the Texas boundary claims by federal payment of $10,000,000 on the debts of the Republic of Texas, and on September 18 enacted the Fugitive Slave Act to provide federal in place of state jurisdiction. And in the last month of this memorable year, the state convention of Georgia accepted the 1850 Compromise, warning that it would secede if that Compromise should ever be violated by the North.

Once again the Bouchard family's wise program of

crop rotation and diversification added to its ever-growing financial strength. In this year, Bouchard cotton sold for about 12½ cents per pound at Mobile, and Matthew Forsden and Luke Bouchard netted a tidy profit through the sale of corn and other vegetables, as well as some twenty steers and as many hogs. Lucien Edmond Bouchard, now twelve, home for the holidays from the Lowndesboro Academy, already displayed the mind of a good scholar. He accompanied his father to the fields while Luke explained the processes of cultivation and harvesting, showed him the cattle and hog pens and made him a Christmas present of a young mare which he promptly learned to ride. As they rode together one early January afternoon, Lucien Edmond asked his father, "Do you suppose that animals could be married like people, so their children can be strong and healthier, Father?"

Pleasantly surprised, Luke nodded and smilingly replied, "I've always thought so, son. I'm sure our local veterinarian might be inclined to agree with you. Now you see, take those cows of mine. I bought the finest stock I could find, and I chose a bull of as good a pedigree as I could be sure of. In that way the calves will be sturdy and they'll grow to make fine beef. The same is true with the sows and hogs. Who knows, maybe one day when you have your own land and farm, you may decide to test your theory and earn your livelihood by it."

CHAPTER THIRTY-SIX

Within three months after the Fugitive Slave Law was signed, some three thousand fugitive blacks crossed the border into Canada, while in some Northern communities, the Negro population organized to prevent the capture of fugitive slaves. Businessmen in the thriving cities of Boston, New York, Philadelphia, Baltimore, Pittsburgh, Cincinnati and Chicago used their influence to quell agitation over the slavery controversy; for thirty years they had been haunted by the fear that the abolitionist movement would result in the secession of the Southern states from the Union.

Yet at first, by the middle of the year 1851, there appeared to be little sympathy for abolitionist agitation. The Free Soil Party, which had been dedicated to the termination of all slavery in the United States, was dead, and most of its newspapers in the Northwest were no longer in existence. Henry Clay sent an open letter to the citizens of New York to declare that throughout the land an immense majority of the people were satisfied with or acquiesced in the Compromise. And so it seemed, at least for the time, that a lull in the gathering storm had been reached, and that perhaps the nation, through calm and cooperative attitude, could weather such a storm if ever it came.

In June of 1852, Sybella Bouchard became a grandmother when Arabella Hunter presented her husband with a black-haired daughter named Melinda, in honor of her mother-in-law. James Hunter's father had died a month after his son's marriage, and James Hunter had given up his law practice in Tuscaloosa to take over the running of the family plantation on the outskirts of Selma, which included one hundred and fifty acres of cotton land and twenty slaves and a fine red-brick two-story house with white Doric columns and a veranda gracing the front. Sybella's son Paul, now twelve, a sturdy, cheerful boy, showed great proficiency as a horseback rider, and had begged his father to teach him how to shoot squirrels and rabbits for the family provender. Fleurette, now nineteen, her sweet face grave and her coppery-red hair drawn back into a huge bun, was distressed at her half brother's proclivities for hunting, remembering how fond she was of her own tame rabbit, Sassy. Somewhat to Sybella's surprise, Fleurette hesitantly asked her mother if she might attend the lectures of a young doctor, Horace Phenley, who had just set up practice in Montgomery and who had aroused considerable scoffing from the capital's citizens by theorizing that women should be trained as nurses to attend the sick, not only in hospitals but also to be able to deal with emergencies at home. Fleurette not only attended this and several other lectures by the young physician, but sent to New Orleans for several medical books and assiduously studied them. Sybella had begun secretly to hope that Fleurette might have found her future husband, when unexpectedly Dr. Horace Phenley was called back to Richmond where his father had just died, and decided to settle there instead and look after his aging mother and an only sister.

On November 2nd, Franklin Pierce, of New Hampshire, was swept into office over General Whitfield Scott by the landslide of 254 electoral votes to 42. But there were ill omens besetting the administration of this little-known President who had served a single term as Senator of New Hampshire and got himself commissioned a brigadier general in the war with Mexico. His first two children had died in infancy, but his third son had survived and at nine years old was the joy of both

504

Franklin Pierce and his obsessively religious wife, Jane. In the interval between Pierce's election and inauguration, the family took a train from Boston to Concord. The train crashed a mile from Boston, crushing the boy to death but leaving the parents untouched. Mrs. Pierce was prostrated and declared that God had exacted her son's death so that her husband would have no distraction in his new duties. And on that fateful inaugural day of March 4, 1853, the sorrowing President urged the annexation of Cuba, where his Vice President William R. King took his oath of office, only to die of fever the following month.

On January 23, 1854, Arabella Hunter presented her husband with a strapping brown-haired son named Andrew, after his dead father. On this same day, Senator Stephen A. Douglas introduced the Kansas-Nebraska Bill which created two territories out of the Nebraska section and repealed the Missouri Compromise, which had banned slavery above the 36°-30' parallel. Although this bill came out of the dispute over railroads, its ultimate effect was to bring the Armageddon of Civil War all the closer.

Missouri slaveholders rushed over five thousand "voters" into the newly organized territory, while Free Soilers countered by organizing the Emigrant Aid Company to help free men move into Kansas and buy homesteads. Within months, Northern "Jayhawkers" were fighting Southerners in open battle, while Southern and Northern speculators scrambled to grab land for themselves and away from the Indians who technically owned most of it. Ill-advised Franklin Pierce protested that the Federal Government had no right to intervene in the rights of a state, dismissing the affair as "mere angry, idle, aimless disturbances of public peace and tranquility." In May of this agonizing year, he further drew calumny upon himself by sending federal troops to Boston to insure the extradition of an escaped slave, while indignant citizens lined the streets to hiss and boo.

In June 1856, the Democratic National Convention met at Cincinnati to nominate James Buchanan of

Pennsylvania for President, with John C. Breckinridge of Kentucky as his running mate, while the newly organized Republican Party had its first national convention at Philadelphia, choosing John C. Frémont of California for President and William L. Dayton of New Jersey for Vice President, on a platform which denounced polygamy and slavery. In September, John W. Geary, newly appointed governor of the Kansas territory, brought in federal troops to disperse the armed Missourians marching upon Lawrence and brought temporary peace to "bloody Kansas."

On November 4th, Buchanan and Breckinridge were elected with 174 electoral votes to 114 for Frémont and Dayton, and only eight for Fillmore and Donelson. And on the last day of the year 1856, Fleurette Bouchard became engaged to Dr. Jonas Morton, a thirty-two-year-old Quaker from Philadelphia who had come to Montgomery two years earlier to visit his older brother and the latter's wife, and had stayed on to aid her through a difficult pregnancy, then decided to set up his practice in Alabama's capital.

But Fleurette's quiet happiness was to be short-lived; on the day before their wedding, which was to have been March 6, 1857, her husband-to-be succumbed to an attack of scarlet fever.

But that day would be remembered through long and dreadful years to come for the decision of Chief Justice of the Supreme Court Roger D. Taney on the twelve-year-old Dred Scott case. In 1846, Scott had sued for his freedom on the grounds that he had lived for four years on free soil. The seventy-nine-year-old Chief Justice wrote in his deciding opinion, "It is useless and mischievous for opponents of slavery to quote the Declaration of Independence, for the 'unhappy black race' in 1776 was excluded from civilized governments by common consent and had no rights which the white man was bound to respect. Congress therefore never had any right to legislate against slavery; no slave can ever become a citizen or sue in a federal court; they are articles of merchandise." Furthermore, the Chief Justice declared, the Missouri Compromise, under which Dred

Scott claimed his freedom because he had been residing in the territory of Minnesota, was unconstitutional to begin with. It was a grave political blunder, one that added fuel to a conflagration which awaited only a spark—and it was to prove the salvation of the newly organized Republican Party.

At twenty, Lucien Edmond Bouchard was as tall as his great-grandfather, as wiry and vibrant with health and controlled energy. His lips were firm and his smile more sober and reflective than irrepressibly good-natured like Paul's. He had the high forehead and the deeply cleft chin and the large dark-brown eyes of his great-grandfather, and Luke was often struck with the similarity of that selfsame twinkle of amusement at the world which those young eyes surveyed, for he remembered old Lucien's contemplative, often whimsical gaze in those early days when he had sought answers to his boyish questions from the founder of Windhaven. Although young Lucien Edmond rode a horse as well as Paul and had learned how to shoot both pistol and rifle, he was far fonder of books than Paul.

On this sunny mid-September day of 1858, Lucien Edmond and his father walked along the rows and the fields of the Williamson plantation, satisfied with the bounteous crop, then moved to inspect the cattle and pig pens. Mara was now twenty-one and a graduate of the Young Ladies' Seminary with the highest honors; she had for the past two years busied herself not only as an expert seamstress and occasional cook for the household, but also made frequent trips to Montgomery on horseback to attend meetings of what the *Journal* editor called, "a society of dauntless rebels with the outlandish notion that women deserve the vote and a place among our legislators." For the past six months, she had had an "understanding" with Bobby Jordan, now thirty-six and the head of the Jordan plantation following his father's death three years ago. His older brother Ashton, uncharacteristically, had become an officer in the state militia. Luke admired his intrepid, outspoken daughter, although he secretly felt that Bobby Jordan was not quite the right husband for her. However, she seemed quite satisfied and had only last week remarked that they might be married early next summer.

"Well, son, we can look forward to another good harvest this fall," Luke smilingly declared. "This experiment with beef and pork has turned out very profitably, and it has certainly improved our diet."

"Indeed it has, Father." Lucien Edmond's face sobered, and he was silent a moment. "If there should be a war, Father," he said, "these animals would certainly be more valuable than cotton. Do you think there will be?"

Luke sighed and shook his head. "This Kansas business is a bad thing. That Indiana Congressman English has just got his bill passed into law to offer the immediate admission of Kansas to the Union and a large grant of public land if the people will accept the Lecompton Constitution, which would make Kansas a slave state. And the Kansas voters have just rejected it. Now that Minnesota has entered the Union as a free state, our country is becoming divided into pro- and antislavery states, and I fear that the new Senator from Illinois, Abraham Lincoln, may have been right when he said in accepting his nomination that a house divided against itself cannot stand, that this government cannot endure permanently half slave and half free."

"I remember, Father. But didn't Senator Douglas just say in his second debate at Freeport last month that the people of the territory could introduce or exclude slavery as they pleased, because slavery can't exist a day unless it's supported by local police regulations?"

"That was an ingenious straddling of the fence, Lucien Edmond, but it will most likely earn the ambitious Senator his re-election," Luke sadly smiled.

"If there really should be a war, Father, what would you do?"

Luke turned toward the river, shading his eyes from the sun with a cupped hand. "Only once in my life did I ever kill a man, Lucien Edmond," he said. "I did it to save the life of one dear to me. It was done out of pure instinct, forced on me by bitter circumstances. Even today, I would answer that I do not think I could ever bring myself to kill in cold blood because other men's convictions differed from mine. Pray God there will be no war—but if there should be, I'd do my share by making my crops and my cattle available to the people who'd need them. I'd try with all my might to preserve life, not take it."

"I think I understand, Father."

"You see, when your great-grandfather came here, he thought of a strong, simple, united country, new and free of the bigotry and ancient hatreds of Europe. Alas, what we now see before us is a division of that country. Yet, while I love this land and all it stands for, I could not in all honesty kill another man because he happened to be born in Minnesota or Ohio or New York. But let's talk of more cheerful things. Do you remember that piece of fifty acres which your grandfather once owned?"

"The one that used to belong to old Granville Murton? Yes, Father."

"Your Uncle Mark sold it to his overseer from Louisiana, but last year that man moved back to New Orleans and sold it in turn to an Ernest Kendall who just last week married a very pretty girl from Huntsville. Well, this morning I received an invitation from the Kendalls and a note informing me their niece was visiting them from Baltimore. So if you've no other plans, I'm sure you'd like to come along with your mother and sister tomorrow evening."

Lucien Edmond gave his father a reproachful smile: "You know perfectly well I have no other social plans, Father, unless it be to study Dubow's *Planter's Manual*."

"Somehow, Lucien Edmond," Luke retorted, "I think it would be far more enlightening for you to meet Mr. Kendall's niece. I understand she's considered somewhat of a bluestocking back in Baltimore, with a brilliant scholastic record. Also, like your sister Mara, she believes that women should have the right to cast the vote and even to hold public office."

Lucien Edmond whistled softly. "Then by all means I should like to meet so imaginative a girl, Father. I daresay I might learn a good deal more than even from an authority like Dubow."

Ernest Kendall was a pleasant, unassuming man in his late thirties, and his pretty wife, just eighteen, obviously adored him. He owned a dozen slaves, but it was at once evident to Luke and Lucien Edmond that Ernest Kendall regarded them as co-workers and that they idolized him. At the supper table, whose ample fare his young wife, Julia, had prepared, he declared that the attractive wooden frame house which he and his wife found so comfortable had been constructed entirely by the hands working in his fields, and that he hoped one day to be able to manumit them.

Meeting a neighbor whose sympathetic views were exactly those of Luke and his son made the evening a delightful one, but Lucien Edmond had eyes only for Maxine Kendall, the Baltimore niece. She was almost as tall as he, with tumbling chestnut curls, an earnest and attractive if not beautiful face, with large hazel eyes and a firm, determined chin. She spoke in a low, vibrant voice, and when the conversation touched on the role of women in present-day society, her face became animated and her eyes sparkled. She wore the modish voluminous hoopskirt and puffed sleeves and full bodice, but it was her voice and her eyes which most fascinated Lucien Edmond.

He had to content himself with this throughout the meal, since Mara, finding Maxine a kindred spirit, zestfully entered into the conversation until both young women were chattering away like magpies, to the indulgent smiles of their elders. At last, when Ernest Kendall and Luke Bouchard went into the sitting room to enjoy a liqueur and cigar, Lucien Edmond had his opportunity and, flushing, asked Maxine Kendall if he might chat with her for a few moments and have her inform him about the cultural and economic aspects of her native city.

Mara acted as a friendly conspirator by giving Maxine a broad wink, remarking aloud: "I will say, Miss Kendall, that while I do not cherish a very high opinion of most young men, I think you will find my brother rather intelligent and the exception."

As Maxine led him through the house on a tour of inspection and talked away, Lucien Edmond knew that he was lost. His one pressing desire was to learn how long this remarkable creature intended to make her visit to her uncle, and was relieved when she nonchalantly shrugged and replied, "I'm quite my own mistress, Mr. Bouchard. My father and mother died two years ago, and my dear but somewhat straitlaced aunt, bless her old soul, is already shocked enough that I dared come across the country all by myself, so I daresay a few more days or weeks won't really matter."

She did indeed prolong her visit, and by November, she and Lucien Edmond Bouchard were formally engaged, and were married in Montgomery on February 14, 1859, the day on which Oregon entered the Union.

The plans of Mara Bouchard and Bobby Jordan—who had been Arabella's first beau when he was only twelve—were delayed by the momentous events of October of this tragic year of 1859. God's angry man, John Brown, raided Harpers Ferry and, with his little army of thirteen whites and five blacks, seized the United States arsenal there. He was captured by Colonel Robert E. Lee and marines, tried and hanged on December 2nd in the public square of Charlestown, Virginia. Facing the scaffold, he wrote a last letter: "I, John Brown, am now quite certain that the crimes of this guilty land will never be purged away but with blood."

In that same month of October, the Wyandotte Constitution was ratified in the Kansas Territory, which would bring Kansas into the Union as a free state. And two weeks after the death of John Brown, Georgia enacted a law prohibiting the post-mortem manumission of slaves by deed or will, and another act which permitted the sale into slavery of free blacks indicted as vagrants. The dreadful issues had been drawn, the battlefields awaited, and the outcome was to endanger even Windhaven itself.

CHAPTER THIRTY-SEVEN

On May 3, 1860, Maxine Bouchard presented young Lucien Edmond with a daughter, chestnut-haired like herself, and asked her delighted husband to let her name the baby Carla in honor of an aunt who had been twice jilted by suitors and who all her life had secretly longed for a child.

Two weeks later the Republican National Convention met in the Wigwam at Chicago and nominated Abraham Lincoln for President on the third ballot, with Hannibal Hamlin of Maine as his running mate. A month later, the Democrats at Baltimore picked Stephen A. Douglas and Herschel V. Johnson of Georgia, and ten days later the Democratic Party seceders from Charleston (who had walked out of their convention in April after a dispute over the platform) met at Baltimore to nominate John C. Breckinridge of Kentucky and Joseph Lane of Oregon for President and Vice President.

On November 6th, Abraham Lincoln was elected by an electoral vote of 180 to Breckinridge's 72 and Douglas's 12. Throughout the South, the talk of secession grew and on December 3 President Buchanan in his annual message to Congress declared that the Southern States had no legal right to secede, nor did the Federal Government have any power to prevent it, recommending an explanatory amendment to the Constitution on the subject of slavery in the last-ditch hope that secession could be avoided.

Bobby Jordan visited Windhaven to tell Mara Bouchard, his fiancée, that he and Ashton were now enlisted in the Alabama state troops and that it would not be wise for them to think of marriage until the safety of the South had been assured, either by conciliation or warfare.

South Carolina's answer to Buchanan's plea was to secede from the Union by unanimous vote on December 20th, and ten days later South Carolina troops seized the United States arsenal at Charleston.

On January 4, 1861, Alabama state troops, in which both Bobby and Ashton Jordan served, seized the United States arsenal at Mt. Vernon, and Forts Morgan and Jaines on Mobile Bay the following day.

Florida, Mississippi, Georgia, Louisiana and Alabama seceded this same month, and on January 29th, Kansas entered the Union as a free state under the Wyandotte Constitution. On February 1st, Texas seceded and on February 4th a convention of delegates from the six seceding states met in Montgomery to form a provisional government of the Confederate States of America. Jefferson Davis, who had been President Pierce's Secretary of War, was elected provisional President and Alexander H. Stephens provisional Vice President of the Confederacy.

On April 12th, the Union's Fort Sumter in Charleston Harbor was fired upon by General P. T. Beauregard and two days later surrendered to the Confederacy. The next day, President Lincoln, declaring the existence of an "insurrection," called for 75,-000 volunteers for three months' service to suppress it. On April 19th, Lincoln declared the blockade of the ports of South Carolina, Georgia, Florida, Alabama, Mississippi, Louisiana and Texas as well as Virginia and North Carolina. And on May 6, the Confederate Congress recognized that a state of war between the United States and the Confederate States existed. What John Brown had foreseen when he prophesied that the land must be purged by blood had now come to pass.

514

That same day also, when the convention of the State of Arkansas adopted its ordinance of secession, Maxine Bouchard gave birth to a son, Hugo, in honor of the great French novelist, Victor Hugo, whose *Notre Dame de Paris* Lucien Edmond so admired.

On July 20th, the capital of the Confederacy was moved to Richmond, Virginia. And a day later, at the first battle of Bull Run, though the Union troops under General McDowell were routed by the gray-uniformed soldiers under Generals Joseph E. Johnston and P. T. Beauregard, both Bobby and Ashton Jordan were killed in battle. At the outbreak of the war, they had jointly addressed a letter to General Johnston asking that they be transferred from state militia to a fighting unit, and their request had been granted.

Laurette Bouchard shook her head admiringly as she listened to her aunt, Fleurette, now twenty-nine, calmly declare how she intended to aid the Confederate war effort. "I think it's terribly brave of you, Aunt Fleurette, but what will your mother say?" she asked.

Fleurette's lovely face, matured with the sorrow of her lost love, was radiant: "Mama thinks it's a wonderful idea. Our boys will need nurses, and after all I was going to marry a doctor, wasn't I? I've studied so many medical books I almost feel like one!"

"Aunt Fleurette!" Laurette gasped.

"Well, I do, and besides, who can care for a wounded or suffering man more than a woman? A woman's made of tenderness and love and patience and sacrifice, and when a man's been in battle, hurt, maybe dying, he'll look to those things. It's little enough I can do. I can't fight, I wouldn't ever kill anyone, but maybe I can save the lives of our brave boys. I've written to Sally Louisa Tompkins, she's just about my own age and a spinster too, and she's in Richmond. She's taken over a friend's house and is making it into a hospital for the soldiers. And if I get an answer back, I'll leave for Richmond right away. But what about you, Laurette?"

"Well, I can make bandages, and maybe knit

sweaters and socks and things for the soldiers, and I guess they can be shipped downriver to Mobile and sent on to the soldiers. Mama's going to do the same thing. We want to be useful. And I've told Uncle Luke that maybe I could take care of a flock of chickens and get eggs from the hens. I don't know if soldiers are going to be marching through here, but there'd be plenty of food for them if they did."

"Each of us has to find what happiness we can in this terrible war, dearest Laurette. I'll find mine by taking care of those who are far from home and in pain. And if I don't make a good nurse, at least God knows I can pray for them," Fleurette Bouchard said solemnly.

Four days later, when the letter did come from Richmond, eagerly welcoming Fleurette Bouchard as an apprentice nurse, Sybella's younger, unmarried daughter bade her mother and stepfather good-bye and left for Richmond.

Luke Bouchard and Matthew Forsden had agreed that raising food instead of cotton would be much more vital to the war effort. From the practical viewpoint also, the continuing production of cotton would be at best a hazardous venture; by April 25th, David Glasgow Farragut and thirteen ships had occupied New Orleans, an action for which he was named the first rear admiral in U.S. Naval history. Shortly thereafter, the important Confederate port of Pensacola was taken, leaving only Mobile. But the Union blockade was powerful, and cotton shipped from Mobile might never reach England. No, it was better by far to devote all the land of Windhaven and the Williamson plantation to producing food for the soldiers and the civilians, although as yet the war had not reached Alabama.

Even though President Lincoln had issued a proclamation on August 16, 1861, forbidding trading with seceded states, the traders followed the armies. Perhaps it was a rule of war from ancient times that one did not trade with one's enemy; yet this was a war not between

516

foreign enemies but the separated halves of an economic whole, who had depended on each other and whose interdependence continued even as the cannons boomed and the rifles whined their hail of bullets. In Nashville, when Buell's troops arrived, all the cotton had been hidden away; but once the traders came, within two months 3600 bales of cotton had been sent north at an average price of $100 a bale, a price at least two and a half times that which had been paid for cotton at Mobile just before the war began. It happened at Memphis, in Richmond too, even where the Confederacy flew the battle standards of its capital.

And it happened in New Orleans as well. One could buy a sack of salt in federally occupied New Orleans for $1.25, and on the far side of Lake Ponchartrain in Confederate territory, each sack could be sold for $60 to $100. A trader who could take a thousand sacks across the lake could make $60,000 with an investment of $1250, and with that profit could buy cotton at ten cents a pound, knowing that he would get at least sixty cents a pound for it once he hauled it within federal lines. Major General Benjamin Butler, an ex-politician and now federal commander at New Orleans, himself was accused of profiteering in contraband.

But there was one who meant to profit still more out of suffering and sorrow. Mark Bouchard, who now ran the enterprises of aging Pierre Lourat, saw that money could be coined hand over fist by purchasing luxuries in England or Nassau, running the Union blockade and taking cover in the pirate swamps of Barataria, thence to haul the smuggled goods into the federally occupied city and dispose of merchandise to Confederates at exorbitant prices.

Neither Luke Bouchard nor his son Lucien Edmond was conscripted into the Confederate Army. At the outset of the war, it was stipulated that all slave-owners were exempt, which drew an angry accusation from many patriotic Southerners that the war would favor the rich and decimate the poor. But Luke Bouchard had visited a Colonel James Warriner, assistant quartermaster for the Alabama district in Montgomery, and offered to turn over half of his crops and his cattle to the Confederacy. This he and Matthew Forsden did in good faith, and young Lucien Edmond himself worked in the fields, as did Lucien Edmond's wife, Maxine. Moreover, Luke Bouchard directed that $25,000 from his Mobile account be offered as a donation to the Confederate cause. "I would be a poor soldier, but I can be a good farmer and serve valiantly, and so can you, my son," he had told Lucien Edmond.

And on September 23rd, when President Lincoln's Emancipation Proclamation was published in the Montgomery *Journal*, Matthew Forsden and Luke Bouchard went out into the fields to tell their workers that at last they were free by the law of the land and that, if they wished, they might leave the soil to seek a new home and a new life. At Windhaven, middle-aged Djamba, standing beside his tall, handsome twenty-two-year-old son Lucas, answered for them: "We have always been free, Mr. Forsden, since we came here. We are your people. Where else would we go? There could be none kinder than you whom we would serve, no matter where we might go. Let us stay with you and work as always."

The next day, a letter came from New Orleans via Mobile and delivered by the captain of the old *Tensaw*, addressed to Luke Bouchard from John Brunton, who now managed the Rigalle bank. He had enclosed a clipping from the New Orleans newspaper, which described the "daring adventure of the well-known merchant and slave trader Mr. Mark Bouchard, in evading yet another trap set for him by the Union blockade and bringing goods which delight the ladies, such as fine gowns and perfumes from France and coffee from the Bahamas."

Paul Forsden had decided to enlist in the Confederate Army at the very outbreak of the war, having already spent three months training in the Alabama state troops, where the Jordan brothers had received their commissions as lieutenants. Neither Sybella nor Matthew could persuade the twenty-two-year-old to seek deferment as a planter occupied in producing food for the soldiers in their rebel gray. "It's my duty," he told them the eve of his departure for Huntsville. "I was born on this land, and it's part of a state that's seceded from the Union. Now it's at war, and I have to defend it. I wouldn't feel right if I didn't fight. I don't want either of you to be sad about my going—but I must."

They had bidden him farewell, these parents whom the turmoil of the last few years had aged; for Sybella, it was hardest of all, because Paul had been the last child she would ever bear, the child of the gentle man who had solaced her grief over Henry, yet in his own way brought her a warmth and happiness even Henry had not been capable of giving her. And when she kissed her son, it was with a foreboding that it might be for the last time; and after he had left, she went up to the tower in which old Lucien had stood so often, to pray for Paul's safety.

At the outset, her prayers seemed to have been answered. Paul wrote cheerful letters back from the battlefields of Belmont in November 1861, and from Mill Springs in January 1862, where he was hit in the shoulder by a rifle bullet, but within two weeks was fit for active duty and back with his regiment. In March, he retreated with his company from the heavy defeat inflicted on the Confederates at New Madrid, Missouri, by the Union General John Pope, and was commissioned a captain for gallantry under fire.

But in the deadly fighting of April 6th and 7th at the Battle of Shiloh on the Tennessee River, in which both sides claimed victory and in which Confederate General A. S. Johnston was killed and Union General Ulysses S. Grant drove back the Confederate forces, Captain Paul Forsden was instantly killed by a Union soldier's rifle in the final skirmish of that bloody standoff.

Ten days later, the letter written by young Forsden's commanding officer reached Windhaven. Sybella, holding back her tears, comforted her weeping husband and prayed for all those gallant young men who, whether

519

clad in blue or in gray, had given their lives for their country.

It was August 23, 1864. The war was nearly over. On this very day, the port of Mobile had been closed to blockade runners through the capture of Fort Morgan by Admiral Farragut. The Confederacy had authorized the use of men between seventeen and eighteen and between forty-five and fifty for military service. Deserters, guerrillas and marauders were preying on the virtually defenseless Southern countryside. A desperate move by the Confederacy of the attempted raid of General Jubal Early upon Washington itself had been blocked by General Lew Wallace, who was to write the immortal novel, *Ben Hur*. The fugitive slave law of 1850 had been repealed by an act of Congress.

At dawn of this day of August 23, 1864, a trim little steamer crept through the fog along the outline of the Gulf, heading for Barataria. It was challenged by a Union gunboat, and when it tried to flee, a light-colored Negro sergeant touched the lanyard of the mounted cannon on deck. The ball tore through a cabin on the upper deck, instantly killing Mark Bouchard, who had boarded the steamer at Nassau, laden with contraband goods. The name of that Negro sergeant was Caleb Zotlow, the adopted son of a childless Cincinnati couple.

Matthew Forsden had aged noticeably since the news of his son's death at Shiloh, and his hair had turned white a few weeks after that tragic news. Sybella, now sixty-two, had grieved as much, but with her indomitable spirit kept control of the château, supervising the kitchen, the garden, the chicken coop and even the hogs and cattle, particularly on those days when Matthew seemed soul-weary and despondent. Luke had tactfully suggested to Sybella that Lucien Edmond might help out with the chores in the fields of Windhaven, as it would be good training for the future, and Sybella had enthusiastically agreed. And Mara, who loved horses, asked if she might go over to Windhaven and stay for a time so as to be near her brother and also try out the many fine horses in the Windhaven stable. But there were two pieces of happier news this grim October of 1864 when the Confederates under General Early were soundly defeated by General Sheridan's Union troops and forced to leave the Shenandoah Valley and abandon all threat to the nation's capital. On the first day of this month, a letter came from Fleurette in Richmond:

Dearest Mama,

I have the most wonderful thing to tell you—I'm going to be married next week to Corporal Ben Wilson. He's a Quaker, just thirty years old, a corporal medical officer in the Union Army. He was brought into Sally's hospital here in Richmond two weeks ago, badly wounded in the shoulder from a sniper's bullet after he had been seen attempting to bandage the wounds of a dying Confederate officer. Because of what he did, Colonel Mattson said he oughtn't to have to go to Libby Prison, especially since he wasn't bearing arms against the Confederacy, so they sent him here. We found so many things in common when I nursed him, Mama. He was going to be a doctor in Pittsburgh, where he was born, when the war broke out. And you know how I've always wanted to study medicine and help sick people—it's just fate that we met. I think we both knew it from the first day when we started to talk.

Anyway, he'll be discharged in two weeks, and we're going to be married here in Richmond. Everybody says the war will be over soon, and Ben has given his word of honor that he won't try to run away, so most likely we'll go back to Pittsburgh as soon as it's possible. But I promise you this, dearest Mama, once there's peace again, we'll come back to see you—and maybe bring you a

521

grandson or a granddaughter, because we both want children so badly.

God bless you, Mama, and dear Mr. Forsden and be sure to let Luke and Lucien Edmond and Mara and Arabella and everybody else know how happy we are, and know that I wish them all just as much as Ben and I look forward to having in our lives together.

> Your loving daughter,
> Fleurette

And Laurette had found happiness too. A twenty-nine-year-old Tuscaloosa merchant, Charles Douglas, who had joined the Alabama volunteers, had been severely wounded by a minié ball above the knee at the battle of Chancellorsville and discharged as unfit for duty, had come to Montgomery to live with his sister and help manage her house and small produce farm. Laurette had met him while visiting his sister to collect some of the produce for needy families along the river, and after a brief courtship had become engaged to him. They would be married in Montgomery the day before this Christmas.

The war was ending, the long, agonizing war that had set brother against brother. Already the Confederacy had sued for peace. On March 4, 1865, Abraham Lincoln was inaugurated for his second term as President, and in his inaugural address displayed his compassion toward the defeated South: "With malice toward none; with charity for all." Andrew Johnson, who had been military governor of Tennessee, became his Vice President.

Major-General James Harrison Wilson, a graduate of West Point and a career officer, had won his laurels in the battles of the Army of the Potomac before being transferred to the West. In the winter of 1864, he went into winter quarters at Gravelly Springs at Lauderdale County, Alabama, where he drilled his cavalry until it was one of the finest fighting units of the entire campaign.

On March 22nd, he left his headquarters with 13,-500 cavalry, marching southeastward, dividing his men at Elyton in Jefferson County. Part of them he set under General John T. Crockston to Tuscaloosa, where they destroyed the University which had been training Confederate officers.

Under his own command, he led his forces south through Montevallo and Shelby Springs, where he destroyed the iron works, and Plantersville on his way to Selma. The Confederate General Forrest engaged Wilson in delaying action, but could not stop him. Selma was defended by 2500 cavalry and the same number of militia manning the fortifications which completely surrounded the city, but it fell to the Union on April 2nd. Here the Confederacy had the largest concentration of ordnance works in the deep South, and Wilson's men set the city ablaze.

Arabella's husband, James Hunter, had enlisted as a private at the outbreak of the war, rose to the rank of major by dint of gallantry in action, and had been mustered out only this February after suffering wounds in the left arm and right leg. Learning of the advance of Wilson's cavalry on Selma, he hurriedly harnessed his two remaining horses to an old carriage, bidding Arabella bring their twelve-year-old daughter Melinda and ten-year-old son Andrew and abandon all their goods except her jewel case and a small iron box containing $5000 in gold coins. Then, even as the first tongues of flame licked the wooden frame houses on the outskirts of Selma, he tugged at the reins, lashed out with the carriage whip and directed the horses toward Montgomery. Ten days later, the authorities of Montgomery evacuated the city and surrendered without a fight—it was the fourth anniversary of the firing on Fort Sumter, and that order too had originated in Montgomery to make the full cycle of war.

"Where will we go now, James?" Arabella turned to her tall gray-haired husband who still wore the gray uniform and major's brevet.

"To Galveston, Bella darling. I've a cousin there who's already been growing cotton the past five years. It's just about the last seaport we Confederates hold, but it won't be held much longer. Pray God things will go back to normal now this insane war is over. At least Melinda and Andrew will have their chance in a new land. Don't look so downhearted, darling. I'll build you a better house than the one we had in Selma, that's a promise. And you'll see, you'll find many friends from our own city, maybe, down in Galveston." He put his arm around her shoulders and kissed away her tears.

But a contingent of cavalry rode on downriver under an ambitious and vengeful captain, Arnold Huxter. His two brothers had been killed at Chickamauga, and he detested slavery and the South with almost obsessive hatred. In his mind, the stately plantations were symbols of the decadence and cruelty of the rich slave owners, and now that the military objectives of Selma and Montgomery had been gained, he meant to reconnoiter and raid and destroy to avenge his brothers.

Three hundred crack troops rode along with Captain Huxter downriver from Montgomery on this fateful night of April 13, 1865. Sybella, standing in the tower which faced in the other direction from that bluff where old Lucien and his Indian wife Dimarte lay at rest, saw the flames rising miles away from the home of the Durlows, an upriver planter family who, unlike the Bouchards, held with slavery and had continually snubbed their tolerant neighbors downriver.

"My God, they're burning the homes! They'll be here next!" she cried out, and hurried down the hallway to waken Lucien Edmond and Maxine, Mara, and her aging husband, Matthew.

"We'll go over to Luke and Lucy's," she explained to them. "Mara dear, hurry to the stable and get Djamba, tell him to hitch up the carriage and to get what horses are left—we've given so many away."

A few minutes later, Djamba and Lucas and Celia came hurrying into the château. Prissy, who had become Sybella's personal maid, was hastily packing her mistress' jewels in a case, while Lucien Edmond and Maxine were dressing their sleepy son Hugo and daughter Carla for the journey.

"Laurette's in Montgomery at Charles's sister's house, I pray God she'll be safe from the Union soldiers," Sybella gasped. "Matthew, do hurry, please!"

"No, my dear, I'm going to stay here. If I can, I'll try to save Windhaven," the white-haired old man insisted. "They won't harm me. I'm old, I've no weapons. I'll try to talk to their officer—surely now that they've won the war there's no need to burn this beautiful house."

"My darling, no, you mustn't—please come with me—"

"No, Sybella, it's the one thing I can do, the only thing that's left to do with honor. I was brought here as an overseer, do you remember?" He put his arm around her and smiled sadly. "Well, that's still my duty. God go with you, and now you must hurry!"

Weeping, distracted, Sybella at last allowed herself to be helped into the carriage by Djamba. "Lots of the workers have run away, Miz Bouchard," he said gravely, shaking his head. "They're cowards, they're not loyal anymore after all these years. But Celia and Prissy and Lucas and I want to go with you, no matter what happens. I've hitched two horses to the carriage, the best ones, and there's one here for Mr. Lucien Edmond, and two for Lucas and Prissy and Celia and me. You'll be crowded there, but those two mares will pull you all to Mr. Luke's place. Let's go now!"

They rode off from Windhaven down along the winding path to the Williamson plantation. There Luke and Lucy and Maybelle, who had been spending the last few weeks with her sister, anxiously awaited them.

Captain Huxter drew up on his reins at the head of his troops and stared through the sparsely moonlit night at the imposing red-brick château beyond. "Here's a castle of vipers, men! Probably one of the richest slaveholders in the South—let's show 'em what we think of profiteering slavers like him!" An exultant roar greeted his words as he waved them forward.

Before the doorway of the château which old Lucien Bouchard had dreamed of since the day Tunkamara had given him this land between the creek and the towering bluff, Matthew Forsden stood, arms folded across his chest.

"There's no one home here. Everyone's gone. Take the food and supplies in the storeroom, but spare this house, I ask you in honor!" he called out to the tall bearded officer who rode up to him.

There was a rifle shot, and Matthew Forsden gasped, his eyes widening. He put his hand to his breast and it came away with blood. He groaned, then fell like a tree before the Union officer's horse.

"Burn it!" Captain Huxter ordered, and with a shout, half a dozen troopers dismounted and ran into the château.

They could see the flames as they huddled in the clearing before the old Williamson house. Sybella sank upon her knees, covered her tear-stained face with her hands and prayed.

"What's to become of all of us now?" Maybelle murmured. "Now we've no one, nothing."

"We've one another," Luke Bouchard said as he reached for his son's hand and nodded encouragement. "It's not the end of Windhaven; it's a beginning. Maybe it's prophetic, even. Do you remember, Lucien Edmond, how I told you that one day you might have a chance to test your theory about sound breeding in animals as one might do with humans? Well, then, why not test that theory and grow cattle instead of cotton from now on?"

"It would indeed be a challenge, Father," young Lucien Edmond agreed.

Luke Bouchard turned to stare at the dark sky upriver, eerily brightened by the dancing flames of Windhaven Plantation. In his mind's eye, he saw, too, the towering bluff where his grandfather and Dimarte lay at peace in their union of immortality that would transcend even the violence and hatred of war. And then, bending to his kneeling stepmother Sybella, he murmured gently, "Weep for those who have gone before us, Mother. Pray for all of us who go ahead to whatever is in store for the living. And bless us all with your strength and courage, for we shall have need of them." Gently he drew her to her feet and kissed her cheek.

Then he turned to Maybelle and smilingly answered her plaintive query: "Why, Maybelle, you're wrong, you know. We've one another, with our whole lives before us. And we've a new frontier, a raw country that cries out for people who can meet its challenge. Yes, there'll be hardship and even danger, but we of Windhaven are used to that. This land we loved will be ravaged by the aftermath of this tragic war. But where we go, there will be land to till for crops and for cattle to graze on, land where we can build a new home that will cherish all the love and unity we knew at Windhaven and thus grow stronger still."

"Do you mean Texas, Father?" Lucien Edmond excitedly asked.

"Yes, Texas!" Luke Bouchard looked up at the crescent moon, and its faint rays burnished his sensitive face. "A country, I'm told, bigger than many of our Southern states put together and with room to spare for people of vision, endurance and a steadfast belief in the rights of all. It will be our new frontier, Lucien Edmond, our new and stronger Windhaven, mark my words!"

Reader's Note

Thus ends volume two in the stormy saga of the Bouchards of Windhaven . . . their beautiful home now a litter of ashes, stained with blood. But neither fire nor death can halt the brave and resolute Bouchards. Temporarily defeated and without a home, they regroup and head for New Orleans, abandoning the hard-won land of old Lucien. They will soon make their way to Texas, to rebuild their lives anew, and create Windhaven Range. With the horrors of the Civil War behind them, Luke envisions a life free from violence and racism. But Mexico is exploding with revolt and the borders are teeming with Comanche raiders, bandits, federalistas, and revolutionaries. Windhaven Range will be built, but Luke and his son, young Lucien, will have to relive many of the hardships old Lucien faced when he first came to the New World of America in 1789. There will be good times and bad, joy and sorrow, but always a Bouchard to carry on . . .

The Legacy of Windhaven